I0740832

Legendary Blue Smoke

by Philip H. Farber

Published by

Hoo-Ha Books
P.O. Box 4431
Kingston, NY 12402
www.hoohabooks.com

Cover image © 2014 DJ Reese.
Design by Hoo-Ha Books.

FIRST EDITION
ISBN-10: 0986214000
ISBN-13: 978-0-9862140-0-4

1. In the Garden

This is a story about what happened after my wife returned from the dead. I know some of you bought this book because you thought there would be juicy tidbits about drugs and groupies, or to help you grok the mind of the creative artist I was when I was twenty years old. Forget that shit. Go buy the *Illustrated Color History of Rock'n'Roll*, if you want that.

I'm sorry about "forget that shit." I've been living up on the mountain for a long time and I learned some habits from the cats and the vultures. And in this part of the story I'm an old man so I sometimes say things like "forget that shit." And it's my damn story. So fuck you.

I was talking to Jane when she came back to life. That wasn't unusual. Talking, I mean. In the fifteen years since she passed away, I spent a lot of time talking to her. When she was alive we talked about everything, all the time. We showed each other our projects or pointed out funny stories in the newspaper or on the web. We had a knack for pointing out the funny, weird, wacky and intriguing everywhere we went, in whatever we did. I never kicked that habit and never wanted to. I knew it was all in my mind, that she had become an imaginary friend, but it was still comforting in a way, like flexing a phantom limb, I guess, if anybody finds that comforting.

Jane always appreciated my green thumb, so I was taking her — or, rather, imagining that I was taking her — on a tour of the garden. Last year, two of the nicer plants were ripped off. It was probably just kids or hunters hiking through, but I went to a lot of effort to move the garden to a new, more inaccessible location. It was a brisk climb up and over mountain ridges to the brink of a rocky escarpment.

When you tell people that you live on a mountain here, they often think you mean the Catskills, but this particular ridge of rocks belongs to the Shawangunks. Locals, if we're looking to impress leaf-peepers up from the city, pronounce that as "shawn-gum" but the rest of the time we just call them "the Gunks." It's a long, stony wrinkle in the Earth that runs north from the New Jersey border through sparsely-populated parts of New York State. Near New Paltz, ten or fifteen miles to the south of my mountain, the Gunks are fairly imposing, a tall rock wall that dominates the view for many miles around. As the ridge runs north it loses altitude rapidly and barely makes it as far as Kingston, where it's no higher than a speed bump. Here on the edge of Rosendale it's a tough climb up a series of ridges to the top, where power lines and cell towers pose against the sky, but it's no Alp.

I didn't have to go all the way to the top. The garden was on the second ridge in a semicircle that I laboriously carved out of the forest with a chainsaw. Beyond that, trees on the tallest ridge blocked a little of my garden's sunlight in the morning hours, but all in all the plants seemed to like it there. I pointed out to Jane how nicely they were coming along, the leaves stretching wide and dark green in the late afternoon sunlight. There were eighteen spread out in the little clearing, three mother plants and fifteen clones. The mothers were almost four feet tall and very bushy, but they had a head start indoors for almost two months while their babies grew roots.

"The clones look great," I commented to Jane, pointing out the little shrubs. "Remember the original Blue Smoke weed, back in '72? I found a film canister of seeds in the back of the old freezer. I don't have a clue how they got there. We bought that freezer in '93. I only got the one good mother plant to grow, but look at these babies!"

Okay, this is one you're not going to find in *Record Beat's Fifty Years of Rock*. Fans and potheads debate this kind of crap, I imagine, so I'll just settle it here. We named the band after the weed, the weed wasn't named after the band. Blue Smoke, the herb, had special properties that helped define the band in other ways, too.

Just about then, there was a noise in the undergrowth that gave me a start, but it was only Bob, the cat.

"Hi, Bob," I said, reaching down to pat his head.

The real Jane never met Bob; he showed up a few years after she was gone, but the imaginary Jane and Bob were old friends. Bob got his name from his obvious resemblance to a real bobcat. He was mostly brown with a silvery grey undercoat and a spattering of fine dark spots down his front legs. And he was not only big, but really broad across the shoulders. He was a big, fearsome wedge of muscle and claws, undisputed King of the Mountain. He even successfully fought off a coyote once, though it did cost about $600 at the vet to patch him up afterwards. Yep, Bob was a scary wild beast who commanded the respect or fear of chipmunks, squirrels, possum, raccoons, rat snakes and probably even bear – but who believed his true place was curled up, purring, on my lap.

Jane and I watched Bob inspect the plants. He would occasionally bite off a leaf and eat it, but that was acceptable payment for his ability to repel pests with generous donations of tooth, claw, crap and pee.

So anyway, it was a really nice afternoon, except for the helicopters. They didn't seem to disturb the pileated woodpecker, who laughed at me whenever I talked to Jane. Or the red-tail hawks who made a brief appearance, circling and calling for a few minutes. But I wasn't too thrilled. They weren't cop copters. They were private-issue, rich people machines. I could tell; they used to fly us into gigs on earlier models of those noisy damn things. They flew over pretty steadily through the early part of the day, finally reaching a peak about three in the afternoon, and then were abruptly gone. But here was one now, following a northerly route parallel to the Thruway, just like all the others.

I knew there was some stupid shit going on over in Saugerties. I saw headlines on the web, but I didn't read that crap. It was tied into some schlocky TV talk show and just entirely failed to catch my interest. But everyone else thought it was hot shit, apparently. The New York State Thruway crossed over White Bush Lane a few miles away and, even at this distance, when the copters and silly-ass woodpeckers were quiet for a moment or two it was pretty easy to tell that traffic was at a standstill. The usual steady thrum of cars and trucks was replaced with an occasional revving motor and a babble of voices. People were stuck in a massive traffic jam and had climbed out of their cars to chat and bitch about it.

Fuck 'em, I told Jane. I might have to get my shotgun if I heard them coming this way.

That's when things started to go funny. First there was a strange, stiff breeze. It smelled really fresh, that's the only way to describe it. Clean. Bob sniffed the air. The babble of voices in the distance hushed and then was replaced with a chorus of oohs and aahs. My old jeans suddenly felt different somehow and I looked down to find that they were clean. They'd never been clean. The breeze died down. The birds and distant voices went silent.

"Damn," I said to Jane. "Now I don't have to do laundry."

"When did you ever do laundry?" I imagined that she asked.

The quiet air held a sense of expectancy. Then, mildly at first but building rapidly, I was overcome with a truly wonderful feeling. It was like my skin was covered with rainbows and my heart massaged by tiny nude virgins. My vision got sparkly and I felt warm tingles inside. I sat down on a tree stump and Bob swirled around my legs, purring very loudly.

"Seems like a late arrival for an acid flashback," I told Jane. "I haven't seen any LSD in thirty years."

"It's no flashback," I imagined Jane saying. "I don't know what it is."

Perhaps the stranded motorists along the Thruway had a clue. There was a chorus of woohoos and hallelujahs that must have been heard for ten or fifteen miles, at least.

"You hear that?" The imaginary Jane commented. "They all feel it, too."

"Okay," I agreed. "Not a flashback, unless they all ate the Owsley, too."

We just sat for a few minutes, feeling damn good, watching the grass grow. Bob jumped into my lap and curled up, his motor still idling loudly. Then the wind picked up again, a warm gust, and POOF! a brilliant purple flash of light seemed to come from everywhere at once. A purple glow seemed to cling to the trees, the plants, the rocks, Bob, my skin. I rubbed my eyes and blinked hard a few times, but it kept right on glowing. Over the next ten minutes or so the damn good feeling kept building in pulses or cycles. It was vaguely erotic, too, and I started to think about when I first met Jane, in 1971. She was so amazingly sexy; in my memories we rarely had our clothes on and while we weren't always in bed, we behaved as if were.

"Damn," I said, "If I could grow weed that did this, I'd be famous – if I ever left the farm."

Then BLAM! there was a much brighter purple flash, the nuclear blast of purple flashes, wiping out my vision in brilliant, unabated, relentless, total purple light. It was purple, right? And the damn good feeling rose to full-tilt woohoo. From the highway, stranded motorists concurred loudly.

A moment later, as my vision returned, I jumped up from the stump, sending Bob bounding into the garden. I wanted to shout, to howl with the masses. I raised my face to the purple-tinged sky and… a vast saucer-shaped spaceship dipped down through the atmosphere, blotting out a big part of my garden's afternoon sunlight and taking my breath away. With a world-vibrating WHOOSH, it soared north, parallel to the Thruway, and disappeared in the distance.

I turned to Jane and…

I turned to Jane and *she was there*. I mean really there. As real as the rocks, the trees, the plants. As real as Bob, who came barreling out from between the plants to swirl around her legs.

She wasn't the hairless, cancer-withered Jane that I most recently recalled. She was the 23 year old, raven-haired goddess who had bluffed her way into the dressing room at the Fillmore to do an interview for a regional zine called *Bop*. She wore a t-shirt that was a size or two too small for her and a pair of faded and patched flare-leg jeans that hung, frayed and tattered, under her boot heels. She was just the way I remembered her – no, she was sharper, clearer, and much more solid than my memories. *She was there.*

Jane smiled. My heart was beating hard, like I'd just climbed the ridge for the second time with a fifty pound sack of bat guano. This was all pretty damn weird, but, hey, I've been through a lot in my years and I've seen some shit. I did some deep breathing and tried to calm myself.

"Hey," she said. Her voice, too, was real, air molecules vibrating all the way from her mouth to my ears. The sound was like a doorway to a thousand moments in our shared past when I heard her and knew that the world had a purpose, that everything was going to be all right, that I was part of this dyadic mind that was greater and wiser than my own.

I gulped. I tried to speak, but nothing came out. I took a step toward her.

Okay, now I know there's some stupid bastard who's going to say that if I had only turned on the damn television, I would have known that something was going to happen. Yeah, *something*. Well, I bet that none of you TV-zombie bastards had any idea that spaceships were going to come down out of the sky and all our imaginary friends would turn real. Did you? Right. I thought not.

In a moment we were in each other's arms, hugging and kissing like it was '72. I managed to forget about my arthritis for a few minutes, and that's pretty good.

When we finally broke, I caught my breath for a moment and asked, "Are you really real?"

"Does this feel real?" she murmured, offering some tactile stimulation.

I had to agree that it did.

2. Better to Burn Out?

The pump for my well is powerful enough to run garden hose most of the way up the mountain and fill a collection of five-gallon buckets. I stash the buckets in a rock crevice and when the plants need water, as often as every day during the hottest part of August, I pull them out and soak the pots. I've got plant food back there, too, custom organics in three bottles that I mix together in different proportions depending on the time of the season and the health of the plants.

Jane knew right where the buckets were and had two of them out before my ancient bones caught up with her. Okay, check it out: I'm 65 years old this coming September. I'm strong enough to chop my own firewood and do the hauling, shoveling and toting associated with a small amount of guerilla farming. I do pretty well for an old bastard. But Jane was in her prime again and made me realize how far I'd come from mine. She was strong, just as I remembered. With both of us working, the plants were watered in ten minutes and, Bob in the lead, we started down the ridge.

As we followed the deer trail down the mountain, I reflected happily on how easy and natural this little miracle seemed. It was like we picked our relationship up again from the beginning, like someone hit the reboot button on the CPU of our lives. Of Jane's life. It could have been a creepy Stephen King back-from-the-dead plot, but it didn't seem that way. Jane showed no evidence of decaying flesh, demonic possession, hunger for brains or, indeed, any kind of homicidal tendency. It just seemed to be her. Except that when I got really close and focused my eyes just right, she seemed, I don't know, almost too real. A little too bright around the edges. But I could easily chalk that up to my imagination, to my heightened mental state from simply seeing her again after she'd been dead fifteen years.

The sunlight, tilting toward evening, made soft golden shafts through green leaves in the grove where I started ginseng plants nearly twenty years ago. A ragtag bunch of the plants survived the first few years and eventually flourished among the roots of the big sugar maples. Even though a few were spectacularly large, as ginseng goes, they were all still really hard to spot among the underbrush. But Jane knew right where they were and paused to admire the glossy dark green of the largest ones.

"You haven't been here since these were just sprouts," I pointed out. "And this has changed. The trail is all different. But you seem to know it as well as I do."

"What are you talking about?" She laughed.

"And you knew where I hid the buckets. I only started using this garden this year," I said.

"You showed me where the buckets were." She looked at me like I was nuts.

That didn't quite raise a memory. "When did I show you the buckets?" I asked.

"Please," she said. "Are you kidding me? You showed me and told me about them pretty much every damn time you've come up here this season, I think."

I had to stop walking to wrap my brains around that one. I looked down at the worn brown of last year's fallen leaves. I looked up at Jane. "But you were…" I stammered. "You weren't here."

She shook her head as if mystified by my typically erratic behavior. "Then who were you talking to when you were wandering around the woods? And wandering around the house. And surfing the web. And reading those old science fiction books. And all the rest of the time. Who were you talking to?"

There was only one thing I could say. "You."

"Well, there you have it." She turned and marched off through the woods.

I just stared at the very worthwhile view of her backside. I cracked open the file drawer in the back of my brain that held my deeper philosophy and thoughts on death, resurrection, ghosts and things that go bump in the night or day. There was a small puff of metaphoric dust and I slammed it shut again. I was pretty sure I didn't want to go there just yet.

What if I discovered she was a figment of my imagination? Or something elusive that would flee before examination? I didn't want that to happen. I wanted her here. If this was a delusion, it was a really nice one. If she was a pod person – I saw the flying saucer right before she appeared – I didn't care. If she wanted to eat my brains, maybe I could convince her to go for sushi instead.

It turned out to be a wise decision. I was a very, very lonely old man and a night with the young Jane was more healing than words can say. You want details? Forget it. I told you I wasn't going to talk about groupies and you think I'm going to tell you stuff about my wife? Go fuck yourself.

I woke the next morning with a sense of optimism that I hadn't felt in a long, long time. The world was suddenly a place of mystery and excitement again. Miracles could happen and love could reign. As I sat up in bed, the morning glittered in my peripheral vision, as if dozens of sparkling fairies were preparing the scenery, just out of direct sight. I smelled coffee.

I threw on my old robe and followed the aroma into the living room where Jane sat on the sofa, cradling a hot mug. She hadn't turned on any lights and the morning sun sent shadows of leaves and branches swirling around the room. She was already dressed, in a silk vest and cutoff shorts. I remembered her wearing those, way back, maybe '76 or '78, but couldn't figure out where she might have found them now. The file of philosophy rattled and I ignored it. She had a sour look on her face, serious and not at all happy. Her fingers tapped a stack of envelopes on the cushion beside her.

I tried to keep it light. "What's up?" I asked.

She looked up at me, her eyes big and dark. "What happened to you, Ian?"

"What do you mean?" I shrugged. "I got old."

She shook her head. "No, that's not it. You don't make music any more. Not anything new, I mean. You just sit around and butcher the old songs, sometimes."

"I quit all that crap," I said. "The music industry can fuck right off. I always hated dealing with those creeps. I don't have to sell my art."

"What art? That argument doesn't work, Ian," she said, putting the coffee mug on the side table and leaning forward. "You don't make any art even for yourself. People used to wear 'Ian is God' t-shirts. Now, nothing. And it's sad because you're probably going to lose everything you own."

"What are you talking about?"

She picked up the envelopes. "Do you ever read your mail?" I remembered that tone. It wasn't going to be good. "Do you ever fucking read your mail? This was my house, too. We both worked hard to have this place." She tossed the envelopes and they scattered on the floor by my feet. I scooped them up and shuffled over to an armchair. I eased myself into the chair and found a pair of reading glasses on the side table.

The first envelope was a dunning letter from a credit card company. Big fucking deal. The second envelope held a thicker packet of papers from the same credit card company: a judgment against me in the county court. The next envelope was a past due property tax notice. And so were the next five envelopes. After that came a notice that I was three years overdue on property taxes and that if I didn't respond damn soon, the county was going to take action to claim my home, studio and land. There was a fresh royalty check in the stack, too, but the amount written on it was embarrassingly tiny compared to the tens of thousands of dollars that I owed. It might buy me some groceries and gas for the truck.

"You used to be exciting," she said, as my mind tried to grasp the situation. "You always had a plan. An optimist. When we were broke and needed money, you always conceived of some project that brought in at least as much as we needed – and sometimes a whole lot more. That's one of the things that attracted me to you. Now, you're a sad sack, an old fart. You're ignoring the decay of your own life.

You're exactly the kind of person we swore we'd never turn into. You don't go out, you don't have friends. We all swore we'd rather burn out than fade away. You're fading and I can't bear to see you like this."

But I knew she was wrong. She may have been right, up until the night before, up until she healed me with the miracle of her presence, with the physical reminder of everything we were. Now she was wrong. Some inexplicable magic had transformed the world and the realm of the possible was now a much, much wider land. A plan was already forming in my mind.

"I don't care if you're old," Jane kept on. "I kind of like it, really. No, the turn-off is the attitude. Or the lack of attitude. Whatever happened to rock'n'roll?" She shook her head. I opened my mouth to protest, to proclaim my transformation and undying love for her, but she continued. "You and I were about life, Ian. About experiencing, being the eyes of the universe, remember? We can't be like *that* if you're like *this*. I don't think we can be 'we.' I'm going away, Ian. I can't stay if you're like this. I can't watch the house and the mountain get taken away. Do something, please. Wake up. Get your life back. I'll come back if you do."

She stood up and smoothed out her vest. She turned toward the door.

I stepped forward to stop her from walking out. "Jane," I started to say, reaching for her shoulder. But she didn't walk.

She didn't fade away and she didn't burn out, either. Before I could reach her, she simply disappeared.

3. Evolution

I know, I know. So far this is the kind of story that would have seemed really miraculous, back before that day in June. But now we live in a world where our dead wives, imaginary friends, six foot tall bunny rabbits, or favorite comic book characters are deeply involved in the day to day fundamentals of our lives. There's a guy in town who hires real deities to light up his front lawn on the holidays. My neighbor, right here on White Bush Lane, keeps some huge, slobbering demon creature under his back porch. I know. I've seen it. I wasn't able to count which it had more of, teeth or eyes. It keeps the skunks from nesting there, he says. I get it. The entities are here to stay, and it's just fine with me. We all needed a little shakeup to our sense of reality. I got mine; you got yours. Hell, I got mine, yours, and some other guy's. And his whole extended family's.

My dead wife left me. If I wrote country songs, I'd have a winner with that one. It hurt. It really did. But I'd missed her for fifteen years and now I had one amazing night with her. It was something I wanted to cherish, to remember perfectly for all time. And in spite of the hurt, much to my surprise, I still felt a sense of optimism. Something long dead could come back to life, as vibrant as before. If it happened once, it could happen again. This was all part of the mystery. And, just maybe, I was coming up with a plan.

The plan that was welling up in my mind came down to one action: call Trenton. When we all went our separate ways in 1981, Trenton and I were the only members of Blue Smoke to have solo careers. When I stopped performing fifteen years ago, Trenton became the only active Blue. The guy had a hell of a solid career, too, even now.

He still sold out the big houses, arenas, and civic auditoriums and his tunes played perpetually on radios and jukeboxes everywhere. Unless you've been hiding under a rock, or living on the Shawangunk Ridge, you hear his stuff all the time. Trenton would know the score. He'd know what was possible, if a Blue Smoke reunion would pay the bills.

When I quit playing, I told the agents and flacks to lose my phone number. Some of them did, I suppose, but over the years I still got plenty of calls from industry weasels and phone monkeys who would say the word "reunion" as if it would blow my mind. Pissed me off every time. And now here I was, as soon as Trenton picked up, intoning the same magic word.

"About fucking time," is what Trent said. He told me he'd call the others and we agreed to meet in Rosendale, at my studio, in one week. In the meantime, Trenton would talk to his management and learn what kind of money might be involved.

Who remembers the names of band members? If you can name all the members of Blue Smoke, you're some kind of fan geek and should find something better to do with your life. Hell, I didn't put too much brain-time toward any of my old band mates over the last decade or so. You *can* find this in *The Complete Rock Encyclopedia: 50s through 80s*, but I'll spare you just this once and run it down. Just this once.

I was a high school sophomore in 1967 when my family moved from Flint, Michigan to Santa Cruz, California. At first I felt isolated. I liked the climate and I liked the looks of the girls in California, but I didn't know a single person and found it tough to strike up a conversation with anyone. I spent a lot of time at home, alone, practicing the guitar. My first week in the new school, though, a strange kid in a suit came up to me and said, "Brown shoes don't make it." He began to walk off.

I knew the line – in fact, I had just listened to Frank Zappa's *Absolutely Free* the night before and the song was stuck in my head. "Quit school, why fake it," I responded automatically.

The kid's head whipped back around to face me, an expression of amazement on his face. "You know that song?" he asked.

That's how I met Trenton Augustus. He was self-isolated, in a way, and our commonality was that we were both outcasts. When everyone else in the school was starting to break loose and experiment with long hair, jeans and hippie gear, Trenton had to go the other way. He wore a suit and tie to school most days. A gray fedora hat, too. He seemed like the nerdiest of the science nerds, and his grades, usually straight A's, supported the con job. But Trenton was deeply weird. While the first, pioneering potheads in school were grateful for a stick of moldy Mexican, Trent had a secret inside line to some real serious shit. He would sniff the bags that kids in school offered and turn up his nose. Some kids thought he was a narc, but after school, when we got to our secret hangout in the woods, he would pull out bags fragrant with real Acapulco Gold, Panama Red and top-shelf Thai. Once he broke out a bag of pineapple-smelling shit that he claimed was Cambodian. We got *high*.

And we played music. In their basement, the Augustus family had an upright piano and a little electric organ and Trent played them both. His parents started him on piano lessons when he was five and had visions that he would be a concert pianist. He could work his way through quite a bit of Mozart, Chopin and Liszt, but when I brought over my old acoustic guitar, we tried to make noise like Howlin' Wolf or Muddy Waters. We listened to records at 45 and 78 rpm, and we tried to copy the sounds. Trent's got a good singing voice, but I could do a fair impression of the Wolf's howling and moaning, so I usually took lead vocals. At first, these attempts would end with us laughing too hard to continue, but after a while we really started to get it.

We tried some more contemporary stuff, too. We could play Beatles and Stones without breaking a sweat. Buddy Holly, Bo Diddley, Chuck Berry, Gene Vincent. It was fun and we were all over it. Our version of "Louie Louie" kicked ass, and usually lasted about forty five minutes.

Over a bowl of sweet Columbian, we formed a master plan that would not only make us popular and get us laid, but would be our ticket to eternal fame and fortune. We would form a band and play all those rock tunes so much better than their originators that we would be worshipped. And get laid. We tacked a few signs to bulletin boards around town and actually got a few wannabe rock stars responding, enough that we had to audition them for three nights running.

All right, all right, I said I was going to list the band members and instead you're reading the unabridged history. Sorry. You'll need to know this to understand the stuff that comes later. If you don't like it, go read *Lion Pulse' Rock'n'Roll Legends*, which does give you a straight list of personnel. And gets it wrong, too. Our manager called them out on it once. Basically, they said "fuck you." Only they said it through a lawyer. Fuck them.

We set up our little make-shift stage platform in Trenton's garage and saw about half a dozen guys who played at typical high school – or worse – levels of musicianship. They just weren't in our league. On the second night of auditions, this short, stocky black guy wandered in, dragging an enormous upright bass behind him. His name was Cleveland White and he was damn good. Cleve got up there and just jammed out some jazz all by himself for a while, rocking that bass to the beat. I asked him if he could play the blues and he laughed and started laying down the rhythm. We joined in and had a tasty little jam session. I don't even remember what song we were playing, but I remember taking a solo and suddenly there was Cleve, weaving that bass line into what I was doing. Right then, I could hear the evolution of our sound, how Cleve's playing created a structure that pulled us together.

The next night we auditioned two drummers. They were both about equally good. One was Bill Mariah and the other was Jason Bowlen. Bill was good, and he went on, as you probably know, to bigtime success as the drummer for Plastica, but we didn't go with him. We went with Jason because he was good and because he laid down this wild rap about music blowing minds and setting the people of the world free. And he said he could get some acid.

We'd heard about acid, read about it in the papers. We saw Tim Leary on the news. We knew the Beatles liked their LSD. We were curious, intrigued, but neither Trent nor I had even seen a hit. Whatever Trenton's miraculous weed source was, it didn't seem to supply anything else. So the promise of acid was an inducement.

Now we had a rhythm section and the four of us, Trent, Cleve, Jason, and me, would remain the core of the band, right up until the end. As a quartet, we played our first gigs at local dances and even a bar mitzvah. We were still a cover band then, though we were starting to explore some extended jams when the situation allowed. Offstage, we worked hard to develop our own sound. By 1970, just after we'd graduated from high school, we were signed to Peach Fuzz records and the first album came soon after.

Other band members came and went. We often had a second guitarist, most notably Will MacPherson on the first album and subsequent tours and Marcus Shane on albums two through four. On *Six Songs*, we had the Speckler brothers as our horn section and Birdie Balam contributing her famous wailing vocals.

Like I said, I hadn't spoken with any of them in a decade or more and I didn't really know what to expect. But for the first time in a very long time, I was excited about Blue Smoke, about playing the old songs again, picking up the thread of creativity where we left it so long ago and weaving some musical magic.

I packed a bowl and went out to the studio.

4. Awake

It was another green and gold June day. Blue jays and flycatchers flickered through shadows and beams of sunlight. High in the air, glimpsed through the branches, a trio of turkey vultures rode an updraft over the first ridge. A breeze shook and rustled the oak trees and sun blazed against the front of the long, low, wood-sided studio building. Winter shutters still covered the windows. I usually closed the place up in the fall and didn't bother to run the heat. I just stayed out.

Now I pulled back the shutters and got all the windows open to let fresh air through and chase the funk out. Inside, with the sun coming in, the studio was bright and comfortable. Guitar racks, amps, and acoustic foam lined the walls. The studio wasn't professionally sound-proof; it was more of a place to brainstorm, jam and be creative. We wrote, planned and rehearsed the last two Blue Smoke albums in that studio. When it was time to record, it was a short drive to Woodstock or Bearsville, where the real recording studios were. But the ridge studio was spacious, quiet and set far enough back in the woods that we could make as much noise as we wanted, even with the windows wide open, and no one would bother us. We could get real crazy in there and, if memory serves, we often did.

I took my old blue Strat down from the rack and plugged in. I switched on the amp and heard a satisfying hum. Setting the guitar gently down on the floor, I lowered my old bones into a chair and fired up the bowl. It was good creative herb, a Nepali strain crossed and re-crossed with shorter-season plants until it could thrive on the mountain. It tasted like the first hash I ever smoked, spicy black temple ball courtesy of Trenton, back in high school.

I filled my lungs with smooth smoke and held it for a few seconds, exhaling a sweet stream of swirling clouds in the sunlight. A couple big tokes and I could feel the first faint buzz crawling up the back of my brain. My attention began to wander around me, noticing the swirling smoke, the flickering greengold of the sunlight, the colors of the guitar bodies lined up on the wall, feeling warm air from the open windows tousling my hair and beard, following a liquid thread of bird call across the treetops, listening to the faint hum of the amp. I took one more deep toke, then set the bowl down and picked up my guitar.

I tuned for a moment and then hit a chord. It sounded nice, ringing off the studio walls. Outside, just under the window, a toad trilled and I tried to imitate it, scratching the pick along a string. It wouldn't have fooled a toad, but it sounded cool anyway. I hit another chord and noticed that the toad-scratch and the chord were pretty close to the opening of "Awake (from the Dream of our Distance)," the first track on *Six Songs.* If you ever came near an FM radio in the last twenty five years, you know it. You know that opening bit, too. If you don't, fuck you, go spend a buck and download the tune.

I played the intro to "Awake" and began to strum the rhythm, imagining that I could hear Cleve and Jason. In fact, my imagination was so keen that day, I could hear every beat, every nuance. That Nepali was some serious shit. Then, suddenly, I could feel it. It was something I hadn't felt in a long time, like the music was pouring into me from the rhythm and filling me up so much that I was ready to burst. If you've heard the records, you know the sound I used to make. It was my trademark, part Howlin' Wolf, part approaching orgasm. It was something I couldn't fake. It had to be real. I had to really feel it. I called it the Primal Moan. The sheet music always transliterates it as "a-awooo." You know it doesn't really sound like that, but for the sake of simplicity I'll use that spelling here.

A-awooooooooo!

The Moan welled up in me and poured forth from my mouth, splashing off the walls of the studio, escaping through the open windows to spill over the trees and rocks.

I started to sing:

"Standing on mountain top

Vast green valleys, crystal peaks

The Earth's sparkling rainbow fire
Filling, willing, rolling, roiling
Am I the only human here?
A-awoooo!"

My mind flashed back through a range of memories: psychedelic lights and crashing decibels the hundreds of times we played the song in concert, focused work in the studio when we recorded it, the days alone with my guitar as I made a demo tape, the experience, the thing that happened that inspired the song in the first place.

The thing that happened involved Jane, of course. No coincidence, really; she was often my muse, the catalyst that switched on my imagination. In this case we both catalyzed ourselves with some very tiny yellow pills. Back then, drugs didn't come with ingredients lists on them. A panoply of chemicals were sold as "acid," "mescaline" or "shrooms." You could make an educated guess, or just trust your source. In this case, my source said, "I don't know what it is, but it's really good." And he poured a dozen or so of these tiny little yellow dots into my hand. Educated guess, with hindsight – some kind of hallucinogenic and empathogenic phenethylamine. In the range of chemicals between mescaline and ecstasy. Empathogenic, do you know that word? It's a good word. Fuck you, look it up.

I swallowed one of the dots right then and there. In a little while the lights seemed brighter and I could feel my heart beating, fast and strong. I wandered out into a northern California summer evening. My memory is a little spotty on how exactly I got there, but I found myself sitting on top of a cliff staring out over the Pacific Ocean. Everything I looked at was throwing off rainbows, rays of pure color that shifted and turned and rotated through the spectrum. The setting sun was spreading a rosy glow across the sparkling waters, feeding the profusion of colors, each of which also somehow produced a feeling in my body.

As the memories filled my mind, I sang the chorus:

"Take a trip with the Tripper

Come awake

From the dream of our distance"

Vast prismatic pinwheels rotated and radiated through the world, riding in and out on every wave that the Pacific threw at the shore. I felt tiny, insignificant, overwhelmed in the wheeling colors. I tried to find some sign of civilization, but there was nothing in my field of vision – or if there was, it was lost in the hallucinatory onslaught. The rays and wheels of color seemed the embodiment of forces of nature, vast, wonderful, penetrating everything, even me. The works and world of humans amounted to little amongst the ever-roiling universal flow of energy.

It seemed an important revelation for me, finally learning my place in the cosmos. I might be a rock star with millions of fans. There might actually be people wearing "Ian is God" t-shirts. Perhaps I was a big deal in the world of humans. But in the measurement of time and space and the processes of everything, I was less than a mote. Collectively, humanity wasn't much more than a speck in an infinite dust storm. It was both humbling and beautiful and it struck me with something that I can only describe as "truth." The knowledge was accompanied by a sense of freedom, as if I was cut loose from the importance I always placed on the objects and activities of my life. I wanted to share the experience, to give Jane a taste of this strange, colorful wonderment.

When I got back to our apartment, the drug was fading and I babbled breathlessly about my experience. Jane grinned and said, "Sounds like good shit."

Later, when I was more coherent, I was able to tell Jane a little more about it and she was eager to give it a try. We waited a few days until our schedules opened up a trip-worthy evening. It was rainy that night, so we opted for an indoor session, just the two of us in the cozy front room of our apartment. Big windows looked out on the lights of our little coast town. Inside, candles in jars gave a mellow golden glow to our collection of embroidered pillows and wall hangings. We each ceremoniously placed a yellow dot in our mouth, then settled back on the rugs and pillows.

Soon the candles glowed with new intensity, throwing prismatic rays across the room. We smoked a bowl as the yellow dots worked their way into our brains. By the time we were roasting the last ember of weed, our cozy front room had transformed into a psychedelic carnival ride. We rode in the pillowed cockpit of a vehicle of rainbow light, a vast radiating wheel that reached into the farthest heavens and the deepest depths. There was the sense that sitting still was an illusion, like when you are in a car or an airplane and can imagine that you remain in the same place while the world parades by. Same feeling, though in the physical sense, of course, we really were sitting still.

The engine of the vehicle was a spinning core of light exactly between us. We both turned to face it, holding our hands out to it, staring into it. Reaching around the light-ball, our hands met and held onto each other. At first it was just a grounding connection to the world of things that have weight and dimension and familiarity. But our touch, our connection, caused the light to intensify, to become denser, and the light-core pulsed and swelled and surged to engulf us. A wave of bliss washed through me, as if every nerve ending, every sensation, every sound, color, and feeling, led directly to the pleasure center of my brain. We both sighed deeply. Over the next hour or eon, depending on your point of view, the trip continued to intensify and we were drawn closer and closer together. At some point our clothes were gone and we were in each others' arms.

And once again the realm of rainbow light blotted out the more mundane world. We were in the center of the ever-roiling universal flow of energy. But it was different this time because I knew, with every drop of attention that I had, that our connection was what made it all. Not just the wonder of rainbow hallucinations, but all that they represented. The interaction of our consciousness was what, I knew at that moment, created the world. It was our experience that sent the rainbow wheel rolling through the void, which tipped all the cycles of nature into another go-round.

When I sat on the edge of the cliff and looked out on the sea, I felt lost in the world, but now, in Jane's familiar yet chemically enchanted arms, the human element – or perhaps more precisely, our conscious awareness – became the most important thing. Part of me was confused by these two seemingly opposite experiences. But something else inside me pressed those two opposites together until years later, while working on *Six Songs* in my Rosendale studio, they burst with rainbow sparks and became something new: a song.

I imagined a psychedelic hero who bemoaned the separation that humans create between themselves and nature, and between each other. He has an epiphany on top of a mountain and seeks to bring humanity the experience of our own connectedness. I thought of him as The Tripper, the man with the psychedelic magic in his hands who would blow the minds of the world and bring us all together.

The reverie faded and I was heading for the guitar solo, where the tune suddenly stretches out and then spirals in again, in swirling psychedelic loops. I was really feeling it and another Primal Moan surged and erupted from my depths. It was so long since I sat in the studio and played – all winter and a good part of the spring, at least – that I was convinced I should be rusty. But somehow it sounded great. Really great. I mean, I took that swirly solo and just played the hell out of it. The riffs that I played so many times in the past were now transformed into something fresh and different, something I would love to share with an audience. It was as if the song came to life again.

Yes, it's true, it was damn good weed, but nonetheless it seemed that all sorts of things were coming to life again.

I played for an hour or so, until my out-of-practice fingers started to hurt, then I closed the studio and climbed the hill to check on the plants. Jane, real or imaginary, didn't turn up for the tour, but Bob did. The rest of the day went pretty much like most of my days, except that everything was transformed. I suddenly saw promise and hope in my activities and I was really looking forward to playing with the band. And maybe seeing Jane again.

After dinner, I felt restless and alone, which was a different experience for me, since I usually did alone so very well. In a sense, though, I really was more alone than usual. I didn't have my imaginary Jane to chat with. She was no longer in my head, but was out there, somewhere, manifest, in the world. I grabbed a jacket in case it got cold later on and climbed into my rusty Dodge four by four. The pickup rattled and farted and bounced the few miles into the village of Rosendale.

White Bush Road followed a curvy route between mountain ridges, both sides of the road marked with archaeological evidence of Rosendale's more prosperous past. Switching back and forth from one side to the other was an ancient rail bed, supported in places by walls and trestles made of great tan blocks of native stone. It was actually the remains of an old horse railway, where animals once pulled carts full of coal and limestone between the D&H Canal and the cement industry at Binnewater. Mostly it was collapsed and in some places cleared away entirely to make room for a double-wide to take root or to allow the New York State Thruway, originally paved with Rosendale cement, to pass through. Along the route of the railway, at the level of the road, were ancient and equally-collapsed brick and stone kilns, more relics of long-gone industry.

At Binnewater, I turned left, driving past Steel Cave, a corporation that stored industrial and governmental records in a nuke-proof facility deep in quarried-out limestone caverns. A huge number of major corporations and federal agencies reportedly used the facility to store primary and backup data about their customer base and constituency.

"They've got millions of lives stashed away down there," is how one local character once described it to me.

No one ever talked much about what was down in those caverns, but once in a while you ran into someone who claimed to have been there. They told tales of vast rows of office building-sized structures, dimly lit and barely glimpsed in the darkness. The above-ground part, a moderate-sized office building all by itself, had a huge blacktopped parking lot, but there were rarely ever more than a few cars there.

The road ran steeply downhill for the next mile, winding back and forth through mountainside woodland to the Rondout Creek, where Route 213 crept out the tail end of town toward High Falls. A left turn and I pulled into Rosendale's short business district and parked along the road.

In late summer, the village played host to a really kick-ass street festival and the one and only street would be filled with partiers. Any other evening, though, there were usually only a few characters out and about – but now the place was almost crowded. As usual, the hub of any action was the Brick & Mortar Tavern. There must have been some kind of party, because at least a few of the people milling around out front were wearing costumes. Some were just inappropriately well-dressed – suits, evening gowns, tuxedos – for an evening in Rosendale. There was some bald guy dressed up like that shiny-headed captain from Star Trek. A bevy of wood nymphs giggled past him and went into the bar. A couple of very familiar-looking Rastafarians were sharing a joint with a long-eared cartoon rabbit. A person with the head of an elephant and a very lifelike, mobile trunk sat on the sidewalk, eating a Dove bar and chatting with a leprechaun. And there were some normal people, too, recognizable Rosendaleans.

Okay, okay, *now* I know they probably weren't wearing costumes. But remember, this is the day after I'm talking about. I just didn't know then. I didn't know the gods were walking the Earth. You didn't either, so fuck off.

The costumed characters brightened up the dimly lit, dark wood interior. The atmosphere was almost festive. A few heads turned to take me in, then immediately snapped back to their drinks and chatter. I approached the bar to order and caught a glimpse of myself in the bar-back mirror. Tall, wiry, a little bit stooped, I wore a brown corduroy work jacket. Originally from Kenco, it usually looked as if it belonged entirely to the Shawangunk Ridge, with plenty of soil and foliage samples to prove it, but today, through no fault of my own, it was clean. But it still looked beat to shit and a little shiny. My beard, mostly gray, hadn't seen scissors or razor in months and my hair, spilling over my shoulders, was no tidier. The bit of my face visible between hair and beard was deeply lined, my eyes fairly bloodshot. I looked like a mountain man, possibly homeless. A hermit. A weirdo. A bum. A madman. I thought I could now understand what repelled Jane and I suddenly got self-conscious. Didn't I used to shave and change my clothes before I went out?

I ordered a glass of locally-brewed stout called Mother's Milk, found a tiny two-top table in the most remote corner of the tavern and sat by myself. As I sipped beer, I recognized the swirling jukebox music that occasionally rose above the voices and clinking of glasses. I had just played that solo myself, this afternoon, even if a little bit different. It was "Awake" and that was a younger, cleaner, more famous version of me playing and singing.

"Take a trip with the Tripper…"

Beer of various shades of amber, brown and black foamed into glasses and gurgled down throats. The throats came in a range of sizes and lengths, from standard issue human to extra-size bull, lion and, I think, anteater. The folks without costumes mingled a little more warily; I thought it was the natural uncool of those who showed up at costume parties dressed as themselves. Some, human and otherwise, nodded their heads to the tune. "Awake" probably lived in the same slot of the jukebox since the machine was installed, whenever that was. Everyone here would accept hearing the song as a natural, inevitable and familiar part of their evening. And I sat there in the corner and mused that none of them made the connection between the song and the crusty old guy with the crazy beard.

A word here about the local folks. Rosendaleans come in several varieties. There is an old-school hippie element, with strong representation by lesbian nurturing-earthmother types and freaky backwoods wizards and witches. The presence of the freaksters can be traced, in part, to fallout from the nearby college, famous as a psychedelic hotspot in decades gone by. Former students who once turned on, tuned in, and dropped out now turned on with The Clapper and dropped by to cash a Social Security check each month. Then there are the mountain people. Their families lived on the ridge for untold generations, perhaps descendants of cement or canal workers, or of the farmers who scraped the rocky soil of the hills to grow wheat and hemp for Washington's troops during the Revolutionary War. Now they lived in bottom-of-the-line modular homes or trailers along country byways like White Bush Road. And there are artists and musicians in Rosendale, as there are generally everywhere in Ulster County. There are more artists of various sorts around here, per capita, than anyplace else outside of certain parts of New York City. So I wasn't the only crusty person, not by a long shot. And I wasn't even the only crusty old guy.

The guy coming toward me, weaving his way around the chairs and tables, was way crustier than me, maybe even a little older. Just to be clear, that means really, exceptionally crusty and moderately old. He looked familiar and for a moment I had the idea that he was another incognito rock star. He was a white guy, thin wisps of mostly-gray hair escaping from a shapeless black leather hat, with a beard that was longer and grayer than my own. The rest of his clothing was leather, too – pants that in their prime would have looked great on Jim Morrison were now worn and stained, hanging limply from his bony frame. He wore a brown leather jacket with fringe that would have been seriously cool in 1972, but now appeared as ancient and tired as its owner. Cosmic bling hung from his neck and festooned his wrists and fingers: crosses, pentagrams, hexagrams, yin-yangs, ankhs, eyes, hands, birds, feathers and crystals. Gandalf the Brown. The Wizard of Odd. A mad shaman from some mythic, proto-Celtic realm that existed before the invention of personal hygiene. He limped a little and his knees popped as he descended into a chair across the tiny table from me.

He closed his eyes as if exhausted from the effort of reaching the chair, but in a moment his head started bobbing and I realized that he was rocking, mildly, to the beat of the song that was playing. It was the second verse:

> "Love aligns our mirror minds
> Endless flow of conscious ocean
> The heart's sparkling rainbow fire
> Filling, willing, rolling, roiling
> Am I only human here?"

He opened his eyes and grinned at me. Had he made the connection between "Awake" and my face that no longer resembled

the Annie Leibowitz portrait that once graced the cover of *Rockin'*
Bones magazine?

"Gonna buy me a drink, brother?" the crusty cosmic guy asked.

"Excuse me?" I said. "Say what?"

"You owe me that much, at least," he said.

"I don't believe I owe you shit," I clarified.

"C'mon, man, I don't have money. Get me a beer and I'll trip
you out." Deft sleight of hand and suddenly Gandalf was holding a
ziploc bag full of dried mushrooms. I recognized them instantly. Long
white stalks with faint blue streaks, curled and gilled brown caps, they
were the real deal, *Stropharia cubensis*, probably picked from a cow pie in
Florida or Georgia.

"I'm getting a little old for tripping," I said.

"You're never too old," crusty said. "It keeps the mind limber.
Besides, you have to change your mind if you're going to help me find
the resonant chamber and sing the song."

I took a long drink of Mother's Milk and tried to decide if I
wanted to get into even the most rudimentary conversation with this
wizardly wannabe. What "resonant chamber"? What song? Change my
mind about what? I wasn't sure I wanted to know. Before I could
decide, he continued.

"I once ate shrooms and journeyed back in time to when I was
a Mayan girl and they tried to kill me to feed a demon," he said, leaning
across the table, his voice rising. "I once dropped acid and went so far
into the future that our entire galaxy had slipped through a giant black
hole into another universe. I drank vine juice and danced with elves
and fairies all night long. Ketamine – holy shit! – blasted my body into
its component molecules and sent the molecules into the void. After a
whole cycle of existence, they came back together and reformed the
world as it is now." He grabbed my forearm where it rested on the
table. "I know the secrets, bro! I figured out what the shaman said! I
know how we can put it all back together again. Come on the trip with
me, man!"

"Unhand me, gray-beard loon," I commanded, pulling my arm
out of his grasp.

He sat back and calmed down a notch. "I need you, man. You and me. We have to go down, way down, and sing the song."

"You have to do it by yourself," I said with as much sincerity as I could muster. "Tell me how it works out, okay?"

He smiled. "How about that beer, then?"

I gulped down the rest of my stout and stood. I fished in my pocket, found a five and tossed it on the table. "Have one on me," I said. "See you around."

As I strolled across the beer-sticky floor to the door, I thought, *kind of reminds me of the old days.*

5. A New Etiquette

In the few days before anyone showed up, I played guitar and worked to tidy the buildings and deploy beds and bath towels. I also put some effort into making myself presentable. The mountain man beard was trimmed to a goatee and moustache. Hair was washed and even combed, then tied back. Clothes were already, remarkably, clean, except for those I dragged through the dirt on my horticultural adventures. Soon I felt ready to face the world again. I wished that Jane could see me.

The first to show up was Don Speckler, three days early. Don and his brother Ed were our sometime horn section, world famous in their own right. Ed passed away five or six years ago and Don was a solo act now, though he had a small entourage with him. Very small. In fact, they rode on his shoulders, a little red devil with a pitchfork on his left and a radiant white angel with a harp on his right. I was still attempting to rationalize these things and figured it for some kind of high tech art project, wearable holograms or something. He rolled up the long driveway in a ten-year-old Porsche covered with more rust and dust than paint. Don didn't look so good either. In the '70s, Don and Ed were short, lean and muscular. Twenty First Century Don was flabby and jowly. He looked exhausted; the short walk from the car to the front door seemed nearly the limit of his ability, even with encouragement – and discouragement – from his entourage. Don seemed mildly embarrassed by his imaginary friends and I decided, for the sake of his comfort as my guest, that I wouldn't mention them. Yet.

I showed him to the little mini-barn that we called The Cabin, where he fell onto a mattress and slept for over a day. The angel and devil waited for him on the night table, playing cards, debating ethics and napping with loud, cartoony snores.

When Don did finally arise, he didn't speak much for a while. He seemed a little dazed, like he was having a hard time shaking off the sleep. When I pressed him on it, he just said, "Ah, I gave in to temptation. Again." That was about as specific as he would get, but I remembered hearing rumors, a long time ago, about Don getting into trouble. Really odd rumors that never quite made sense to me, something about a dentist, a hooker, and a plate of escargot. I didn't press him about it too hard.

I packed a bowl and led Don out to the front porch where we sat on the steps and looked out over the expanse of mowed grass and weeds that I affectionately referred to as the parking lot. I lit up and held the bowl out to him.

Suddenly the little red devil popped up on Don's shoulder, smiling from ear to pointy ear, crying out, "Oh baby, yes! Smoke that shit!"

Predictably, the angel sprang into being on the opposite shoulder. It looked at the bowl, it looked at Don, it looked at the devil. "Oh, what the fuck," the angel said. "I could use a bit of that myself."

I passed the bowl to the angel, who took a big hit and handed the pipe to Don.

It was just around then that Trenton cruised up in a black town car. I guessed that he flew in to New York City from Oregon and hired the car for the three hour drive north to Rosendale. Accompanying him was a chubby middle-aged man in a dark suit who immediately set about removing luggage and keyboards from the trunk, a short, blond woman wearing a rather conservative skirt and jacket who poked compulsively at a personal communications device of some sort, and a statuesque, black-haired goddess in a toga who did an excellent job of looking beautiful and very, very radiant.

"Just in time!" I called as Trenton emerged from the car. I snagged the smoldering bowl from the devil and held it up. Trent came hurrying over. I noticed that age added a very slight stoop to Trenton's tall frame and a few lines to his face, but there was no gray in his sandy hair. He had long since stopped wearing suits on a daily basis, but still dressed nattily in black silk slacks and some kind of hand woven shirt with stylized faces on it.

He took a great big toke and coughed his lungs out. "Smooth," he chuckled.

We hugged. He shook Don's hand, made a point of ignoring the imaginary friends, and introduced us to his posse as the bowl resumed its rounds.

The chubby fellow with the luggage was Oswaldo, no last name given, who acted as Trenton's general gopher, driver, and joint-roller. The blond was Karen, also with no surname offered, and she was Trenton's business manager and road manager when he was on tour.

"And this is Esty." Trent gestured toward the toga woman as if I should know who she was.

"I'm just a fan," Esty said in a voice that was like a choir of sighs.

Trenton leaned toward me and whispered, "I don't think she's real. Anyway, 'backstage rules'."

I grinned at him. I hadn't heard that phrase in ages.

Don Speckler was flabbergasted. He stared at Esty and pointed, his mouth open wide. The angel and devil on his shoulders were similarly slackjawed. "You're… you're…" he stammered. "I saw you on TV. I…"

"Holy crap!" Esty exclaimed in six-part harmony. "You're Don Speckler. Of the Speckler Brothers! I have to get your autograph."

"*My* autograph?" Don squeaked.

Pay attention now. This is an excellent example of how television turns you into a moron. Don, like just about everyone else on the planet, had been glued to the Idiot Box on June twenty third and apparently young Esty was a star of the whole whateveritwas. So Don, an intelligent and accomplished individual, could barely croak out a complete sentence in Esty's presence. I was engaged in wholesome, outdoor activities that day, so my mind and vocal abilities were entirely intact.

"Trent thinks you're not real," I blurted out.

"I know," Esty smiled. "I'm real, though."

"We're real too!" the angel and devil called.

We all shook our heads. Don looked embarrassed.

"Toke?" I asked, holding forth the pipe.

"Don't mind if I do," Esty harmonized with herself.

Later that evening, Trenton and I managed to slip upstairs to my office to talk business. I planted my ass in my desk chair and swiveled around to face Trent, who lowered himself into the antique armchair under the window. The lower branches of a very large maple tree, silvery shadows in the moonlight, waved just a foot or two from his head.

"I need to make twenty five grand." I laid it out. "To save the mountain and the studio. Uh… Jane came back. She wants me to make it right. I've got to do this, so she'll come back."

"Jane?" Trenton asked. "She came back but you need to do this so that she'll come back? Huh?"

"She was back, Trent. Her ghost, maybe. She was young. And real. I could… touch her. But then she read my mail and got pissed about the mess I've made of it all. Said she might come back again if I make it right. Then she just… disappeared."

"Hmmm." Trenton thought for a bit. "There's been a whole lot of weird shit going on lately. Crazy shit, Ian. Ghosts, gods, demons, Bugs Bunny. I don't fucking know. But Jane. Wow. That's intense."

"Twenty five gees, Trent. Can I do it?"

"You can't make that farming?" he asked.

I explained that I really just grew weed for myself. Some years I had a nice surplus and could sell a little, if I had the connections, which I usually didn't. Other years, bad weather, hungry deer, or rip-offs would lead to a smaller crop. Twenty five grand would require a surplus of ten pounds or so, and that was pretty doubtful whatever the weather. I needed a sure thing.

"You'll make that in the first few nights," he said.

"First few nights of what?" I had an idea, but still had to ask.

He shook his head. "The first few nights of the reunion tour, that's what. I had dates booked for my own tour that will now become Blue Smoke dates. We start in ninety days. We hit a couple smaller cities to warm up, then it'll be two months visiting major venues around the globe. Arenas. Stadiums. A Blue Smoke comeback is so ripe. We will each make millions. Is that enough?"

"That would do it," I said, thinking not just of my taxes and Jane's return, but also entertaining a brief fantasy about a new indoor grow room with hydroponics and state-of-the-art LED lighting. "Are you sure? People want to see us? Even if we're old and shit?"

"Even if we're old and shit," Trenton replied. "Some of our fans are old and shit, too. Plus a generation or two of new fans."

In the few days since Trent and I spoke on the phone, his management team pieced together the main highlights of a tour and were still adding in dates. The tour would begin nearby, at the Mid-Hudson Civic Center in Poughkeepsie, a concert hall with seats for about three thousand, followed by a show at the twenty thousand seat TD Garden arena in Boston. Then down to the Meadowlands in northern New Jersey, a huge stadium that now boasted a corporate name that neither of us could remember. Nikea or Smalmart or something. But it was bigtime, the kind of arena where you'd expect to see U2 or Aerosmith or a Led Zep reunion. Then on from there to Atlanta, Dallas, Chicago, and a half dozen west coast dates. Then we would work our way through South America, Asia, Africa, Australia, Europe and finally back home, probably exhausted and hopefully with a big-ass check to cash at the local bank.

I liked it. I was ready. I was excited. I wanted to see and hear and feel an audience in front of me again. I wanted to rock.

"One more thing," Trenton said before we went back down to join the others.

"Yes?"

"I want to get some weed from you."

I just stared for a moment, trying to figure out if I heard him right. "*You*," I asked, "want to get some weed from *me*? What happened to your connection?"

"My connection is the same as ever," he said. "But when your harvest comes in. I want Blue Smoke."

"The good lord willin' and the creek don't rise," I told him. "Sure thing, if I've got it." Light dawned. Sort of. Blue Smoke was something you couldn't get these days. But… "How did you know I was growing Blue Smoke?"

He shrugged. "Just a hunch."

"A hunch…" I began, but Trent cut me off, pulling a fragrant baggie from his pocket. It was the kind of fragrant baggie that could reek out a room even if it were double wrapped and stashed in the back of the sock drawer.

"Genuine Kush," he said. "From the Kush Valley, you know, not a grow room down the street. The real thing. Shall we?"

I was forced to acquiesce.

Downstairs in the living room, Don Speckler was gazing worshipfully at Esty, his angel and demon holding a protracted whispered conference behind his head. I grabbed a big pillow and propped my old bones on the Persian rug. Trenton dragged a wooden chair from the kitchen. He handed the baggie to Oswaldo, who began to twist up a fat doobie.

"Many of the bands we think of today as legendary," Esty was saying as we settled in, "didn't make a dime when they were active and fresh."

"That's true," nodded Karen. "The Who were hardly popular at all in the USA until years after their prime. The Doors sold most of their records after Morrison was already gone. But management principles have changed a lot since those days."

"How do you know all this stuff?" Oswaldo asked Esty. He lit and puffed on the joint and then continued. "You are… much too young. I've never heard of half these bands you talk about, myself, and I'm at least ten years older than you."

"My father was a musician," Esty harmonized. "He died when I was little, but he left his record collection. I was listening to Hot Tuna and Captain Beefheart while the kids in my school were mostly into, I don't know, Hannah Montana. I've read a few books about rock history, too."

"*Headbanger's Guide to the Galaxy of Rock Stars?*" I asked.

Esty laughed like wind chimes in a summer breeze. "Yes, I read that one."

I changed the line of questioning. "What did your dad play?"

"Whatever instruments he could get his hands on," she said. "But he was probably most famous for his guitar. He was in a band called The Gestures."

"I played with The Gestures, on their *Somnolent Dance* album," Don Speckler spoke up. "Eddy and me."

"I know," Esty smiled. "You played a great clarinet solo on 'The Dance of Pan'."

Don actually blushed as he mumbled a thank you.

"Your father was Jack Westheimer?" I propped myself up a little straighter.

She nodded. "Cool, huh?"

"So what do you play?" I inquired.

"The ipod," she replied in heart-wrenching multiple tones. "Though I've been thinking about doing some singing."

Most of us laughed. "Let me know if you need management," Karen said.

"Show biz is sure going to benefit," Trenton said. "You know, since June twenty third."

"Oh, I was like this before the hoo-ha." Esty continued to smile sweetly. "Really. I'm human. I'm not an entity. Or mostly human, anyway."

Trent looked skeptical. I took her at her word, at least provisionally. You probably watched that shit on TV and read Esty's Kiwipedia page, so you're having a good laugh at us. Fuck you.

The next day, toward noon, Cleve White and Birdie Balam pulled up. They'd been friends and stayed in touch over the years and when it came time to travel they arranged to ride together from JFK in a rented Honda. Cleve still lived in northern California – Euriah, or Areka or one of those places. Birdie lived in Austin, Texas. They saw each other perhaps every few years, but after three hours in the car they seemed like an old married couple, helping each other with their bags and leaning together when their travel-wobbly legs weren't quite doing the job. They mostly ignored the very large jungle cat, a jaguar, which slid from the back seat and swirled around Birdie's legs like Bob when he's hungry or looking for some lap time. She absently pushed the hundred and fifty pound animal away with her foot. The rest of us, who had come outside to greet them, backed away from the cat, giving it ample room to sniff around the porch.

Cleve's short-cropped 'fro and neatly-trimmed beard were now white as snow. Always on the stocky side, he could now add roly-poly to his resume. Birdie, a bit chunky back in the day, was now somewhat closer to obese. Her hair, still shiny and black, fell over one shoulder in a long wave.

Cleve grabbed a flat instrument case and a wheeled suitcase from the trunk. Trenton and I stepped forward to handle the three monstrous suitcases that accompanied Birdie. The jaguar, who was making friends with Bob in the bushes, traveled light.

"Hey, Bob," I called. "Finally, a cat who can kick your ass."

Bob gave me a look which I imagined meant, "Are you kidding? This pussy?"

"Don't encourage the jaguar," Birdie suggested, either to me or to Bob, I'm not sure. "I'm trying to get it to stop following me around."

"You let it follow you all the way here from Austin?" I asked.

"It's like an old joke," Birdie explained. "Where does a hundred and fifty pound jungle cat sit?"

No one had to say the punchline, we all nodded and grunted understanding. I just wondered if the jaguar prowled the aisles of the airliner or if it had some more mystical means of travel and was waiting for Birdie when she landed in New York. I didn't ask. It was becoming obvious even to me that we were somehow plagued by strange entities of all sorts and that a new etiquette was necessary. What was the proper thing? Did one mention the ten foot tall, squid-like, eldritch creature escorting an acquaintance? Or was it best conversationally circumnavigated, like a zit or a hunched back? Fucked if I know.

"It's a pest," Birdie continued. "But I can't shake the feeling that it's trying to tell me something."

"You mean like an omen or something?" Esty asked. "A dream symbol?"

"Maybe that too," Birdie said. "But more like, if it could talk, it would have a message for me. I don't know how to explain it. Just a weird feeling I get."

"I get that from Bob, sometimes," I said.

Birdie looked at me like I was nuts.

The final Blue still alive and able to make the reunion was our drummer, Jason, who showed up in a shiny maroon minivan forty five minutes before our first rehearsal. He pulled the van close to the porch, climbed out and looked furtively around. He then immediately set about hauling big black drum cases and blue storage boxes from the back of the van. Trenton and I stepped up and joined in.

"Nice to see you, Jason," I said.

Jason had left music behind as a career in favor of literary pursuits. He wrote three books about the hard-partying, orgy-filled, strange-drug-gulping life of rock stars. The books made him the go-to guy for anecdotes about rock culture or drinking ether before meeting the President and he maintained a moderate media presence as a professional celebrity. It also helped him score a gig as an associate professor in the Cultural Studies department of a small, well-endowed liberal arts college in New Jersey. He had a second wife, two kids from one marriage and one from the other, all fully grown, and these days drank scotch rather than ether. It looked like he worked hard to maintain the look that he had when we were a band. His dark hair brushed the shoulders of his worn-thin t-shirt. A bit of a belly poked out over the top of his Levi's, but just a bit. His face showed his age the most; saggy skin around the eyes and wattles under his chin gave him a basset hound look.

"Yeah, nice to see you, too, Ian," Jason said. "Let's get this stuff inside."

"Did you come alone?" Trent asked.

Jason stopped and looked around again. "I think so. C'mon, hurry. Let's get the drums inside."

"Uh, yeah." I toted a drum case through the door.

It took only a few minutes to get the stuff in. Jason closed the door behind us, checked the windows, and then took a breath. "Hey!"

he enthused. "I made it! Reunion, right? Blue Smoke! Woohoo! Let's party!"

Trenton passed the current joint his way. Jason took a tiny sip of smoke, coughed politely and then passed it to me.

6. Backstage Rules

Our first rehearsal in decades started on time. And we didn't sound half bad. After a few false starts, we managed to get all the way through some of our favorite songs. We all took turns contributing to the arrangement and I thought I felt a little of that old collaborative feeling. I don't think anyone consumed anything stronger than my Shawangunk Nepali, but it did seem a little trippy with an angel, a devil, a very attentive and alert jaguar, the jaguar's new best buddy Bob, and Esty among our select interspecies and perhaps interdimensional studio audience.

Mostly we kept it pretty basic. Jason was keeping it the most basic, in the pocket, but not risking any pyrotechnics or anything resembling a solo. Don Speckler sounded pretty sweet on alto sax and added some major swing to the whole afternoon. Birdie sounded great, too, and we all immediately took it for granted that she would be singing most of the back-up on everything, not just the tunes she originally sang. Cleve warned us that he was rusty, and he was, just a bit. Trenton occasionally played a couple of Blue Smoke numbers in his own act, so he was all over it on those tunes, but worked hard with the rest of us on everything else. When we hit the groove, it was okay.

It was work, mostly, without revelation or peak experience. And it was a pretty good beginning. The unspoken consensus was that it could happen and everyone was in, which was cause for celebration.

Jason refused to use his minivan for the after-dinner beer run, so I gave my truck keys to Cleve and Don. The pickup rattled off into the twilight and I went to sit on the porch and roll a joint.

There was an old green and yellow plaid sofa on the porch, a bit weather-beaten but not too mildewed. I extricated the bag of bud from my jeans pocket and lowered myself onto the couch. Several months of accumulated junk mail rested on the arm of the sofa and a cardboard used-car circular became a nice surface to break up the weed. It was a bit of my Lemon Bud, an energizing sativa strain with a bubbly, euphoric high. The lemon meringue aroma rose to meet my nose as I crushed the bud between my fingers. I was lining up the pulverized ganja in creased rolling paper when the front door creaked open and a six-toned voice said, "I thought I smelled something good."

I looked up to see Esty, radiant as ever in a long, flowing white gown.

"Join me?" I offered.

"Don't mind if I do," she smiled. "You've got the best shit."

We passed the joint in silence for a few minutes. Treefrogs and crickets were beginning their evening chorus. Somewhere in the distance a mad or horny owl hooted repeatedly. From further away came a faint susurrus of cars sliding up and down the Thruway.

As the bubbly euphoria began to rise through my chest and head, Esty asked, "So, you don't have any imaginary friends?"

"Maybe you're my imaginary friend," I said.

"You don't watch TV." It was a statement, not a question.

"I have a DVD player," I explained.

"Right," she said. "I keep telling everyone, I was like this before the hoo-ha. I did this to myself. I'm not anyone's imaginary friend, nothing against imaginary friends. Hey, I was there when this all started. I helped make it happen."

"This…?"

"The gods walk the Earth," she said. "All the characters and beings of our tales and mythology are solid matter now. Or sort of solid, anyway. Solid when they want to be."

I worked the roach for another hit. "What did you do? How did you make it happen?"

"There were a lot of people involved, even at the, er, climax, though Joe and I were the ones on camera. On one level, it was a big marketing stunt, an exercise in memetics and media that twisted thought patterns a little bit. On another level, it was a symbolic sex act that pushed the attention of the world beyond the mere information, the memetics and so forth. And on yet another level, it was part of an inevitable cosmic process that began in the very early moments of the universe and manifests throughout time and space. Now we see, feel, hear, taste and smell the entities who formerly just inhabited our imagination."

"But how is that possible?" I asked.

"Hell, I'm not really sure, either," she said. "But remember, everything you think you experience is an interpretation, created in your brain. Humans have mostly always behaved as if their gods and demons were real, and the gods and demons have sometimes changed the world. Now we see and hear and feel them, too. It's just a slightly different way for our brains to represent them. Or, at least, that's my theory. Alternatively, the newagers say that when Joe and I, er, when we performed the ritual that made the hoo-ha manifest on worldwide television, the boundaries between our world and the next one began to dissolve."

"What does it take for something, someone to become real?" I asked. "I mean, is it only gods and things that millions of people believe in? Or...?"

I thought I heard something rustling in the bushes next to the porch. Leading suspects were cats, large and small, so I let it be.

"I'm not sure 'believe' is the right word," Esty said. "Maybe 'relate to' or 'delineate' would be better. It doesn't seem to matter how many people are involved, more a matter of how well the entity is defined, which happens when we relate to it in some way. We think about it, make offerings to it, write or read books about it, tell tales about it, make movies about it, tell our innermost secrets to it, tell it our wishes and prayers, and so on. The delineation is in the details. Do we call it he or she or pansexual and polymorphous? Do we offer it candy, cigars and rum or the blood of our firstborn child? Do the stories we tell about it concern cleverness, avarice, beauty, murder or compassion? I think that if more people are involved, relating to the same entity, it could really get, um, really real. Realer?" She laughed and it sounded like sparkling rainbow light. "More details, anyway. But if one person had a particularly well-defined entity, it could very well walk among us, too."

A scraping noise from next to the porch. My THC-enhanced paranoia spiked sharply.

"We're not alone," Esty whispered, which did nothing to allay the paranoia.

I got up in time to see a dark shape shuffle into the deeper darkness next to Jason's minivan. By the time I went down the steps and around the side of the porch, I could see nothing there at all. I went back to my seat.

"What if that's just an embodiment of my fear?" I asked.

"You don't seem like the kind of guy who would be afraid of trespassers," Esty intoned.

"They should be afraid of me." I reached behind the sofa and pulled my old Mossberg from the hidden holster I had wired there.

"Whoa," she said.

"Shotgun," I grinned.

"Whoa," she said.

"I only ever use it to scare off bear and coyotes." Then I spoke louder, in the voice I use to address arenas full of people. "But in the event I catch someone sneaking around on my property, I will not hesitate to shoot their ass with this vintage but fully functional shotgun!"

I was rewarded with a bit of scuffling from the side of the house, and we could hear the door of the minivan click shut.

"Go get Jason," I told Esty. "Tell him there's someone in his van."

She ran inside, a blur of flowing white fabric, and I stalked down to the parking lot, shotgun in hand. I stood behind the van, in a position that would let me see if doors on either side opened.

"Okay," I boomed out in my best cop impersonation. "I know you're in there. Step out of the vehicle."

Something whimpered from within the van, which shook a little bit, betraying internal movement. But no one stepped out.

"Come on," I ordered. "Get out of the vehicle with your hands above your head. I have a shotgun."

I pumped a shell into the chamber, always a satisfying sound. The whimpering increased and the minivan shook even more.

Just then, Jason emerged from the house, Esty, Oswaldo and Birdie right behind.

"I'm going to shoot your ass," I called.

"Wait," said Jason. "Wait! He's…" He looked around. He looked down at the ground. No one else said anything. A treefrog trilled. "With me. It's…"

We listened to the treefrog for a moment more. I was still clutching the gun.

"I just like the song," Jason finally continued. "It was stuck in my head that day. June twenty third. Now he follows me around. I thought I'd lost him coming up here."

I lowered the shotgun and went around the side of the van. I peered in the window. In the dimness, I could make out a shape that may have been an old man dressed in layers of ruined clothing, cowering in a near-fetal position. He apparently saw me, too, because he began whimpering and shaking more violently.

Jason joined me at the side of the minivan. "You have to know how to talk to him." He gingerly opened the side door of the van a crack. "Don't you start…" he said to the old man, who whimpered even more frantically. Jason coughed, shook his head, and began again. "Aqualung my friend," he said.

"Aqualung!" several of us, including me, exclaimed. "Aqualung?"

"Don't you start away uneasy," Jason continued.

"Are we going to have to pay ASCAP for this?" Birdie asked.

"You poor old sot," Jason said.

"Not if we keep interrupting," I said to Birdie.

Jason turned to us. "Shhhhh. You have to talk to him like in the song."

"Like in the song?" Oswaldo asked. He was obviously not a Tull fan.

"You see it's…" Esty multi-toned, by way of explanation.

"You see it's only me," Jason told the old man.

Aqualung quieted: no whimpering, no deep sea diver sounds, just a few sniffles.

"I think that's fair usage," Birdie said.

"Come on out, Aqualung," Jason urged the old man. "Come meet some friends."

Mild grumbling could be heard from inside the vehicle. Jason pulled a silvery flask from his back pocket and held it up.

"Look what I've got! Single malt!" Jason called cheerily, shaking the flask.

Aqualung emerged hesitantly, a crop of gray, dirty, matted hair rising from the minivan door. His nose, as the song quite frankly describes, was the source of a prodigious amount of mucus. Shabby clothing was quite smeared with grease, or worse. Narrowed eyes roamed the length of Esty's gown with what can only be described as bad intent. Really, he looked at all of us and it was tough to say whether his intent was bad or if his face was just stuck that way. His squinty gaze finally came to rest on Jason. He snatched the flask from Jason's grasp and we watched his wrinkly Adam's apple bob for a few moments. Finally he handed the flask back. Jason wiped it on his shirt, took a swig himself, and replaced the cap.

"What..." Aqualung began in a hoarse voice. He cleared his throat, wiped goop from his upper lip onto his shabby sleeve, and then began again, his voice just as hoarse. "What do you mean... like in the song?"

Jason opened his mouth to answer and then closed it again. He scratched his head. It was another one of those etiquette problems. How do you tell someone that they're just a character from an old pop song?

Jason was spared by the rattling return of the pickup truck. Aqualung stared after us as we walked out to meet the beer.

Don hopped out from the passenger side.

"That was quick," I observed.

"We went down to Crumby's," he said, referring to a gas station and convenience store just a few miles away on Route 32. "Hey, we met someone there. A fan. This guy really knew a lot about the band, about the songs. I was impressed. Anyway, we brought him along for the party."

"You brought a fan?" I asked. In the old days we had strict rules about fans. Other than our personal guest list, only beautiful women and guys who had good drugs could make it backstage, though we did make exceptions for a few fans who were actually fun to hang out with.

Cleve appeared from around the truck. "It's cool," he said in a low voice. "The guy's got some…"

"Whoa," said a male voice from the direction of the pickup. Someone lying in the truck bed now sat up and became dimly visible as a shadow in the shape of a torso and head. "I was lying here, looking at the stars as we drove and went around the curves. I suddenly had this sense of how we're always moving relative to the stars, walking or driving around on the planet, the planet spinning around and whirling around the sun, the sun spiraling around and around the big cosmic drain at the center of the galaxy. Whoa." He clambered out and as he stepped nearer the light from the porch, I could see that it was the panhandling shaman-wannabe from the tavern.

"Shrooms," Cleve said into my ear.

"Big cosmic drain?" I asked.

"Ian, man," the old shroom guy said. "There you are! I promised to trip you out."

"Can you even remember the last time you saw shrooms?" Cleve enthused close to my right ear.

"Last week," I said. "With this dude."

"They're really good shrooms." The shroom dude giggled suddenly. "Woooo! The ancient Aztecs used to serve psychedelic mushrooms at all major public celebrations, to mark out the experience as something special."

"What's your name, my old friend?" I asked.

The crusty guy stopped giggling abruptly, looked like he was taking me seriously, and then said, "You can call me The Tripper."

"Great," I said. "Stay out of the house. You can party out here with, uh, Aqualung. You're both from songs, you'll get along nicely."

Aqualung and The Tripper eyed each other suspiciously while we carried the beer into the house.

"Ian, why are you making that man stay outside? Where's your sense of hospitality?" Cleve asked.

"I'm hospitable to people who tell me their real names and smell like human beings. Sorry, man, I don't mean him any harm, but this is where I live and only friends get invited in here," I explained. "If we had backstage rules about access, this is so far beyond backstage that I should require DNA tests and a background check."

"Uh, sorry, man," Cleve said. "But thanks. Now I feel special about being here."

"I'll tell you what," I reconsidered. "The Tripper can hang in the studio, if he promises not to touch the guitars, and we can all party in there for a little while. But not Aqualung. Not without delousing."

So, a short time later, the band and our combined entourage gathered in the studio and set to work on the beer, a big bag of Shawangunk Nepali and, yes, the mushrooms.

7. The Shroom Version

The swirly things that were haunting the edges of my vision, originally a gift of the cannabis, were now morphing into interlocking Sun Wheels, kind of an M.C. Escher-meets-the-Aztecs motif. The whirling geometric designs flowed over the walls and furniture. The studio and people took on a unique significance. Our presence at that particular moment was important, sacred, destined. A new era was born in which the psychedelic message would be carried forth once again. Sure, my imagination was running amok, but that's half the fun of tripping.

At some point, Trenton asked The Tripper, "So who are you really? And where did you get these shrooms?" That may have been a few minutes ago, or it may have been hours, I couldn't tell. The Tripper was deep into a rap about his travels and shamanic initiations and I wasn't sure it made any sense, but then my mind wandered a bit. If I closed my eyes, I gazed into vast, jewel-like landscapes and cycling pastel proto-machines that dominated and then became the landscape, endlessly repeating and mutating. Yes, it was pretty cool and don't try this at home, kiddies. Fuck that. If you can score shrooms as good as those, do them up. But enjoy the trip in the comfort of your home. Stay put. Turn the lights down. Put on a Blue Smoke CD. Stay on the sofa. Don't do something stupid. Like we did.

"I was Dennis McKenna for a short time, in South America," The Tripper was babbling. "And I was Terence for quite a while. I visited Tim Leary in his later years. I never got to be Robert Anton Wilson, but I did hang around him for a time. And mostly people you never heard of, in other parts of the world. It's nice to just be myself for a little while, you know? Once I was a shaman's apprentice in Peru and…"

Birdie was lying on her back on a worn throw rug, in a nest of pillows, the jaguar and Bob curled up by her side. The cats hadn't snacked on shrooms, but felines seem to pick up the psychedelic vibe. They were purring and beaming fuzzy attention at us through luminous eyes. I didn't know that jaguars could purr, but it was loud enough to be heard over the ambient clouds of sound that Trenton conjured from a keyboard.

"So the prophecies were always true for those guys," The Tripper ranted, "because it wasn't something external, but part of their epistemological makeup, if you catch my innuendo. Like snow to an Inuit. And the shaman had the whole story, too. He had it spelled out, letter by letter, for years to come. He claimed that he came by it through metaphysical powers, but I think he had some technology, some way to travel back and forth through time and space, to anywhere that he wanted to go. He was always really well stocked with herbs and drugs and such and there was nothing but grass and scrubby little trees for a hundred miles around. So when he told me about the quest, hell, I said I'd go anywhere, even Rosendale."

I let that slide. "What quest?" asked Oswaldo, who had been staring off into space and giggling sporadically for the last half hour or so. He was lounging in a threadbare armchair, a green beer bottle resting on his round belly. Now he tilted his head just slightly toward The Tripper. Over in the corner, Esty and Don Speckler stopped whispering and giggling to each other and also gave their attention. Karen, stripped down to her bra and panties, sat in lotus position on the sofa, making soft "wooo" noises and giggling. Cleve was lying on the bare wooden part of the floor with his eyes closed. I had no idea whether or not he was with us. I didn't know where Jason was, but had a hunch he was outside, polishing off his flask with help from Aqualung.

"Oh, well that's the thing," The Tripper said. "Even though we were all convinced the shaman could travel through space and time, at least in spirit if not in actual body, no one could really understand what the fuck he said. It was all in stories and riddles and symbols and shit.

But I figured him out. You see, he'd always be puffing on a pipe, or chewing some herb, or stuffing some goop up his nose while he was talking and he would kind of rock back and forth and fall into a rhythm. So I thought maybe if I could get into the same headspace that he was in, I'd understand the way that he thought and…"

"The quest, my man," Cleve said loudly, without opening his eyes. "What the fuck did he say about the quest?"

"We're all on shrooms, man." The Tripper laughed. "So I have to tell the shroom version. Someone get me a drum."

"The drums are Jason's," I said. "And he's not here to ask."

"Oh, not those drums," The Tripper said. "A shaman's drum. A hand drum. Like that dumbek over there by the wall."

The dumbek, in a black faux-leather case, had lived over there by the wall for at least fifteen years and hadn't seen the light of day in all that time. It was Jane's, a metal and plastic Alexandrian, pretty near indestructible. I figured she would rather that the drum came out of its case from time to time and I gave The Tripper a nod. Nobody else moved, so he crossed the room to fetch it himself. The drum looked as shiny and clean as the last time Jane played it, years ago.

The Tripper held the drum upside down and it looked like a giant hourglass-shaped golden grail. "In Egypt," he pronounced, "they fill these with beer and then play all night, once they have drunk."

He flipped it back upright, whacked it with his thumb and it made a satisfying *pong*. He smiled and settled into his chair, the drum between his knees. *Pong-bop. Bop bop. Pong pong.* The Tripper got a feel for the drum. He actually looked like he knew what he was doing. *Pong-bop pong-bop pong-bop pong-bop.* He found a rhythm, a bright, resonant heartbeat, and held it steady as he spoke. Trent, still spinning auras of sound from his keyboard, began to incorporate the rhythm.

"Back in the ancient days," The Tripper said in low, serious tones, "in the days of our ancestors, the gods walked the Earth every now and then. It was a rare and sacred occasion when they did. When there was a special need for it, the shaman said, a god or gods would incorporate – inhabit a solid body – and get the job done.

"In the first days of time, the world was perfect and harmonious, but as human beings took over from the gods, their inexperience and imbalance knocked creation awry. The world became more and more cacophonous. People complained about their lot in life. The weather sucked. People drew lines on the Earth, showing where they would fight other people who crossed or tried to redraw the lines. They knocked down great forests, massacred mighty herds, fouled the oceans with their waste, and smashed the crust of the Earth itself in search of gold and oil. They fought over resources which, if they but looked and imagined, were really plentiful."

Pong-bop pong-bop pong-bop pong-bop.

"To set it right, the gods called forth six beings who had the spirit of the first days in them, full of song and awareness of the many voices and tones of the world. There was Bernard, the…"

"Wait, wait," interrupted Birdie. "Bernard?"

"It's a very ancient name," The Tripper asserted. "There was Bernard, the smart one of the group; Perzanto, who was…"

"Wait, wait, wait," Birdie cried. "Perzanto?"

"Also a very ancient name," The Tripper said.

"If ancient means you just made it up," Birdie said more quietly, "sure. But I don't mean to stop you. Go on with your story."

The Tripper took a moment to gather his thoughts.

Pong-bop pong-bop pong-bop pong-bop.

"There was Bernard," he reiterated, "the smart one of the group; Perzanto, who was strong and could lift boulders and push down mighty trees; Beezel…" The Tripper paused for a moment, shooting a glance at Birdie, who just smiled. "…who could sing directly into a person's heart; Dondelakavin, the cute one of the group; Mortimer…"

Birdie burst out laughing, a mushroom-fueled laughing jag that could easily have escalated.

Pong-bop pong-bop pong-bop pong-bop.

"Mortimer," The Tripper said once more in a louder voice, "the messenger of the gods; and Gardangulon, the leader of the group, who carried an axe and a thunderbolt. The six beings were sent off from their homes in various, diverse parts of the world. Their mission was to meet in a place called The Valley of Roses. In the Valley, protected by the thorns of magical rose bushes, was a gateway to the underworld, to a special place where the Earth would resonate with power. When the six beings met in that secret, subterranean cavern, they would sing a song together and the vibration of the song would pass through the rock, the soil, the oceans, the crust, mantel and core of the planet. It would vibrate every part of the world, which includes not only the earth, but the air, water, trees, animals, and human beings."

Pong-bop pong-bop pong-bop pong-bop.

"The shaman was very specific in describing the gateway. It was thirty feet across, twenty feet high, and was an arch of eroded, brown limestone. It was set into the base of a cliff and the magical rose bushes that protected it had great clusters of pure white flowers. Each of the beings had a map to the place, each had magical powers, and each was a great warrior who traveled with a squadron of fighting men. Their travels took many years and spawned even more tales and legends. In time, they should all have made it to the cave."

Pong-bop pong-bop pong-bop pong-bop.

"They should have?" I asked.

"They should have," said The Tripper, "but something went awry. The shaman didn't know what. The song was never sung. The Earth remains discordant and out of balance. The tales of several show that they made it here and…"

"Excuse me," I interjected. "Here? They made it *here?*"

"Oh yes," The Tripper explained. "Don't you get it? The Valley of Roses? Rosendale? Plenty of caves here, too. But there's one cave just on the other side of this mountain." He gestured toward the back of the studio where the lowest ridge could be glimpsed through the windows, rising up and out of sight. "It matches the description perfectly."

"Hey! That's on my property," I said. "Have you been snooping around on my mountain?"

"Uh, it was the shaman, man. But Ian, that makes it even better, that you own the cave. Because now we can go there and you guys can play a song." The Tripper smiled and whacked the drum.

Pong-bop pong-bop pong-bop pong-bop.

Birdie giggled. Trenton made some loopy sounds. Karen said, "woooo."

"So that's the quest?" Cleve asked, still staring at the engrossing view inside his eyelids.

"Yeah, man," The Tripper said. "That was my quest, given to me by the shaman. To find the greatest rock band ever and get them to play a song in the sacred cavern in the Valley of Roses. It's just a little bit more way-cool synchronicity that the band's front man owns the property where the entrance to the sacred cavern is found." He giggled a shroomy giggle.

"Mick Jagger has a cave on his property too?" I asked.

Pong-bop pong-bop pong-bop pong-bop.

"I'll go play a song in a cave," Trenton spoke up. "Just please stop with the *pong-bop*, okay?"

The Tripper set the drum down.

"I'll go too," said Birdie. "It'll be an adventure."

"I wouldn't mind being outside for a bit," Cleve offered.

"I bet the acoustics in the cave are amazing," said Don. "All that resonating and vibrating."

They were all looking at me. "There might be dangers," The Tripper said. "We don't know what happened to Bernard and Gardangulon and those guys. There were supposed to be guardians in the cave who would fight to protect the sacred vibration point of the planet. There might be people living in there."

"On my property?" I asked. "People living on my property?"

"Yeah." The Tripper nodded. "Under it."

"Fuck. Yeah, let's do this." I grinned. "I bet Mortimer didn't have a shotgun."

Oh, like you never did anything stupid.

8. Down

And so, the preternatural glow of mushroom hallucinations lighting the way, we set off on our quest. Well, most of us. We found Jason and Aqualung sitting in the perennials, in front of the porch, and Jason made Aqualung look like the designated driver. The only thing keeping our drummer sitting upright was the dose of psilocybin running through his brain.

Perhaps because he wasn't there when the rest of us agreed to this thing, Jason was unmoved by our holy purpose. "Wander around the mountains? In the dark? Looking for a fucking cave?" Jason took another swig from his flask. "You gotta be nuts. Man, I'm not gonna fall off a mountain into some fucking hole, 'cause I'm following some hippy nutjob around, 'cause I'm tripping. In the dark. Nope. Not me. Me and the 'lung here, we're just gonna hang and wait for you to get back."

"Shorry, Jay," slurred Aqualung, shakily getting to his feet. "I'm going on the quesht."

We gathered up our instruments and loaded gear onto the non-musician members of our party. From the back of Trenton's hired car came a trio of battery-powered electronic amps, the latest thing from some electronics corporation that wanted to bask in the aura of Trent's P.R. image. I distributed ropes, flashlights, and bottled water. I crammed a big bag of 'Gunk bud into my guitar case along with my 1961 SG Les Paul and slung the old Mossberg over my shoulder.

So we set off, a caravan of aging hippy gypsies and our imaginary friends, stumbling and giggling our way up the side of the mountain. The Tripper led the way and I made an effort to stay up there with him, to make sure no one strayed from the path, as it were, into the garden. The Tripper was toting the dumbek, now back in its pleather case. I had both shotgun and guitar, straps crossing my chest like bandoliers. Esty, who had a surprisingly long and graceful stride and a portable amp on her back, was just behind us. Oswaldo was only a little way behind her, in spite of being the most loaded with stuff. He looked like a chubby little burro, piled high with equipment cases and big, snaky coils of cable. He stomped along cheerfully, mushrooms lending looseness to his limbs.

Trenton, Don, Cleve, Birdie and Karen walked so close to each other that they kept bumping together, the angel and devil fluttering frantically into the air every time. More often it was the gear strapped to them that took any impact, and the result of the minor collisions was mostly giggling and a tendency to stray from the path. But they weren't the slowest members. Shuffling along, way back on the trail, was Aqualung, definitely starting to make some deep sea diver sounds as the trail began to climb the ridge.

The jaguar silently kept pace with us, staying off the trail and flowing between the trees. Bob was nowhere to be seen.

The moon and stars were laser bright and our pupils widely dilated, so no one switched on a light. Silvery patterns of light and shadow flickered and merged with psilocybian geometrics as the bramble-filled logging road switched back and forth up the ridge. The trail dipped into the narrow valley between ridges and we walked through a grove of mature white pines, a carpet of needles cushioning our step. When the giggling stopped for a moment, the forest was deeply quiet.

The trail became steeper and narrower, winding between oaks and maples as we ascended the second ridge. I lost track of Aqualung entirely and was mostly aware of the others from the sounds of footsteps, collisions, and giggling. Esty had somehow gotten ahead of me and her white gown reflected dappled, ever-shifting patterns of moonlight, shapes that left long, trailing retinal burns in my field of vision.

"Robert Heinlein," I said to her rocking hindquarters, "proposed that our world was myth. That our universe was a fictional creation, parallel to the mythic worlds we find in books and movies."

Esty turned and dropped back to get a little closer to me. The trail was too narrow at this point to walk side by side, but she got close enough so that she only had to turn a little bit to see and speak with me. "Pantheistic Multiple-Ego Solipsism," she pronounced.

"That's it," I said. "I was trying to remember the term. Thanks."

"Any other esoteric terms I can help you with?" she asked. "In spite of my appearance, I am a certified geek."

"I had a feeling," I said, then paused for a moment. "What's happening to our world.… UFOs, Aqualung, angels, devils, the jaguar, my dead wife.…"

Esty gave me a penetrating, wide-pupiled gaze. "Oho! Your dead…? So you do have an imaginary friend!"

"Yeah, yeah," I said. "But she's away, for now."

"I bet you say that to all the girls," Esty grinned.

I knew she was kidding around, but it still made my breath catch. "I mean, Pantheistic Solipsism, it kind of explains what's going on."

"Could be," Esty averred. "Our cultural myths and our personal myths wandering out of their, um, mythic universes, their stories, into ours? That's one way of understanding it. And maybe our brains have learned that these universes aren't as separate as all that, that they all converge wherever there's a point of consciousness…" Her multi-voice trailed off into shroomy contemplation for a moment, then snapped back. "Well, this sure isn't a Heinlein novel. Too much weed."

"What about him?" I aimed a thumb up the trail where we could glimpse The Tripper stomping along through the trees. "Human or entity?"

"Entity," Esty said. "For sure."

"Yeah," I nodded. "That's what I was thinking."

"That makes two for you," she said.

"He's mine?" I asked.

Esty shrugged. "You wrote the song."

The trail dipped slightly again after we crested the second ridge. Between the second and uppermost ridge, there was a wide, flat expanse with an occasional cedar or stunted pine. In the moonlight, pale shapes bobbed and shifted in a slight breeze. When my shirt caught on a thorn, I remembered that the wild roses were blooming in big white clumps.

The official flower of Rosendale is, not surprisingly, the rose. But Rosendale wild roses aren't your grandmother's big old garden flowers. They are tiny, delicate little things that grow in great numbers on formidably thorny, sprawling bushes. When the flowers fall away later in the season, each leaves behind a sour little rosehip no bigger than a malnourished pea, on the end of each twig.

The Tripper suddenly stopped in the middle of the trail and turned to face us. "Behold the Valley of the Roses!" he called melodramatically.

There were a few oohs and aahs from the group, and more giggles.

"Stay on the trail," I added, nearly as loud. "The thorns are dangerous."

More oohs, aahs, and giggles.

The trail wound through the shallow valley and then suddenly began to ascend the top ridge, trees and roses giving way to bare rock. We climbed fairly quickly, even our less athletic members now fully energized by the psilocybin. In about fifteen minutes we were at the summit, a flat shelf of rock spattered with bird poop that glowed eerily white in the moonlight. The view was awesome, as always. Lights from as far away as the Hudson twinkled in the darkness: bright homes full of cozy people tucked into the woods, the lamps of cars and boats flickering in and out of existence as they passed beneath trees and behind buildings and hills. The cliff fell away a hundred feet to the woods below. Long ago, a glacier had scraped and pushed enormous blocks of stone off the top of the ridge and they lay in cracked and broken profusion below, glimpsed in the half light as square shadows and pools of deeper blackness. In one of the pools of deep blackness was the cave mouth.

Our hike up to the summit had its steep moments, but from this point on the terrain became increasingly vertical, mostly in the downward direction. I knew how to scramble down to base of the ridge, but I wasn't sure I knew how to safely guide our group of giggling rock stars and industry flacks that way. Hell, I wasn't sure I'd try it myself in the dark, let alone while I was hallucinating rotating neon gears and sun wheels all over the rocks. The Tripper, however, already had a course charted and damned if we just followed along. We walked single file, slowly, on a sloping, narrow path that zigged and zagged down the escarpment. It had precarious moments and got several squeals from Birdie and at least one from Don.

As we descended, someone began to chant: "All the way, all the way, all the way down."

I'm sure you know this song, too. Track three on *Six Songs*, the last cut on side A. Plenty of radio time over the years. "Down" had a bit of a revival in the mid '80s and got a lot of airplay, a whole damn lot of airplay, for a few years. It still pops up here and there.

A few more of them joined in. I heard Birdie start to improvise around the melody.

"All the way, all the way, all the way down."

The chant went on for a timeless while as we crept carefully down the trail. I was the only one who could break the trance, I knew. No one else would sing the verses with me there. I was the one who had to sing it. So eventually I gave in to the urge.

"I went down to see my baby…" My mouth was too dry and the words barely came out. I forced myself to swallow and waited for it to come around again.

"I went down to see my baby

Gonna make that girl my bride."

I couldn't quite give it full power because I was paying attention to the trail and generally not falling off the cliff, but it was working anyway.

"All the way, all the way, all the way down."

"I went down to see my baby

But when I found my girl she cried"

I let the chant carry the rhythm as the trail descended around a tricky turn, until I felt sure of my footing.

"All the way, all the way, all the way down."

"What's gettin you down my baby?

What's gettin you down my girl?
She dried her eyes
And made more sighs
And then she left this world."

The moon disappeared as the trail wound down into the shadow of the cliff. Mushroom-enlarged pupils aside, it got pretty damn dark.

"All the way, all the way, all the way down."

"Hey!" The Tripper called suddenly. "This is it! We're here!"

The procession took several minutes to actually come to a halt and stop giggling for a moment. Before us was a big patch of darkness in the middle of a great jumble of smaller patches that were almost as dark. The big patch of darkness swirled with bright geometric shroomy images, all the brighter for the contrast. A cool, steady breeze flowed out from the blackness, the rotating mushroom visuals floating on the chilled air.

I unclipped my flashlight from my belt, clicked it on and sent a piercing arrow of light into the darkness. Mixed limestone and conglomerate, all of it mottled brown in the dimness, formed a massive archway around the beam. More lights came on and we could see that the cave mouth, shaggy with ferns and hanging plants, was down in a hole. It would be necessary to descend about twenty feet before we could stroll into the cave and play a song.

I took a look at some of the heavyweight band members. I took a look down into the hole. "Ropes!" I called. "Who has the ropes?"

Okay, I know that this is probably not in the American Spelunking Club book of recommended practices. Some of our group had likely never stepped in a pothole, let alone explored an honest-to-the-creepy-god-my-neighbor-hides-in-his-basement actual limestone cavern. We had some ropes and flashlights - a collection of LED lights I'd bought cheap at Jolly's Bargain Outlet in Kingston; they were bright and would run for a year on a set of batteries – but no helmets, and no real climbing gear. And we were tripping and following an entity of some sort who was very likely nuts. What can I say? It seemed like the thing to do at the time? Fuck you! It did seem like the thing to do.

It took all of our ropes, a whole lot of muscle power, and an indeterminate amount of time. Eventually we stood before the cave entrance, probing our flashlights into the big dark. The darkness swallowed the beams and the sense of the massiveness of the stone archway stilled the giggling. For one long, solemn moment.

"C'mon dudes!" The Tripper invited us cheerfully. "Let's go in and get down!"

The giggling resumed.

We followed his hallucinatory ass into the cave, keeping flashlight beams aimed close to us, lighting the next step rather than trying to push back the pervading darkness. I had a pretty good idea what was coming next. I'd seen the gaping maw of the cave from my treks along the cliff, but I'd never been in before. Didn't matter. I knew what was in most of the caves around here. Hell, if we looked hard enough, we might find the nether end of my well pump.

"Water!" exclaimed The Tripper.

Flashlight beams played across the darkness as our expedition spread out along the shore of a large underground lake.

"Is there any way around it?" asked Trent.

"I doubt it," I said. "Most of these caves are full of water. It's kind of cool here, though." I gazed for a moment into the psychedelic funhouse. "We could play a song right here."

"The water's right to the wall on this side," called Don from somewhere down the shoreline. "No way around."

"Pretty deep and wet over here," harmonized Esty from the other direction.

I unslung my guitar. "Who has one of those little baby amps?" I asked.

We were all plugged in and set up within minutes, sitting or standing on smooth rock that inclined just slightly toward the water.

"Hello Bats and Troglodytes!" I called into the void. "It's great to be here in the cave tonight! Always a fantastic audience!"

A weird, rattling echo returned from the darkness.

I began the chant and the others fell in with me. "All the way, all the way, all the way down."

The chant went around a few times and I started on the verse.

"I went down to see my baby
Gonna make that girl my bride.
I went down to see my baby
But when I found my girl she cried"

"All the way, all the way, all the way down."

"What's gettin you down my baby?
What's gettin you down my girl?
She dried her eyes
And made more sighs
And then she left this world."

It was working. We were falling into synch much more easily than we had in our rehearsal. I shut up and played my guitar, a solo of long, plaintive notes that swooped off into the distance and managed their own, stony reverb without benefit of a pedal.

The others jumped back in with the chant, Birdie improvising a bluesy wail.

"All the way, all the way, all the way down."

"I went down to see the preacher," I sang.

"Ask him what became of my young bride.
I went down to see the preacher
Asked him if my girl had died."

The chanters chanted and I could have sworn, somewhere deeper in the cave, I heard a splash.

"He said it was the work of the Devil
Said he'd taken her from this world
He closed his eyes
And prayed on high
Said the Devil took my girl."

I did hear a splash. Over the semi-unplugged rock'n'roll, I could hear a rhythmic sloshing. It was drawing closer. I stopped singing and one by one we all stopped playing until it was silent, except for the approaching noise. I set the guitar down, balanced on the dinky little amp, and swung the Mossberg around into my arms.

"Hello?" called an uncertain voice from the darkness.

I realized then that not all the glare shining into my eyes was from our own theatrically-aimed flashlights. One light was moving toward us, about fifty feet away on the surface of the lake.

"Don't mind me," the voice said. "I… uh, I'd like to hear the rest of the song."

"Come closer and show yourself!" I suggested.

"Yes, okay. Already on my way."

By now it was obvious to even the most shroomed out mind that the rhythmic splashing was the unknown fan's oars dipping in and out of the dark water as he rowed a small boat. They were powerful strokes and the boat and lantern surged closer and closer. The glowing light and splashing oars made a moving, but highly visible target.

In just a minute, the boat was close enough to see the really big man laboring with his oars beneath a sphere of light that apparently floated over his head. It's not that the guy was tall, though he was fairly tall. What immediately impressed was how very, very wide he was. His shoulders were mountains, his arms the trunks of mighty trees, and his bare torso, what was visible above the gunwales of the boat, was a pile of muscles like boulders. He made Arnold in his prime look like a girlie-man. He could have made a fortune on the pro wrestling circuit squashing contenders between forearm and bicep. The guy was strong, right?

And there was something about him – I swear it was not just the shrooms – that seemed remarkable, otherworldly, mythic. I was starting to catch on by this point and I thought *entity*. Then, as the boat scraped up the rocky beach and he stepped into our circle of lights, I revised my appraisal to *god*. His legs, emerging from tattered cut-off jeans, were even more tree-trunky than his arms. He radiated in a way similar to Esty. While she exuded beauty and sexy wisdom, his aura bathed us in strength and more strength, tempered with a bit of personal insecurity.

"Please," he said in a quiet, hesitant voice. "Go on playing. I did not mean to interrupt."

"Who the fuck are you?" I greeted him politely. "And what are you doing on my property? Er, under my property." I made my peaceful intent known more clearly by hefting the Mossberg and sighting along it at his large, lumpy head. It's okay, I hadn't pumped a shell into the chamber.

He peered at me. "Gardangulon?" he asked.

Birdie giggled.

"Ian," I said, still aiming the gun. "Ian Better."

"Thou art a god," he said, and began to grovel on the floor.

"Um, no," I explained. "Just an old fart with a shotgun and a guitar."

The big man looked up at me. "I saw a t-shirt," he said.

"Don't believe everything you read on shirts," I told him. "Now who the fuck are you?"

"My name is Perzanto," he said slowly, "and I have been down here a very long time."

9. Perzanto's Tale

I lowered the shotgun. We all looked around at each other. The Tripper grinned. Aqualung had somehow found his way into the cave without benefit of flashlight and lurked at the edge of the pool of light. Water dripped from the end of an oar into the lake with a crystalline tinkle.

"Please," urged Perzanto, "finish your song. I want to hear how it ends."

I slipped the strap of the Mossberg back over my shoulder and picked up my guitar. "All the way, all the way, all the way down," I began and the others joined in. I started on the last verse.

> "I went down to see the Devil
> Ask him why he took my bride
> I went down to see the Devil
> I found my girl right by his side
> She said, 'gonna be the Devil's baby'
> 'I'm gonna be the Devil's girl'
> She flashed her eyes
> And stroked her thighs
> Said, 'I'm a Queen here in *this* world!'"

I joined in with the chant as we took the song into the final jam. Don favored us with a spacey but intense solo, angel and devil hopping up and down in excitement on his shoulders. Cleve slipped from the blues into a deep dub rhythm, and then back again. Even The Tripper added some tasty fills on the dumbek. We ended with a big, dramatic finish and our small audience – Oswaldo, Karen, Esty, Aqualung and Perzanto – gave us a standing ovation. They'd been standing already, but it was enthusiastic anyway.

When he finished clapping, Perzanto shook his head. "It is a sad song," he said.

"Not for the Devil," Trenton remarked.

"But for one such as I," Perzanto sighed. "Very sad. I have, how you might say? Abandonment issues."

"The song would sound better," The Tripper explained, "if we played it in the resonant chamber."

Perzanto gasped. "You *do* seek the resonant chamber! Hmmm. You would replace a missing god with a guitar god?" He gestured toward me with a finger like a salami.

"That's, um, the general plan," The Tripper acknowledged.

"The resonant chamber is across the water," Perzanto said. "Come, I will take you across."

"I'm not really a god," I said.

"You sure about that?" Esty grinned.

Perzanto's boat was sturdy but small and he took up a major part of the available space. It took us two trips to get the humans and equipment across, and one more trip to pick up Aqualung and the jaguar. Perzanto didn't seem at all intimidated by the jaguar and, indeed, spent some time scratching it under the chin after the ferrying job was done. Birdie was silent, perhaps hoping that the big cat would bond with the muscle-bound god and leave her alone.

The trip across the water took about fifteen minutes each way. Perzanto's inexplicably floating lantern created an eerie bubble of light in the darkness. The water looked black and the true colors of the surrounding rocks only emerged from total blackness when we passed close to them, which wasn't often. The splashing of the oars and the rocking of the boat was hypnotic and the mushrooms were still making their presence known, although our situation in general was weird enough that I had difficulty telling shroom weirdness from general weirdness.

As far as I could tell, we traveled over open water for a time —
a long slow echo following every splash suggested that the ceiling was
pretty far up there. Then we moved for a while through a smaller,
narrower space; I could hear the water lapping against the stone walls
of the passage. Perzanto guided the boat through an unseen maze,
turning and dodging around boulders and solid walls of rock that I
didn't even suspect until they were in our wake. At one point he told
us to keep our heads down and we ducked to avoid stalactites that
dripped chilly water down the back of my neck. Finally, the boat
scrunched against a sandy beach and we climbed out.

We waited there until everyone, human, animal and entity,
came across. Seated on a reasonably flat rock, I noodled around on the
guitar and wondered where Bob was and what Jane might think of this
adventure. I had no real answer for either of those. The giggling
among the others became increasingly sporadic and conversations kept
drifting off into dreamy mumbling. When our own sounds ceased for a
moment, we heard the drip of water echoing endlessly through the
cavern. It was darker here, this deep in the cave and, if anything, the
shroom visuals were brighter than ever, pastel-glowing, rotating
geometrics that would suddenly flash and merge into alien landscapes,
architecture, and interstellar space.

"Hey, Cleve," Esty called in the semi-darkness, "how come you
don't have any imaginary friends?"

"I don't believe in any of them things," Cleve said. "Angels,
gods, power animals, web-footed… um… No, ma'am. I only believe in
the one God."

"Who? Ian?" snickered Birdie. There was a bit of giggling.

"There's only one god," Cleve asserted. "Thou shalt have no
other gods before Him."

"Oh," Birdie remarked. "*That* god."

"He's not an imaginary friend," Cleve continued. "Not
imaginary at all. No offense to the rest of you, but I'd prefer not to
have all these things following me around, buzzing around my head."
He swatted an imaginary angel. "I'm glad I've always believed in God.

Now I'm not pestered by angels, aliens, Aqualung, or gigantic man-eating pets."

"Don't rule out Aqualung or pets," I said. A blob of orangey light floated toward us from the darkness – Perzanto and the final ferry-load. The light swelled rapidly and the boat soon splashed and scrunched onto the beach. Perzanto stepped out, the jaguar leaped over the gunwale and trotted like a housecat to Birdie's side, and Aqualung slowly and dazedly climbed ashore. The old sot looked like he needed a drink. Or maybe some Dramamine.

"Okay," I said. "Show us to the resonant chamber. Let's rock this cave before our shrooms wear off and we're ready to go home."

Perzanto looked surprised. "The resonant chamber is deep inside," he said. "At least a day's march. Tonight you will be my guests and in the morning we can begin our journey."

"A day's march?" I repeated. "How about rowing us back out now, and we can come back for that march another time? Like in a month or so. We need to get ready, rehearse, work out, get in shape…"

"I will not row you out now," Perzanto said firmly. "This is a good plan. We can make this happen. I have waited here too long, and now there is a chance. Please. It is late. Stay at my home tonight and in the morning we can discuss this more. Come."

He set off up the beach, his lantern swinging along above him. Without a better option, we all shuffled to our feet and followed. Perzanto took us into a wide tunnel with a more-or-less flat, gravelly floor. The passage curved gently, first to the right, then to the left, and went steadily, gradually downhill.

The Tripper and Esty hurried to catch up with Perzanto and I got close enough to hear what they were saying.

"How long have you been down here?" The Tripper asked. "What happened to the others?"

"We came here at different times," Perzanto said. "I was here first. I've been living in these caverns, waiting for all of the six to arrive, for nearly twenty thousand years. I waited almost five thousand years before Dondelakavin showed up. Beezel showed up about a hundred years after that. Then it was a long wait until Bernard got here, only about seventy five years ago."

"And Mortimer and, uh, Goldang…?" Esty attempted.

"I've seen or heard nothing of Mortimer or Gardangulon," Perzanto explained. "When your group arrived, I thought it might include one or both of them."

"No," said Esty. "But Blue Smoke is a really kick-ass band. Legendary. Greatest rock band ever, according to *The Golden Book Encyclopedia of Music.*"

Perzanto nodded in agreement. "I have 'You Need to be Free' on vinyl," he said.

I snorted and changed the subject. "You've been living in my cave for twenty thousand years? Damn. How come you didn't all get here at the same time, when you were supposed to?"

Perzanto was silent for a moment. The trail climbed back uphill a few steps and then went into a narrower tunnel that swerved back and forth through dripping-wet rock. The closeness of the walls was a reminder of how deep we were under the mountain and I imagined the great mass of rock and earth that was between us and the sky.

"Come inside," he said. "Have some refreshment. Make yourself comfortable and I will tell you."

He stopped where a big wooden door, a slab hewn in one piece from some ancient tree, was set into the tunnel wall. Perzanto produced a big, rusty key and fiddled with the lock for a few moments. The door pulled back to reveal a tunnel even narrower and darker than the one we were in. But when Perzanto stepped inside, a string of odd-looking lights suspended between stalactites blinked into life. Or at least that's what it looked like. On closer inspection, there was no string or wire or anything else except glowing points of light. The lights, without bulb, wick or anything else, floated in thin air, with no evidence at all how they were produced.

There was a step up onto a hardwood floor made from giant old growth trees. Hundreds of years, at least, of Perzanto's footsteps had worn the wide planks smooth and shiny. Walls were also covered in paneling and the only exposed rock was on the ceiling, which was quite dry for a cave and mostly free of stalactites. Perzanto led a Spartan life, but the sheer amount of time that he had lived there was evidenced by the accumulation of stuff. It was almost geological, forming strata representing past epochs of history. Twenty years made my mountain home a bit cluttered. Twenty thousand years made Perzanto's place look like a cross between a museum and a landfill. I won't criticize. I'd probably have to move out of a place and burn it to the ground after only a century or two.

In the nooks and crevices of the archaeological evidence, as if some crazed squirrels used the cave for secret storage, were piles and scattered patterns of acorns. I moved one off the arm of my chair and noticed that it had a single strange mark drawn on it, a squiggly sort of thing that might have been a letter in some unknown alphabet.

Perzanto cleared seating for us, a strange collection of chairs from historical and geographic origins that I couldn't even guess. Mine was the size and shape of an ordinary kitchen chair made from some kind of stone, but very light and slightly warm to the touch. Birdie reclined on a sort of chaise lounge decorated with strange cuneiform markings. The jaguar, thoroughly scratched and petted by Perzanto, curled up on a small rug next to Birdie and immediately went to sleep. Aqualung selected a tall-backed, polished wood chair, but Perzanto shook his head and motioned toward a park bench near the door. Perhaps the big guy was a Tull fan. Don settled himself in the chair and the angel and devil perched on the high back, flipping each other off and doing imitations of Don's facial expressions. Trent found the only actual armchair in the room. It did, technically, have arms, although it appeared to be a large mound of sculpted sand. Trent kicked back and looked very comfortable.

Anyway, we all found things to sit or lie on and I got busy rolling a fat joint. Perzanto took a long stride, stepping over Esty who lay, eyes closed, on a bare patch of floor, and leaned over my spliff-making operation. He pinched up a small bud between huge fingers and gave it a sniff.

"Ah," he exhaled. "Kan Sha. It has been many centuries since I've had this herb. But I remember it fondly."

I lit the doobie and passed it to Perzanto, who toked deeply, burning down a third of the spliff, and then exhaled a mighty room-fogging cloud of sweet secondhand smoke.

"That's the stuff," he sighed, passing what was left of the joint to Trenton. I started to roll another.

"Mushroom?" The Tripper offered.

"No, thank you," Perzanto said. "Cold beer?" The response was unanimous. He disappeared into the back of his cave and returned a moment later with two dripping six-packs of Merkin. I noticed a Crumby's sticker clinging to one of the cans. "No refrigerator," he commented, "but the water down here is plenty cold."

A little beer and pot is a fine way to mellow out the tail end of a shroom trip. As we sipped and puffed and grew very mellow, indeed, Perzanto began to speak.

"In this age," he said, "most people believe that humanity is more, um, technologically advanced than were ancient civilizations. If we go beyond ten or twenty thousand years ago, historians will agree that humans were hunter-gatherers who could make a tasty dish from slugs and beetles. They would say that the ancients were only starting to figure out civilization and tools were limited to whatever you could make from rocks and sticks."

"And that isn't true?" Trenton asked.

"Oh, we had our share of knuckle-draggers back then," Perzanto replied. "But, hey, every age has its, how shall I say? Boneheads. Technology was much more fun and interesting then. Our cars were better. Our phones were better. Our computers were faster, smarter, and better. Our spaceships were better. And we had stuff that would just debilitate your mind. Perhaps I am saying that wrong. Blow your brain?"

"So how come we don't know about this ancient technology?" Trent inquired. "How come we haven't found any ancient phones or spaceships or brain blowers lying around?"

"We were also better at cleaning up after ourselves," Perzanto said. "And it is also possible that you wouldn't recognize any of those things if you saw them. Our technology was of a different order than yours. You build gadgets, we built thoughtforms. Most devices that you use are about processing or transmitting information in some way. If the brain can conceive of a way to do that processing, it can probably do the job, too. So the physical component of our gadgets might look to you like nothing more than a pebble or a crystal or a leaf, but when activated could lead the mind to process or transmit information. Echoes of our technology survive today as superstitious beliefs and tales of witches and wizards, magic wands, crystal balls, talismans, and sigils.

"You must also realize," and Perzanto leaned forward and gave each of us a penetrating gaze, "that this English language I am now using is lacking in many concepts that were taken for granted in my time. What I say about these things – calling them gadgets or phones or thoughtforms – can only be an approximation of what I could tell you in my native tongue. It is difficult, but I will make the metaphor as useful as possible. Please keep this in mind.

"I was born about a thousand years after the first gods retired. Already, some of the gifts of the gods were forgotten and others went awry or were misunderstood. But still, compared to what *you* think of as the peak of civilization…" Perzanto shook his big head. "Since then, when I go to the surface, I see the affairs of humans rise and fall, but mostly fall. I realize now how fortunate I was to be born into such a time, when human society was still near its zenith. I do not mean to be insulting. I am sorry. It's just that your civilization is so…" Perzanto shrugged a massive shrug.

"I was born in the part of the world you think of as China," he continued, "long before there were Chinese people or language. My family lived in a grove of nut trees in a temperate climate, a little milder than in the Valley of Roses. Nuts." He laughed. "Nuts! Nuts were everything. My earliest memories include hauling sacks of nuts. Every day I lifted many nut sacks."

There was a bit of giggling, mostly from Don's little red devil.

Perzanto looked around. "What? These nut sacks were very large and very heavy. I would not laugh at them. I grew very strong, lifting them. And my family became very wealthy, although our idea of wealth was very different than the acquisitiveness your culture often mistakes for wealth. We provided raw nuts in bulk for schools, research facilities and manufacturing. And we offered a full range of nuts inscribed as things you might refer to as phones and computers. I learned a moderate amount of inscribing, enough to keep up a basic level of civilization, at least. But I wasn't a great inscriber. My sister was the best. Even when she was a small child, she could write with almost anything, on anything, and get a connection to the information flow. She designed most of our new products and taught the rest of us how to copy her designs.

"So my childhood was a wonderful time, until the Master Inscriber showed up. I had heard tales that such people existed, that there were humans who could connect so completely to the information flow that they had intimate knowledge of past and future. He was truly like someone from a legend; he could transmute any one thing into any other and always seemed to know everything beforehand. Reality in his presence was both less real and more real. Being near him was like eating some sort of mushroom!"

Pong-bop, pong-bop, pong-bop, pong-bop.

We all glared at The Tripper, even the angel, and he put the dumbek back in its case.

Perzanto ignored the interruption. "The Master Inscriber gathered together all the inscribers in the land, and all who worked to uphold the traditions of the first gods. He told the gathering, who were all in awe of his powers, even the oldest and most experienced, that as the ways of the gods were forgotten, the world would become increasingly out of balance. He said he would choose one from among us, a strong young man, to undertake a mission to restore the balance. Altogether, six men would be chosen, from different cultures and geographical origins. The six would journey to the Valley of Roses and meet in a sacred chamber deep in the cave. There they would play a song that would, vibrating through the planet, inscribe a new way of being for all people.

"I was very sure of myself in those days. Everything seemed very clear. When I heard of the Master Inscriber's message, I knew immediately that I was the one. There were better musicians than I, and better inscribers, but I could handle the basics of both playing and inscribing and I was young and strong. Very strong. I knew that I was the perfect choice for the mission, but I still had to prove it to the Master Inscriber.

"Young men came from all over the countryside to be tested by the Master Inscriber. When I arrived at the Central Grove, it was already full of men, playing instruments, practicing inscribing skills, and wrestling with each other. I had never seen so many people all at once doing such things and I figured that my best course was to sit and watch for a while. From the top of a grassy rise at one end of the Grove, I could see only one candidate who was larger or stronger than I and he seemed slower and not as skilled. But there were inscribers conjuring fantastic flying machines, robots, computers, and display projectors, some of these far beyond my own inscribing ability. There were also a few that I recognized as well-known musicians, drawing clusters of people to listen, watch and play with them.

"The activity was non-stop, intense, and a bit frantic and it only got more so when the Master Inscriber appeared and took a seat on a dais opposite from where I sat. His impassive gaze panned across the Grove, taking it all in. Wherever he seemed to be looking, the players and inscribers and wrestlers tried to show off their skills and great airships, giant three-dimensional talking heads, glittering objects beyond description, and no-holds-barred rumbles sprouted from the throng. Beautiful songs from all parts of the Grove crashed and bashed each other into pure cacophony. I saw the Master Inscriber's gaze follow a shining blue dolphin through the air and as the mechanism or phantasm passed between us, our eyes met. I could have sworn that he smiled a little bit, but at that distance it was hard to tell. I was so frightened that I almost, uh, let loose my... um... but the moment passed as he continued to scan the crowd.

"I thought the Master Inscriber would make an announcement, set the rules, and organize the tests, but he seemed content to watch the competition that naturally ensued. At first, I thought I would wait on the sidelines and save my strength for whatever official challenges would come, but as time went on and no decrees were issued, my confusion increased. I thought perhaps I should enter the Grove proper and challenge someone or join a jam session, but I couldn't decide what to do, which part of the chaos I wanted to be a part of, and I continued to sit.

"The losers of the wrestling matches were the first to leave the field, battered and bloody. Their ranks were soon swelled by long-faced musicians who flubbed a solo or couldn't keep up with more dynamic players. Next came sad-looking inscribers who made devices that malfunctioned or didn't transform at all. After a while, there were only a few competitors left in the Grove. I recognized the really big man I had seen earlier, a popular sqwth player of some note, and my cousin Mehrvyn, who studied inscribing with my sister. They stood looking at each other and I thought for a moment that the big man was going to trounce the smaller men. I almost got to my feet, but then they all turned to look at the Master Inscriber. He shrugged, his expression blank.

"'I am the strongest one here!' the big man yelled.

"'But can you play Erbeth's Number Twelve Concerto on the sqwth?' the musician countered.

"The big man looked down. 'No,' he mumbled. 'I cannot play concertos of any sort.'

"'Can you inscribe a sqwth on an elm twig?' cousin Mehrvyn asked.

"The musician paused for a long moment. 'No, probably not,' he said sadly.

"'I will crush you both!' the big man bellowed.

"The Master Inscriber cleared his throat. He reached out an arm and pointed a preternaturally long finger past the contestants, directly at me. 'You!' the Master Inscriber called across the Grove. 'Come closer.'

"I stood and walked down the little hill into the Grove itself, joining the remaining candidates.

"'Closer!' the Master Inscriber commanded.

"I approached the dais and looked up at him. He wore a richly embroidered vest, filled with swirls of gold and purple, with tails that hung nearly to the floor. Beneath that was a robe of flawless white silk. His hair was a thick shock of darkest black and a thin beard dangled on his bony chest. Bushy eyebrows helped to frame a gaze that pierced me like, what do you call them now? Laser beams.

"'Can you best this big man in a fight?' he asked me, gesturing toward the largest candidate in the Grove.

"'He may be larger and stronger than me,' I said, 'but I have watched him wrestle and I believe I am faster and smarter. I think I could best him in a fight.'

"The Master Inscriber nodded. 'I believe you,' he said. He looked at the big man. 'Thank you,' he said. 'You may go.' The man's mouth opened as if he were about to protest, but then he shook his head, closed his mouth and reluctantly left the Grove.

"The laser gaze focused on me again. 'Can you play Erbeth's Number Twelve Concerto on the sqwth?'

"'I've never played the sqwth,' I said. 'But I suspect I can learn how. I can play the mrrlnx part of Erbeth's Number Twelve, though. It's simpler than the sqwth part, but…'

"'Fine,' the Master Inscriber interrupted me. 'I believe you.' He looked at the musician. 'You may go,' he said.

"The piercing eyes panned back in my direction. 'Can you inscribe a sqwth on an elm twig?'

"'I've never tried,' I said, 'but I can inscribe a mrrlnx on a nut.'

"'Good enough,' the Master Inscriber offered. 'Especially since you don't play the sqwth.'

"Cousin Mehrvyn shot me a glance and then slouched away from the Grove.

"Then the Master Inscriber stepped down from the dais, wrapped an arm across my shoulders and said, 'It doesn't really matter any way. I spotted you as soon as I came in. I knew you'd be the winner, because I can see through time. But most importantly, you were the only one with enough sense to sit your ass down and wait. If it came to a wrestling match with any of these.' He swept wide his free arm to conversationally include the grumbling losers on the sidelines. 'You would certainly win. You are rested and fresh, they are all battered and worn. And you display a quality that is more important than mere physical prowess, musical or inscribing skill.'

"I waited for him to say what that was, but he left my side and began to walk away. He climbed back upon the dais and turned to face the Grove. He raised his arms over his head and stood there. In only a few moments, everyone noticed and quietly watched him, waiting for a word.

"'The candidate has been chosen!' he called, triumphantly. There was a small amount of grudging applause. The Master Inscriber looked down at me. 'Get your ass up here, kid,' he said. I climbed up and stood beside him. He spoke to me in loud, ceremonious tones. 'You have been selected to make the journey to the Valley of Roses where you will find the five other candidates and descend to the resonant chamber to play a song. You are a fine, strong young man. You have knowledge and skill. But that will not be enough. Only a god may play the song in a way that will return harmony to the Earth. There was a ceremony when you were born and there was one when you became a man. This gathering, this ritual is the ceremony of your becoming a god.'

"He aimed a long finger at me and, in his mind, inscribed a figure upon me. And I transformed. I grew larger, stronger, smarter, more talented. Things happened in my brain that I could feel, neural pathways rewiring. My perception of the world shifted. Everything became richer, more imbued with information. I could feel the information flow everywhere, as I'd never been able to do as a man. I became the entity that you see before you now. There were gasps from the audience. Then applause.

"I felt wonderful, remarkable, fantastic in my new form and everyone scrambled over each other to be in my presence. I was offered food, wine, kan sha, sex, and happy conversation all night long. I accepted as much as I was physically able to bear and, being a god, I was able to bear a mighty amount. I was very happy to be a god, then, and wanted the worship to continue forever.

"But morning eventually came, and with it, two of the Master Inscriber's apprentices. One handed me a magical map of the world.

The other one pointed toward the horizon and suggested that I start walking that way. I protested, for I was still disentangling myself from the limbs of playmates I had exhausted during the night. The man just shook his head and pointed. That's how my journey began. If I'd had any idea how it would turn out…"

Perzanto paused here, draining a can of beer in a single gulp.

"What kind of instrument is the mrrlnx?" I asked.

He smiled and set the beer can down on a rough wooden table. He scooped a handful of acorns off the tabletop and began to sort through them, peering carefully at each one before tossing it back onto the table. In a moment he selected one and let the rest of the massive handful rattle back into a heap, several of them escaping and bouncing across the floor. He ignored the errant nuts and held the one that he had selected before his massive face. He concentrated and, with a faint snap, he no longer held an acorn. In his hand was a long, flat black object, about four feet long, six inches wide and less than an inch thick.

"The mrrlnx," he said, resting one end of the thing on his shoulder. He stroked it with an enormous hand and a long, deep note reverberated in the cave. His big fingers danced across it and rocked a fat bass rhythm.

"Can you play the blues?" Trent asked.

Perzanto chuckled, a sound almost as deep and booming as the mrrlnx. "Perhaps later we can jam," he suggested. "I would be honored indeed to play with the mighty Blue Smoke." With another faint snap, the mrrlnx was gone and Perzanto tossed the acorn onto the table.

"I journeyed for a hundred years," he said. "Mostly I walked and took whatever local transportation was available. Cars, wagons, horses, oxen, rickshaws, unicycles, canoes, steamboats, hang gliders. Whatever. Sometimes I had to inscribe a conveyance, which took some work for me, back then, figuring out all the details. When my first five boats sank, I tell you I wished my sister were there. I went a long way north and east, then across a land bridge to this continent, and finally across the continent on a long, zig-zag route. The inhabitants and cultures I encountered were diverse and very, very different from what I grew up with – and even more different from your own country. I had numerous adventures and often found myself involved with people and events that compelled me to deviate from my path. I stopped and lived for years sometimes, sometimes forgetting my sacred quest entirely. But I never felt entirely comfortable, I never really fit in and eventually the quest would pull me on. I began to wonder if it was taking me too long, if the other five were waiting for me or if they had given up on my ever showing. I wondered if I were messing it all up, if my late arrival would prevent the world ever returning to harmony.

"At long last, I rowed a boat up the wild, young river that would one day be called the Hudson. I hiked through dense forest along a rivulet that your people would name the Rondout Creek and finally came to the Valley of Roses and the entrance to the caverns." He gestured, presumably back toward the cave mouth. It took me a day to work out the details to inscribe a boat to cross the water and another two days to find my way through the water-filled passages to this place, here. I made a temporary camp, stacked my nuts and sticks, and began to explore the deeper caverns.

"You'll have to understand that my sense of time became skewed. The journey that took a hundred years and would have filled volumes with tales of adventure now seemed only a day. A month or a year spent finding the resonant chamber would seem like an instant. So I explored the caverns methodically, gradually getting deeper and deeper, down toward the resonant chamber.

"This part, this is an ordinary cave, but further down it changes. There is an ancient place known to the gods where the thoughtforms that we call *shebangs* are stored. Some myths tell of this place, talking about threads that represent lives. Others talk about books that hold destinies, wherein is written our fate. These are not threads or books, more a place where the information flow swirls into a deep, deep pool. Think of a place where the information forms entrances to other worlds, worlds that follow the patterns of the entities that inhabit them. And they are inhabited, indeed, by more entities than crowd upon the surface of the Earth. It is a strange place, exciting and mysterious, infinite and diverse. You will find out. We will pass through it tomorrow. The resonant chamber is in the center of it all, deep inside.

"Below us there is a series of large caverns. They have seen various uses over the many years. Animals hibernated in them. Native tribes conducted ceremonies in them. For a while, they were temporary home to escaped slaves heading north to freedom. When I arrived, there was no one, only bats and bears. At the lower end of the caverns are openings that lead to where the shebangs gravitate. Near one of those openings something was happening.

"A torch set into the wall of the cave illuminated the scene in dim, flickering light. Two shadowy figures did a kind of dance in the firelight and the sound of feet shuffling on loose rock echoed through the caverns. The murky light and distance across the great cavern didn't matter to my senses – I knew they were something other than human, more like what I had become than the masses of men and women I lived among for a hundred years. I came closer, hoping that these might be my companions, Bernard and them. I could soon see that one was smaller and female and one much larger, male and clad in heavy armor. I took a breath to hail them, but the breath caught in my throat as the small woman suddenly and viciously attacked the man. I ducked back behind a large rock and watched as best I could.

"The woman was a surprisingly fast and powerful fighter. She leapt and rebounded off the tunnel walls and kept coming at the armored man, but he continued to repel her. A clatter of metal upon metal filled the cave and I could see that the woman wielded a short sword with which she hacked and slashed at the man. I could see that she was making hits, even though he would dash her back to the stone floor with a sweep of a steel-clad arm. His armor was showing scratches and dents and exposed skin on his cheeks and the backs of his hands bled in fat droplets. Finally, he threw her to the ground and stepped on her with a massive metal boot. Her arms and legs flailed uselessly and he looked as if he were about to bear down and crush her flat.

"I stepped out from my hiding place and switched on my light. I cleared my throat. I have a large throat and the sound filled the cavern. The armored man looked up from his victim and turned his head to find me.

"'Gardangulon?' I asked.

"'I am Snorx, the guardian of the Deep Place,' the man said, 'wherein lies the Pool of Shebangs. Turn back now. No man or woman may enter here.'

"'What of her?' I asked.

"'She is no woman and she may not leave,' the guardian said.

"'I am much larger than you,' I reasoned, 'and you are already bleeding. Do you think you can stop me?'

"'You cannot pass me,' the guardian told me. 'It is the way of things. It is not just my job, it is what I am, a barrier to keep these,' he glanced down at the woman pinned beneath his metal boot, 'in and you out. I may appear as a man and I may even appear to bleed, but these are appearances only. Think of me as an impenetrable wall.'

"'Have you been here a long time?' I asked.

"'Thousands of years,' he said.

"'No vacations? Sick days? Kan sha breaks?' I inquired.

"'I do not know these things,' Snorx said.

"'Do you read? Or listen to music? You know, entertainment?' I further inquired.

"'What is entertainment?' the guardian asked.

"'Allow me to demonstrate,' I said, fishing in my pocket for acorns.

During my hundred years of travel I had ample time to practice both music and inscribing. Indeed, I started to learn that I could play a song and inscribe something simple on a small object through the music. Nothing very complex, just effects mostly, but it added a nice touch to a musical performance. Strategically placed nuts or sticks could be triggered to become colored lights or streamers or laser beams at appropriate moments during a song. I'd paid for my dinner and lodging with musical magic more than a few times along my journey.

"I found a nut with the mrrlnx inscribed on it and I made it become. Snorx watched skeptically, as if I was performing cheap sleight of hand and he would catch the trick. I started to play.

"There is a children's tune that my people know. It has a simple melody, easily played on the mrrlnx and somewhat infectious to the brain. The melody is short, just a few bars of music, and at the end is a pause."

Perzanto caused the mrrlnx to reappear in his hand and he played ten seconds of a bouncy, catchy melody.

"Each time the pause comes around," he continued, popping his instrument back into acorn form, "the children shout and it becomes a competition to shout the funniest or most outrageous thing. I encountered no other people during my travels across a large part of the planet's surface who knew this tune and this game. So when I played it, it was brand new for everyone and the shouts, which I embellished with flashes of colored light, pyrotechnics, and holograms, were a crowd-pleasing surprise every time

"As the melody bounced into its second iteration, the woman relaxed. When the pause came around, I added lights to the shout. The guardian, entranced and distracted, removed his boot from her torso. She did not fight or run, but sat up and watched me, her eyes wide. As the glow of my – how do you say? – special effects faded away, I saw how beautiful she was, even bruised and battered from the fight. Her eyes were large and dark, her hair was glossy yellow, tied back in a thick braid.

"I used even brighter and bigger flashes the next time around, pyrotechnic color splashing off the rock walls of the tunnel and the greater cavern, and Snorx gasped and oohed with pleasure. I played the next round louder and deeper and as the caesura approached something strange happened.

"I was about to aim the music at a handful of acorns scattered onto the cavern floor, to make a monstrously big, dazzling flash and use the distraction to run past the guardian – or overpower him if necessary. But as I was aiming the inscription, my attention was drawn toward the woman. She had gathered herself into a crouch and was also preparing to take advantage of any momentary distraction. And somehow I aimed the music, the inscription, at her.

"I couldn't do that with humans. I knew it could be done. The Master Inscriber did it to me. But I was not that adept. A large nut was my limit of complexity. Or maybe a log, if what I made was very simple. But inscribing a human was way beyond me. When I looked at her, though, I saw that she definitely wasn't human and I knew instantly how to do it. It took no thought, no figuring out. It was just a blast of intent carried on the music. And I fired off some flashy nuts, too.

"The woman transformed. She became larger and much stronger and she glowed. Her hair was now free, a thick wave of golden light that flowed down her back. She wore shining black armor and her short sword was now a six-foot blade of gleaming steel. This mighty and radiant being was already in mid-attack. There was a blast of light and a blast of energy and she subdued the guardian, who whined pathetically in her grasp. She looked at me.

"I popped the mrrlnx back to an acorn. 'Allow me,' I said, taking the whimpering guardian from the woman. I hurled him across the cavern, where he landed in the dark with a series of clanks and yelps. "This is a good time to run," I suggested to the woman, and then took off into the Deep Place, running as fast as I could.

"She started to run after me. I stopped. 'Weren't you trying to get out?' I asked.

"'I was leaving,' she said, 'because I needed to find more, to learn more. But I think I might be better served to study with you. I want to learn how you do… these things. And… I owe you.' She looked down at herself and saw in the torchlight the body and limbs of a mighty battle goddess. 'I like this,' she said, 'and now you are the only one who matches my physique.' She gave me a sidelong glance. 'I would like to stay with you. Who are you? What are you doing here between one world and the next?'

"'I am Perzanto,' I said, 'and I seek the resonant chamber.'

"'I am Liana,' she told me, 'and I think I was looking for you.'

"I cannot deny that I was pleased. She was beautiful before the inscription and now she was a goddess, transformed nearly as much as I had been by the Master Inscriber. In my travels across continents, I slept with the occasional woman curious about sex with a being such as myself. I even stayed and lived with a woman for a decade. But I always knew that I must move on and could never fully give myself. And the women were human, simple and small, no match for me. In one hundred years, I wanted many, but yearned for none in the way that I did for Liana. I took her hand and we ran together, fleeing through the tunnel toward a vague hint of light in the distance ahead.

"After a run of some duration, the tunnel opened out in a wide area that was so bright it was almost blinding, after the dark of the tunnels. Near us, a campfire burned with a bright crackle. Beyond the fire, a tall column of brilliant yellowy-white light rose up into the vastness of the cave. Beyond that column, two more columns, and beyond those a great forest of light, filling an enormous cavern.

"Around the campfire sat a small party of men and women in clothes of shiny fabrics, sipping from steaming mugs and chatting amiably. They looked up at us and their eyes went wide.

"'Hello, neighbors,' Liana said as we walked up to them. She smiled and raised a hand in greeting.

"And the neighbors stumbled from their seats and backed away, chairs tipping, mugs spilling.

"'It's me,' Liana said, continuing toward them.

"'It's her!' they gasped, stumbling further back.

"'And some really big guy, too,' said one of the bunch.

They turned and fled, abandoning their fire.

"'What got into them?' Liana asked. 'I had breakfast with Morn and Dana this morning.'

"'You've changed,' I said. 'It must scare them.'

"'Hmmph.' Liana folded her arms across her mighty chest. 'I think I look hot like this.'

"'And maybe a bit scary to the little people,' I said. 'Or maybe it was me who scared them.'

"I stared off into the bright cavern. The columns of light were almost too bright to gaze at directly. Throughout the cave I heard evidence of scattered civilization, voices, the rattle of pots and pans, and even some percussive music, far off. I was figuring that these people weren't human, as Snorx had said of Liana. 'This must be the Pool of Shebangs,' I exclaimed. I gazed at Liana. 'And you are not human – you are a shebang entity!'

"'I'm a what?' Liana asked.

"'I began as flesh.' I thumped my chest like this." Perzanto pounded a fist against his vast sternum. The sound reverberated in my body. "'You are thoughts, information that interacts with my brain to make me think you are flesh.'

"Liana laughed and thumped her breastplate. 'You doubt that I have flesh?' She stepped into my arms and pressed her lips against mine. They felt like flesh. We kissed and then she pulled back.

"'The nature of your flesh is fine with me,' I said, 'whatever it's made from.'

"'Show me,' she said. 'Show me how you do your magic.'

"I searched my pockets and found a remaining nut. I held it out on the flat of my palm and inscribed it with the First Inscription, the one we teach to the youngest children. The nut transformed into a ball of yellow light that got brighter for a moment, then diminished and disappeared. With a large nut and a darkened room, it can be an impressive display, but near the Pool it seemed dim and inconsequential.

"Liana was nevertheless enthralled. 'How? How?' she asked.

"Wondering if a shebang entity would have the ability, I snatched a coal from the campfire and drew the sigil figure large on the bare rock floor, without making it an inscription. Then I held out another acorn. 'In your mind, draw that figure on the nut and as you do, feel the light expanding out from it. You have to imagine the light exactly as you would like it to appear. Then you feel the acorn in your mind and adjust your imagination. When your imagination matches the feeling of the nut, it will transform. I will do it along with you so that you can experience how I do it.'

"I placed my other hand on her shoulder and held the acorn close to us. I started to inscribe, very slowly, and felt her join along with me. The acorn burst into a fairly bright light.

"'Now we must go,' I said. 'I'm so close to the resonant chamber. I can feel it pulling on me.'

"'Wait! Wait!' she cried. 'One more! Let me do one by myself.'

"I agreed, provided that we hurried on as soon as she was done. I had one last nut, deep in the bottom of a pocket and I handed it to her.

"Her inscription was relatively slow and careful and, in just a moment, a ball of yellow light burst from her palm. She was delirious. She laughed, she jumped up and down, she grabbed me and hugged me and showered my face with kisses, all the while professing her deepest thanks.

"'Now,' I said, 'let's go!'

"We walked between the mighty columns of light, ever inward, deeper into the cave. Residents of the Pool scurried and darted out of our way. It soon became evident that the Pool of Shebangs was a great shallow dish of smooth limestone and our path sloped down toward the center. After an indeterminate time hiking through the cavern, the luminous columns ended. At the center of the great dish was solid stone with tunnel openings cut into it.

"There were no residents this far in and for a moment, other than our own breathing, it was quiet. I was looking around for something to inscribe as a light, before we went into the tunnel, when we heard commotion from all sides. We looked up to see several groups of people approaching us. I never got a clear look, but I knew who it was. It was my brethren, come to meet me and descend into the resonant chamber for our song.

"I turned to face the nearest group, but at that moment a great voice boomed out from the nearest tunnel entrance. 'TIME!' the voice echoed from the rock. 'TIME!' I turned back and saw the Master Inscriber standing in a halo of bright light.

"'I'm glad to see you,' I said, walking toward him. 'I didn't know if I made it here on time.'

"'Now!' the Master Inscriber commanded. 'Down to the chamber!'

"'Does that mean I *am* late?' I asked. He just turned and strode rapidly into the darkness. Liana and I followed. I assumed the others, who I thought I'd heard in the cavern, would be behind us.

"The tunnel tilted down for a long way. I had nothing that I could inscribe to make a light and the Master Inscriber didn't seem to need any. We followed as closely as we could. After some time he slowed and we could hear his boots on stone steps, which turned out to be a very long stairway down into further darkness. Finally, after another period of time, a dim light became visible a long way down the stairs. The light grew brighter as we continued to descend. It was a bright, yellowy glow, almost the same color as the First Inscription flash.

"Further down, we came to a landing and a smooth stone archway through which the light was shining into the stairway. The Master Inscriber commanded Liana to remain outside the arch and beckoned me into the chamber.

"The chamber was a perfectly flat and polished stone floor with a parabolic domed ceiling. The light emanated from every surface so that it seemed as if we walked inside a brilliant bubble. The Master Inscriber walked to the center of the circular floor. From behind me, I could hear footsteps and clattering on the stairs, the others of my kind and their people approaching.

"Before they reached the landing, however, the Master Inscriber suddenly produced a long gleaming staff of crystal and, using the staff as a stylus, quickly inscribed a giant sigil on the stone of the chamber itself. He raised the staff, pointing it at the high-arched ceiling. For a moment, nothing happened. I could hear the clattering sounds of people on the landing.

"Then, with a deafening boom louder than thunder, the chamber shook and vibrated. I fell to my knees. My ears hurt from the noise and from a sudden change in air pressure. My vision skewed, the world seeming to slide away in great, uneven fragments.

"Then, suddenly, there was silence. Total silence, the rocks and air now still, as if they had never been disturbed. And I was alone in the chamber. There was no trace of the Master Inscriber. I ran to each of the arched doorways that surrounded the chamber. There was no one. Liana was gone. The others, who had almost joined me there — gone. I called for Liana. I called for the Master Inscriber. I called for anyone. There was no answer. I was alone."

Perzanto paused. He looked down.

"What happened?" I asked. "What did the Master Inscriber do?"

Slowly, Perzanto's big head lifted. His eyes scanned our faces.

"Time," Perzanto told us. "He scrambled it. In the beginning of my adventures, all our stories were in the same time, the same overall narrative, represented in the same shebang. Bernard, Beezel, Mortimer, all of them. Our journeys would have ended simultaneously. We would have found each other. But somehow, the Master Inscriber changed it all and our stories were separated by aeons. Dondelakavin, Beezel and Bernard, when they finally got here, had no memory of making the journey before. They just had their one set of memories. Somehow, perhaps because I was in the chamber at the time, I remember it both ways.

"And Liana," Esty inquired, "what happened to her?"

"I never saw her again," Perzanto said sadly.

"Why did he do that?" Cleve asked. "He was the one who sent you all there in the first place."

"I don't know," Perzanto whispered. "Maybe because of me."

"Because of you? Bah!" I snorted. "You did what you said you'd do. You got there ahead of the others."

"I shouldn't have," the big man said. "I was distracted from my purpose and dallied along the way. I took a hundred years to get there. I stopped, even at the moment of my arrival, to teach Liana an inscribing trick. My intent was impure. I deserved this." He paused and shook his head. "But maybe the end is finally in sight. Maybe my punishment is almost complete and we will sing the song and set the world aright."

We all nodded and agreed. The shrooms were wearing off, we'd been through some weird shit, and everyone was looking a bit sleepy.

"Is anyone hungry?" Perzanto asked.

Birdie sat up from where she'd been lying on the floor. "What you got?"

"Cave slugs!" Perzanto smiled. "And beetles! I made a casserole."

We all politely declined, though Aqualung looked like he was thinking about it.

Perzanto showed us where we could sleep. I found an old brown rug and curled up against the wood-paneled wall. I drifted off on the tail end of the psilocybin and the next thing I knew, it was much later. The lights were out and snores, both gentle and not-quite-so-gentle, came from various parts of Perzanto's cave home. Something lumpy was pressed against the small of my back. I reached down to feel hard muscle covered with silky fur.

"Bob?" I whispered.

"Yeah," Bob purred. "It's me."

Comforted by his familiar presence, I slid back into dreamland.

10. Steel Cave

When we all woke, Perzanto served us a fairly slug-free breakfast of hard rolls and deli meat from plastic Crumby's wrappers. There was even coffee, brewed in a device that reverted to a dried pea when it was done, and some kind of powdered cream substitute. We descended on it like vultures after the first spring thaw. I was ravenous and it all tasted just fine.

We packed up the remaining food, gathered up our gear and Perzanto led us back out into the labyrinth of subterranean tunnels. For just a moment I thought the night's adventures were a mushroom delusion and that he was going to take us back out into the open world, but of course we were headed all the way down.

What the fuck, I thought. If we find the resonant chamber, we'll at least get some rehearsal time.

As our merry band straggled through the tunnels by acorn-light, Bob came bounding up by my side.

"Hi, Bob!" I said. "You *are* here!" He swirled around my legs. "I had a dream about you, kitty. I dreamed that you could speak. Can you speak, Bob?" I was just rapping, you understand. Just saying silly things to the cat. I did that a lot, more since I stopped talking to Jane. What? You claim you don't talk shit to your pets? Fuck that. You know you do.

"Yeah, dude," Bob said. "I can speak."

That stopped me. In spite of the weirdness of the last week — spaceships, dead wives, and entities of all sorts — hearing my own cat, occupant of my lap for so many years, speak in clear, unaccented English was pretty damn surreal. In the 1980s, Jane and I took a course in lucid dreaming and we learned a series of tests to find out if current experience was a dream or not. I did a quick check — nope, couldn't fly, the word "Mossberg" embossed on the barrel of my old gun read the same way even after I'd glanced away, and my companions appeared to be, okay, not normal, but only as strange as I expected them to be. I looked back at Bob, but he was already off, setting up to ambush the jaguar.

We continued on, down a narrow, sloping tunnel of damp brown limestone and pale red conglomerate.

Okay, okay, I know you're probably still wondering about some of this shit. Well, so was I. I mean, I saw a spaceship there, up on the mountain, like a great, glittering effect from an old Spielberg movie and all this other stuff followed, including, now, a talking cat. My mind kept insisting that, assuming this wasn't all a dream or an endless shroom hallucination, there was cause and effect. Alien spaceship arrives, dead wife and other entities appear. It was aliens, right?

"I saw the spaceship, too," Esty told me as we walked along, her multi-toned voice reverbing faintly from the stone. "But for me it was well down in the sequence of events. As Perzanto's story suggests, time doesn't seem to be particularly linear outside of our brain's interpretation. Our language implies linearity of time and cause-effect relationships, but it's often an illusion. Most English-speaking people, for example, represent time as moving forward. The future is ahead of us and we leave the past behind. In other languages, it's just the opposite. In ancient Greece, the past was ahead and the future behind. That's also been observed in modern times among the Aymara people of Peru. In their language they move forward into the past. And those are languages we know about. There are many other ways to represent time that don't involve straight lines, forward and backward, at all. Transforming myself into the person you see now involved learning to think of time as a cloud."

"So you think this wasn't caused by aliens." I interpreted.

"Millions of people think that Joe Maloney and I caused it, when we did that thing on June twenty third," she said.

"Did you cause it?"

"I don't know. We were part of it." She thought for a moment. "We performed a ritual…"

"What kind of ritual?" I interrupted.

"Sex magick," she harmonized.

"Do I really want to know about that?" I mused.

"Do you?" She grinned. "Google it some time. Anyway, we did the ritual, live on television and the web, with the participation of millions of people all over the planet, and then the entities appeared. All kinds of entities: gods, goddesses, angels, demons, elementals, fictional characters, cartoon rabbits, allegorical figures, dead rock stars and, yes, aliens. While my gut feeling is that the ritual did cause these things, when I think about it, I can't really be sure. Maybe we'd still be hip-deep in entities even if there had been no ritual at all. I think I would rather say that the ritual was synchronous with the events. It was an inevitable part of a greater process."

"So you just happened to do the ritual at the same time all this weird stuff started happening?" I hadn't smoked yet and I was struggling to process.

"We only have the edited version of reality, created by our brains and language, and we have a pretty good clue that time is not what we think it is."

"So then it could have been aliens," I said.

"You would not be the first to propose that theory. Or maybe the aliens were simply among the first entities to appear. Spaceships and their inhabitants are powerful archetypes."

I was intrigued and wanted to contemplate these ideas, but I hadn't rolled any joints. "Hey," I called ahead. "Can we take a rest stop?"

"No," Perzanto's voice boomed back through the tunnel. "Not here. Not now."

"When?" I asked.

"Some other time."

The tunnel rose and fell but ultimately continued to slope down into the Earth. More and more side tunnels opened into it, suggesting that the cavern was becoming even more labyrinthian. Indeed, we soon followed Perzanto through a bewildering series of turns and then through a wide chamber where the ceiling was so low we had to stoop to walk through. Beyond the chamber we went into a passageway so narrow that our larger members, particularly Perzanto, had to work hard to wedge themselves through. I was wondering if I could find my way back by myself and was wishing that I had brought a pipe or a one-hitter so that I could get high without waiting for the rest stop.

The lemon squeeze eventually opened out into the widest tunnel we'd yet seen. The rock was smoother and relatively free of stalactites, suggesting it had been artificially widened. A slight breeze cooled my face. Trent started to clap a rhythm that echoed off the walls. It sounded like "Shining Girl." You know it. *Six Songs*, side B, second to last track. Number four on the U.S. charts and number one in the UK. I was just about to jump in with the vocal when Perzanto shushed us.

"Quiet!" he hissed. "Quiet!"

The tunnel ended abruptly and we stepped into a vast cavern lit with rows of streetlights. Regular human-style, four hundred watt, metal halide roadside illumination cast a harsh blue-white glare across asphalt roadways and dark buildings of steel and stone. There were enough buildings for a small city's business district. They were three to ten stories in height, as wide as warehouses – in the case of one that I could see nearby, as wide as a city block – and they had few windows. And it didn't look like anyone was home.

"Whoa," said the Tripper. Everyone else stared in silence. Aqualung blew his nose.

Bob came and sat next to my leg. He looked up at me.

"I know what this is," I said and everyone turned to look at me. "It's Steel Cave."

They continued to stare.

"It's a records management company. The entrance is a building along Binnewater Road, a few miles from my house. They store government and corporate records in a climate-controlled, nuke-proof cavern."

"This is climate controlled?" Trent asked.

"These caves stay at fifty five degrees F all year round," I explained. "And the buildings must have some system to control humidity."

"Let's play a song," Trenton said.

"No!" Perzanto told us. "There is a guardian here. And in the last week, there have been other things as well. We must be stealthy. Wait here quietly while I reconnoiter." He looked stern and godlike for a moment. We waited and he stalked off into the shadows around the periphery of the cave.

I sat on the stony floor, my back against the cavern wall, and extracted a fat bud from the guitar case. Crumbling it onto my palm released a cloud of sweet and spicy terpenes. With Bob watching alertly, I twisted two extra large wraps into a fair sized spliff. The most motivated potheads, Esty and Trenton, came over and sat down by me. As soon as I sparked it up, pretty much everyone else gathered around too. I took a nice big hit and passed it on the left hand side to Trent.

Some of us were toking deeply, but I saw that Karen, who hadn't yet puffed, was practically hyperventilating.

"What the fuck are we doing down here?" She sputtered for a moment. "What…?"

Someone passed her the joint and she took a deep hit, coughed, turned bright red and coughed some more.

"Do you need help?" Oswaldo asked.

After a moment Karen looked up and smiled. "No, I think I'm okay."

The Gunk mountain shit works every time.

Okay, so the THC was starting to find its way into my brain and the wheels were beginning to turn. Time was weird and subjective. The ritual preceded the aliens, but maybe that didn't matter either. The entities, like time, had something to do with the way that we perceived them; they were also weird and subjective. Maybe even weirder. How could I make sense of these thoughts, find a thread of reason that unified them? The spliff came back my way and I took another deep hit.

"Hey!" someone yelled. "Hey, you!"

In the cavern, emerging from between two squat stone buildings was a tall man in a uniform. A shiny badge pinned to his breast pocket glittered in the pale light and he aimed a big, black metal flashlight in our direction.

"Stay right there!" the man called.

The beam of light caught me holding the joint up to my lips. "What the fuck," I said, springing to my feet as quickly as arthritis would allow. Guitar and shotgun swinging wildly, I sprinted back into the tunnel. There was a disorderly stampede of humans and entities behind me. The cats, loving this kind of game, leaped ahead. Bob jumped over the jaguar; the jaguar batted him out of the way and took the lead. I made a sharp right into a side tunnel. The further from the underground city I got, the darker it became. I came to a place where an ancient, cracked and rotten plank crossed a crevasse. My wimpy little flashlight beam was lost in the deep darkness and there was no way I was going to attempt that dubious bridge to somewhere I couldn't see – so I turned left again, back into a brighter tunnel.

The tunnel curved around and the cats and I came skidding to a halt back in the main cavern, in an alleyway behind a large building covered in corrugated steel. For the moment, we seemed to be alone. I didn't hear the others behind me, so I figured they didn't keep up when I took evasive action. That was okay. As far as I knew, I was the only one with a half pound of Gunk bud in his instrument case. If caught, they might get off with trespassing, but I was well over New York State's decriminalized maximum of three quarters of an ounce. Some of the cops around here were mean redneck motherfuckers who listened to country music; I could do jail time. I considered ditching the weed somewhere but, hell, I'd already run. If I kept running, I could keep my bud, too. I was, after all, pretty close to home. Where was the exit?

I figured I would circle the cavern counterclockwise, along the outer wall until I eventually came to an exit. I stayed as close as I could to the buildings and set off, Bob ahead of me and the jaguar behind. We covered some distance pretty quickly, but then I heard a voice from behind. I pressed flat against the cinderblock face of a building and turned to look. I saw a man in a very different kind of uniform – green and formal, with lots of brass bits. Damn, I cursed silently. Why was the army down here? He was facing three-quarters away from me, apparently talking to someone hidden from my view by the dark stone wall of a warehouse. Keeping in contact with the building, I started to back away from the soldier.

I made it pretty far, too, a good twenty or thirty feet, almost to the corner of the building, when Bob spontaneously bounced into the air and ambushed the jaguar's tail. The big cat seemed to roll under itself and came up scrambling for Bob the way Bob might go after a mouse. The housecat leaped high in the air and twisted, landing triumphantly on the jaguar's head.

The soldier turned toward the commotion. He looked to be about fifty years old with craggy features and a few bristles of short, dark hair showing beneath an officer's cap. He saw the cats, but I'm not sure he saw me. "Hold right there!" he commanded, drawing a sidearm and swinging it toward the frisking felines.

The cats stopped and looked up at the soldier.

"There's some kind of damn leopard here," the soldier called into the alleyway. "I'm going to take it down." He raised the gun, holding it with both hands, and sighted along the barrel. It was an M1911 semi-automatic .45 and I was pretty sure it could do some damage.

"Wait!" I yelled. "Don't shoot! It's…"

"Who the fuck are you?" the soldier demanded. The gun swung toward me. I didn't give him time to aim; I ducked low and ran, dodging around the corner of the building into another white-lit alley. Again, the cats managed to get ahead of me. For a moment, it seemed that I was alone. I planned to cross the side street and then make the next right turn, attempting to keep my counterclockwise direction. I took one step, though, and a group of three soldiers appeared in the intersection ahead of us. Behind, I could hear the pistol-toting officer call, "Where are you, you old freak?"

I went flat against the wall, but of course the cats didn't and I could see the three soldiers turning toward them.

"Hey," whispered a voice, very close behind me. "In here, quickly now."

I turned to see a heavy steel security door open a crack and a shadowy, long-haired figure lean out. He wasn't wearing a uniform and did not look at all military, which was a plus, and he seemed vaguely familiar. While I was momentarily considering this, Bob bounded into the open doorway, followed by the jaguar. No choice now, I noted, jumping in after them. The door clanged shut behind me and the long-haired guy rattled bolts and banged latches.

We were in a gray stairwell. A bare lightbulb in a metal cage high up above us cast a dim, yellowy light.

"Let's get away from the door and into a safer part of the building," the man said, gesturing us up the stairs.

We climbed two flights and went through another big metal security door that was bolted and latched behind us. A short utilitarian green hallway with a textured steel floor led us into a great room with shelving that towered up to a distant ceiling. A wide concrete avenue ran down the center of the hall, the only part of the room with any amount of lighting. Up ahead, though, it was brighter, light and movement shining though an open archway at the far end. As we got closer, I could also hear voices. I kept one hand on the shotgun; so far this seemed like a safer deal than I had with the soldiers, but I still had no clue who these people might be.

The hairy guy led me through the arch and into what must have been intended as a place to sort or read documents. Movement in one corner caught my eye: a bank of small, black and white television monitors, each with a different view, some outside and some inside the building. On one monitor, I could see a few uniformed soldiers having a powwow. Another monitor showed the alleyway we just came from, the army officer stalking down the center, pistol drawn. A couple of long, wooden tables dominated the center of the reading room. Around the tables and scattered in various parts of the room were bright orange fiberglass chairs with spindly metal legs. And seated in the chairs was, unmistakably, the Terran International Party, better known to '60s and '70s media as the Trippies.

They were unmistakable because they were iconic. Remember Barry Kaufman on the cover of *Rockin' Bones* in a shirt made from an American flag? There he was, shirt and all, sitting in front of me. And the long-haired guy who saved my ass from the soldiers was Perry Wilson, who once brought the government of the United States to a halt by tossing a bagful of dollar bills onto the floor of the Senate. In the '80s, Perry cut his hair and put on a suit to become a business advisor and motivational speaker. This was the younger Perry, circa 1971 perhaps, in an electric blue silk shirt and faded jeans. The short guy with curly hair who looked barely out of his teen years was certainly Mark Ratner, underground journalist and editor, who showed up to testify at the trial for the Columbia Five tripping on a hit of windowpane. About a dozen other very familiar-looking people also sat in the cheap retro chairs.

I was in awe; these were some of the heroes of my youth, but I was starting to learn. Entities. They had to be. Kaufman was dead and Wilson and Ratner were older than me.

"Holy crap," Ratner exclaimed. "It's a tiger! Is that thing safe?"

"It's a jaguar," I said, "and it seems safe enough. Just don't mess with it."

"All right," he replied with a wary grin. "It's a cool cat."

Bob and his jungle buddy began a thorough inspection of the environment, noses and tails twitching as they poked their heads into every corner.

"Thanks for letting me in," I said. "I wasn't getting on too well with the soldiers." I nodded toward the security monitors.

"Yeah, they're assholes," said Kaufman. "You know, you look a little bit familiar."

"I met you once," I explained. "In '74. You came to one of our shows and jumped onstage. Blue Smoke? At the Hollywood Bowl?"

"Blue Smoke!" Kaufman cried. "I love that band. What are you, pops, their manager?"

Pops?

"Lead guitar." I patted my instrument case. "And vocals."

They gawked at me for a long moment. I took the opportunity to unstrap my gear and lower my ass into a chair.

"What happened to you?" Wilson wanted to know.

"What do you mean?" I asked.

"You look like crap."

"I got old. Do you know what year it is?"

"Damn it!" cursed Wilson. "I knew it. They just got us out of the way, didn't they? Kidnapped us and made us disappear. Kept us tucked away while King Richard and his fascist regime took over."

"Nixon resigned," Ratner said. "A couple years ago."

"How long do you think you've been here?" I asked.

"I dunno," said Kaufman. "There's no night or day. Um…"

"A few days?" asked Ratner.

"A week?" asked Wilson.

I tried to explain to them what I thought happened on June 23 and that the '70s were a long time ago.

"You mean they've had us on ice?" Kaufman asked.

"No one has had you anywhere," I said. "You lived your life, man. You were a famous radical, you were a fugitive, you were a celebrated author and lecturer. I'm not sure what you are or why you're here now. And I'm not sure you are really that guy or not the original one, anyway. Ever since last week, dead people have been coming back. Aliens, too."

"What about this stuff?" Wilson pointed to piles of paper on the table. "It's proof that they were watching us. Files. Dossiers. Photos. Real personal stuff, too. They had reasons to lock us up. Weird, insane, fascist reasons, but reasons nonetheless. Check this out." He picked up a sheet and read, "Perry Wilson is an anarchist, a communist, and a weak-willed drug-addicted pervert with an agenda of treason against the United States. This Office recommends detention for the foreseeable future."

I picked up a manila folder, stuffed with about an inch and a half of yellowing paper. The tab on the folder said "Ratner, Mark Ethan." I flipped through the stack of documents. Surveillance reports, interviews with acquaintances, media clippings, candid photographs. One report suggested that Ratner was part of a terrorist cell on a mission to dump LSD in the New York City water supply – or grow magic mushrooms on Spiro Agnew's compost pile, it wasn't clear which. There was a photograph of him with a t-shirt that bore an image of Che Guevera and a clipping of a satirical piece Ratner wrote claiming that Nixon was addicted to injections of horse tranquilizer which he took while masturbating in the White House bathtub.

Conclusion, dated 1974: "Ratner, Mark Ethan is a ranting, unrestrained lunatic and a potential threat to national security."

I looked at the small, smirking man in front of me. He seemed cool by me.

"Where did you find these?" I asked.

"Back in the stacks," Kaufman told me. "Where they had us first."

I had a hunch I wanted to test out. "Can I see?"

"Yeah. Yeah, man," Kaufman said. "You're Ian, sort of. You were a god. Come on, I'll show you the stacks."

He led me back into the main hall where he opened a gray metal circuit box bolted to a pillar and flipped a big, black plastic switch. The switch made a resounding *clunk* and, high overhead, rows of 1000 watt lights began to buzz and glow. With a few disconcerting flickers, the lights brightened to full glare and we set off between rows of oversized shelves.

"Here we go," Kaufman said as we came to the end of one stack.

At the very end, the shelf or one of its supports had buckled, probably just from sheer time and weight, and a couple large cartons of file folders had tilted onto the floor. The edges of the cartons were chewed by mice and a fine layer of dust covered the folders splayed upon the concrete. Who could guess how long ago they spilled? Years? Decades? It didn't matter. I theorized that the people described in the dossiers were well-delineated enough to become entities on June 23 and I knew how to confirm my theory.

I pulled another big cardboard carton from the shelf. A gold foil seal was glued to the top: NSA. With a thumbnail, I severed the packing tape that held the box shut and pulled the top off. It was packed full of folders, not quite as thick as the dossiers on the Trippies, but thick enough, I figured. I picked one at random and pulled it out.

The name on the tab, inscribed in hard-edged black by the courier type-ball of a long-gone IBM Selectric, said "Eftweather, Reginald." I opened it and skimmed a statistics sheet on top. Mr. Eftweather was born in '47, had two wives – not at the same time –

four children, was involved in various church and municipal volunteer services, and liked to purchase and resell surplus bomb parts on the black market.

"Ahem," Mr. Eftweather began.

I looked up to see a short, tubby man with a black mustache like two little spider legs and a few thin strands of dark hair combed over a great expanse of bald head.

"Reading my personal file, are we?" Mr. Eftweather inquired.

I looked over at Kaufman. "Cool," the Trippie leader said. "That was very cool. One moment, it's just us, the next, he's here. Far fucking out, Ian!"

"What is this place?" Eftweather aimed the question at Barry Kaufman. Perhaps the flag shirt made him look more official. "What am I doing here?"

"Oh, man," Kaufman complained. "You're asking the heavy questions."

"There are millions of lives stashed away in this cave," I said.

"I have a feeling it's going to get really crowded in here." Kaufman gazed at the towering shelves with new appreciation.

I nodded and we walked back to join the others, Eftweather following us like a lost puppy.

I did my best to explain to the assembled Trippies that they were entities, created from information that the NSA and other agencies collected about them a long time ago.

"Well that is some shit," Ratner commented.

"But you don't have to live like this," I said. "Now that you're here, you can go anywhere, I think."

"It's not so bad here," Ratner quipped. "Though a few joints sure would help pass the time."

I unstrapped my guitar case and opened it on the table.

"Whoa," said half a dozen voices at once. "Holy shit," said half a dozen more.

"Ian is God," Mark Ratner confirmed.

"Oh, my goodness," said Mr. Eftweather. "Drugs."

We got really high.

"Okay," Perry Wilson said to me a short time later, "I want to try this entity thing again. We're in the Twenty First Century and… one week ago, gods, aliens and imaginary friends just started appearing?"

"That's right," I said.

"I mean, how do you deal with that, man?" Wilson asked.

"I don't know." I took a hit from a roach that was, somehow, still making its way around. "It's an existential dilemma. You just live with it, I guess. We like to think that we're in charge of our world, but I think that humans are really just fleas on the back of a big dog. The dog makes the decisions. If Ol' Rover takes a dip in the river, the fleas endure a flood, though they can't possibly grok Rover's trajectory or motives. Humans have survived ice ages, plagues, the development of agriculture, the taming of fire. Fuck, we've survived television. So far. Why do these changes happen when they do? Is there some thread of meaning to any of it? Is there some rule that says humans have to understand? Fucked if I know. All this stuff changes our world and we adapt. Or we don't."

"So you're saying," Kaufman asked, "just go with the flow?"

"I'm just saying, 'Fucked if I know'," I explained. "The world is full of ambiguity, but too many people are too damn certain. I'll wait to find out. Maybe I never will. In the meantime, 'Fucked if I know'."

"Hey," said a middle-aged woman toward the far end of the room. "Look!" She pointed at the security monitors.

There was movement on several of the little black and white screens. I took a step closer so I could see better.

Way down at the end of one street, very difficult to make out on the tiny TV, there was a commotion involving, it seemed, quite a few soldiers. And maybe a few other people. As they slowly came closer to the camera, it appeared that they had prisoners who were being marched along at gunpoint, hands tied behind their backs. I knew those prisoners – they were my bandmates and friends. All of them, it seemed, except Aqualung and Perzanto. And along with them, also tied and captive, was the security guard who had spooked me earlier. I could see now that he was just a rent-a-cop, a poor guy with a low-paying and previously very boring job. He was probably the guy who made rounds in a golf cart and checked the security monitors in the individual buildings.

On the edge of another monitor, I caught a brief glimpse of something humungous, stalking behind the soldiers and their hostages. Perzanto, I thought.

"All right, Trippies," I announced. "The time has come. It's time for us to overtake the soldiers. I want to save my friends and you need to get your Trippie asses out of this building."

"While I definitely support the idea of getting the fuck out of here," Mark Ratner said. "I would like to point out that those soldiers have a lot of guns."

"They've got the guns," I said. "But we've got the numbers."

Ratner looked around the room. "Fifteen people and a jaguar? I admit the jaguar is pretty fearsome. And that housecat has a mean look, too."

"There are many thousands of lives in this building," I waved a file folder. "Free the people!"

Kaufman grinned. "Free the people!"

"Free the people!" cried the other Trippie leaders.

"Free the people!" yelled the rest of those in the room.

"Ahem," said Reginald Eftweather. "If I understand correctly, those shelves are full of radicals, terrorists, and miscreants of various kinds. Do we really want to free them all?"

"Mr. Eftweather has a point," I said. "Is there a directory for this building? A listing of what's stored here?"

Perry Wilson reached beneath a table and hefted a very large and heavy binder onto the tabletop with a resounding *thud*. I came around to take a look.

I pulled the cover back and began flipping through the documents. "This is amazing," I said. "Great organization. About half of the building seems to be records for retired policemen. So fuck that. But the rest..."

"Yeah?" Kaufman asked expectantly.

"Radicals, terrorists and miscreants of every kind. Let's free the people. "

"Are you sure?" Eftweather asked nervously. "I mean…"

"Check it out," I said. "This section is all anti-war protesters. Over here, anarchists! I mean, real anarchists! In this section – look at this! – the Clown Fellowship, the Brotherhood of Bread, the League for Symbiotic Development, the Church of the Subgenius, the New Cut-Ups, the Guerrilla Ontology Liberation Front, Students for Collateral Damage… Wow, I can't believe the government was compiling information on Mothers for Corresponding Measures!"

"I never heard of that one," Ratner remarked. "Were they some bad mothers?"

"In the 1990s," I began, "there was a White House intern named Monica Lewinsky. The President got caught with his, um, cigar in her mouth and it became a scandal that ended with Bill Clinton being impeached, but magically retaining power. Anyway, some clever fellows in the Russian Duma noticed that when President Clinton was getting head, he was a pretty peaceful fellow, but when left unsucked, he tended to drop a lot of bombs in various impoverished parts of the world. They suggested that the USA open an Office of Corresponding Measures, to make sure the President got properly hoovered on a regular basis. For world peace. The Duma passed a resolution on the suggestions, but the idea went pretty much unnoticed in the United States, except for one or two peace organizations that worked to promote Corresponding Measures. Mothers was the coolest one. Their leader, Mona Ramona, offered to blow the President herself. They did a lot of very personal lobbying, you know, in Congress."

"Free the Mothers!" Ratner cried.

I grabbed my gear and, cats and all, we marched into the stacks. I scanned the lids of cartons and cross-referenced with the index binder, which some of the Trippies dragged along. I found a shelf marked COINTELPRO, pulled the top off a box and selected a folder.

A tall, stooped black man in his late 30s winked into existence and stood blinking for a moment under the bright sodium lighting. I grinned at him. He was someone I'd wanted to meet, Captain Head Charge of the Poetic Alliteration Alliance. The PAA flew helicopters over the estate of the federal drug czar at dawn, bombing his backyard with fifty pounds of marijuana and scaring the crap out of his household staff. I thought it was a waste of good weed, but it was poetic. Head Charge created a national conspiracy to buy hookers for televangelists and far-right congressmen. Allegedly financed in part by stroke-book mogul Larry Fink, the prostitutes came equipped with condoms, sex toys, and hidden recording devices. Head Charge and his proto-hacker buddies tapped into a communications satellite and jammed the feed for the Super Bowl, replacing it with a surrealist documentary about a linoleum-covered enigma entitled "The Slant Step." Sports fans across the country were admitted en masse to mental hospitals. As their final act, the PAA broke into a secret military chemical warfare plant and poured fresh water into a reservoir of toxic acid. For making the solution slightly less poisonous, five PAA members were arrested and charged with terrorism and a list of other charges. Captain Head Charge was rumored to be a John Doe who somehow disappeared during transportation. During the five or six years of the '80s that the PAA ran its course as a movement, Captain Head Charge never showed his face in public, but here he was.

I introduced him to the Trippies who, once upon a time, released three large canisters of laughing gas into the Pentagon air system. It was a little bit freaky, but I figured they were destined to be friends.

Within the next hour, the warehouse became crowded with all manner of suspicious characters. There were thousands, of every size, shape, motive, and preferred method. There were indeed a few scary, potentially bomb-wielding types, but for the most part it seemed like the FBI or NSA or whoever created the files spent a lot of time watching the civil disobedient and creatively dissident. We had Black Panthers, Gray Panthers, and Cougars for Peace. There were two full squads of the Clown Fellowship, who spread through the crowd stealing neckties and performing acrobatics. We had Students for a Democratic Society, Students for a Socialized Democracy, Demagogues for Strident Speechification, and the Corporate Hog Elimination Squad. A band of Mothers for Corresponding Measures strolled through the crowd, like Charlie's Angels with stretch marks. We had Marxists, Anarchists, Masochists, Situationists,

Environmentalists, Nudists, Dissident Linguists, Obstructionists, Artists, Radical Orthodontists and the Justified Ancients of Mu-Mu. Twenty or so men and women, mostly past middle age and with beatific expressions, worked the crowd, embracing anyone who looked confused: the Free Hug Happiness Corps. Judging by clothes and hair, the records we unleashed as radical entities began during the Truman administration and ran up through the reign of Bill Clinton. I imagine that was when computers fully took over from cardboard file boxes.

I set my guitar and shotgun on a shelf and climbed up onto a step ladder. "Hello, everyone!" I called in my best rock-arena voice. The room quieted and faces turned toward me. I did my best to explain the situation. Everyone had witnessed the process of their peers and comrades appearing from cartons and folders, so I thankfully didn't have to try to explain the nature of entities. "I think all of you ended up in this building because you cared enough to try to change the world for the better," I said. "And you ended up in these files because the government or someone powerful didn't like that. They still don't like it and they want to keep us all in here. There are soldiers outside right now, some of them with guns, who are trying to keep us down. The soldiers had the Trippies pinned inside this building for the last week. Even worse, they have prisoners. They have some of my friends, my bandmates. Some of you know them as Blue Smoke." There was a scattering of applause and a few enthusiastic shouts. "But now, my brothers and sisters, there are more of us than there are military motherfuckers. A lot more, I hope. And there's someone else out there, a really big guy, sort of a god, I guess, and he's on our side, too. So I ask you this: Shall we chase out the army bastards and get liberty and justice for all?"

There was a fantastic cheer of approval that almost blew me off the step ladder. It was way beyond anything I could have imagined, like the roar of a crowd after a perfect show. I wanted to howl. I wanted to pick up my guitar and play an encore.

"All right!" I shouted. "Follow me!"

I stepped down from the ladder, grabbed my axe and gun, and pushed off toward the front of the building. The cats, the Trippies,

Captain Head Charge, and Mona Ramona, queen of Corresponding Measures, walked with me. The horde of dissidents fell in behind us and our instant unarmed army flowed down the stairwell and into a small front lobby. In a moment the lobby was packed and more of us were coming down the stairs so I pushed open the door and led the entities into battle.

11. The Battle

I did my best, my whole life, to stay away from war. The late '60s and early '70s were a damn tough time to do that, but somehow, even with a career as a rock star, I managed to stay matriculated at U of C Santa Cruz long enough to avoid getting sent to Vietnam. The record company helped a bit with that and Trenton and I got course credit for touring and studio time. When we were in town, we took film and literature courses and may even have learned a few things. Cleve had some kind of medical deferment and Jason famously showed up at his draft examination tripping hard on STP and wearing lingerie.

Not that I'm entirely a pacifist. I know how to handle a gun and I can think of a few things I'll fight for. Freedom is one of them, particularly when it's my personal freedom and running is out of the question. I'll fight for my friends. I'll fight for principles, if it ever comes to that. The Vietnam War was fought for none of those things, so I felt no call, no duty to fight there and I was happy to stay in the states and play music at peace rallies. Fuck you if you don't like it. Behind the bullshit ideological domino theory rhetoric, that war was fought for control of heroin and money and those are stupid things to kill for. I was hoping to avoid a fight in Steel Cave, too, but this was about freedom and friends and the Mossberg and I were ready to kick ass if we had to.

The soldiers must have suspected that something was up because four guys in green waited for us outside. As we burst from the door, they pulled guns – three M1911 handguns and one M16 rifle – but we overwhelmed them so fast they didn't have time to fire. In a moment, there were hundreds of us. A few minutes later, thousands. I lost sight of those soldiers entirely.

All right, I just want to get this out of the way. I know there are some of you who think I was a traitor of some kind for avoiding military service or taking a stand against the soldiers in Steel Cave. Do you know what a traitor is? A traitor is someone who betrays the spirit, the nature of a nation. A traitor is someone who works their way into the highest places of power and then uses that power to strip away our freedoms, to curtail our liberty, to fight wars on behalf of intelligence organizations, international crime and weapons dealers. A traitor is someone who ignores the founding principles in favor of big government defense contracts and the greed of corporations. A traitor is someone who tears down the edifice of human rights upon which our nation was built when they commit atrocities in the name of America. A traitor is an unthinking soldier who follows those atrocious orders without protest. When I was growing up, I learned that America was the land of the free and home of the brave, that we only fought to defend ourselves and that we stood on the side of liberty and the rights of human beings. I'm a patriot for that America, motherfucker. The Trippies were patriots. Captain Head Charge was a patriot. The Mothers for Corresponding Measures were patriots. Got it?

Columns of soldiers in full combat gear marched from a building up the street, a stocky officer in the lead, shouting orders that echoed off the cavern ceiling. There were, I quickly estimated, about a hundred, equipped with light body armor, serving bowl helmets, and belts laden with clattering gear. Most carried guns, either the M1911 or the M16, both weapons that were no longer standard issue in the Twenty First Century. Their combat fatigues, too, were as retro as the afros on our Black Panthers. They formed ranks and began marching toward us. Behind me, dissidents continued to stream forth from the building.

"Hey," said Bob, slinking along beside me, "over there." His ears and nose were aimed up a side street where a large lumpy figure lurked in a doorway.

The figure stepped under a street light where I could see him, out of sight of the soldiers. Perzanto, of course. He held a finger like a knockwurst to his lips and beckoned to me with the other enormous hand.

"Keep everyone here," I said to Barry Kaufman. "Just hold your ground for now. I'll be right back."

I took Captain Head Charge with me and Bob tagged along. As we walked away, I could hear Kaufman exhorting the troops: "Okay, ladies and gentlemen. This is Civil Disobedience 101. We are going to peacefully hold this space. But if you can think of any good chants, that could be fun too…"

We met Perzanto in the shallow doorway of a stone building. Head Charge gave Perzanto the once over and gave a long whistle. He looked back at me. "Is he the god?"

I nodded.

"Damn, you're a big dude," he said to Perzanto. "You must be like three people wide. Three big people. Linebackers. Do you know how to box? Can I be your manager?"

Perzanto looked at me, enormous eyebrows raised.

"Perzanto," I said, "meet Captain Head Charge. He's good at this stuff. Trust me."

The big guy looked skeptical but engulfed the Captain's hand in his and shook.

"So how do we do this?" I asked. "We need to get Blue Smoke away from the green people and we want to get all these people free."

The two of them, and Bob, stared at me.

"Well?" I asked. "Any ideas?"

"Oh, I thought you would have the plan," Captain Head Charge said.

"Right," said Perzanto. "That's what I thought."

"Me?" I adjusted my guitar case. "I don't even know where they've got our friends locked up."

"The soldiers are based in one building," Perzanto said, "the big, gray stone one that the troops came marching from. They took the prisoners in and up the stairs. That was as much as I could see."

"Head Charge, how did you get into that chemical weapons plant?"

"Easy," he grinned. "We made uniforms. They looked just like the real thing. Hats with shiny brims, medals, laminated plastic name tags and everything. Then we just marched in like we owned the place."

"Maybe we could steal a few uniforms…"

"Wait," Perzanto said. "There is another way." He stared for a moment at Captain Head Charge. His massive brow furrowed with concentration, he took a deep breath and let it out. There was a snap like a dried pea turning into a coffeemaker and Head Charge was now a private first class, in vintage 1970s combat gear exactly like the troops that were marching across Steel Cave.

"Whoa," Private Head Charge exclaimed. "Damn. What the…? How did you do that?"

"Never mind how," I said. "It worked. You look good."

Head Charge looked at his green-clad arms and legs, checked out the insignia on his uniform, and pulled a pair of tinkling dog tags out of his shirt. "Not good enough," he scowled. "How come the black man is always the private? How come I'm supposed to take orders from the man? Shit."

"What do you want?" I asked.

"Shit," he repeated. "Make me a general! Not just any general. Make me the goddamn general in charge. Head Charge in charge, that's how it should be."

Perzanto looked at me and I nodded. The god concentrated again and with a snap, Captain Head Charge was in a more formal uniform, with lots of brass and medals. His chest looked thirty percent larger, his whole head was bigger and his jaw was now square and huge.

He checked himself out. "Now that's more like it!" His voice was deeper and he tried out a command. "All right, men," he snapped. "Atten-hut!" We snapped to attention. Head Charge giggled. "Okay, I can do this. But, damn, it'd be much more fun if I could get high first."

I opened my guitar case. General Head Charge's massive jaw dropped.

We got a little bit stoned. Okay, maybe more than a little.

"Can I score some of that from you?" the general inquired.

The cannabis accelerated my creative thought processes. A plan started to form in my mind. A general was unlikely to sneak in and out the way a private might, but there were other advantages to the rank. "Okay," I said. "Here's how I see it. General Head Charge, if you and Perzanto can keep the bulk of the troops occupied, I'll get into the building and free our friends. Then we'll work on getting the dissident horde out of the cave. Can you do it?"

"Can we do it?" Head Charge used one sleeve to polish a large gold medal pinned to his chest. "Can we do it? I'm a *goddamn general*. I can do anything I want!"

"Can *you* do it?" Perzanto asked me. "Can you get in there and get them out?"

"I'll have some help," I said.

The god and the faux general put their oversized heads together and began to confer so Bob and I started back toward our group of dissidents.

Through our short conference with Perzanto, we heard the level of noise behind us continue to rise as more and more people issued from the building. Now I could make out a chant, a couple thousand voices calling, "Army guys smell like pee! People in the street got to be free!"

I found Kaufman, Wilson and Ratner at the head of the crowd, grinning from ear to ear and pumping their fists in the air with the chant. We faced the advancing soldiers, who were now barely a block away.

Ratner suddenly turned and faced the crowd, waving his arms. "Wait! Wait!" he yelled. "I've got another one." As faces turned toward him, he started a new chant. "Free marijuana! Free marijuana!" The crowd joined in.

Wilson grabbed Ratner by the shoulder. "What the fuck?" he shouted over the chanting.

"What?" Ratner asked. "You don't want free marijuana?"

Just about then, they caught sight of me.

"Well, speak of the devil," Ratner exclaimed. "See? The chant worked!"

I realized I still had a smoldering roach in my hand and I gave it to the Trippie. The crowd, apparently realizing what they'd been saying, started to quiet down and the chant devolved into chaos. As the noise level diminished, we could hear the sound of boots on asphalt. Lots of boots. The dissidents got very quiet. We could all see the phalanx of soldiers, only half a block away.

Wilson turned to face our mob, arms raised, ready to direct them with another chant. "All right, everyone! This is it! All together…"

"Wait." I put my hand on his shoulder. "Just a second."

As Wilson lowered his arms, another voice boomed out.

"COMPANY, HALT!"

The soldiers stomped to a full stop. Unsuccessfully suppressing the giggles, General Head Charge stepped out into the street. As his brass caught the light, the soldiers snapped to attention and saluted. Head Charge swaggered along the front rank of men, eyeing them with a fair simulation of official appraisal, before returning the salute.

"Officers! Front and center!" Head Charge boomed. A dozen men with insignia on their fatigues stepped out from the ranks. "Fall in!" the general ordered, pointing to an empty patch of asphalt near the intersection. The officers marched over and formed a double line. "Your mission," the general informed them, "is to enter that side street and engage in reconnaissance operations."

The officers marched efficiently around the corner and disappeared down the street. We heard repeated thumping, clatter, several loud crashes, and an empty helmet rolled out from between the buildings. We all watched as it spun for moment on the pavement. The general turned toward me and gave a thumbs up. The dissident horde watched in amazement.

I looked at the colorful diversity of radicals, terrorists and miscreants around me. Through the throng I could see a bobbing head of blond hair and I elbowed my way to get to Mona Ramona, queen of Corresponding Measures. Mona was almost as tall as I, in her early thirties (although I reckoned she would actually be close to 50, in her real, physical form), wearing a leather miniskirt, calf-high boots and a white spandex tank top.

"Mona," I said, "I need you."

"What?" she asked. "Are you running for office?"

"No. I'm trying to save my friends and I need your help." I explained my idea to her. She formed a cadre of Mothers and they accompanied us to the rear of the crowd where we ducked down a side street and went behind the building. We walked along the outer cavern wall, back along the way I'd originally come. Bob stayed close to me and the jaguar joined us from the shadows, trailing silently behind.

As we got closer to the soldiers' building, we could hear sounds and voices from the other street, a block further into the cave.

General Head Charge's booming voice: "…remove your shoes! That's an order, soldier! Now march!"

Crashes, thumps and grunts of pain.

Head Charge: "Atten-hut! Now waddle like a duck! One, two, one, two… My grandmother waddles better than you, soldier!"

Repeated battering. A whimper.

The soldier's huge, squat, stone building was buttoned up tight on our side. There was one big set of metal doors, locked from the inside and we couldn't budge them. As I pulled fruitlessly on the door handle, the jaguar sauntered up to Bob and made a low growl. Bob tilted his head with interest, his tail swirling.

"Tim says around the corner," Bob told me.

"Tim?" I asked.

"The spotty dude." Bob's nose pointed toward his jungle friend. "He wants to find Birdie."

We followed the jaguar around the corner. Sure enough, there was a gray metal security door with two guards posted outside. I nodded to Mona. The cats and I held back as the Mothers formed a flying vee with Mona at the point and advanced on the soldiers, strutting and rolling their hips with precision that transcended the military by a bucket or two of hormones.

My plan was pretty simple. I figured that the troops dated from an era when women didn't serve in combat and that there must be few, if any, females in that building. Even if the Mothers for Corresponding Measures were a few years older than the soldiers, they had enough conscious pulchritude packed into miniskirts and spandex to distract and possibly overwhelm the sex-starved soldiers. This is what they were good at, what they trained for. If Mona and the girls couldn't talk or shimmy our way in, they might at least offer an opportunity for me to apply a little shotgun persuasion.

One of the guards swung his rifle toward the approaching Mothers, but the muzzle dipped toward the pavement as distraction overwhelmed his aim. The other soldier never even took a defensive position; he stood slack-jawed and wide-eyed. In a moment the guards were surrounded by Mothers, who pressed soft flesh against them and cooed inanities about what gorgeous men they were. Soldier brains turned to mush as circulatory systems sent vital blood and hormones to other parts of their bodies. In just minutes we strolled through the door. So far, so good.

Inside was a square foyer with industrial green walls, barely big enough to hold all of us, and a set of doors leading to a stairwell. Three more soldiers came to attention, their bloodflow quickly redirected by the Mothers. The cats and I hung back behind the women, letting them work their seductive sorcery, trying to remain as inconspicuous as an old fart with a shotgun and an oversized jungle beast could. Soon the procession, led by delirious, drooling soldiers, started up the stairs.

We came out into a big, echoing storage room, much like the one in the Trippies' building, wide shelves climbing up toward blazing white sodium lighting. A few dozen soldiers loitered about, sitting on the concrete floor or wandering through the stacks.

"Hello!" Mona Ramona's sweet voice echoed around the space. "How are you boys doing today? Feel like having a little company? How about a party?" She cocked her hips and stood there, the Mothers in a line behind her, as the soldiers took notice. The jaguar and I stayed back, watching as pheromones pulled the soldiers to the Mothers like ants to sugar. Bob disappeared into the shadows of the towering stacks.

The army temporarily placated with corresponding measures, I figured it was a good time to look around. Staying as far from the soldiers as we could, Tim and I circled around toward the stacks and the far wall. As we walked, I scanned the stored boxes. Veterans

Affairs. On the next row, Pentagon. Beyond the Pentagon, a whiskered face popped out between boxes.

"A couple rows over," Bob said. "There's a door with two guards. Smells like entity soldiers in there, and our humans, too."

"Lead on, big cat," I told him.

Bob dropped into a bird-stalking crouch and crept forward. Tim and I moved as stealthily as we could behind him. Stealth only worked so far, though. Where the stacks came to an end there was only open floor and no way to sneak up on the guards. I stepped out as dramatically as I could, pumping a shell into the Mossberg and taking aim. The jaguar leaped out beside me, back arched, and spit a blood-curdling yowl. Bob also hissed and growled, but it didn't have the same kind of effect.

"Place your rifles on the floor," I ordered. The soldiers, eyes darting back and forth between the fat muzzle of the shotgun and the exposed fangs of the jungle cat, hastily complied.

"Open the door," I said.

"We… we can't," one of the men stammered. "It can only be opened from inside."

"Get them to open it," I told him.

He nodded and turned to the door, knocking a quick code on the door. I realized my mistake as the door flew open and six heavily armed guys in dark green body armor burst forth. I dropped the Mossberg and Tim closed his mouth.

"Mona!" I called to the rafters.

An officer swaggered out to join the troops. I recognized him immediately: the craggy-faced, middle-aged man who pursued me earlier. I don't know military insignia; I'd guess his rank was Major General. He looked me up and down and one side of his mouth lifted slightly in a vague suggestion of a grin. Behind the officer, before someone still inside the room could get the door slammed shut, Don's little red devil fluttered out.

"The old cat freak," the officer snarled. "I had a feeling we'd meet again." He nodded to the soldiers. "Get them inside. Goddamn, there's some weird shit down in this cave."

The devil landed on the man's shoulder and crossed his tiny arms over crimson chest. "So, whatcha gonna do?" he smirked.

The officer swatted at the little entity, which evaded him with a flap of leathery wings. "None of your damn business, you... uh... whatever you are," he scowled.

"I give good advice," the devil called, gaining altitude. "And you're gonna neeeed it!"

Behind us there was a clatter of boot heels on concrete. Mona and a few of the Mothers came running up. They stopped and posed to display a maximum of thinly-wrapped curvature.

"What seems to be the problem, officer?" Mona asked.

The soldiers seemed instantly captivated, but the Major General was unmoved. "Keep the whores out here. I want the old freak and the animals inside."

A private reluctantly rapped out a code on the door and it swung open.

"You don't like Mona?" I asked.

"Don't ask," the officer warned.

The soldiers grabbed me, but then there was another commotion from the stacks. We heard shuffling, stumbling, mumbled cursing and then Aqualung shambled from the shadows.

"Hold it right there, bum!" the officer ordered. Three of the soldiers aimed their guns toward the old sot.

"I'm jush lookin' for Ian," Aqualung explained.

"Stop that bum!" the Major General commanded.

"Freeze!" one of the soldiers yelled.

Aqualung continued forward. "Ian, man, I was lookin' for ya..."

"Stop right now or we'll shoot!" the soldier elaborated.

Aqualung stumbled forward. "I jush wanned to tell ya..."

And three soldiers squeezed the triggers of three very large guns.

Nothing happened. Not even a click. Aqualung kept walking as he delivered his message. "Their gunsh don' work," he said.

The soldiers kept trying, frantically squeezing the triggers, working the bolts and banging on the gun mechanisms with their palms. The soldiers who held me released their grip and brought their own guns to bear, with similar lack of effect.

Aqualung was right. The soldiers had impressive guns – but they didn't work. Maybe there wasn't enough information about ammo in the files, or maybe guns just don't reincarnate properly. I don't know. I dived for the Mossberg. I jumped back up with as much speed as arthritic knees would allow, took aim at the ceiling and fired off a booming shell. The sound echoed through the space and everyone froze.

"All right, motherfuckers," I said in my best action-hero voice, pointing the muzzle of the shotgun at the closest soldier. "Just hold it right there."

Tim bared his teeth in a fierce grin and growled at the soldiers. Jaguars can make some pretty freaky sounds. I felt a chill run down my spine and, judging by their expressions, so did the soldiers.

"Weapons on the ground," I ordered.

They lowered their useless guns to the floor.

"Mothers," I asked, "can you handle these unarmed gentlemen here?" I waved my gun toward the rank and file. Mona and the Mothers smiled at them and they suddenly looked less defeated.

"You," I said to the officer, "inside." I gestured toward the open door and we went in, followed by the cats and Aqualung.

There was one more soldier inside and he lowered his weapon to the floor when he saw the shotgun aimed at his CO's head. The room was small relative to the vast spaces of Steel Cave and brightly lit by incandescent bulbs in metal cages. Our friends were in there, tied to chairs with packing straps and plastic pipe cinches apparently scavenged from various parts of the building. Musical instruments and gear were stacked against a wall.

There was a weak cheer from the prisoners. I directed the soldier to untie them, although Tim got to Birdie first, snapping her bonds with dagger-like teeth. When they all stood, rubbing and stomping the circulation back into wrists and ankles, I ordered the Major General to sit and sent the soldier out to join his company. Birdie gratefully scratched and petted Tim. I sat next to the officer and

Trenton grabbed the seat on the other side. Esty and Don circulated through the room, checking on everyone, the angel and devil fluttering along behind, arms around each other's shoulders.

"I was worried about you," the angel said.

"Ah, the guns didn't work," said the devil.

"Yeah, but you didn't know that," the angel replied.

"Don't worry," the devil said. "I'd never leave you alone with the human. You'd warp his mind."

Karen, Oswaldo and the security guard swapped breathless instant retellings of their peril. Cleve did his best to dodge Aqualung, who careened up against a wall and slid down into a fetid heap at the bottom, succumbing to a brief, snotty bout of D.T.s.

"What is it that you freakazoids want?" the officer asked.

I propped the Mossberg across my lap. "We just want to play some music," I explained. "And maybe get high every now and then."

"Like I told you," Trent said, "we were just passing through."

The officer looked down, then up to meet my gaze. "What is this place? Is this… Hell?"

I sighed and explained again about the way the world was and the nature of entities and the function of Steel Cave. At the end of my spiel the officer looked more confused than convinced, but that was my best shot.

"So, you…" he began. "You are a real human and I'm something else?"

"Yeah," I confirmed. "And my gun works and yours doesn't. Don't get me wrong, though. There's nothing wrong with being a recreation of a human being from an earlier time. It makes you a unique being. Very unique. Be proud of what you are."

"Did you just call me a freak?" He clenched a fist. I raised the shotgun a tiny fraction of an inch and his hand relaxed.

"I said 'unique'," I told him. "But if the shoe fits…"

"Well, you have me," the man said. "A shotgun at my head, my troops in disarray. I take it we're to negotiate a surrender. What are your terms?"

"Terms? Order the troops to cease and desist all hostile action. Are you the guy with the power to do that?"

"I am."

"It might be a good idea," I said. "Since we already kicked their asses."

He sighed. "Anything else?"

"Yes, one more thing," Trent spoke up. "You and as many of your men who would like to, come to the concert. Three hours from now, in the center of the cavern."

Trenton has a lot of really good ideas.

12. In the Morning

With dissidents and soldiers pulling their weight as roadies, we were soon ready for the show. We cannibalized shelving to make a quick and fairly sturdy stage, in the process freeing another thousand entities from their files. We set the portable amps on the front of the platform and did a quick sound check. Trent played around with the settings on the little gizmos and figured out how to get them to emulate the sound of old Fender amps, like the kind we used on our first tour. The acoustics in the cave were surprisingly good. Sound seemed to concentrate and hang in the air. Each note seemed to have its own aura of sound. The Gibson SG Les Paul has a clear, warm sound, with fantastic sustain courtesy of the big, heavy brass whammy bar; I sent some long, soaring notes off into the cavern and a bright scattering of applause returned to me.

Through all the pre-concert industry, the Steel Cave security guard sat quietly and watched, making no objection even when we raided buildings for chairs, tables, and pretty much anything else not bolted to the floor. With the sound check completed, there wasn't anything to do until show time except hang out and get high. I unfolded an ancient gray metal chair and sat by the guard.

His brown rent-a-cop uniform was disheveled, shirt tails hanging loose; his hat and tie were long gone and his shiny brass badge was askew. He was in his early thirties, tall and generally thin except for a round belly that was only partly restrained by his belt. The guard greeted me warmly, introduced himself as Frank, and apologized for scaring me off.

"Just my homegrown paranoia," I explained. "Don't worry about it. It ended well. I got some exercise, we freed a whole shitload of entities, and we made peace with the military. Next time, though, maybe you won't shout so fucking loudly at an old man."

"I was excited!" Frank said. "I thought I saw a famous rock band on the monitors. This cave has always been a little strange, you know. Sightings and shit, lights and creatures. My granddad used to tell us stories from when Steel Cave was a quarry. But things started getting really weird last week. The soldiers, the hippies, your extra-large friend…. But seeing Blue Smoke, that was pretty cool. Seriously, I've got CDs! I had to check it out. I figured you were real, too, I mean human, because…"

"Because?"

"Uh, because you looked old."

"That we do." I gestured at the throng gathering by the stage. "Aren't you supposed to be stopping this? Or reporting it or something?"

He laughed. "Right. They pay me barely enough to be worth it when nothing happens. I don't make nearly enough to deal with anything like this. Who cares, anyway? I should have quit my job last week. I want to see you play. Front row at the first Blue Smoke concert in thirty years! I am so there."

"Thirty two years, I think. If you want front row," I suggested, "you might want to stake out some turf now."

He thanked me profusely, folded his chair with a metallic creak and carried it off.

I caught a quick toke as I watched the crowd gather. Freaks and soldiers mingled freely, enemies no more now that everyone understood the way of the world, the nature of file entities and all that stuff. A few boys in uniform had Mothers on their arms as did, I could see, Barry Kaufman. Captain Head Charge, still a general, was making friends with Mona Ramona. Perzanto sat on the edge of the stage, calmly watching.

A few minutes later, Oswaldo whirred up in an aged brown Steel Cave golf cart and drove me to the back of the stage. As the band climbed onto the converted shelving, the street lights went out and the cavern was plunged into darkness. We used flashlights to find our way to the instruments and stood for a moment in silence. Then lights around the stage flashed back on, bathing us all in brilliant, blue-white glare, and we rocked. We rocked hard. We rocked well. We kept it real simple. We played the five Blue Smoke songs we knew best, filled them with energy and made them as loud as we could with the baby amps. The Tripper did a surprisingly good job on the dumbek, really filling in creatively for the missing drum kit. Cleve was miraculously back up to speed and he really held it all together with solid rhythms. Don was as soulful as ever. Birdie was even more soulful than ever. And Trenton was his usual excellent self. The angel and devil fluttered overhead, the cats strolled around on the stage, and Esty danced. Karen worked the lights, switching street lamps on and off from a utility shack along the cave wall, watching the show on the ubiquitous monitors. Oswaldo took a well-deserved rest, though he did dance a little.

Then, just because it seemed like the thing to do, we jammed on some old favorites. Perzanto joined us, booming out deep rhythms on the mrrlnx, and we played Bob Marley's "No Woman No Cry," Pink Floyd's "Time," Bob Dylan's "All Along the Watchtower," and Howlin' Wolf's "Smokestack Lightning," the first tune that Trenton and I ever played together. It was fun. We *played*. I wished that Jane was there. She would have loved it.

There was a lot of applause, we waved to the crowd, and suddenly it was decision time. All the entities were now, apparently, free to do as they pleased. They could leave Steel Cave – Frank the security guard showed us a set of double doors beyond which an elevator led to the office building on the surface – or they could stay. And we had the same decision. *I* had the same decision to make. I knew that I could just climb those stairs and come out on Binnewater Road. I'd have a five mile hike home, but that was at least a definite quantity. Continuing further into the cave was a complete unknown.

Thing is, I was having fun. I got high with some of my childhood heroes. I got to fire the Mossberg and scare the shit out of some army guys. That earned a chuckle every time I thought about it. We had a jam session just for the thrill of it and a bit of applause. That felt great. And we had another gig already booked, as it were, in the resonant chamber. It was a warm-up tour, it was an adventure, and there was still plenty of weed in my guitar case. I was a little concerned about what we'd do for food. I figured there was no artist hospitality in a cave. But Frank had the food thing under control. He took his car into Kingston and loaded up on groceries at the big Canafford near the Thruway roundabout.

I decided I'd stay in the cave at least for the night. I reserved the right to change my mind in the morning, but it seemed that some of the others were taking it as a sign that the quest would continue. The whole band was still with me, Esty, Oswaldo and Karen, too. Aqualung appeared to be unconscious and no one really wanted to know his decision, anyway. Perzanto, of course, took it for granted that we would continue on. Mark Ratner joined us, although the other Trippies planned to leave. Captain Head Charge, a battalion from the Clown Fellowship, a small squadron of soldiers, a confusion of guerilla ontologists, and at least one dissident linguist also chose to come along. The Mothers for Corresponding Measures, however, declined.

"We really are mothers," Mona Ramona explained. "We want to see our kids. And maybe even our husbands and boyfriends."

"They'll be much older," I said, "and your human versions are probably still around, too."

"I know," Mona told me. "But I want to see how they turned out."

I didn't envy her the etiquette questions. When you meet yourself, do you just nod and move along or do you buy her a beer? "It's a weird world now," I said. "You never know, you might like yourself."

Mona gave me a warm kiss on the cheek and with rustle of spandex and creak of leather, the Mothers sashayed toward the exit.

Perzanto transformed acorns into comfortable foam mats. We each grabbed one and made camp in the Trippies' building. I wandered into the stacks for a little privacy and quiet. Tall shelves rising into unseen darkness, it was like a gothic shrine to the half-forgotten paranoia of governments gone by. A moment after I lay down, Bob slid out from the shadows, purring and kneading the acorn mat with his big front paws.

"So Bob," I said. "Tell me about the talking. Have you always been able to?"

"Yeah," said Bob. "But only in the cave, and usually much farther in. I would have told you about it but, obviously, you know, I couldn't."

"You've been down here before?"

"Hey," he said, "it's my mountain."

I didn't dispute it. "What about Tim?" I asked. "He can't talk?"

"He can talk," Bob said. "Just not so you can understand him."

"But you can?"

"That's right." He curled up on the mat, his furry back pressed against my leg.

"Does he say anything interesting?"

"He talks about Birdie." Bob sat up, stretched, turned around, and curled up again. "He has something to tell her, but, you know, he can't."

"Do you know? Do you know what he wants to tell her?"

Bob uncurled and stretched. "The jaguar's a little loopy, dude. He keeps saying that Birdie is a jaguar too. She is… how does he put it? Big Jumbo Protector Between Worlds. Something like that. Something and Protector and something about worlds."

Odd messages from jaguars seemed only slightly nuttier than talking to my cat. "We could tell her," I suggested.

"Yeah," said Bob, yawning. "In the morning."

"In the morning," I agreed. I reached down and rubbed his fuzzy head. "You're a good boy."

"I know," he purred.

Excitement, exercise and copious cannabis throughout the day encouraged a deep and dreamless sleep. In the eternal cave-time I had no idea when it was morning, but the sound of people talking and moving about in the building woke me. Perzanto had one of his coffee makers set up in the reading room and I gratefully accepted a steaming cup and a large bagel with cream cheese. Aroma and caffeine started to wake up my brain and I thought about the decision that faced me. On one hand, I wanted to get back to the mountain and check on the plants. They were probably okay, but I did like to check most days. On the other hand, this journey to the center of the Earth could be completed in a day and there was adventure and music to be had. I figured that after breakfast I'd roll a joint and give it a think, but just as I was washing the last bite of bagel down with a gulp of coffee, Birdie Balam burst into the room.

"Cleve," she gasped. "Cleve is gone!"

At moments like this, some idiot always has to restate the obvious. If you say, "Cleve is gone," someone inevitably has to say, "Cleve is gone? What do you mean?" That idiot, this time, was me. Aw, hell, if I didn't say it, someone else would have.

She folded her arms across her breast and switched on an intense glare. "I mean he's gone. Gone, as in somewhere else. Not where he was. Missing!"

I risked another glare. "Where did he go?"

"If I knew that," Birdie growled, "why would I say he was missing?"

"Birdie," I said, "just calm down and tell us what happened."

She took a deep breath. "We both camped out on the first floor, in the small reading room down there, near the entrance. I went to lie down, but Cleve said he needed to unwind a little before he could sleep. He went for a walk and I fell asleep. When I woke up, he wasn't there. His pad and his stuff were exactly the way he left them. He never came back from his walk."

"Maybe he got lucky," snickered the devil.

Don swatted at the fluttering entity and the angel, roosting on his shoulder, stuck out its tongue.

Birdie ignored the chatter. "What do we do?"

We ran through the building, calling Cleve's name and peering into dark corners with flashlights. We went outside and snooped around the buildings. We stuck our heads into other buildings and shouted. We found Aqualung, who looked like he had a very, very bad headache but was otherwise more sober than we'd seen him. We didn't find Cleve. It quickly became apparent that, even with the fifty or so people and entities still in the cavern, it would take days to search everywhere. And Steel Cave, as we well knew, was part of a much greater network of caverns and tunnels. Not to mention the exit to the greater world on the surface. Cleve was never very impulsive, except when improvising music, but I hadn't spent time with him in many years. Maybe he changed. Maybe he made a sudden decision to join the lines of entities that were still straggling toward the exit.

We stood outside our building moping about the situation when Frank rolled up in a cart.

"Why didn't you come to me first?" the security guard asked when we explained about Cleve. "We have ways."

"Ways?" I asked.

"You know all those little tv screens in the buildings?" Frank asked. "Half of them feed into a bank of video recorders. Hell, that's the worst part of the job, changing tapes and labeling all that shit every morning. If they would upgrade to a computer system…"

"We'll be looking through a lot of, erm, tapes," Aqualung said, with only a minimum of mucus. "It'd take just as long."

"No," I said. "We start with the cameras near our building, around the time that we think Cleve went out. Frank, show us how it works."

Through the double doors that led to the exit, on the right, before you came to the big freight elevator, was another, regular size door. Elderly steel covered in geological layers of brown paint bore the word Security. Inside was a small concrete room with a few crappy desk chairs and considerable shelving full of video tape machines, all humming away. Bright blue and green LED displays counting lengths of VHS tape projected weird, flickering hues through the rest of the room.

Frank sorted through a box of tapes while Birdie, Trent and I stood fidgeting. After a few minutes he stacked half a dozen next to an aged, industrial-looking VCR. We started to watch.

We found Cleve on camera pretty quickly. We watched from two different camera angles, in grainy black and white, as he strolled from the building. Frank scrambled to find more tapes and we watched Cleve walk down a narrow side street toward the cavern wall. At the wall, he did something I didn't expect. He kneeled down on the asphalt, placed his hands together beneath his chin, and he began to pray. I could see his lips move but whatever he said, he didn't get to say much of it. Two large, dark-skinned warriors appeared from one side of the screen. They wore armor made of leather straps and hammered metal disks, helmets adorned with glittering stones, and they carried very large spears with wicked-sharp leaf-shaped blades.

Cleve looked up at them, surprised but calm. There was a short exchange that we couldn't hear and the warriors roughly grabbed Cleve by the arms and frog-marched him into a tunnel where they passed out of camera range.

We looked at each other and for a long moment, no one said a word.

Finally, Frank spoke up. "They work for her," he offered.

Perzanto, who had been inspecting the grungy concrete floor, looked up. "Her? You've seen her?"

"She's a witch," Frank said. "Or a queen."

"A queen bitch?" Birdie suggested.

"I saw her once," Frank said. "And her men a few times. She was big and wore armor like the warriors, only much nicer. Really long, flowing blonde hair. Rapunzel, only she'd kick your ass before you knew it. Nah, she had more of a Xena vibe than Rapunzel. Hot but kind of scary."

Perzanto grunted.

"Her men travel in twos or threes, from what I've seen in Steel Cave. She's got magic powers, but they're just assholes."

"Magic powers?" I asked.

"She turned me into a newt." Frank giggled. I think he may have had a wake and bake with one of my roaches. "No, seriously, I saw her turn one of her guys into a horse."

"A horse." Birdie harrumphed.

"Yeah," said Frank. "A big damn horse and she rode off on his back. I've got it on tape here."

So we all watched the tape of a huge blond witch queen turning her warrior into a horse. It was grainy and all the action took place low in one corner of the screen, but the warrior-into-horse thing was unmistakable.

"I hope she turned him back into a man when she finished riding," Esty commented mellifluously.

Birdie harrumphed again and shook her head.

"What do you think, Perzanto?" I asked. "Who is she?"

"She ruled the Pool of Shebangs and the inner cavern before I ever arrived here. I never saw her, though," Perzanto said, "during the years that I lived inside. She rarely emerged from her castle and even then would go by surrounded with people or in a carriage. But I was curious…"

"Yes?" Esty prompted.

"Because I was told that she is my size," Perzanto said after a moment. "And she is, now I see. And it bothers me that she…" He blinked and swallowed. "Never mind. She is cruel and arrogant. She holds her people in oppression. She is hard and without mercy. Those who were my friends, inside, were sworn to fight against her, but they were few and never a match for her legions of warriors."

"Is that why you left?" I asked. "Is that why you came out of the depths?"

Perzanto shook his big head. "No. I came out so that I could look for Gardangulan and Mortimer. What if they arrived and turned back at the first water, as you would have?"

"We have to get Cleve," Birdie said. We all agreed that she was right, but no one moved.

"Legions of warriors?" Don asked.

Perzanto nodded.

"Turns people into animals?" Trent asked.

Perzanto grunted. "That warrior wasn't a person. Not human, anyway."

"Okay," I said. "Maybe she can't turn us into toads, but she can turn her legions into whatever she wants."

Another nod from Perzanto.

"Can she turn them into anything that can't be stopped by a shotgun shell?"

He grunted and shrugged. "I do not know."

"How many shells do you have?" Trent inquired.

I pulled out my ammo and counted. There were four 70mm shells in the magazine and seven in my hands. "Eleven shells," I said.

"Eleven shells won't stop legions." Don shook his head.

"They don't know I only have eleven," I said. "Believe me, using the Mossberg is more of a show than a massacre. I just have to make it look scary."

"Scarier than them?" Birdie asked.

I snarled and brandished the gun. Birdie harrumphed.

"Does anyone have a better plan?" I packed the shells back into a pocket.

"We must cross her realm to reach the resonant chamber," Perzanto said. "We must go there anyway."

13. Snorx

Perzanto warned us that there would be no smoking in the tunnels, so I finished off a roach as we made ready to go. He also told us that we would have to be completely silent while sneaking up on our enemies. Once underway, though, it became obvious that our best attempt at silence consisted of a low rumble of shuffling feet, collisions and mumbling. Noisy enough, considering that we'd added thirty or forty radicals and soldiers to our ranks. Despite our best efforts, no one could make Aqualung stop his burbling snorts and undersea Foley. Nor could we dissuade him from following. Respiratory condition aside, though, Aqualung seemed to be sobering up steadily. He even offered to carry gear. Nobody wanted him touching anything important so he was entrusted with a loop of orange extension cord we figured we'd be unlikely to use in the caverns.

We shuffled and mumbled through a crack in the Steel Cave wall into a series of stalactite-adorned tunnels and chambers. Rivulets of mineral-rich water flowed through cracks and wrinkles along the tunnel floor and the sloshing of shoes added to our traveling symphony of sound. We wandered through a maze of limestone walls and columns for hours, finally emerging in a cavern so vast that our beams faded before they could find the far wall.

We couldn't see anything, but our beams could be seen. Somewhere off in the deep darkness a lantern answered ours, a tiny fleck of light, very far off.

"Hellooooo!" I called, my voice echoing from ceiling and tunnels. There was no response except some muttering from behind me. I looked at Perzanto and he nodded, so we set off toward the distant light, picking out a barely-seen trail through a field of knee-high stalagmites. We must have hiked well into the day by the time we could see that the fleck of light was a rather large lantern and holding the lantern was a rather large man in armor.

"That is Snorx," Perzanto hissed in my ear. "The guardian of the Deep Place."

I swung the shotgun into my arms. "This is Mossberg," I told him. "Guardian of my ass."

Perzanto nodded and we stepped into Snorx's circle of lantern light. Perzanto and I led the way, our troops behind us. Snorx was a big guy but only half as wide as Perzanto. Thick black eyebrows and dark eyes glared from beneath a metal helmet covered with glittering spikes. His armor was black with spikes of steel that gleamed like chrome. Perzanto physically took up more space, but Snorx seemed kin to the limestone walls and columns, solid and immovable.

"I am Snorx, the guardian of the Deep Place," he said, "wherein lies the Pool of Shebangs. Turn back now. No man or woman may enter here."

"Don't we have to answer three questions?" I asked.

The allusion was lost on Snorx. "No questions. No one enters."

"Except him." I gestured with a thumb toward Perzanto.

Snorx's eyes went wide for a moment, his voice was a low growl. "You."

"And I think there were three others like him," I added. "Beezel, Dondelakavin and Bernard."

Snorx looked at me and snarled. "*You* will not enter."

"Well, you never know, do you?" I hefted my gun.

Perzanto stepped between us. "I recall that you enjoyed music," he said to the guardian.

Snorx grunted, his eyes slits beneath brushy brows.

Perzanto gestured me back a few paces. With a snap, the mrrlnx appeared in one hand. I could see that the other huge hand held a bushel or so of acorns. He began to tap out a melody on the face of the mrrlnx, deep notes vibrating the stalactites. Snorx watched impassively. Perzanto found a bouncy groove and I got my guitar out of the case, to lend accompaniment, if I could. Perzanto took the simple little melody to a climax and gave a great, startling shout.

"Damn!" Captain Head Charge exclaimed, with nearly as much volume as Perzanto's noise. "That shit hurt my ears!"

Snorx bent his knees, twisted his torso so that he led with a shoulder and slowly raised his lead hand. He moved like Bruce Lee on acid.

Now we all had our instruments in hand and plugged in and we jammed along as loud as we could. The Tripper whacked the dumbek like a jackhammer. Don fired chaotic blasts from his horn. Birdie wailed and howled. Trenton's little synth sounded like a giant steam calliope and my guitar screamed. At the end of the phrase, Perzanto detonated his nuts in a great, booming star of yellowy light.

Undeterred, undistracted, before we could make any kind of offensive move, Snorx attacked. I twisted my shoulders and the guitar swung behind me, the shotgun coming around and dropping into my arms. I might be an old fart, but this was stagecraft I'd practiced a thousand times, switching guitars in mid-song. In one motion, I pumped a shell into the chamber, aimed at Snorx and pulled the trigger. The blast caught him as he leapt toward us. And it stopped him.

Just for a moment. As the concussion reverberated through the cave, he looked down at his armor. It was scratched and dented where it took the shot, but Snorx himself appeared undamaged.

He snarled and leapt again, aiming for me but, just as I thought my world was going to end, there was a great dull thump and Snorx was intercepted by Perzanto. For a long moment they were motionless, arms locked around each other, muscles straining and neither budging even a fraction of an inch. Then, suddenly, one of them tipped the balance – it was impossible to tell which – and they were grappling furiously among the stalagmites. They twisted and turned so quickly it was a blur in the dim light, but we could hear the grunts and the pounding blows that echoed around us. Their rage took them from wall to wall, from floor to vaulted ceiling and back again. Both were pummeled by mighty blows and kicks and both did their share of pummeling. They endured punishment that would have squashed a human flat. Snorx's armor was bashed to oblivion and he fought in a pair of tattered have-a-nice-day-smiley-face boxer shorts, apparently all he had worn beneath the leather and steel.

The cave itself vibrated as if dynamite had been detonated deep beneath us and I realized that some of the noise, the sounds of destruction that I had attributed to the fight, was coming from somewhere deeper in the cave. Even Perzanto and Snorx paused, ears cocked toward the tunnels.

In that moment of relative non-violence, the ground shaking beneath our feet, a strange, reedy voice spoke up. "What is it with everyone today? Everyone seems so edgy."

A man stood inside Snorx's line of defense, in a tunnel opening. He reminded me, at first glance, of people I'd met on our first tour through England in 1973. For a moment or two of rock'n'roll history, Carnaby Street hippy fashions collided full on with the glittery androgyny of glam rock. This guy in the cave looked like Ziggy Stardust after an unfortunate accident with a flock of ostriches. His sequined jumpsuit was adorned not only with gigantic plumes of feathers, but with the equally long necks and tiny heads of the birds. He held one of the severed bird heads in his hand and idly petted it. The beak opened and gave a mild squawk.

Perzanto and Snorx looked at each other, shrugged, and the battle continued, the two warriors crushing stones, boulders, stalactites and stalagmites in their mighty struggle.

The ostrich guy beckoned to me. "C'mon," he called over the noise of the battle and the mysterious background rumbles. "If you're coming across, do it quickly, while the guardian is distracted."

I took a step toward him and was instantly thrown back into the throng of radicals and soldiers by the impact of Perzanto's body, like a ton of big rocks, right in front of me. Perzanto rolled, returned to his feet and pushed off again after Snorx. I tried again, and this time Snorx himself smashed into the stone, blocking my path. The guardian snarled at me, was knocked flat by Perzanto, and they continued grappling. Fists and feet slammed bodies and stone. Columns of limestone were reduced to dust. The shrapnel alone made passage unlikely.

Our feathered friend shrugged and, from somewhere I couldn't see, pulled out a giant hat that looked like a wedding cake and flopped it onto his head. Candles on the cake illuminated a wide circle of cave floor around the man. He strolled a little closer to the invisible line over which we couldn't cross. He folded his arms over his chest and watched, smiling slightly, as the great battle continued.

Perzanto hauled Snorx over his head and dashed the guardian against a stone wall. Snorx rebounded and dived toward Perzanto, rolling and sweeping his leg in a circle, knocking the god's feet from underneath him. Perzanto fell like a truckload of concrete blocks, executed a perfect back roll and closed on the guardian again, trapping him firmly in a headlock. Snorx bent and threw Perzanto over his shoulder. Perzanto was momentarily airborne, tucking for a roll as he collided with a group of soldiers and they went down in a heap. Snorx, now back in his territory, watched smugly as Perzanto untangled himself and returned to his feet.

There was a deep rumble in the distance.

"Great Shtumpfen!" exclaimed the ostrich guy, clutching his abdomen. "I apologize. Never eat bean burritos for breakfast."

His accent was pronounced, but I couldn't place it. I almost believed him about the burritos, but there was a second rumble, quite distinct from any flatulence, and getting louder.

The man wedged his hand into an opening on the back of his skin tight, glittery jumpsuit and rummaged around in there for a while, deep and persistently enough to make many of us uncomfortable. Finally, with a sigh of satisfaction, he pulled a long, bluntly shaped object from the general area of his ass. There was a collective groan of disgust from our side of the border, but the object didn't seem to be a turd. It was nicely wrapped in silver paper with gold ribbons and we all watched as he carefully removed the wrappings.

It was, after all, a turd, long and moist and, apparently, steaming.

We all stared. There were moans and groans and various noises of digestive unease, but everyone kept watching, even Snorx and Perzanto.

"Dondelakavin," Perzanto called, "what in the name of the Master Inscriber are you doing?"

"I'm buying you some…" Dondelakavin started to say.

There was a great blast from the nearest tunnel entrance. It shook the floor, nearly knocking me off my feet. Bits of rock sprinkled down from the cave ceiling and a great cloud of dust rolled out from the tunnel. We all stepped back, except for Snorx, who took a step closer to the explosion.

"…time," the ostrich man concluded, brushing bits of gravel from his sequins.

As the cloud of debris expanded through the cave, three figures emerged. Two of them were unscathed and one, the blonde witch queen, was seriously scathed. Cleve supported her from one side and from the other an old man with a great white beard gripped her arm. Cleve and the old guy were a bit dusty, but otherwise appeared to be in good health. The queen, however, was slightly charred and a bit despondent. They set her down on the stone.

Snorx advanced on them. "My lady," he cried. "Are you all right?" He glared at the two men and snarled.

"Tell your guardian to stand down," Cleve told the queen. "And let these people into the Deep Place."

The queen mumbled something. Cleve shook her firmly.

Snorx jumped toward Cleve – and was stopped instantly by a thunderclap and an explosion of rock and dust at his feet. The old man with the beard chuckled and blew across the tip of his finger like it was a smoking gun.

"Tell him," said Cleve.

"Stand down and let these people do whatever the hell they want," the queen ordered half-heartedly. "The Scrambler has defeated me. For now." Snorx stepped back and sat on a rock. He looked exhausted.

We crossed the border to where Dondelakavin stood grinning. There was no sign of the turd or its wrappings. The cats sniffed him suspiciously. Don Speckler went over and shook his hand. I wasn't that reckless.

Perzanto pushed past us and walked right up to the queen. She looked up at him meekly. "You," she said.

Perzanto snarled at her. "I did not know you were the queen, Liana. If I had known…"

"Yes?" she prompted.

"If I had known, I would not have loved you these many centuries. You are not the person I thought you were." He spit at her feet and walked off.

Birdie embraced Cleve and gave him a peck on the cheek, while keeping a suspicious eye on the giant white woman in battered armor.

I clapped Cleve on the shoulder. "We were worried about you, man."

"Don't worry about me," Cleve told me. "I put my faith in God." He looked toward the old man who smiled humbly.

"Really?" I asked. The old guy fit the profile. Tall, long white beard, long white robe. Piercing eyes. Thunderbolts.

God stuck out his hand and I shook. He had a strong grip for an old man.

"I'm Ian," I said.

"I know."

"Jay's a fan," Cleve said. "Show him, Jay."

"Jay?" I asked.

"I never liked Jehovah," God explained. "It's a stodgy name. Old-fashioned. Please call me Jay." As he said this, he fumbled with the front of his robe and pulled it open.

Under his robe, Jehovah was wearing a t-shirt that said *Ian is God.*

14. The Power of Prayer

"I just wanted to stretch my legs," Cleve told us as we rested and regrouped, "maybe find a quiet spot for some thinking and praying. So these two assholes with spears grab me and drag me into the tunnels. I learned later that people down in the cave heard us rock the concert last night and Liana sent her goons to check it out.

"They dragged me pretty fast, like they had some big, important plans for my ass. I couldn't keep up, so after a while I went as limp as an old, damp dishtowel and made them carry me. And they did. They hauled my ass down narrow little tunnels and through big old caverns. We met the guardian, the guy in the colorful underwear over there, and he waved us past like it was business as usual. We went down long sloping tunnels, one after another, into the bowels of the Earth, until we came to a place with tall columns of light that rise up and kind of disappear into the distance, even though you know there's a ceiling up there somewhere. There were thousands of them, everywhere you looked. We went between them, following some path that the guards knew. There were other people there too, a whole lot of foot traffic going in and out and around the shafts of light. A regular bustling metropolis of light and crazy people.

"I saw a lot of guards. And they were some mean ones, too. Damn, it looked like L.A. out there, except the cops were beating everyone, black, white, yellow and green. I didn't get a whole lot of time to sightsee – we moved pretty quickly and the guards weren't stopping. But I saw a lot of serious shit.

"Pardon my French," Cleve said to Jay.

"Fuck that," the deity replied. "I never told anyone they couldn't say shit. I told 'em not to take my name in vain."

"Okay, then," Cleve continued. "I saw some *nasty* shit. A crowd of people being electrocuted. Beat downs with these wicked, spiky batons they use. Mostly they used rocks, though. Just mowing motherfuckers down with big boulders. These bastards were treating me like royalty, compared to the stuff I saw them doing. But I didn't know what kind of nasty shit they had planned for me. So I started to pray.

"I was in it pretty deep, so I made that prayer a masterpiece. It's tempting when you're in a tight spot to whip off a quick one but, you know, that's not how it works. You have to give your mind to the prayer, fully and completely. It's like rock'n'roll. You have to let it build up and build up and take you over, from head to toe. You have to fill it up with beauty and detail so that it touches you in your soul, before God will hear it. Isn't that right?"

"I do like it when people make the effort," Jay said.

"I said, 'Dear God,'" Cleve went on. "'Ruler of Heaven and Earth, you who made the birds fly and the fishes swim; thou art mighty. Oh merciful one who smiteth the wicked in their misdeeds. Oh righteous one who maketh the lamb to lie down and the falcon to swoop. Good Lord, who causes the sun to shine and who gives us our daily bread, our daily wine, our daily music, our daily television, please take a moment in Your busy schedule to hear this, my earnest prayer to You, who led the Israelites through the desert and fed them with manna…'"

Jehovah grinned broadly, buffing His fingernails on the front of his robe.

"Can we get to the point?" insisted Birdie. "Where did the goons take you?"

"Well, I kept praying the whole time," Cleve said. "And it's a good thing that I did."

Birdie harrumphed.

"Those a-holes dragged me for a long time and I was working on my prayer the whole way. Finally they hauled me to a shaft of light guarded by a squad of leather goons. They made way for us like we were on a mission from the President and we went right into the light. It was a really weird feeling, going into that glowing column. It was kind of like suddenly falling asleep and then waking up somewhere else. Sort of like the whole world, the cavern and the guards and all the other shafts of light dissolved into nothing and then when the world came back and I woke up, it was a different world. It's hard to describe, but it's the damnedest thing.

"Everything was suddenly different. The only thing that was the same is that the a-holes were still dragging me around. But now I was in a place with a blue sky and a wide green lawn like a golf course. There was a warm breeze blowing and a big flock of gray birds were squawking and making a racket. Across the lawn was a castle. It wasn't one of them fairytale castles. It was a real-looking kind of thing made from big blocks of red stone. It looked like it could have been the site of ancient battles or where the Frenchmen hid the Holy Grail.

"I was just coming to the juicy part of my prayer, where I finished calling upon the Most High and started to lay out what I needed. 'Oh, Lord,' I said, 'I know that I'm only a sinner down here on planet Earth with millions of other sinners all asking You for stuff. I have no right to petition You, who has given me everything, for anything more. I know that You work in the most mysterious of ways and I may not understand everything You have given to me. I am but a wart upon thy mighty foot, Oh Lord. No, I am a speck of dust upon the hair that grows from the wart on thy mighty…'"

"Oh, Lord, will you get on with it?" Don's angel fluttered past Cleve's head.

"Yeah, dude," said the devil, flying along right behind. "What the fuck?"

"Really, Cleve," said Birdie. "When did you get religion, anyway? No, wait, don't answer that. Tell us what you asked the Lord for."

"I'm getting to it," Cleve told us. "While I was praying, they dragged my ass into the castle. It was real nice in there, too, like a really nice hotel. Remember that place in Hong Kong where we stayed on tour a couple times? Like that, sort of. Lots of exposed beams, oriental carpets, and glass cases with old pottery in 'em. Big rooms with comfy sofas and fireplaces. I thought it would be the kind of place I'd like to retire to, if it wasn't owned by whoever took me prisoner. But I kept praying and they kept hauling me down these big, wide hotel corridors. Finally we came to the biggest room yet, an acre of stone floor with a fat strip of purple carpet down the center and great fires roaring in fireplaces all up and down the place. There were a lot of well-dressed people standing around, talking, waving handfuls of paper at each other, and giving each other orders. The a-holes dragged me clear across that big room and threw me at the feet of their queen. The lovely Liana here."

Liana, tied to a column of stone with a length of slimy orange extension cord, glared and growled.

"At first glance, before I realized who or what I was dealing with, I fell in love," Cleve continued. "I mean, I never had a special thing for blond chicks, you know, but she was a woman and a half. Still, I kept praying. I was thinking that maybe she would be my salvation, the tool that God used to work his will in the world."

"The tool?" Oswaldo asked. "I'm not sure I understand."

"That's how it usually works, you know," Cleve explained. "God usually doesn't show up in person. He uses events and people and the stuff around you in the world to carry out His intentions. So I hoped that this beautiful giant angel of a woman would take kindly to me and let me go."

"Did she?" I asked.

Cleve laughed. "Oh, no. She had me thrown to the ground! You've been thrown to the ground, I'm sure." He looked around at us. I nodded. The radicals and soldiers eyed each other and agreed that, yes, they'd sure as hell been thrown to the ground. Mark Ratner burst out laughing. Only Jehovah Himself had never been thrown to the ground. "Then you know how much that shit hurts!" Cleve went on. "She poked me with her foot and prodded me with her staff. That hurt, too. I kept praying. 'Dear Lord,' I said, 'I am a captive in a foreign land. I have been carried away from friends, imprisoned, poked and prodded. I beseech you, Oh Lord, bring some understanding to these, mine enemies, so that I may love them and turn my cheek. Let peace and compassion be unto them, that they may release me and we may co-exist as brethren and sistren in this strange land.'

"'What is your mission in the cavern?' Liana demanded. I said that we just wanted to play some music, you know, and maybe get high every now and then. She struck me with her staff." Cleve pulled up his jacket and shirt to show us a fat purple bruise on his side. "Hard," he said.

"She stared at me for a long time and she kept drawing shapes in the air. It reminded me of how Perzanto stares at things before they turn into appliances and shit.

"'You are not like us,' she told me. 'What are you? If I kill you now, will you stay dead?'

"I assured her that once dead, I'd stay that way until God called me forth to everlasting life in Heaven. She kept asking me things and hitting me with the staff. But I did not despair. I called upon the Lord of Mercy, the Lamb of Kindness, the God of Love. And He appeared."

"Jehovah," I said.

"No," Cleve told me, as if it were obvious. "Jesus."

"Jesus!" Birdie snorted.

"That's right," Cleve said. "Jesus appeared. He wasn't as tall as I thought he'd be and he was a little scruffy, you know, with the beard and sandals."

"Jesus was a black man, right?" interjected Captain Head Charge.

"Hell no," said Cleve. "He was, like, Arabic-looking or something. Swarthy Semitic type of guy with a big nose. He had the most gentle smile and kind dark eyes.

"'Please,' Jesus said to Liana and the a-holes, 'love one another.' He smiled and held out His hands. That smile was so beautiful. It was the very symbol of compassion for all living things. If I were an old Renaissance painter, man, I would have painted The Boy right at that moment. Shit. Didn't last long, though, because Liana's guards kicked the living crap out of Him. He turned the other cheek and they kicked that side, too. Damn! They worked Him over like they were pimps who didn't get paid.

"I was getting pissed off now and I was thinking they really shouldn't have done that to Jesus, so I started to pray again. 'Oh Lord,' I said, 'they have trampled upon Your Son. They have poked me and prodded me. I beseech You, Lord: Smite My Enemies!'"

"At least that was to the point," Birdie commented.

"Jehovah?" I asked.

"That's right," Cleve went on. "That's when Jay showed up in a burst of glorious flame and smoke. It was spectacular. When the smoke cleared and we stopped coughing, there He was, looking like, well, looking like God.

"'Father,' Jesus moaned from where they'd left him on the floor, 'forgive them. They know not…'

"'Screw that,' Jehovah said and he started blasting away with thunderbolts. He blasted the guards, He blasted Liana, He blasted the stones of the castle itself. That's when I ran. I ran my ass off until I got back outside. I turned and saw the castle crumbling in on itself in places and exploding out in other places. The noise was deafening and the ground shook. Stones and bricks and sofas flew through the air. Guards and civilians fled from every exit. A big cloud of stone dust rose into the air as the ground shook from the thunder. From out of that cloud came Liana, running with everything she had, laying down a contrail of dust like a 747 through the stratosphere. She tore a trench in the turf sliding to a stop, then turned to face, you know, God, as he literally flew after her. Liana hurled something toward Jay, like a major leaguer looking for strike number three. Whatever it was burst in the air like a grenade, with big-ass orange flames and it was loud, too. Hurt my ears. But God just kept coming.

"Liana turned and made a gesture with both hands. In front of her, a slit of light opened up and she dived into it and was gone. I watched as the light, like a crack in the surface of reality, kept widening for a few seconds, then started to close up again. Before it was gone, Jehovah, like a meteor in a nimbus of smoke and flame, followed her in. What else could I do? I took a chance and ran for it, right into that brilliant crack in creation.

"And suddenly I was back at the Pool of Shebangs, between towering columns of light. I had to put on the brakes pretty fast and stop myself from running right into another one of those things. Liana and Jay were still moving, though, dodging around columns and people, heading for the tunnels on the outer edge. I tried my best to keep up. I'm not a runner, you know." Cleve patted his pudge and there were a few chuckles.

"Where the stone floor sloped up away from the Pool, Liana let out this horrific yell. Remember that chest-thumping noise that Tarzan used to make in the old movies? Like that, only with feedback, like she was too close to her own monitor. Just awful. It was a signal and her leather goons came running from every direction. They tried to get between her and Jay, but God kept striking them down with blast after blast. Liana kept backing toward the tunnels, shouting orders to her troops. As more and more of them appeared, they formed ranks and stood their ground before the Almighty, which I thought was brave and very, very foolish.

"I saw one of the goons hand something to Liana, a handful of something that ticked and clattered into her palm. She tossed the things into the air and whatever it was snapped and popped like fireworks on Chinese New Year. A big pile of something or other fell to the stone floor with a loud clatter and the leather warriors started grabbing things off the pile. Weapons. Big, mean-looking guns, like a cross between one of them old blunderbusses and a Star Trek phaser. The goons squatted on the ground and started firing at Jehovah. The guns made a big blast, a long orange flame, and hurled shot or gravel or some kind of crap, along with a whole lot of smoke. A lot of recoil, too; they were knocking themselves over with those things, which would have been pretty funny if I wasn't praying to stay alive.

"So it's just getting louder and louder in there and that huge cavern is filling up with smoke. People who didn't know what was going on were diving for cover and I ran behind a big boulder. The goons were blasting and falling over. In the chaos, Liana made a break for the tunnel. Lot of good it did her. Jay was right on her ass. He waved His hand and scattered her warriors like they were toy soldiers in a high wind. He followed her into the tunnel and I ran after. They were a lot faster than me and got pretty far ahead, but I could follow them easily enough from the blasts and screams."

"Screams?" Don asked.

"Oh, they were all hers," Cleve replied. "Jay was blasting and Liana was screaming. Then there was one big blast and she was quiet. I came around a turn in the tunnel and found them there. She was already His prisoner, kneeling on the cavern floor with her hands behind her head and a look on her face like she was four years old and someone stole her candy. The dust and smoke from all the blasting made me choke, so I kept going and Jay and his prisoner were right behind, trying to get out of the tunnel. I prayed then that I would be reunited with my friends. And then we found you. The power of prayer."

"Oh, please," said Birdie.

"It's true," Jehovah explained. "I always listen. Though I usually don't give a crap. Humans mostly pray for the stupidest things. 'My old auntie is ill. Please, God, make her better.' Who do I look like? Asclepius? Aunt Eunice is 98 years old and cranky most of the time! Let her go, dumbass. If it's not health, it's money. Am I an A.T.M.? C'mon. I don't care how much you want that overpriced big screen TV. Even if that model wasn't a piece of crap, like you really need to sit and watch Seinfeld reruns until the end of time? And if it's not money, it's sex. And with such desperation! As if the human race would die out if George Dewayne from Lubbock, Texas didn't get his rocks off. As if you people had nothing better to do with your time! Stupid, petty, selfish, boring prayers. And not really my area of expertise, if you know what I mean. Back in the day people prayed for a good smiting! That's where I kick ass, you know. Smiting, floods, laying to waste, pillars of salt…"

Liana moaned.

"She believes," Cleve said.

"I'm starting to believe," said Oswaldo. "Wow! You're God!"

Jehovah bowed.

"I'm still an agnostic," I said. "Fucked if I know."

"Now that's just being stubborn, man," Cleve told me. "How can you not believe, in the face of God Himself?"

"Aw, Cleve." I said. "He's an entity, just like Aqualung. I still haven't decided if these things are real or not. He's everything we would expect from Jehovah, so maybe it's the same as him being God, after all. Fucked, as I said before, if I know."

"But I believed in him, as he appears before us now, long before any of this entity bullshit," Cleve said.

I shook my head. I was still way out of my depth with these etiquette situations.

"Cleve, Old Buddy." God grinned broadly. He extended a long forefinger toward Liana. Miniature lightning played around his hand. "Shall I smite the shit out of her? Finish her off? Do a little Sodom and Gomorrah on her ass?"

Cleve slowly shook his head. "No, Jay. I think I'd like to show her a little mercy." He began to untie her.

Jehovah harrumphed loudly and lowered his finger.

15. Forever, Until Now

Jehovah did admit to a talent other than smiting. He could make food. If you can call that manna stuff food. Jay wasn't exactly Wolfgang Puck, if you know what I mean. Hell, he wasn't even Ronald McDonald. I'm an omnivore, but I don't mind tofu if it's cooked right. Manna is sort of like sticky tofu that's been in the fridge too long, only not as tasty. I remember reading a theory, a long time ago, that the biblical manna was some kind of goopy insect poop and I can believe it. Terence McKenna argued that it was magic mushroom mycelia. Bug crap or fungus, I wasn't having any. Jay tried to convince us that it was sweet and heavenly, but I took three bites and went to find a bag of Doritos from Frank's supermarket run.

I sat on a smooth rock and shared the chips with Esty, who also couldn't stomach God's gift to the culinary arts.

"His son's a better chef, I hear," Esty commented. "We could have had tuna sandwiches, at least."

We crunched and watched as Cleve handed Liana a large blob of manna. She raised it cautiously to her face and gave it a skeptical sniff. She made a face as if she'd just unwrapped Dondelakavin's package, but to our surprise she didn't hurl it at Cleve or God. She stared at the goop for a long moment and then, with a sticky pop, the manna turned into what appeared to be a very large slice of chocolate cake. Liana shoveled the pastry into her mouth.

"Hey!" I said. "How did you do that?"

"Is that chocolate?" Esty asked. "Can I have some?"

Liana looked up at us. "You do not know how?" she inquired, as if she naturally assumed that we knew.

"The inscription thing? Heh, not likely," I explained.

Liana snorted and returned her attention to the cake.

"Do you think we could even have the ability?" Esty asked.

The witch queen gave us a long look. "You are both more than human, yes?"

"I'm just human," I said. "One hundred percent proud homo sap."

"I'm mostly human," Esty offered.

"I cannot tell you how I did it," Liana grumbled, shooting a glance at Jehovah. "I am a prisoner."

"Prisoner of love," Esty grinned.

"What do you mean?" Liana snapped.

Esty shook her head. "You don't see the way Cleve looks at you?"

"Hey!" protested Cleve. "I look at her the way she deserves to be looked at."

Liana grunted. "It would not work," she said sadly.

"How do you know until you try?" Cleve attempted.

"I am older than your entire civilization. You are an infant."

"Yeah, but you've held up really well," I interjected. "And Cleve is very mature for his years." She snarled at me.

"We're not even the same kind of being," she added.

"Do you think the relatives won't approve?" I asked and, growling, she started for me but Jehovah wiggled his finger and she reluctantly settled down. I was glad; the Mossberg was already in my hands, but after my experience with Snorx, I wasn't sure it would stop her.

"Also," she grumbled, "I learned many aeons ago never to date musicians."

"I thought you had a thing for Perzanto," Esty said. "He plays mrrlnx."

"Not professionally," Liana said, "and besides, that was aeons ago."

"How long have you been down here?" Cleve asked.

"God knows," Liana sighed.

"No," Jehovah interjected. "I don't, actually. Maybe I could know if I wanted, but I really don't give a shit about all the little details of everyone's life. I mean, can't you people keep track of your birthdays without me? Damnation, woman or whatever you be, you've probably been down here forever and that's too many birthdays for me to even think about keeping track. Next you'll want me to know how regular your bowel movements are. Feh."

"I've been down here so long it might as well be forever," Liana elaborated. "Different shebangs have different cycles of time. And the cave has no time at all. The mountains have shifted and I think that continents have moved around us, but the Pool of Shebangs and the resonant chamber remain always the same. This is the Heart of Time. There is only the rhythm of the eternal, which is no rhythm at all. You want me to tell you how long I've been here, in the time units you are familiar with, but I do not know that time. I do know that you would have lived and died a million times while I reigned in the Deep Place. While it lasted, it was eternal."

Esty chuckled, a sound like tiny icicles raining on a crystal bell. "Your story must have a beginning, at least. Perzanto told us you were outside the resonant chamber when…"

"When that damn fool…" For some reason at this point, Liana gave me a sharp glance. I looked up at Jehovah, to make sure he was still on the job. "…fucked everything up and sent me spinning into eternity, into the aeons in which I ruled the Deep Place forever. Until now."

"Ruling forever," Cleve commented. "That doesn't sound too bad."

"It gets old after an aeon or two." She shook her head. "I was in the stairwell outside the resonant chamber and I could hear people approaching, coming down the stairs, very close to me. And through the doorway I could see the Time Scrambler and Perzanto in the resonant chamber. The Scrambler raised his staff toward the ceiling. There was a deafening noise, like the mountain was being torn in half, and a big part of the world slid away into nowhere – and then it was all back again and he was gone. They were all gone. I wandered into the resonant chamber, calling for Perzanto, for anybody. I was alone. It was very still in there, just the silence and the yellow glow.

"I climbed back up the stairs to the Pool of Shebangs. The Pool was empty, save for the columns of light."

Liana was interrupted by Perzanto's voice booming over the commotion. "It's time! Gather your belongings and let's go!"

Some of the soldiers took up the cry. "Move 'em out!"

I brushed Doritos crumbs from my clothes, checked my guitar and gun straps and got to my feet. Esty sort of flowed upright, a wonderful sight to behold. Liana ignored the orders. Jehovah cleared his throat and nonchalantly examined his index finger. With a pained expression, Liana stood, Cleve hovering nearby in case she needed help. In a few minutes our procession hiked into a long, downward-slanting tunnel.

We'd used our flashlights through many hours of hiking and exploration over the last couple days and some of the ones we'd looted from the Steel Cave security office had begun to burn out. The LED lights I contributed were still holding strong, but I mostly kept mine switched off. I did the best I could with the light that others held against the darkness. That was not limited to electric devices; Esty had a bit of natural radiance and mostly eschewed the electric light. Perzanto had some kind of illumination without a source, which would float or fly at his command. Jehovah had a flaming nimbus, adjustable for changing conditions. For the moment it was a gentle, flickering glow.

All of which was a good thing because we were way the hell underground. Every now and then, when I wandered into a patch of greater darkness, I would get a momentary sense of how deep we were, and how large the mountain of rock above us was. I think I was not alone in these feelings. As the tunnel sloped inexorably down into the Earth, conversation became sparse and we hiked in silence.

Well, not quite silence. We'd tried the silence thing before without much luck, but for the moment our cacophony was at low ebb. Even Aqualung stopped sniffling. The rhythm of our steps became the only way to mark out time and since we all walked at a slightly different pace, it was as if each of us were in our own little bubble of time, as if time were flowing in different streams all around me. It was an odd feeling, though not entirely unexpected given that my personal bubble of time included a lit doobie.

The tunnel continued on, deeper and deeper into the Earth, in immeasurable cave time. Eventually it opened into a cavern, small compared to Steel Cave but still roomy enough for our contingent to gather. We had another meal and by now I was hungry enough to choke down a few more bites of manna, though that was my limit. Scavenging through Frank's grocery bag yielded granola bars, miniature bags of M&Ms, and more Doritos. Frank must have been high when he went shopping; it was all snack food.

I scooped up another blob of manna from the flat rock where it materialized and showed it to Liana. "Can you turn this into a cheeseburger? Please?"

She bared her teeth and growled. "Why should I help you? Why would I aid the forces that have plagued me for so long?"

"Lady," I said, "I just met you and I haven't plagued you much at all, tempting as it might be."

"Lies," she said.

Jehovah prodded her with a sacred sandal. "Do it," he commanded. "Render unto Ian a cheeseburger." He turned to me. "Do you want anything on that?" He asked.

"Lettuce, tomato, pickles and Russian dressing," I said. "And a side of fries."

"Do it," Jehovah commanded.

"I don't even know what this 'cheeseburger' is," Liana said through clenched teeth.

"Oh, bullshit," Jehovah barked. "Surely the shebangs hold cheeseburgers as well as everything else." He flexed a lightning-charged finger and his nimbus flared.

"Oh," Liana grumbled. "A *cheeseburger.*" She took the sticky blob of bug shit from my hand, held it before her eyes and gazed intently.

Now this time I paid careful attention as the witch queen focused her thoughts on the manna. I couldn't really know what she was doing, but I did notice that her breathing slowed and became deeper. There was a sense of expectancy in the air and I could somehow feel a shape forming in the manna. And then she was holding an off-white china plate containing a cheeseburger deluxe. She even threw in a tiny paper cup of cole slaw and a sprig of parsley. She snarled and held out the plate.

"I should have ordered a Happy Waitress," I said, taking the burger and fries. I hefted the sandwich to my mouth and took a bite. It was juicy and delicious. "Thank you," I said, finding a place to sit and eat. "It's perfect."

Now everyone had the idea and every rocker, soldier, radical and semi-human entity among us wanted their manna converted to real food. Some of the pleading and begging was downright disgusting and, enjoying my cheeseburger, I was feeling a wee bit less sympathetic than I might have just a few minutes before. Liana, at first, seemed highly annoyed, but in a few moments she stopped snarling and started taking orders. She handed a plate of sliced, roast turkey with gravy and all the trimmings to a soldier. Manna morphed into filet mignon with garlic potatoes and she passed the plate to Captain Head Charge. She stood to reach the blob of stuff being handed to her by a clown fellow whose big shoes were making it hard for him to get through the crowd. The blob transformed into something that went *boing* when the clown poked it with a fork. He seemed happy with that. Liana accepted some manna from a short, Black Panther-looking woman with a big 'fro. After converting bug poop to an egg salad sandwich, she carried the plate to her customer as if she were about to point out something very important next to the garnish. When the woman leaned in close to look, Liana suddenly turned, grabbed her and locked a powerful elbow around her throat.

The area around the witch queen and her hostage cleared out fast. People and entities stumbled over each other trying to get back. I did the best I could to remain where I sat. Damn it, I was still eating! My plate got a good jostling, but in a moment it was just Liana, her hostage and me in a bare circle of dimly-lit cavern floor. I started on my fries.

"Stop right there!" Jehovah ordered, his nimbus flaming.

"Yeah, right," Liana said, backing up with her hostage in the direction of a tunnel entrance.

God pointed his staticky finger toward the queen.

"You'll have to blast through her," Liana said. "And she's one of yours."

"She's not one of mine," Jehovah said, taking a step closer. "I think she's a Buddhist."

The hostage nodded. "Yes, that's right," she said, then gulped, her eyes widening.

God's nimbus flared, momentarily bringing daylight to the cavern. "Ian," the Big Guy said, "I think you might want to move back a bit."

I swallowed. "Oh, don't blast her yet. She hasn't run. I think she has something to say to us. Liana?"

"What?" She tightened her grip on the hostage, whose eyes were beginning to bulge. "I… I do have something to say."

I'm not a hostage negotiator, but all those years out on the road, you get into some situations, you see some shit, you learn how to give people what they want, even if they don't know they want it. I was a little rusty, but in my prime I convinced Keith Moon not to blow up a tour bus (there were people on it, otherwise who cares?) by promising him he could flush an M80 down the toilet at the hotel. The Waldorf Astoria banned him for life after that, but the record company paid the damages and no one was hurt. I remember one night in Paris when a psycho groupie chick kidnapped Jason and used gaffer's tape to tie him, naked, to the bumper of her car. Oh, wait, that's not a good example. I tried to talk her out of it, but it turned out that Jason, who was kind of wasted, had paid her to do it.

Anyway, I could see in Liana's eyes that she just really wanted to tell us off. I figured, why not? Get her talking and there might be an opening.

"Where is he?" Liana demanded. "Where is the Scrambler? I want him to hear this."

We looked at each other. Scrambler?

She glared at me. She was damn good at glaring. "Is it you? I did not see him well and it was long ago, but you could be him."

"I'm Ian," I said. "Only thing I've ever scrambled is eggs."

She hissed. Okay, it wasn't the snappiest comeback. Fuck you, too.

She turned on Jehovah. "Is it you? Are you the one who has tormented me all these centuries?"

Jay held up his hands. "Not me, lady, though I'm hoping to make up for lost time."

"The Scrambler is a legend," said Perzanto, stepping out from the shadows. "For the shebangs, the Scrambler is like the Satan of the manifest world. He is the adversary, always tearing down what people build up, killing, destroying, lying, and cooking with improper meat products."

"And legends *have* been coming to life recently," I noted.

"You," Liana accused Perzanto. "You saw the Scrambler. You let him send me back to the beginning of time. You alone know what he looks like. Is he someone here?"

"I saw only the Master Inscriber that day," Perzanto explained. "I don't know your Scrambler."

"A lie," Liana said. "Can't you understand? That was the Time Scrambler disguised as your master."

"Improper meat products?" asked Dondelakavin.

"That was the Master Inscriber." Perzanto looked down. "But it was my fault. It was because of me that he scrambled time."

Liana hissed, a mixture of skepticism and loathing. "If it was because of you, then why did he pursue me through the aeons? Why did he plague my existence for so many centuries?"

"I've been here for 20,000 years," Perzanto said. "Where... er, when did the Master Inscriber send you?"

She cursed. "I was here before anyone else. Before humans walked the Earth, before life itself resonated from the shebangs. There were no caverns, only the Pool and the resonant chamber, embedded deep in warm rock. A single narrow tunnel, many miles long, ran up to the surface. Where the light of the shebangs faded, the stone glowed and illuminated the corridor with dim red light. But there was nothing up there. Rocks and water and a bad smell in the air. No trees, no animals, no insects, no life anywhere, so I returned to the Pool. I went into the greater shebangs, the columns of light, and they were empty worlds too. After a while I grew hungry, very hungry, but there was no food. Although I am not like you, the hunger weakened and sickened me. I knew I would die if I did not eat and I thought perhaps that was a good thing. I would come back from death only when there were others who thought of me, and that would not be until my own proper era.

"But I didn't die. The hunger continued for a very, very long time and I lay there, weak and suffering. I came to believe that if I didn't find some food, I would stay in that state – just alive enough to know how miserable I was – forever. I remembered the things that I saw Perzanto do and what he taught me and I wondered if I could somehow produce food that way.

"But what could I inscribe? The only things I could find anywhere were rocks. I tried the inscription that Perzanto taught me on some small pebbles, but nothing happened. I thought that maybe I wasn't doing it right, so I tried again and again. Nothing happened. I searched through the Pool and on the surface for anything else that I might use. Weak though I was, I hiked for many days away from the tunnel entrance, each step an enormous effort, telling myself that each one would be the last. The landscape was the same, endlessly, the same kinds of rocks, the same bad-smelling pools of water, the same acrid mist on an ever-present wind. I stopped trying to inscribe the rocks and kept shuffling forward, hopefully to my end.

"The end never came. Eventually, I found a place where the rocks looked different. A small crop of crystals clung to the inside of a depression in the stone. They were clear, shiny points, unlike anything else I'd seen so far. I feebly aimed an inscription at one and, much to my surprise and relief, it burst into yellowy light. It wasn't very bright and it only lasted a moment, but it worked! I sank to my knees, right there on the damp and steaming rock. I tried again on another tiny crystal, this time using as much concentration as my weakened state allowed. The crystal transformed into a bright glow that dazzled my eyes for a full second."

Liana's voice drifted off, mesmerized by the brightness of her own memory. She seemed to be relaxing, just a little, her grip on the hostage loosening slightly.

"So you were able to make food?" Perzanto asked. "I only taught you the first inscription."

"At first I could only make light," Liana explained. "I experimented in every way I could imagine. I changed the way I thought about the light. I changed the shape of the sigil in a thousand different ways. I tried everything. For a long, frustrating, hungry time nothing at all happened. It seemed fruitless, but then, little by little, I started to gain control over the inscription. I learned to tap into a flow of information that is all around us and was all around me even at the very dawn of time.

"I cannot say how long this all took, but it was a very long time. The sun rose and set over the barren world countless times. Crawling across the naked stone, I sought out more deposits of crystals and other stones that might work. I grew weaker and weaker. My body consumed itself and my skin shrank around my bones, but I was encouraged by my small successes. And finally, after perhaps tens of thousands of attempts, I created a tiny blob of gruel. I scooped it up in my bare hand, gulped it down and scrambled across the ground looking for more crystals to transform. I made gruel blobs until I was sated and rinsed my hands clean in a puddle of foul-smelling water. I rested for a long time and then began to collect crystals. I removed my armor and used it as a carrying case, hauling as many of the tiny things as I could. When I had all that I could carry, I began the journey back to the Pool."

Liana's grip loosened entirely and her hostage was as good as free, but the woman stayed right there, fascinated by the witch queen's tale. Perzanto, Jehovah, Cleve and Trent crept closer and now stood just behind me.

"Over many years, I learned the basics of inscription and began to extend and refine my technique. I returned to the surface several more times to collect crystals for my experimentations. One day, I followed my original route into the wasteland, intending to prospect further in that direction. After days of walking I came to the place where I first was able to create food. But that place had changed. The water, which had been murky and foul-smelling, now had a disgusting scum on the surface, through which fetid bubbles slowly rose and burst. And some of the scum had spread onto the rock. I had an odd feeling, an urge to aim an inscription at the puddle, which I did. To my surprise it boiled and popped as tiny bits of something burst into light. Whatever was now in the water could be inscribed. Unfortunately, it was not enough to really amount to anything, and it was the only scummy puddle I could see."

"Life," said Perzanto. "There was something living in that puddle."

"Yes," Liana agreed. "I learned that only such things that can represent or be represented as a shebang can be successfully inscribed. A crystal, a leaf, a spore, a seed, an insect, an entity…"

"And sometimes the creations of men," Perzanto added.

"Or men themselves," she said, giving him a direct gaze.

He grunted and looked away.

"That was my final trip to the surface," Liana went on. "Soon after I returned to the Pool, there was a mighty earthquake. The mountains shifted and heaved for nearly a day. Rocks and stone shook loose and fell in the tunnel, rumbling and rolling into the Pool. But that stopped as the tunnel became plugged. When the Earth was again quiet, I saw that there was little damage to the Pool itself, and none at all to the resonant chamber. The mountains rose and living rock rearranged itself around the inner, secret cavern, flowing around the Pool like water around a stone. The Pool was unharmed, but I was sealed inside, with only my latest haul of crystals to last for the rest of my life.

"I was despondent. I could not believe that I was the victim of two world-changing calamities. I was still angry at the Scrambler for the first cataclysm and I knew, I just knew, that my current imprisonment was also his doing."

"The Master Inscriber would not create such an earthquake," Perzanto said. "What would be the reason?"

"Then maybe," Liana suggested reluctantly, "the Scrambler is not your Master Inscriber. But I am not sure. And that was only the beginning. The Scrambler pursued me through the aeons, my every step dogged with disaster."

"How did you live?" Esty asked. "I mean, for so long, with only a limited number of crystals?"

"Something happened," Liana explained, "in the shebangs. Just as the pool of water on the surface yielded traces of life and things that could be transformed, the Pool of Shebangs started to bubble with forms. Like whatever was in the water, at first it was barely perceptible, specks of things that would flicker with light if I inscribed them. But soon, if I stepped into any of the columns of light, I found lichens and tiny plants, then eventually forests and animals and people. And I learned that I could transform almost anything in the shebangs from one thing to another, that every little speck of whatever in the Pool reflected every other little speck, so that every pebble, mushroom, oak tree or mountain was, in its own unique way, a representation of the whole shebang."

"Heh heh," snickered Don's devil. "The whole shebang."

Don swatted the devil and it went fluttering off into the darkness.

"The Pool of Shebangs is rich and deep," Liana said. "My life could have been an eternity of wonder and joy, but instead, every time I got comfortable, every time things seemed peaceful and prosperous, there was disaster at the hands of the Scrambler. When my people lived in the cavern, earthquakes and molten lava wiped them out. When we lived in the columns of light, death and destruction came in many more ways. There was famine, flood, war and blight. The Scrambler sent spies, assassins and agitators against me. I raised an army to defend our homes. I built an intelligence network through all the shebangs, agents and cells in countless worlds, reporting back to me on everything that we could detect about the Scrambler. I transformed an entity into Snorx and set him as guardian, to prevent the Scrambler and his minions from entering the Pool through the caverns. I raised an army of transformed entities to fight the incursions and terrorism of the Scrambler and all those who might oppose the peace and prosperity which I tried to bring.

"Over the millennia, some of the people, the entities, in the shebangs allied themselves with the Scrambler, for whatever misguided reasons they had. I was always trying to help them, to protect them and motivate them. But the Scrambler recruited them into his army and they rebelled against me countless times. My life became a living hell. I must be constantly on my guard, always alert for those who would secretly move against me. It wasn't so bad at first, but after many thousands of years it began to wear on me, to obsess me and cause endless misery.

"You must understand that it is difficult to fight against an enemy you cannot see, who uses soldiers and spies who cannot be killed. The best we can do is to disrupt them for a bit, destroy the physical bodies of his minions and force them to re-corporate somewhere else."

"Re-corporate?" I asked.

"Oh, yes," Liana said. "I understand that you humans do not come back when you die. But we who are composed of the reflections of shebangs, we do not die. I know this. I have hanged agents of the Scrambler, and they were back the next week, working the same mischief."

"Maybe they weren't, uh, properly hanged?" someone asked. I turned to see a sober Aqualung standing not too far away.

"It's not how they are killed," Liana explained. "I have hung them, dismembered them, buried them alive, broken them on wheels, nailed them to crosses, electrocuted them, poisoned them, shot them with arrows, pierced them with spears, filled them with bullets, struck them with stones, crushed them beneath boulders and tore out their hearts with my bare hands. Sooner or later, every one of them came back to strike at our society again and again. It's not how they are killed; it is the nature of their existence. Our existence." She thumped her breastplate. "We are information encoded in the structure of the world itself. You are encoded in your own structure. Kill you and the information dies with the cells of your body. Kill us and the information goes on and we are still here."

"Would it not be easier," Perzanto suggested, "to transform them rather than kill them? If you turned one into a snail, I would think it would stay a snail."

"For a time I did that," Liana explained. "Though I care not for snails. Furniture, that's what I like."

"You turned your enemies into tables and chairs?" I asked.

"Sofas," she said. "And ottomans. Deep armchairs. Furniture with nice upholstery."

"I saw those sofas!" Cleve exclaimed. "They were very nice. I thought they had character."

"Thank you," Liana said and, just for a moment, she actually smiled a little bit. "Though you can have only so many sofas. All right," she said. "I no longer believe you are of the Scrambler's legions." She turned to her former hostage. "I'm sorry," she said. "You may go free."

I reflected that she was now convinced of our innocence, even if we did little explaining. She did most of the talking and somehow changed her own mind. Now, having heard her tale, I no longer thought of her as the Hitler of the underworld. Make no mistake, I could see that the aeons had driven her way around the bend of the deepest and twistiest tunnel. And I don't care how quickly her victims might come back to life, getting crushed by a boulder is still going to hurt like nothing else. I bumped her down a notch from mass murderer to mass torturer.

As the hostage straightened her clothes and went to rejoin her file-entity friends, the stand-off ended. Cleve, with a look of puppy-dog love on his face, went to Liana's side. Birdie harrumphed.

I stood and put my empty plate on the stone. "Is everyone all right?" I called to the assembled company. Everyone seemed to be okay.

"We must continue on, to the Pool," Perzanto said. "We can get there before night and make camp."

"Night?" Mark Ratner asked. "How the hell do you even know it's day?"

"No camp necessary," said Dondelakavin, appearing suddenly by Perzanto's side. "You can all stay at my place!"

Perzanto sighed. "That's a fine offer, Dondelakavin, but we couldn't possibly…"

"Oh, sure we could!" enthused Birdie. "Damn, what I wouldn't give to sleep in a real bed for a night. You got beds there?"

"Beds? Of course!" Dondelakavin exclaimed. "Beds for everyone!" There was a thin cheer.

"Oh, hell," said Perzanto and we began the march down to the Pool.

16. Avatar of the Jaguar Spirit

The tunnel was wide, the floor worn smooth and flat. It curved gently, back and forth, as it sloped down to the Pool. Birdie and Tim came and walked beside me.

"Damn," Birdie griped, "do my feet hurt!"

As the most obese of our aged band, I had really expected Birdie to give up a long time ago. I was impressed that she was still hauling her considerable bulk along.

"We'll rest for the night soon," I said.

"Ah, that's okay," she told me. "My feet fucking hurt, but I can handle that. Other than the calluses and blisters, I haven't felt this much energy in years! It's like the deeper we get into this cave, the more alive I feel! Actually, I'm a little more worried about Cleve."

"Cleve?" I prompted.

"Yeah," she said. "With that damn oversized witch bitch. He's gone goofy." She shook her head, glossy black hair undulating down her back.

"Birdie, don't tell me you're jealous."

"Oh, please," she scoffed. "There was a time… Way back when… But, no. I still care about him, though. He's a friend. And that bitch is scary."

"The Lord is by his side," I reminded her. "I do think Cleve's got the upper hand this time."

"Yeah, well," Birdie muttered. "I hope he's all right. If she hurts him in any way…"

The jaguar seemed to be following our conversation closely, watching our faces with luminous eyes. He let out a low growl. Something brushed against my leg. I looked down and there was Bob. He made a throat clearing noise.

"Hi, Bob." I stooped to pet his head.

"Tim wants to tell her," Bob said.

"Excuse me?" Birdie stopped walking. "Did that cat say something?"

Bob, Tim and I had to stop also, and turn to face her. I wasn't entirely sure what to say. Other members of our group had to squeeze past us to get by; they were polite about it.

"Sure," Bob replied, the tip of his tail swishing back and forth. "Got a problem with that?"

Birdie stared for a long moment. "Oh, what the fuck," she finally said. "No, no problem at all. Can the jaguar speak, too?"

"His name is Tim," Bob explained. "And he can speak fluent feline in three different dialects."

"But no English?"

"No," said my cat, "but he hopes to learn one day."

Birdie shook her head. "I've had a feeling all along that, er, Tim had something to say to me. All right, little kitty cat, what's his message?"

Bob stared coolly at Birdie. He doesn't think of himself as a little kitty cat and as cats generally go, he's not one. Compared to Tim, though, it was more or less accurate and Bob let it pass, though I imagined that he was thinking about pooping in Birdie's shoe.

There was a short exchange in feline dialect.

Bob cleared his throat again. "Tim says, 'The ancient Mayan kings and queens were named for the jaguar spirit, Balam. But that name was not merely a word. Royalty were protected and given wisdom by the nagual, the mystical jaguar who crossed between worlds.'"

Bob looked at Tim. The jungle cat lowered his muscular haunches and sat, delivering a short discourse in feline yowls. "'I am that nagual,'" Bob translated. "'and the royal blood of the ancient kings flows through your veins. The jaguar spirit is part of your heritage and you are the last of the line. As with kings and queens in many lands, those of Balam blood were considered to be gods as well as humans.'"

"Hey, Ian," Birdie exclaimed. "Who prints your t-shirts?"

"Excuse me?" I asked.

"Birdie is God," she said. "Er, Goddess."

Jehovah, who was trying to walk past our tunnel-clogging pow-wow, cleared his throat loudly and glared at Birdie. I couldn't help it, I had to laugh.

Tim roared and we all shut up.

"Tim wants you to shut up," Bob told us.

"Yeah, we got that," I said.

There was a short exchange of yowling and meowing.

"'This is not to be taken lightly'," Bob continued to translate. "'There is power in your station and also great responsibility. As the last avatar of the jaguar spirit, Birdie Balam, you are the Guide and Protector Between the Worlds. You have complete freedom to travel through all the realms and you reign supreme in the shebang of those who have passed beyond. It is your birthright.'"

"I reign supreme?" Birdie asked. "That sounds cool. Does it pay well?"

An exchange in cat talk and then Bob said, "'An entire world is yours and you reign over billions of souls. Yet to rule is also to have the fate of all those entities in your hands.'" Bob looked at Tim, who uttered a short snarl. "'Also, travel is required.'"

"So where is my world?" Birdie asked.

Mmmrrrrryyyyooooowwwww!

"'You can go there whenever you wish'," Bob relayed. "'As soon as you know where it is.'"

"And where is it?" Birdie, predictably, asked.

Tim gave a short growl, turned, and padded off into the tunnel toward the Pool of Shebangs.

17. Lakavinland

"Well, damn," said Birdie as we hiked down the long slope toward the Pool. "If I'm Queen of the Underground, how come I don't have, like, some zombie flunkies to tote my gear?"

I chuckled politely. I wasn't sure how serious to take Tim's message. Given the amount of weird shit that we'd already experienced, I figured it deserved at least a little thought. Throughout our journey, Birdie showed a remarkable ability to scoff. I'm all for skepticism, but when weirdness shows up in the form of a supernatural jaguar – or for that matter, a resurrected wife, a talking cat or a mystical quest to the center of the Earth – I tend to be a little more open-minded. Don't get me wrong – my brain wasn't flapping in the breeze; if Bugs Bunny appeared I might accept him as Bugs Bunny, but I wouldn't fall for that old rabbit-in-a-dress gag. Anyway, Birdie was in deep denial and I wondered when this particular loaf of weirdness was going to hit the fan.

I'm not sure how long we hiked, but I was getting tired by the time there was a light at the end of the tunnel. It was a real, non-metaphoric light that started as a general glow, far off, and after a while became quite bright. Finally we came out of the tunnel into a vast open area. You already know what the Pool of Shebangs looks like: endless towering columns of light and a smooth stone floor sloping inexorably down to the resonant chamber, unseen in the distance and glare. I'm not sure if the descriptions offered so far have quite captured the awesomeness and brilliance of the Pool. So take it from me: it was both awesome and very, very brilliant. Breathtaking. Add a couple fog machines and it would be the ultimate rock'n'roll stage set. I wanted to take a picture for our next album cover. I marveled that this fantastic place was deep beneath the funky little town of Rosendale, though I was really unsure how far we hiked or in what direction, other than down. We could have been under the Catskills somewhere, beneath Kerhonkson or Ellenville, or somewhere else entirely.

Our party stumbled to a halt at the edge of the Pool. Band members, file-entities, gods, goddesses and creatures of various sorts stood dazzled and blinking in the light of the Pool. Really, the glare made it tough to see for a few moments, though my eyes, tearing a little, soon began to adjust. Dondelakavin beamed at us and made a grand, sweeping gesture, as if he were the proud proprietor and originator of every last bit of illumination.

"Come on," Dondelakavin called. "Right this way." He led us down between the columns.

I could now see that the Pool was populated. People – or shebang entities that were indistinguishable from humans, if you prefer – had well-lit enclaves and campsites scattered throughout the cavern. Clothing styles were diverse, unique and, more often than not, unfamiliar. But the things they did were familiar and even comforting in their ordinariness. They talked. They shared food. They drank. From one small group seated in a circle on the stone floor came the rich and pungent aroma of burning ganja. I felt as if I had just arrived at the site of a rock festival or a big party at which Blue Smoke was booked to play.

"Do all these people live here?" Esty asked.

"Live here?" Dondelakavin laughed. "No. They live in their own shebangs. In the columns of light. They come here for some, how shall I say? Inter-world cultural exchange. It's a great way to score drugs, too. And all kinds of stuff you'd never find in your own world. There's a bit of shebang rivalry, but people are generally friendly out here. Except for these jokers."

Three jokers in leather and metal uniforms marched up and saluted Liana by thumping their chests and shouting.

"Do you need assistance, my Lady?" One of the guards inquired. "Shall we kill them all now?"

"No," she commanded. "They are here to assist us in our fight against the forces of the Scrambler."

That was news to me. Jehovah scowled, but Cleve kept smiling.

"Let them pass," Liana continued. "And let them go where they will. With your accompaniment. Stay with them." She looked at me. "To serve you," she said, "and protect you."

"Sure," I said, "Just like the LAPD." Los Angeles, as you'd know if you read *Cash Box* magazine, was the only place I've ever been busted. Well, L.A. and Fort Worth, but everyone gets busted in Texas.

"Don't sweat it." Cleve nudged me in the ribs and glanced at Jehovah who was nonchalantly examining an index finger.

"We're going to Lakavinland," Dondelakavin announced. "And the officers are welcome to join us. Right this way." He strolled down the slope into the glare and we followed, a long line of humans and entities snaking between the towering columns.

I don't think any of the descriptions so far really capture the psychedelic nature of the Pool of Shebangs. The light from the columns was all-pervading, soaking into everything, into every pore of my body. We've all been describing the light as columns and from outside the pool they certainly look columnar. Within the Pool I guess they are still sort of columnar, but there's a sense that the light is everywhere and that it just gets much denser and brighter in some places. As if the light were water and the columns were drains that the water flowed into, except that they were vertical and it's a lame metaphor. If what you take away from my attempt to describe the Pool is that it was an experience difficult to express, then you get the idea.

After we'd walked between the columns for half an hour or so, Dondelakavin suddenly paused, grinned at us, waved, and leaned in to one of the columns. And he was gone. Liana, her goons, Jehovah and Cleve followed without hesitation, disappearing into the light. Perzanto sighed deeply, shrugged his mountainous shoulders, and he too was gone. The rest of us stood looking at each other. I took a single step closer to the column and reached out a hand to touch it before I committed to diving in. It didn't take any more than that; suddenly the bright world fragmented into sparkling motes that twinkled away and I was somewhere else.

As tough as the Pool was to put into words, Lakavinland was even worse. I'll give it a shot because I figure you've read this far and deserve the effort on my part. But if it seems like nonsense, fuck you. Don't say I didn't warn you.

Reality reformed or coagulated or defined itself. I was standing at the edge of a forest. Incredibly tall trees filled the sky before me with verdant fullness, small animals and long-tailed white birds flitting among the branches, calling to each other. Directly above, where the trees ended, a profusion of swirling stars and comets shone down bright as daylight, though it seemed to be night here. Ahead of me, walking deeper into the forest, I could see Perzanto's broad back.

I took a step to follow and suddenly realized that what I'd taken for great, leafy oaks or maples were really towering palm trees, each one sprouting a profusion of expanding, multi-colored umbrellas. And by the time I took another step, the umbrellas were fountains of sparkling green, red and blue wine. Bubbles and blobs of falling wine spiraled and transformed into flocks of ducks and geese that quacked and barked and shouted in French as they flew into the distance.

Behind me, with a muted greenish flare and low-pitched popping sounds, Aqualung, Captain Head Charge, Karen, Trent and Don Speckler appeared, one after the other, like soap bubbles blown from a wand. A herd of purple and blue lawn tractors, driven by extra-large woodchucks, emerged from the forest (which was now a broad highway surrounded by clusters of rotating yellowy streetlights) and rolled, grumbled and chattered around us, finally disappearing into a small complex of industrial buildings that grew from the ground. My companions sighted me and started forward, the rest of our entourage appearing behind them.

"What the…?" Captain Head Charge exclaimed.

Trenton grinned and nodded like he was getting off on a big dose of acid. Aqualung stared, slackjawed.

Karen started hyperventilating. I fished in my pockets for a roach and lit it for her.

Don looked around in amazement. "Woohoo!" he shouted, after a moment.

"Oh, no," his little angel opined. "Here we go."

"That's right, baby!" the devil enthused. "Now we're talking! Which way to the party?"

"Where did they go?" Trent asked.

I pointed toward the shopping mall made of Swiss cheese, where Perzanto could still be seen beyond a collection of freestanding, neon bright, pink kiosks. As we watched, the cheese melted and flowed into a lake of undulating yellow and green fluid, while the kiosks began to rotate and grow into oversize purple woolly mammoths. The mammoths formed two lines and danced the Cowboy Boogie as we strolled down a grassy lane between them. They trumpeted to the beat of their stomping feet. The cats came bounding up behind us, Bob leaping high in the air after a glowing blue butterfly with black and orange spots. By the time Bob's trajectory carried him halfway to the insect, it became a ball of Silly Putty that stretched and snapped itself out of paw's reach. Tim made snorting noises that sounded like jaguar laughter.

The constant, kaleidoscopic transformations continued and the sun, big and green and blobby, was rising in the west as we caught up with Perzanto.

"This," Don said breathlessly, "is really amazing. I want… I want…" His eyes fixed on something behind me and he stumbled past, angel and devil flapping furiously to keep up.

"Please stay together," Perzanto suggested. "It's easy to get lost here."

"Yeah," Captain Head Charge said. "Like, for instance, where the hell are we?"

"Dondelakavin went that way." The big god pointed toward a jungle of pinwheel-sprouting vines that climbed and hung from the fossilized carcasses of enormous winged dragons.

As we started in that direction, the fossil dragons became huge living anteaters covered with parabolic dish antennae and there was a loud, angry squawking from behind us. I turned, the shotgun swinging into my grip, and saw, a dozen paces back, Don Speckler gripping a six foot emerald green monitor lizard by the throat. The lizard wore a grey fedora hat with a blue feather stuck in the band. Man and lizard were surrounded by a circle of more lizards, along with giant frogs in tophats, men with the heads of orange tabby cats, and a scattering of small blue box turtles. The animals and animal-headed ones were taking bets, great sheaves of funny-colored money passing back and forth between them. The angel and devil were flapping around Don's head offering suggestions.

"Hit him with a right!" the devil yelled.

"Get out of there!" the angel called. "Violence is no way to settle your differences."

"He's a lizard," the devil argued. "How's he going to understand reason?"

"I'm not talking about reason," the angel said. "I'm talking about what you know in your heart is right."

The emerald green lizard snapped at Don's right ear. "Hey!" the angel yelled, barely managing to fly out of the way in time.

"Still holding on to that non-violence?" the devil inquired, leering.

"Kick his scaly ass!" the angel commanded Don.

By that time, though, the lizard's ass was no longer scaly as he was rapidly morphing into a medium size greased pig with boxing gloves. Don lost his grip on the creature and dodged as the pig thing took a swing at him.

"Don!" I called. "What the hell are you doing?"

"I want that hat!" Don shouted, advancing on the pig. The lizard's feathered fedora, however, had become a small blue bird that hopped back and forth between the swinish ears. Don dodged another roundhouse swing – the pig's arms were pretty short – and he leveled a blow at the animal's snout. By then, however, the snout had become a very large and crispy-fried spring roll, held in the hand of a short, swarthy waiter in a checkered vest. The spring roll burst into shards of cabbage and baby shrimp which became sparkling bits of confetti as it sprayed all over Don and the waiter, who was now a big lizard again, only still wearing the checkered vest. The hatbird, grown now to the size of a turkey vulture, flew off and perched on a traffic sign that said "Traffic Signs Ahead."

"Don," I yelled. "Quit fucking around!"

"No! No!" the devil countered. "*More* fucking around! More!"

"Ian's stealing my lines!" the angel protested. "Quit fucking around!"

Don backed away from the lizard as it began to grow larger and larger. The giant gophers and snails, formerly box turtles and cat headed men, furiously wagered sticks of cinnamon chewing gum and what appeared to be tiny refrigerators. The lizard sprouted four sets of glittering dragonfly wings and gently rose into the air. Don backed away faster and more furiously, then turned and made a dive toward the hat vulture only to find the creature hanging limply from the jaws of a large jaguar that steadfastly remained a jaguar. The dead bird, however, transformed into a limp Salvador Dali clock, then into molten chocolate which dripped to the floor. Tim gave it a lick and shook his head in disgust; the chocolate was now rainbow-colored crayon wax.

The flying minivan that once was a winged lizard in a vest kept rising and rising and was soon followed by a retinue of dancing badgers – formerly gophers, snails, lizards, and frogs in tophats – who expanded into big Macy's parade balloons and soared off into the swirling sky.

Don stood dazed.

"Damn," the devil declared. "You wanted that hat!"

"I wanted that hat!" Don repeated.

"Give me a break," complained the angel.

"Oh, shit," said Don, staring down at the oily patch on the fuzzy, fizzing ground that had been the hat. He looked up at me and then at Perzanto, who was standing off to one side. "Sorry," he said.

"I lost sight of Dondelakavin," Perzanto told us. "We'll have to find his place ourselves."

"I can't imagine finding anything here," I said.

"Dondelakavin is the god of this world," Perzanto explained, "which makes him a little bit easier to find. Only a little, though."

"Why don't we wait here?" Trent suggested. "When we don't show up, he'll come looking for us."

Perzanto sighed. "There's no such thing as 'here' here. Or at least, not for long."

It was true; as we stood there, mountains rose and fell, trees and buildings and things I have no words for grew, moved, transformed and self-destructed.

"We have a saying in the Hudson Valley," I remarked. "If you don't like the weather, wait five minutes. We'll amend that for Lakavinland. If you don't like the scenery, well, there's no waiting at all."

"Excuse me," said Aqualung. "I think they went that way." He pointed a gnarly old finger toward a great city of glittering steel and glass rising on the horizon. A golden aura pulsed above the skyline. Stars and fireworks twinkled and exploded. Unscathed by the skyrockets, airplanes and great, gooney, Dr. Seuss birds took off from the city or circled for an approach. Enormous neon arrows blinked on and off in five different colors, pointing to the glittering towers.

It sort of made sense. I figured that the most important guy in the shebang would be in the biggest city. However, there was no guarantee that it would still be a city, rather than an orange orchard, used car lot or electronic duck farm, by the time we got there. For want of a better plan, we started walking that way.

"Why is Lakavinland like this?" Esty asked Perzanto as we walked along a yellow brick asphalt superhighway. "I thought that each shebang was a reflection of the world at large. This is just crazy."

Endless strip malls along each side of the highway made it look a bit like Orlando, Florida. The storefronts looked fairly normal, until you peered closer and read the signs. "Beaver Mating," said one. "Transistor Elocution Depot," said another.

"Every shebang is a reflection of the whole, yes," Perzanto agreed. "And each one has its own bias. It's what makes the shebangs different worlds instead of identical clones. Just as people are also reflections of the whole, some may be more sedate, some more chaotic. And we will find a wide range and the extremes, too."

"So this shebang is the Salvador Dali of worlds?" Esty asked.

Perzanto nodded. "More specifically, it is the Dondelakavin of worlds."

"He's that nutty?" I started to ask, but was interrupted by a troupe of capering leprechauns who rappelled down from purple moiré helicopters.

"You're coming with us!" one of the leprechauns announced.

"Grab him!" the devil yelled into Don's left ear.

Don, with a look of intense glee, tried to grab the little man.

"Stop it!" the angel commanded.

It didn't matter. The leprechaun was now a very prickly, four foot tall hedgehog. Don jumped back.

All the leprechauns, perhaps a dozen of them, were now hedgehogs, skunks, possum and a mall security guard, a woman with big shoes and a brown uniform.

"Come with us," the rent-a-cop said, her uniform morphing into a very sexy hotel bellhop outfit. "Right this way."

"Yeah!" chimed a possum. "Right this way!" The various animals snickered.

"Do we have to tip?" Mark Ratner pondered.

"I don't tip hedgehogs," said Captain Head Charge.

"What is that, some kind of racist attitude?" one of the hedgehogs badgered.

"Doesn't matter anyway," said another, "'cause we're not hedgehogs anymore."

It was true. All of them were now Brownies and Cub Scouts in tye dye uniforms, and the former bellhop was their leader. They ran around, tugging at our pant legs, shouting "Come on! Come on!"

"Do you know where Dondelakavin is?" Perzanto asked.

Overhead, the helicopters, now glowing blimps, were coming lower. They grew feet which turned into long ropy tentacles. We all scrambled to get out of the way as the blimps, now soft and squishy, settled to the earth with great farting sounds.

"Whatthefuckavin?" one of the cub scouts asked.

"Fuckavin! Fuckavin!" the others chanted.

"Dondelakavin," Perzanto said grimly. "Your god."

"Latke Vin? Waka Tin? Crocka Sin? Laka Dial! Stinky Pile!" the little scouts chanted, dancing around the flailing tentacles of the giant octopi formerly known as blimps.

"Come on," said the den mother, who was now also growing tentacles. "We'll take you where you're going. You can't stay, you know, here."

"Yeah," said Don with an odd grin. "There is no here!"

"No here! No fear! No beer! Faux cheer! Dough tear!"

Don jerked, his body spasming. He twitched and danced convulsively until he fell to the ground and began rolling back and forth, laughing and sputtering.

"It's too much for him!" the angel cried, fluttering over Don's twitching body. "It's overload!"

"Yeah," the devil agreed. "He's cracked! He's flipped! He's gone gaga!"

"And he didn't even have to pay for a hooker," the angel remarked.

Don laughed, hooted and babbled nonsense along with the cub scouts (who were now yapping Chihuahuas). I was amazed. I'd never seen him like this. While I'd heard rumors of his odd behavior over the years, and seen occasional evidence of excess, well, hell, that's fairly normal stuff for a musician. I spent some evenings, back in the day, hanging out with Jim Morrison who was about as out-of-control as any of my friends, Keith Moon included. Who's to say if the path of excess is the road to wisdom or the highway to hell? Don's behavior seemed to be something else, though, a fit of some kind, an episode. Insanity.

The ground, which previously looked like a field of blue-green grass, was now a rapidly growing garden of dense, spiky plants. A dagger-like spike caught me in the ass and I cursed. Yelps and cries soon followed from other members of our party.

"Quickly, now," the den mother, who was now a giant nursing rottweiler bitch, urged, "into the squidlocopters!" She gestured toward the glittering squid-like things that had formerly been octopi, blimps and purple moiré helicopters. We didn't have much choice. Perzanto grabbed Don and hoisted him, still laughing, babbling and twitching, onto one shoulder. The angel and devil landed on the god's other broad shoulder and held on as he began to run. A big orifice on the side of the closest squid squooshed open and, dancing as best we could around the pointy plants, we ran for it and dived inside.

Inside the squidlocopter it was soft, pink, and fleshy. Folds in the flaccid hull made long, couch-like rows of seats on both sides, now partially occupied by a pack of large rats in vests and dark sunglasses. Bob and Tim, leaping through the door, skidded to a halt, sniffing at the rats suspiciously. The rottweiler den mother, now making a sinuous transition into some kind of big weasel, reorganized the troop of rodents with a long-fingered paw and sat down among them. Perzanto jumped through the pulsing orifice with Don, angel and devil still in tow. He tossed Don onto the seats and we sat down on either side of the giggling sax player. I leaned guitar and shotgun against the soft pink stuff, clearing the way for Bob, who jumped onto my lap for the ride. Birdie, Trent and Aqualung squeezed through the doorway, which irised shut with a loud slurp behind them. Through a translucent panel on the opposite wall, I could see the rest of our company, pursued by the growing spiky plants, hurry into the other squids. With a lurch, we were airborne.

My ass hurt where the plant had jabbed me. I shifted onto one cheek and slid my hand back there to check on things. It felt like a pretty good welt or bruise, but there wasn't any blood, so I figured it was safe to sit on.

"Hey! What are you doing?" Bob was trying not to slide out of my tilted lap.

"Yeah," commented Birdie. "Please."

I took my hand out of my pants and settled down.

"The wounds will heal on their own," the giant weasel squealed.

"Hee hee hee," the rats tittered. "But they're gonna get worse, first!"

"Where are we going?" I asked.

"We're off to see the wizard," the weasel said.

"The lizard!" one of the rats cried.

"A mizard! The shnizard! Shit lard! Pushin' hard!" the other rats chanted, bouncing up and down in their seats. "Pushing too hard on meeeeeeee!"

The squidlocopter gained altitude and banked. Through the translucent hull, I could see a kaleidoscopic landscape, transforming endlessly, rotating through an infinite profusion of colors and shapes.

"Does that mean we're going to where Dondelakavin hangs out?" I asked.

"Lakavin! Hakavin! Where ya been? Going in!"

"What does he hang out?" The weasel looked puzzled. Its face became more and more human and its body flattened and grew shorter until it looked like a large duckbilled platypus with the face of a tubby blond woman.

The squid banked again and we could see, rising rapidly from the ground below, some vast, complicated structure. Like a time-lapse film of plate tectonics forcing the Himalayas up to the highest heights, the thing grew enormously, exponentially. The squid pushed for altitude, making a sharp turn around the obstacle. As it climbed up past us, we could see that it was an endlessly repeating pattern of monkeys standing on big, red and white striped rubber balls, balanced on the heads of monkeys who were standing on balls. The monkeys waved and jabbered and pointed at us.

Don's eyes were wide, his mouth open, a little bit of drool running from the corner. As we turned away from the monkey mountain, I could see an avalanche beginning, monkeys and balls falling and toppling more monkeys and balls. As more and more of them fell, hundreds and thousands, the monkeys became giant salami and the balls turned into whirling pinwheels attached to the salami with ropes, slowing their descent. Don was breathing hard.

"Don," I asked. "What the fuck?"

He turned toward me, for the moment marginally rational. "Ian," he panted. "Ian. When I was ten years old. A kid. A skinny little kid with a saxophone…" He trailed off, eyes wide as something in a state of furious mutation zoomed past our squiddy window.

"Don," I said.

"Oh. Ian. What?"

"When you were ten years old?" I prompted.

"When I was ten years old, I was a skinny little kid with a saxophone," Don repeated. "And a box of frogs."

"I had frogs too, when I was ten," Trenton said.

"Yeah, me too," Aqualung added.

"Ew. Little boys are gross," Birdie told us.

"Gross! Dose! Nose! Rose!" The rats were now green glowing guinea pigs with tiny bowler hats.

"My frogs were different," Don said. "Only I could see them."

The guinea pigs flattened and their fur matted into smooth, shiny skin. In a moment, they were leopard frogs, the kind they made us dissect in high school, only considerably larger. Their green skin, mottled with black markings, suddenly started to rotate through a spectrum of dazzling, electric colors. They stood up on their seats and danced, a remarkable feat given the swerving, undulating flight of the squidlocopter.

"Imaginary frogs. Okay." Birdie rolled her eyes.

"Hey, I had an imaginary llama," Trent said. "But that was when I was six. By the time I was ten, I had an imaginary Steinway."

"Oh, no," Don said solemnly. "They weren't imaginary. My frogs were real. Not even Eddie could see them, though. They were green and purple and invisible."

The angel and devil, now back on Don's shoulders, crossed their eyes and twirled fingers by ears: crazy.

"Sometimes I would go in the box with the frogs and they would take me to their pond."

The squid, turning and banking on its indirect course to wherever, now gave us a view of terrain covered with blue and red squares like an election-year map of the United States. As we watched, the colors began to swirl together and I realized that we were seeing vast herds of blue and red animals of some kind – they were too far away to tell what – mingling together. We all watched, fascinated. Don was breathing hard and once again lost the tenuous thread of his tale.

I was a little leery of Don's story. I wasn't sure how entirely sane he was at the moment and the story had veered off into absurdity from the start. But curiosity got me anyway and I prompted him. "Frogs. Taking you to their pond. When you were ten years old?"

Don laughed. "Frogs! Yeah, they took me to their pond. It was a fabulous place, with neon tadpoles, magical flutes and horns, headless chickens, and big, glowing, bloodshot eyeballs. There were cookies that tasted like ham, hamburgers that tasted like oranges, fruit that tasted like my mother's famous chopped chicken liver, and horseflies that tasted like prime rib. The frogs danced in a long chorus line, always beckoning me to join them. I did the frog dance while the… while the… uh…"

The angel and devil face-palmed themselves, sighing and moaning. We could now see six other squidlocopters flying beside us, only they had become big, translucent geese, flapping impossibly long wings. Our own 'copter was apparently just as goosey, glassy wing-feathers dipping into view. Inside the body of the nearest gooseplane, I could see Esty and Captain Head Charge along with a troupe of Clown Fellows and a pack of purple beavers. Esty waved as their goose banked away from us.

"You did the frog dance," I prompted.

"Say what?" Don asked.

"The frog dance, in the pond, when you were ten."

"Oh yeah, the frog dance. I joined their endless conga line. We danced through water, through air, down into the earth and up into the sun. We danced through airport lobbies and bowling alleys and lingerie departments. We jumped and hopped through the biography section of Brains and Noballs. We swam along the highway of obsolete technology. We jitterbugged through the Graveyard of Paper Cups and we tangoed near an animated billboard for the Miami Serpentarium. Boy, those froggies could really get down!"

"Get down!" the candy-striped beavers, formerly frogs, repeated. "Down town! Big clown! Pig clone! Priced to own! Hormone!"

The angel and devil fell to the floor and feigned melodramatic anguish. Tim came over and sniffed them; they froze like scared rabbits by the highway.

"I'm sorry," said Birdie. "But what the hell does this have to do with anything? Wrestling with lizards, epileptic fits or convulsions or whatever. He's talking nonsense. This man needs to be medicated."

I grinned and opened the guitar case.

Birdie scoffed. "That's not what I meant."

I turned toward the giant platypus woman, who was now a small, heavily armored blue dinosaur. "Is it okay to smoke in here?" I asked.

"Smoke," she affirmed, producing a long-stemmed Dr. Grabow's pipe and puffing blue clouds. The beavers likewise lit up cigarettes that made rainbow-colored smoke, all except one who was toking gently on a tall, ornate hookah. The smoke wafted neatly into gills or flapping vents along the ceiling of the gooseplane.

I rolled up a fat one and sparked it into life. I passed it to Don. The angel and devil both urged him on and he took a deep hit. The goose turned again and we could see a fabulous vista, an ever-changing cityscape, a confusing conglomeration of crystalline structures that grew and multiplied as we watched. Chaser lights fled along the edges of buildings until the buildings ceased being buildings and the lights spilled off onto whatever was below. Great flashing, colored signs spun up from streets, swelling and bursting in crescendos of neon. We banked again and began to head directly for the crazy quilt city. Don exhaled and the smoke wafted into the gills.

I urged him to take a couple more tokes before passing the spliff. He needed it. Hell, maybe we all needed it a little. I kept thinking that Lakavinland might make a little more sense if I were stoned. At any rate, I figured it couldn't hurt.

Man, was I wrong.

Don's insane laughter subsided into ganja giggles and his babbling settled down into – ah, hell, it was still babbling, but less annoying. The gunk mountain shit works every time.

A little more relaxed now, Don continued his tale of hallucinatory froggie paradise. He insisted that the details of his exploits in the pond were relevant, but I'll spare you. His descriptions of dancing frogs and their environment sounded an awful lot like a

DMT trip to me. DMT is intensely trippy stuff that comes from weird jungle vines in South America or from clandestine laboratories – and there's also a little bit made in our own brains. It probably helps us dream, but every now and then we can accidentally trigger a serious and total trip-out, just on our own brain chemicals. One time in the early '80s, Jane and I were driving home from a festival and I was running on too few hours of sleep. I volunteered to drive first and when it came time for Jane to take over, I decided to force myself to stay awake, to keep her company and help her stay alert. I did okay for an hour or so, but then suddenly started slipping in and out of a very strange reality. It wasn't quite dreaming – I was definitely still awake, I think, but it was another world with different rules, much of which I can't even remember now. When I came to myself, Jane was staring at me, quite freaked. She claimed that I was speaking very excitedly about how time was an ocean full of starfish. I have no idea what I said, but the sleep-dep experience was remarkably like the time I smoked DMT with Hunter Thompson out at Kesey's place.

So I don't know if ten year old Don was tripping on his own brain chemicals, but he got quite used to visiting the frog pond.

"When I hit puberty," Don explained, "it all started to fade. I remember it now, the frogs, the creamy skies, the musical poop, the…"

"Yeah, yeah," Birdie said. "Musical poop."

"But usually it's not so easy. Mostly, I'm not even sure it ever really happened, like I'm remembering a dream. It's something about this place. Lakavinland. It's like the frog pond. It brings it back. And as I started getting interested in sex, there was still some part of me that craved the weirdness. As I stopped going with the frogs, I started to make weirdness in my own life. And, uh, I was a horny kid." The devil started to titter uncontrollably. The angel swatted it with his halo. Don ignored them both and continued. "You know how puberty can do that. It all started to get mixed up. My yearning for anything outside the boundaries of rationality and my adolescent quest for poontang. My craving for anything that punctured the surface of consensus reality and my hormonal compulsion to shoot my load as much as I could.

"And, against all of that," Don went on, "I tried to exercise some control. I had to be normal in public and get my ya yas out in secret. Or as secret as I could make it. It was a constant struggle. I imagined that I had an angel on one shoulder, telling me to behave like everyone else. And a devil on the other shoulder, urging me on. And the last week or so…" he gestured at his entity companions who posed smugly.

Throughout Don's rant, the goose's flight became more and more erratic. We were losing altitude rapidly and swerving from side to side. The dinosaur and beavers, now a delightfully prim Victorian schoolteacher and her gang of saber-toothed squirrels, became very agitated. The squirrels chattered and jumped up and down on their seats. Through the translucent goose wall, I could see the other geese, high above us, still holding altitude and a somewhat straighter course.

"We're going down!" the devil shouted. "The goose is cooked!"

"The goose is *baked*!" the angel yelled. "I told you not to burn that shit."

"You did not," the devil said. "And you were bogarting the joint, too. I saw you."

"I'm afraid your smoking material was a bit stronger than our own," the schoolteacher said in clipped, precise tones. "We are indeed, as the small red gentleman so aptly put it, going down." She changed into a clown with puffy yellow hair and enormous red shoes. With a beep, the clown adjusted her glowing blue nose and grinned.

Alas, the gunk mountain shit does it every time. Honking joyously, the goose continued to plummet.

"This is it," the devil informed us. "Does anyone have any last words?"

Don was unfazed and his rambling account continued. "At first," he said, "when I, you know, waxed the bishop, I'd listen to Spike Jones and look at pictures of household appliances that I cut out of magazines and glued to the backs of plastic turtles. Then I would…"

"Whoa!" Birdie exclaimed. "Too much information! And I think we'd better assume crash positions or something."

We held on as best we could as the goose executed a sloppy loop-the-loop and then hit the ground with a jolt that launched us all from our seats. The floor was soft, but my already sore ass landed on the guitar case, which wasn't. The goose ran and stumbled to a halt, honked loudly and opened its orifice. We gratefully piled out, checking ourselves for injuries. Neither guitar nor ass seemed broken but, man, my butt cheek hurt! Another journey to the interior of my pants revealed that the injured area was forming a lump or knot that was painful to touch.

The goose, which now resembled a giant, deflated bagpipe, had deposited us on the outskirts of the great city, or whatever the fuck it was at the moment. Looking up, far in the distance, I could see the other gooseplanes disappearing over the skyline.

18. The Terrtrych

I was limping a bit, but we had to keep moving. The landscape, like everything in Lakavinland, was in flux and we needed to adapt quickly and constantly, my sore ass reminded me. Sickly green bubbles rose up from the ground around us and we worked hard to avoid them. The cats seemed particularly offended by the bubbles and hissed loudly whenever one appeared in their path.

I'll continue to refer to the bizarre and overwhelming conglomeration of things before us as a city, even though, from moment to moment, that was debatable. The city roared, crooned, boomed, tweeted, whistled, and hummed. The sound of it all was simply incredible and a little bit maddening. I wished that I had a way to record some of it. Every part of the city changed constantly, and every element of change seemed to involve flashy colors, bright lights, and loud noises. Mostly it was chaos, but every now and then, inexplicably, all the changing parts would synch up and transform into the same color, brightness, rhythm or shape at the same moment. One thing did, sort of, remain the same. The city had a heart, a center from which all the other insanity emanated. It too kept shifting and changing, but it held its location and remained the densest, brightest, loudest part of the place.

Our hosts, last seen as a clown and a squad of saber-toothed squirrels, were now a small herd of very tiny deer, led by a large moose or elk. The elk nodded its antlers in the direction of the city's heart. The tiny deer chanted in helium-heightened tones, "This is the way, but only today, follow us now, we'll show you how!"

They picked up the pace and we were forced to jog to keep up. It wasn't easy to limp at that speed. Perzanto was in the lead, Don once again over his shoulder, and Trenton not far behind. Birdie was doing surprisingly well, though her weight still slowed her. Aqualung and I brought up the rear, which was slightly humiliating. We dodged and swerved through shifting streets, mutating markets, bizarre buildings, and an endless supply of objects and beings that I simply could not identify. The deer seemed to have an infallible instinct for how things changed, mental maps that took time and transformation into account. They would lead us down a safe avenue that would change into giant flashing blades or a pit of bright, bubbling, psychedelic lava only moments after we were past. We worked really hard to stay with the tiny, fleet-footed critters.

After a lengthy, somewhat harrowing jog through confusion, the big elk dodged into a doorway and we followed into a moderate-sized room. The deer came to a stamping halt and then transformed into a flock of colorful and noisy jungle fowl, presided over by a zebra-striped flamingo. The room was interesting mostly in that it remained a room, at least for the time being. Walls and exterior seemed to be going through some changes, but the open space in the center of the floor remained open and the floor remained a floor. I wondered how long it would last. I figured the flock of fowl would let us know when to vacate, before the room turned into a Volkswagen or a bagel with cream cheese.

Perzanto released Don on his own recognizance and we took a few minutes to catch our breath. Ornate, claw-footed antique furniture evolved from the floor and most everyone sat down. My ass hurt too much and I remained standing, leaning when I could against a big overstuffed armchair.

"Hey!" said a tiny voice. I looked around. "Hey! Let me outa here!" No one else seemed to hear, which was good because I was convinced that the reedy little voice was coming from my pants. I figured that denial was my best plan and I ignored it.

"We will be there soon," the flamingo informed us. "But we must wait a few moments before we continue."

From outside the room, we could hear the sound of the city's heart, now close by. It was a mighty roar, somewhat muted by the walls. It rose and fell in volume and tone, but mostly seemed to get louder and deeper the longer we stayed there. Don kept looking in that direction and, after a few minutes, actually went to the wall and put his hand on it, as if he could feel the power of the throbbing chaos.

"Come on," Don urged. "Let's keep going! Let's go there!"

"Yeah, yeah," the devil agreed. "Come on!"

"I don't think that's such a good idea," the angel said, shaking its head.

The devil, riding on Don's left shoulder, leaned close and whispered something in his ear.

"No, really," the angel insisted. "It's not…"

Don howled, a spine-tingling, lunatic cry, and bolted out the door. We ran after him as far as the entranceway where a forest of very sharp-looking crystalline trees suddenly blocked our path. In the distance we could see Don leaping and dodging around infinitely changeable obstacles. The angel and devil fluttered desperately to keep up.

The flamingo shook its striped head. "He will die," the bird said.

"We have to go after him," I said.

"You cannot," the flamingo squawked. "You will die!"

"It's no lie! You will try! You will cry! You will die!" the smaller fowl confirmed.

"Damn," I said. "He's a friend! And a great sax player. Legendary. We can't just let him run off to his death. It's like watching Morrison drink himself into the big sleep. Or watching Elvis swallow his final bucket of pills."

"Don looked like he was doing okay to me," Trent said. "I didn't think he could move that fast."

"You knew Elvis?" Aqualung asked.

"No," I said. "But I saw him in concert once, in Vegas."

"We'll catch up to Don," Birdie spoke up. "I imagine we're all heading to the same place, right?" She looked at the flamingo, which was preening a wing.

The bird straightened its long neck and slowly shook its head from side to side. "Oh, no. I do not think so. Legendary sax player wants the terrtrych. We are for Dondelakavin."

"Aha!" I crowed. "So now you'll say it! That is where we're going! We're going to see Dondelakavin."

"Lakavin! Hakavin! Where ya been? Going in!"

"What is the terrtrych?" Trenton asked.

"It is the heart of change." The flamingo pointed its large bill toward that which dominated our reality, the roaring, crazy center of the city.

"That's not where Dondelakavin hangs out?" I asked.

The flamingo gave me a blank stare.

"I knew this was a bad idea," Perzanto bemoaned. "I should have stopped us before we ever set foot in Lakavinland."

"You're no fun!" the fowlettes cackled. "Grab your gun! Time to run!"

The birds ran, flapping, clucking, and squawking, right out the door. We grabbed our shit and took off in pursuit. My butt was really sore and my hip wasn't working too well, but I pushed for whatever strength I had. The guitar case banged against my ass wound and the pain almost stopped me in my tracks. What did really stop me, though, was the tiny voice that shouted "Hey! What the fuck?"

"Uh, hello?" I said to my own buttocks.

"Quit hitting me with the guitar! Hey! Why are you stopping?" the tiny voice called. "Hurry up! Run! Move your ass before…"

The ground heaved up beneath me and I sprinted after the flock of friends and fowl. Another second in that spot and I would have joined the barnacles on the hull of the huge ocean liner that burst from the ground and steamed, full speed ahead, into the sky. The ship boomed out a blast on its horn and turned to avoid a tall, flashing billboard for something called Bed Breezer.

"Thank you," I said to my ass as I ran. "You saved my life."

"Think nothing of it," the voice said. "Just let me the fuck out of here as soon as you can, okay?"

"Deal," I panted. "After we finish running."

I pushed through the pain and managed to get closer to our crew. We dodged through an alley full of shiny, blue blocks of stone that randomly shot up from the ground or dropped from the sky. We slid down a long, undulating tube into a chamber that was full of squishy stuff, like the inside of a pumpkin. From there it was out onto a loop of raised highway with a roadbed that writhed like a serpent in heat. The squirming pavement passed very close to the city's heart, which was entirely overwhelming now, blotting out any thoughts except keeping up with our avian guides.

Our formerly avian guides, I mean, because by this time they were transforming into blue monkeys and a big, orange orangutan. The monkeys swung from the swervy road onto a series of ladders that climbed into the noisy, flashing sky. We followed. The jaguar raced up ahead, as if the ladders were jungle trees. Bob did pretty well too, scaling the vertical supports like he did the big oak in my front yard, occasionally using the rungs for a little added push. The rest of us climbed as best we could, taking one rung at a time until we came up through the floor of – hell, I don't know what to call it. It was a crazy marketplace where vendors constantly moved and swapped their booths and wares; it was a labyrinth with high walls and a forest of flowering trees; it was the grand entrance to a museum of Dadaist art; it was a palace designed by a psychotic architect with a penchant for paradox. The place was dense with an incredible diversity of people, talking animals, animated objects, and self-mobile things that transformed too quickly to pin a name on. Or at least that's what it was like at the moment.

We followed the scampering simians through this ever-evolving craziness for a short time until we came to an area that was doing a good job of holding its shape as a room. Surrounded by people and things of various sorts, sitting in a big, tall-backed office chair at one end of the space, was our weird pal, the resident god of Lakavinland, Dondelakavin. He wore a mountainous red robe, with a phallic hat that would have made the Pope jealous. In his right hand he held a rubber squeaky toy in the shape of a rat. In his left was one of those rotating spiral wheels used by hypnotists in old movies.

"Chumps!" Dondelakavin called. "I mean, Chimps! You found them!"

The monkeys, who were indeed now chimps, chattered around Dondelakavin. Our own friends – Esty, Karen, Oswaldo, Captain

Head Charge, Mark Ratner, Cleve, Liana, Jehovah, and other file entities and humans – gathered around us. I could barely stand up, my butt hurt so much, and Perzanto offered an enormous arm to support me and help me to an object that might loosely be called a chair. I couldn't sit, though, and I had made a promise to my ass. I dropped my pants.

There was a collective "Whoa!" and I really don't think anyone was looking at my privates. I craned my neck to look back at my ass as much as I could. Something was moving there. Something was sticking out of my ass and waving its tiny arms.

"Come on," the thing said. "Get me outa here!"

"Oh shit," said Mark Ratner. "It's a talking hemorrhoid!"

"Fuck you," the thing said. Apart from the fact that it was painfully embedded in my butt cheek, I was starting to like the little guy, or whatever it was. "Come on, Ian. Give me a pull."

"What the hell is that thing?" Birdie wanted to know.

"I don't know," I said. "It's where I got jabbed by that pointy plant."

"Hey," Captain Head Charge said. "I got jabbed, too. It hurts like a son of a bitch, too." He started to pull up his pants leg.

I reached behind me and I grabbed that thing and gave it a good yank. There was a sucking sound and it came free in my hand. I looked at it. It was about three inches tall with short, stubby arms and legs. The head was disproportionately large for the body, with big, yellow eyes, a wide, toothy grin and no nose to speak of. Its skin was thick and nubby. It looked like a cross between a Troll Doll and a horny toad.

"Thanks, dude," the little thing said as I set it down on the chair. Bob came and sniffed it. It didn't seem to mind.

My ass still hurt and I could feel a deep crater in the cheek, rimmed with a hard ridge of thickened skin like a callous.

"Ow," I said.

"No fear," the thing told me. "It'll close up."

I pulled up my pants.

Dondelakavin climbed out of his throne and came over for a look, acres of red robe following him across the floor. "Nice one!" he said. "They usually don't get that big."

"Yeah," said Captain Head Charge, "mine's a lot smaller."

Sticking from his calf muscle was a thing like an inch-long sea horse. It grinned at us and blinked. "Hiya!" it said.

Half a dozen soldiers, two clowns and Karen also discovered tiny critters embedded in their flesh.

"What the hell are they?" Birdie asked Dondelakavin.

"Oh sure," the Captain's sea horse thing complained, "talk about us like we're not even here."

I looked down at mine, who was lounging on the chair. "Got an explanation?" I asked.

"You must be from out of town," the little thing said. "The pattern of life, the spark of consciousness – it's not a fixed, solid thing. That's just a trick that happens because of your brain. It's information. And it can flow through things and change."

"My ass is a solid thing," I told it. "Usually."

"An illusion," the critter said. "Your ass is information, too. And a little bit of my information got into your information when you backed into the plant."

"Sorry," I said. "It was an accident. I didn't mean to… Hey! I didn't back into the fucking plant. It grew at me! With malice!"

"Not malice," my little assfriend explained. "It's a…" He mumbled something that I couldn't quite make out.

"It's a what?" I prompted.

"It's personal!" the thing protested. "Not in front of everybody."

"Whisper in my ear." I lifted it up and held it close to my head.

"Reproduction," the little thing hissed.

"Reproduction?"

"Shhhh. It's personal, remember?" the thing told me. "Would you like it if I talked about your sex habits in front of your friends?"

"Sex?" I hissed.

"Well, not sex as such," the entity said. "It's how I spread and grow and adapt."

"By poking innocent people in the ass?"

"Or wherever I can manage to poke. And may I add that your ass is very pokeable."

"Hey!" I exclaimed. "That's rape!"

"You didn't complain when it was happening."

"Yes I did!"

"What's going on over there?" Captain Head Charge called.

"We're almost done!" I said.

"You see, I can't help it, man," the entity said. "I really have to, you know, spread my information. Bees are compelled to sniff out flowers. Salmon have to swim upstream. The mighty targtargulon must dance all night under the podupery tree and sing exactly three verses of his national anthem through his engorged fragnortal organs."

"He does what?"

"You know, so he can win the right to inseminate the host larva. And I have to do what I have to do, too. Doesn't mean I can't enjoy it, though."

I put the thing back down on the chair. "We've been fucked," I said to Captain Head Charge. "The damn things reproduce by cloning themselves in passing hosts. You're a mother…"

"Shut yo' mouth!"

"No, really, you're a mother. A mom. A maternal parent. Hurry up and pull that little fucker out of your womb."

"Ewww," Head Charge complained, pulling the little sea horse thing from his leg. All the way out, we could see that it had little stubby legs. Head Charge placed it on the ground and rubbed at his calf.

Dondelakavin chuckled and said, "Since you're all here, I was really hoping you could play a song. I'm told that you are the greatest band of your day and I saw a t-shirt once…"

"Wait!" I said. "We're not all here!" I explained about Don.

"Too bad," Dondelakavin replied. "He doesn't stand much chance out there."

"We have to find him!" Birdie exclaimed. "We can't just let him wander off to his death."

"Bats!" Dondelakavin called and a flock of very large bats appeared, lead by a dark, furry woman in a vampire costume. "Go find the one you lost! Find him now!"

"Find him! Fondle him! Foodle him! Feed him!" the bats chanted and then flew off.

"We should go, too," I said. "He's our friend."

"You were already poked in the ass by a pattern entity," Dondelakavin reminded me. "There are far crazier things out there, especially this close to the terrtrych. You would not survive. What's Don like?"

"He's crazy as a loon," I said.

"Good. Then he might make it until my minions find him. If he is enough like mentally ill water fowl." Dondelakavin suddenly turned and marched back to his throne chair. He sat and laboriously arranged his robe around him. His hypno-wheel spun and he held the plastic rat where its beady eyes could reflect the spiraling design. "So. Let us have a song!" he cried.

"Birdie, Trenton and I just climbed six miles of ladders to get here. We need to rest a little."

Birdie harrumphed. "Speak for yourself, kemo sabe. I feel fine."

I looked over at Trent. "Remember that time in '75," he began, "we were heading to Amsterdam to play a big concert at the Museumplein? Our flight was delayed because of storms, we didn't sleep for nearly a day, our gear got ripped off at the train station and we had to walk halfway across the city in a thunderstorm because the trams weren't working. And we still played a kick-ass show. I think I can handle a song."

"We had acid back then," I argued feebly.

"That might be overkill here." He gestured toward a great multicolored something or other that wobbled close to us, throwing off big, luminous blobs of neon oatmeal — and beyond that the whooping roar of the terrtrych. I shrugged. No argument; Lakavinland was trippier than orange sunshine.

So I was overruled and shamed into it and a few minutes later we were set up and plugged in. I looked out across the audience. In front were recognizable people – Aqualung, Oswaldo, Karen, Ratner, Esty, Head Charge, Jehovah, Liana and her leather goons. Beyond them, a chaotic throng of things and entities less easy to describe. And beyond them, the maelstrom of weirdness that was all around us.

"The name of this song," I announced, "is 'I Am You.'" I looked back at my band to make sure they were with me. They nodded and smiled.

You might not know this song. When the album first came out the track didn't get nearly as much airplay as some of the other tunes from *Six Songs*, but it was a well-crafted piece, if I do say so myself, and one of my favorites for very personal reasons.

The Tripper started the rhythm on the dumbek. It was fitting. The album version, as you may know, had a bongo intro and the single hand drum gave a nice variation. Trenton came in on keys, a bit of free jazz that flowed through the drumbeats like water down a rocky streambed. The intro left a lot of room for the roaring, tweeting, and whooping of Lakavinland to blend in. Dondelakavin dropped his hypno-disk and toy rat into the mouth of a giant toad and sat listening with an expression of extreme bliss. The throng shifted and morphed continually, though most of them did seem to be paying attention. It was only slightly more distracting than your average rock audience and perhaps slightly less distracting than playing to a rock audience while tripping on acid, which we did more than once back in the early days.

As the intro ran its course, I came in with vocals. The first part was spoken, slowly and with lots of space for Trent's piano to play through: "When I first saw you, I recognized you. Something about the way your hair moves in the breeze, the corners of your mouth crinkle when you smile, the way you push your hair back from your brow."

When I wrote those words, I was thinking about the first moment that I saw Jane. It was a memory, a few years old at the time. Now, forty-some-odd years later, the memory was just as vivid. I could see her face, as I did every time I heard or played "I Am You." Perhaps it was even easier now, because I'd seen the young Jane just a week or so ago, looking like she did when we first met. Her features, after all these years, were as familiar to me as my own. More so, because I spent so many years looking at her, not at myself. But that first moment that I saw her, backstage at the Fillmore, she seemed just as familiar, like I'd known her my whole life, as if time and memory were ass-backward and all the years to come cast their influence into the present.

The tune began to rock and I started building the guitar riff that would ultimately peak in the climax of the song. While percussion was scaled back to the single dumbek, Cleve and Perzanto were booming on bass and mrrlnx, the rhythm urging the audience to move. Trent wove a thread of Middle Eastern melody, actually a few bars of Moroccan music we heard while touring in Africa. We didn't have sax, but Birdie was filling in any possible empty space with soulful wailing. Feet tapped, heads bobbed, and all sorts of body parts – and various colorful, flashing transitional things – boogied to the beat.

I sang:
"Turn your ears my way
Tune in to vocal vibration
Each word takes you deeper
Every breath draws you in"
Birdie sang the next line, working it for every syllable.
"Deeper into the dance"
My line came next:
"Ev-er-y chance thought"
Then Birdie:
"Deeper into the trance"
And we sang togther:
"Everything turns on this moment"
If you've looked at the liner notes to *Six Songs*, you know that Jane had the lead writing credit for "I Am You." Other than the spoken word intro, the rest of the words were hers, but she never sat down intending to write a song.

As my fingers picked and slid along the strings, my mind wandered back to the summer of 1974, an arc of time I've highlighted in my memory again and again over many years. Blue Smoke had just returned from a fabulously successful world tour. One of many wonderful experiences while on tour happened during some days off in the Netherlands, when I fell in with a group of pothead hippies. In those days, there were no cannabis coffeeshops in Amsterdam, but there was still a thriving commerce in all things clandestine and a big community of mystic stoners. This particular group of denim and fringe-wearing freaks was enamored of a guru who claimed to be a genuine Shiva Sadhu from India. Sadhu Guru, as he was called, was a thin, dark-skinned fellow with dreadlocks down to the backs of his knees. He wore a rough and dirty piece of cloth, supposedly his only garment, though once when he bent into asana, the robe came open a bit and it looked like he was wearing a clean pair of BVDs. Anyway, Sadhu Guru's gig was teaching people how to smoke great big chillum pipes full of powerful ganja while meditating.

Now, I knew a lot of musicians who were into meditation. Three out of the four Doors met in a Transcendental Meditation class. The Beatles loved the Maharishi. Carlos Santana spent a lot of time raising kundalini with Sri Chinmoy; so did John McLaughlin. Pete Townshend was into Meher Baba. But somehow meditation never caught my interest. It was too passive, definitely too boring and, hell, if I wanted to relax and groove with the cosmos, I could just smoke a joint. But when Sadhu Guru explained his thing in halting, Dutch-accented English, I could suddenly see the appeal.

As my mind wandered in memory-time, Birdie sang the next part:

"When we were children dancing free
Perhaps when we were two or three
We knew the trance, we had the key
We just had to breathe, just had to be"

The song pulled me from my thoughts for a moment as we all sang together:

"And you call me and
I hear myself
And I call you and
You hear yourself"

As I continued to remember the origins of the song, each bit of memory seemed to feed into my playing. I felt haunted and full of mystery and the feelings were coming out of the little amp. The audience was transforming wildly, which I took to mean that they liked it.

Do you know what a chillum is? It's a kind of ganja pipe they use in India – and in Jamaica, too, sometimes – that's kind of like a narrow chalice or wine glass. It's a little bit of a juggling act keeping the thing vertical while you cup your hands around the stem to create a smoke chamber. With some practice, you can get huge hits, toking through the gap between your thumb and forefinger. It's a great way to get high, if you don't mind your hands smelling like a bong. Applying the chillum liberally, Sadhu Guru taught us the sounds to activate the chakras.

I didn't have a clue what a chakra was and I'm still not entirely sure. But, damn, smoking and chanting and feeling the energy in my body was fun. I got wonderfully, blissfully high. And when I got home, I wanted to share it with Jane.

My verse again:
"Turn your gaze on me
Focus on visualization
Every sight takes you deeper
Every breath makes it clear"
Birdie:
"Colors of the dance"
Me:
"Ev-er-y chance thought"
Birdie:
"Colors of the trance"
Both of us:
"Everything turns on this moment"
Jane sometimes came on tour with me, but I couldn't realistically expect anyone who wasn't being paid to sit through eighty or a hundred shows in a row, no matter how much they loved me. At this point in time, too, Jane was producing theater projects and needed

to stick around and shepherd them through to completion. So after all that time on the road, I was really glad to see her and wanted to show her all my souvenirs and tell her about every weirdo that I met in every strange and exotic city. I had a few tangible souvenirs — some trippy-looking lapis lazuli beads I'd picked up in London, a clean, unused chillum from Sadhu Guru, and some tour shirts from other bands we met along the way — but we always enjoyed experience over material stuff. I wasn't stupid enough to carry drugs of any kind through customs, so this chakra thing was a cool way to share my Sadhu Guru trip.

It was simple, really. There are seven chakras running in a line from the base of the spine to just above the top of the head. Like I said, I don't have a clue what they are, but I could still imagine them as glowing blobs of light right in front of me, with tails that went into me and connected to my spinal cord. The blob at the very base of the spine was red and the mantra was "Lam." A few inches above that, the chakra blob was orange and the sound was "Vam." At the solar plexus, it was yellow and "Ram." The heart chakra, in the center of the chest, was green and the sound was "Yam." The throat chakra was blue and the mantra was "Ham." Above that, the third eye chakra blob was indigo and the sound was "Aum." The crown chakra, on top of the whole shebang, as it were, was violet and was observed in silence.

Birdie sang:
"When we were children dancing free
Perhaps when we were two or three
We knew the trance, we had the key
We just had to breathe, just had to be"

Sadhu Guru's special technique involved a big blast from the chillum before chanting each chakra, imagining that the smoke was flowing into the colored blob. Then you would chant the appropriate sound at least three times before moving on to the next chakra. Practice by yourself was a great way to get extra high. Practicing with someone else gave the feeling of being strongly in tune with each other, vibrating together in a way that pumped up the blobs even more. So

Jane and I sat facing each other and I guided her through the meditation just like Sadhu Guru did for me.

Birdie and I harmonized:

"And you show me and

I see myself

And I show you and

You see yourself"

It was my turn to solo and I had some fun playing around with that Moroccan melody and then just rocking out, expressing a bit of chaos, before Trent had his turn.

So the chakra meditation with Jane was great. We broke in the new chillum with a bowl of Jamaican lambsbread, if memory serves. And by the time we got to the crown chakra, we were stratospheric. I watched Jane's face to see if she was delighted by this traditional (or so Sadhu Guru said) yoga technique. I suppose she was. She looked really blissed. And she started talking.

I had a tape recorder running through our session because I thought the chanting might be something fun to play with in the studio, so I had a complete record of what she said. She talked for about twenty minutes and each word she said got me higher and more involved, until, with just seven hits off a chillum, I was tripping like it was LSD. I felt totally connected to her; it was like her spirit, totally apart from her physical presence, pulled and gently guided me into another realm. In that realm, we flew over an endless plain at jet speed, as the essence of our beings seemed to swirl together. It was all quite recognizable as cannabis-inspired closed-eye hallucination, but really detailed and with a powerful full-sensory impact. And through it all: her gentle voice.

Oh, hell. I missed my cue to sing and had to wait for it to come around again. Trent filled in with another solo and the audience never noticed.

"Take my hand in yours

Feel the touch of excitation

Caress takes you deeper

Every breath swells your heart"

Birdie:
"Movement into the dance"
Me:
"Ev-er-y chance thought"
Birdie:
"Movement into the trance"
Duet:
"Everything turns on this moment"

Five or six years later, I played back the tape again and transcribed Jane's inspired words. They were as beautiful written as they were spoken, but there was no way I could use all of it. I had to pick and choose and pare it down to a few verses that would fit into a five or ten minute cut. I don't think the song captures the depth and intensity of the experience that Jane drew me into, but it's a good song.

Birdie sang:
"When we were children dancing free
Perhaps when we were two or three
We knew the trance, we had the key
We just had to breathe, just had to be"
I joined her with:
"And you touch me and
I feel myself
And I touch you and
You feel yourself"

My solo reprised and returned to the Moroccan melody and then we all dropped out except Trenton, who ended it with a burst of jazz, notes scattered in our wake.

Dondelakavin stood, applauding wildly. A few members of our own crew stood as well. The greater throng of relentlessly transforming entities cheered exuberantly and turned their transmogrification up to ten. Arms, legs, heads, hands and feet turned into flippers, tentacles, socket wrenches, tree branches and hors d'oeuvres. Families turned into fire hydrants, automobiles turned into Republicans and paisley dolphins danced on their tails and transformed into floating spheres of swirling light. They winked, they blinked, they clapped, they stomped, they whistled like steam engines, they flicked their lighters, and a few of them exploded. Blue Smoke has played for stranger audiences, but not many.

Dondelakavin cleared his throat and waved his arms, long red streamers trailing from his sleeves in a breeze that I could not feel. The crowd fell, well, not silent but they settled down a bit. In fact, it was *really* not silent, although the noise did not seem the fault of the crowd. Dondelakavin was practically shouting to be heard.

"Thank you, thank you, my friends." He continued to gesture grandly, really working the streamers. "I hereby formally welcome the members of Blue Smoke and all their colleagues and associates to Lakavinland!" He waved to include the whole crew of humans, felines and file-entities as he bowed deeply. "Partake of our bounty! Drink of our wine! Drive our luxury sedans!"

"Luxury sedans!" Birdie snorted.

"Could I get some kind of sandwich?" Captain Head Charge asked. "Maybe a cup of coffee?"

"You shall dine upon the fat of the land," Dondelakavin promised. "And if you don't like fat land, we can whip up a bowl of tofu and marmalade soup! Now everyone please rise for our national anthem!"

Some stood, some rose without standing. The Lakavinland national anthem sounded like a truck full of bricks and flowerpots falling off a cliff in a thunderstorm. And yet, it wasn't quite loud enough.

"Stop! Stop!" Dondelakavin yelled over the din. He removed his hat and cocked his head, listening. The anthem rumbled to a halt and we could all hear that the background noise level, the sound of the terrtrych, was now much, much louder. And coming closer.

Given the constant chaos of Lakavinland, I took it in stride. But Dondelakavin didn't.

"The terrtrych has come loose!" he shouted, flailing his streamered arms and running in a circle. "Who?! What?! Why?!"

"I take it that it's not supposed to do that," I said.

"No," Perzanto answered, "I don't think it is."

Dondelakavin closed on us and pointed at me. "What did you do?!" he demanded. "You played your song and it called the terrtrych! It's moving! How did you do that? I'm the only one who can move the terrtrych!"

"It was just a song," I said. "I don't know anything about your terrtrych."

"We'll be crushed! We'll be destroyed!" Dondelakavin yelled. "It's out of control!" He paused and took a breath. "Isn't this fun?"

The whistling, hooting and roaring of the terrtrych was very close now. The wall of the room, always in flux, was now fluxed up beyond all recognition. It seemed to bow inward, swirling, twisting and spinning off objects that changed too fast to even identify. And suddenly everything was moving and transforming much too fast to track.

"Run!" Dondelakavin called. "Run for your life! Run for *my* life! Ruuuuunnnnnn!"

He had a good point. Except that I didn't know where to run. It was like I'd been dropped into the middle of a busy Manhattan intersection at rush hour, without a car, and the traffic lights weren't working. Instead of cars and trucks, though, strange, twisting, changing forms barreled past me: A pink rhinoceros that was changing into an antlered, twelve-legged, thirty-foot long beetle; killer whales in a variety of pastel colors; a flock of whirring blenders that grew wings and sprouted Mickey Mouse ears; upside down canoes piloted by green naked women; a dentist drill as long as a javelin, trailing clouds of butterflies; an eyeball the size of a Volkswagen that burst open, showering us with tinkling gold coins. I dodged frantically and didn't seem to get very far in any direction. I was getting pretty damn tired, too. We'd come to Lakavinland to rest and, instead, it was one overly athletic adventure after another. When I was a kid, I might have enjoyed it, but now my arthritis was killing me, I was breathing really hard, and my ass was still sore.

"Hey! Over this way!" called a thin, reedy voice. I looked around, but in the confusion I couldn't see who was speaking. Hell, I'd totally lost track of any of my friends. "Quick!" the voice called. "This way!"

I took a step toward the voice and something small collided with my leg. I looked down; it was my little trollish assfriend, hanging onto my pants leg. A steel-toed work boot large enough to stomp me flat roared through, right where I'd just been standing.

"To the left now!" the little creature called. "Two steps. Now stop."

I followed his direction and boulders, flaming in neon colors, slammed and bounced past on either side of me.

"Forward now! Keep moving! And duck!"

I moved and ducked. Mayhem surrounded me and something with sparking, whirling blades roared over me. The sparks from the blades scattered onto the ground like buckshot from the Mossberg, narrowly missing me on all sides as the little creature guided me on a dodging path.

"Do you have a name?" I asked when I could catch my breath.

"Species name only," he told me. "Diverticulonium. Go ahead, name me. It seems right."

"Um, no," I protested. "I'd rather not."

The discussion paused as we dashed and turned through the confusion.

"Left," he ordered. "Left again, quick! Now back a step. Please name me?"

"You won't like it," I told him, ducking my head to avoid decapitation by a low-flying biplane covered with lampreys, piloted by a large turtle. The plane did a barrel roll, lampreys hanging on by their teeth, and disappeared into the mayhem.

"I'll like anything you suggest," the little guy said.

"Assfriend." It just popped out of my mouth.

We narrowly avoided collision with a herd of giant, rolling machine gears.

"Assfriend Diverticulonium." He tried it out. "Assfriend. It has a nice ring to it."

"All right. Then Assfriend you shall be. Um, Assfriend? I've got a couple questions."

"Ask away," the little thing chirped.

"Why are you doing this? Helping me like this?"

"You're family," he said. "There's a little bit of you in me – just like there was a little bit of me in you!"

"Nasty," I commented. "Next question: Aren't we going the wrong way? Shouldn't we be going *away* from the terrtrych?"

"Look!" Assfriend pointed up through a cluster of giant mutating berries. Something fluttered out from a gap in the chaos. Its skin was bubbling and shifting colors, bumps and complicated protrusions were forming on its little leathery wings. One horn seemed bent the wrong way. But it was unmistakably Don Speckler's devil.

"Aren't you looking for your friend?" Assfriend asked.

The giant berries morphed into even huger bowling balls and began slamming to the ground all around us. Assfriend guided me between them with a series of quickly barked orders.

"Is Don in there?" I asked when I had a chance.

"*In* there?" Assfriend shook his little head. "That *is* Don."

"No," I said. "It's the terrtrych."

"Same difference," Assfriend told me. "Now."

"How do you know this stuff?" I asked.

"Everything and everyone that is a part of this place," the little guy explained, "knows how everything else flows and changes. When your friend ate the terrtrych, we all knew it. Now we have to do something about it."

We dodged and ran further into the kaleidoscopic center of weirdness. The devil flew crazily above us, bouncing and tumbling between moving obstacles. If he were flesh and blood, I thought, he'd be hamburger. In a moment we saw the angel, too, clutching frantically to something that changed and twisted and morphed constantly. Hell, everything was changing constantly now, too fast to identify anything for more than a glimpse. The angel's wings were tattered, its halo askew, its white skin now dirty gray and lumpy.

Assfriend guided me through a bunch of things that exploded into mutating colored blobs before any of it took on definite form and there, all of a sudden, in front of us, was a human-shaped figure. Its skin, or whatever was where skin should have been, was a three-dimensional paisley that threw off colors and sparks and things that grew and changed and expanded. This was the apparent center of all weirdness; everything that churned and whizzed past us emanated from this being. It was shaped like Don, but about three times as large, and I couldn't make out any distinct facial features. As the weirdness moved and shifted around, though, I became quite convinced it was him. A shiny, metallic object lurked there in the confusion, revealing bits of itself as everything changed and flowed around it. It was a saxophone.

"You said that he ate the terrtrych?" I asked, dodging tons of flying mutation.

"That's right. Now duck and get over there." He pointed urgently.

"Don!" I called as I followed Assfriend's instructions. "Cut the shit!"

"Yeah," the angel called weakly from where it was being crushed between iridescent rotating blobs. "Cut the shit!"

Don turned fully in our direction, which was a problem because a whole lot of crap flew right at me. I managed to dodge most of it, but something struck me hard in the shoulder and I lost my balance, falling to my knees.

"Ian?" Don's voice was loud, but distorted and altered, like he was speaking through an effects processor.

"C'mon! Move!" Assfriend shouted. "Left! Now!"

I tried to get to my feet but I wasn't fast enough. Something hit me like a punch to the gut and, as I doubled over, something else slammed into my head. I went down. My field of vision filled with twinkly lights, there was a loud humming noise and everything went dark.

19. The Great Attractorizer

I woke up in bed, Bob curled by my side. I'd love to say that all was calm and well, but it wasn't very calm and my body was a mass of aches and pains. My head hurt like the time some moron on Quaaludes knocked a stack of amps onto me during a show in Philadelphia. The bed and the room seemed to be holding onto their functions for the time being, but I was still in Lakavinland and everything else was in flux. The background din, which in all fairness was considerably less than it had been in the presence of the terrtrych, was making my brain throb.

"You're awake," said the reedy little voice of Assfriend, who was resting against the side of my pillow. "Good thing, too, because that won't remain a bed for much longer." He gave a loud whistle and a shout. "Hey! He's awake!"

Trent was the first one in, followed by Birdie, Esty and Perzanto. Behind them, arms around each other's shoulders, came Dondelakavin and Don Speckler. Don looked more Don-like, although he was now wearing a moiré-patterned suit that changed color as he moved. The angel and devil were back in their rightful positions on his shoulders, even if they did look a bit wiped out. They clung to him and barely said a word.

"What the hell happened?" I asked. Bob stretched and raised his head.

"I'm so sorry," Don said. "As soon as I realized it was you, Ian, I pulled it way back. My control isn't perfect, yet. I hit the wrong notes here and there, but I'm learning. Check it out."

The color-changing whorls of his suit suddenly whorled and whirled in three dimensions, an aura of flowing chaos projecting at least a foot from his head and body. It flowed for a moment and then settled almost, but not quite, all the way back into Don.

"It's inside you?" I had to ask. "The terrtrych?"

He nodded. "I couldn't resist. I just had to… I had to…"

I got to the point. "What the fuck is that thing?"

Don tried to wrap some words around an explanation, but ended up scratching his mutating head and shrugging.

"You've heard of a strange attractor?" Dondelakavin asked. "The terrtrych is sort of like that."

"That's a math term, right?" I asked. "I don't get that kind of math. In simple terms, please? How is the terrtrych like a strange attractor?"

"It's strange," he told me.

"Yeah. And?"

"It's damn attractive."

"Do you really think so?" Don asked, extruding a swirl of weirdness.

There were a few non-committal murmurs. Don took it as a compliment and grinned ridiculously.

"Have you not learned the art of attraction?" Dondelakavin asked me. "A god such as yourself…"

"I'm not really a god," I explained.

"God or no," he said, "it is now time to arise. The rest of us have been up for hours and your bed is about to turn into something much squishier."

"Yeah," snickered Assfriend, "and smellier, too."

"Come with me," Dondelakavin said, "and I shall tell you the tale of the terrtrych."

I sat up, creakily swinging my legs over the side of the bed. Bob jumped to the floor. I stood carefully, feeling every sore muscle. I looked around for my gear. Esty held the Mossberg, which she handed to me. Perzanto had the guitar; he gently placed the strap over my head. Assfriend jumped from the bed onto the neck of the guitar case and clung there, grinning. I figured he'd saved my ass enough times to have earned a free ride and I refrained from swatting him onto the multi-colored, corroding floor.

"This way," said Dondelakavin, gesturing to the pulsating orifice that currently served as a door.

"I could really use a cup of coffee," I commented as I followed him toward the chaos that waited outside. Behind us, the bed turned to iridescent blue sludge and bubbled down into a conveniently-placed storm drain. The scent of hot vomit chased us from the room. "And a painkiller. Can we stop for a few tokes?"

"I am fond of the traditions of your civilization," Dondelakavin said. "It is all so exotic and wonderful. Bottomless cup of coffee! Supersize it! Tokes until your brains come out!" He shook his head, smiling. "I thought perhaps, lunch while we talk. Or, for you, breakfast. A schmoozing."

"A what?" Birdie inquired.

"A schmoozing. Where we talk with our mouths full."

"Breakfast sounds perfect," I said. "With the wake and bake special."

"One wake and bake special!" Dondelakavin crowed. "Coming right out! This way, please."

I followed him through ever-changing terrain to an impromptu outdoor café. A variety of natural features had adapted themselves to service as tables, chairs, plates and napkins. At Dondelakavin's invitation, I pulled a very comfortable tree stump up to a wide shelf of polished stone that balanced on boulders and giant mushrooms. Our party filled up the available seating, everyone crowding as close to Dondelakavin and me as they could. A seven-foot-tall chickenoid took our orders and served coffee with deft movements of her wing feathers. I started to crush a bud on the wide, floppy leaf that seemed to be my napkin.

"I have not always been this carefree and wild," Dondelakavin explained as I gulped hot coffee and started to twist a joint. "My culture was a very restrictive one. I had a very confined and narrow role to play and very few options to change anything."

"I find that hard to believe," Birdie commented.

"No, really," Dondelakavin protested. "We lived in a very conventional spheroid. We had a tarantula garden, a snapbox in every room, a white picket fence, big green eyeballs painted on the windows, a poochscraper and other trappings of traditional scoobootay life. Just like on all the snapbox pleasers. My life was very ordinary."

There were a few chuckles. "Doesn't sound very ordinary to me," Birdie said.

"Perhaps it loses something in translation. Didn't you all have the snapbox? The tarantula garden – it is the very symbol of the common human, totally scoobootay. Surely you understand the symbol of normalcy."

"The white picket fence," said Esty.

"No, no," Dondelakavin replied. "We were the only ones with pickets for fences. That was my family's one uniqueness, our claim to difference and we were ostrich seized by some. It is the only thing that kept me from going out of my mind with boredom, truly."

"Ostracized," corrected Perzanto. "I believe that is the correct English word."

Dondelakavin shook his head. "They seized three of my favorite ostriches." He sniffled. "I miss those ostriches even today, so many years later."

I pulled out my lighter and torched the doobie. "Conventional? Restrictive?" I asked between puffs. "Seems pretty weird and wonderful to me. I mean, spheroids, ostriches, tarantulas…"

Dondelakavin chuckled. "You are too funny. There are no tarantulas in a tarantula garden!"

"In my world," I said, "all that stuff would be pretty damn weird. But surely it couldn't have been that boring. There must have been some change from time to time."

I passed him the joint. He looked at it for a moment. A thin stream of smoke rose toward the multi-colored sky. "Change! Sure there was change, constant, stultifying, superficial change. *Everything* changed, except the things that really matter. Ah, but the things of the modern world, of your world, I dare say, seem pretty damn different and exciting to me. Free. Liberating. Extreme. I love it." He took a medium-sized toke, coughed politely, and handed the doobie to Trent.

"So there I was," he continued, "living each day the same, getting up, eating breakfast, climbing into my jumpgear to go to my laborium, making exciting genital reproductions for everyone else, but never finding any excitement for myself."

"You made genital reproductions in your labia?" asked Birdie. "I don't even know what that means."

"Laborium," Dondelakavin corrected. "Where everyone goes in the morning to engage in their societal obligation to produce value and worth and synthetic novelty items designed to induce sacred distractibility and holy commerce."

"Oh," said Birdie, "you mean your job!"

"Yes, and day after day, I put on my big green shirt and my stretchy purple pants and lined up with everyone else on the jumpway to go to my, as you say, job. The same route, every day, the same movements, all of us in green and purple – first the left leg, up, then the right leg, up, then the left leg down, then hop, hop, hop, then up, down, leg, leg…"

"The dance!" Don Speckler exclaimed. "The frog dance!" He got up, his suit swirling with green and purple, and performed a few steps of a country line dance.

"Yes! Yes!" Dondelakavin exclaimed. "That is a jumpway navigation sequence! Do that again."

Don seemed to grow larger, his suit jacket glowing green and his trousers blinking purple. He danced and Dondelakavin jumped in next to him, their steps synchronized. They looked like the backup band for an underwater Elvis impersonator. Most of us burst out laughing. But, hey, we were a little bit stoned by then.

The sax player and the lord of Lakavinland stopped dancing and grinned at each other. "That would have taken you to Outer Spoofield, if you began the sequence at the Less Than Central Station," Dondelakavin explained.

There were a few more giggles. The angel and devil, who had taken to the air during the demonstration, flapped their way back to Don's shoulders.

"What a loon," the devil commented, rolling his eyes at Don.

"Sheesh," said the angel. "You're not kidding."

Don ignored them. "My god," he said, staring at Dondelakavin. "You were one of my frogs!"

"Perhaps not me, specifically," Dondelakavin replied, "but people like me, all the little, uniform, froggy members of my society, trapped in their humdrum laborium ponds and their jumpway dances. Or so it seems, though I cannot guess how you traveled so far back in time to dance the Outer Spoofield commuter shuffle. That exit was combined with the Porvory Circle downjump when I was a teenager. And that was over fifteen thousand years ago!"

We all puzzled over that one for a few moments. The roach returned to me and, after a final puff, I set it on the saucer next to my coffee cup. The chickenoid, now a kind of buck-toothed dinosaur, topped us all off and took our breakfast orders.

"Well, now," the lord of Lakavinland continued. "You see how restricted and narrow my life was." I think most of us were a bit unsure on that count, but no one said anything. "So it was natural that when the Great Attractorizer appeared, offering a quest to redeem the world, that I should apply. I might have grasped at any opportunity to get out of that place, but the Great Attractorizer was so different than anyone I'd ever met, I was immediately fascinated by him. It seemed very, very right."

"The Great Attractorizer?" Trent asked. "Is he the same as the Master Inscriber?"

"I have heard Perzanto's tale," Dondelakavin said, "and I think it likely that they were allied beings, if not the same person altogether. I arrived here five thousand years after Perzanto. If the Great Attractorizer was the Master Inscriber, he would have been very old."

"You're fifteen thousand years old," I reminded him. "Or so you say."

"Indeed," Dondelakavin nodded. "And it was the Great Attractorizer who bestowed long life upon me and the others who were to meet in the resonant chamber, so it would have been within his power, I would imagine."

"Feh," Birdie scoffed. "Everybody here has a story about being fifteen thousand years old, twenty thousand years old, or knocking around since the beginning of time. It's pretty freaky down here and it sure might seem like it was twenty thousand years, but I think you're all tripping."

Tim, who was lying at her feet, made a small growl and tucked his head under a paw like a catcher's mitt.

The buck-toothed dinosaur returned with food. She slid an omelet and home fries in front of me, with a side of toast, and a plate full of jiggly blue and orange cubes for Dondelakavin.

The lord of Lakavinland grinned at his food, stuffed a bit in his mouth and spoke as he chewed. "I thought I was, as you say, tripping, when I first met the Great Attractorizer. In fact, I was hallucinating a bit from the salad I had with dinner, but I was used to that. The cosmic herbs and fungi were half the fun, as the salad vendors were always reminding us. 'Melts your mind, not your mouth'." He chuckled, a little bit of blue food dribbling back onto his plate. "And I'd had a few drinks, but those don't usually make me hallucinate. And some Chi Bah, of course, though it was not nearly as fine as yours." He nodded toward the roach, deceased beside my coffee cup. "Also, I may have swallowed a handful of confusion nuggets. It was so long ago, and I was so confused, it's hard to remember, which makes me suspect that I did. It was a regular evening, really, and I may have doubted my senses at first, but I know what I saw."

He forked a jiggly orange cube and aimed it into his mouth with the ceremony and precision of spaceships docking. We waited. The stone expanse of the table turned to wood, then transformed into imitation wood-grain vinyl. I worked on my home fries.

"What did you see?" Aqualung finally croaked.

"Yeah, dude," said Bob, looking up momentarily from a saucer of salmon. "I was wondering if you were tripping right now."

"Well, I saw the Great Attractorizer," Dondelakavin said around a blob of orange mouth-meal. "Didn't I say that already?"

"You may have," I said.

"He came out of nowhere," Dondelakavin continued. "I was leaning against a wall out behind some laborium structures, slightly out of my brain from all the salad and the other stuff. Suddenly there was a sound like an enormous bleemer and…"

"What's a bleemer?" the devil yelled. The angel shushed him.

"You know, when your ass wind makes that sound like *bleeeeeeeem?*"

"Feh," said Birdie.

The angel and devil, and several humans, giggled. Aqualung grinned and nodded.

"I don't think my ass makes that sound," I said.

"You're a bunch of children," Birdie proclaimed.

"So there was this sound," Dondelakavin went on, "and a big burst of yellowy light, and this guy tumbles to the ground, from out of thin air. He was a tall, skinny fellow with a little bit of a beard. He wore a shiny suit and a silvery cape. Very conservative, I mean. I wasn't too impressed at first. He fell down in a heap and stood up slowly, with many curses.

"'Oh, hell,' the skinny guy says. He looks up at me and his eyes get wide for a moment. 'Oh, it's you,' he tells me, as if I didn't know I was me. 'Am I here already?' he asks, as if the answer weren't perfectly obvious. 'Okay,' he says, 'I hope I can remember how to do this.' And he starts squinting at me and pointing his finger, waving it around.

"'What are you doing?' I ask him.

"He lowers his finger and says, 'I'm not doing it right, am I? Oh, yes, I was supposed to explain to you about the quest, first.' And he goes on to explain about the six beings and the resonant chamber and all that. He told me there was a hole in the ground near a Valley of Very Fucking Thorny Plants with Little White Flowers. He told me it was near a river, but the fellow did not seem to know where he was and couldn't say whether or not the entrance to the resonant chamber lay on the same continent where we stood or another. He explained that he was collecting delegates, men and women who were like unto gods, for an unprecedented adventure. I protested that I could not be one of the sacred beings, that I was just an ordinary person wearing ordinary, everyday jumpgear, having eaten an average amount of herb salad.

"'You play an instrument, right?' the guy wants to know and I tell him that I play several, but mostly the lipsquacker. 'And you do some kind of magic, turning one thing into another?'

"I scratched my head, hoping that the confusion nuggets would wear off, that is, if I took some. And if not, I was hoping that this strange character would make a little more sense. 'I make no magic,' I said. 'And the only things I turn one into another are the reemslabs at work, which I turn into finished product, genital reproductions for novelty purposes only. I create an attractor and the 'slabs flow into form. It is the usual method.' I began to explain the technical specifications of my job, how attractors draw the reemslabs into their final form and how I create the attractors based on the various templates… but he interrupted me.

"'It doesn't matter,' the man said. 'I know you. Just fucking hold still a moment.'

"'Wait!' I said. 'Who are you?'

"'I am the Great Attractorizer!' he told me and then he aimed his finger and I changed.

"It felt like some kind of luscious explosion inside me, a little painful but also very pleasant at the same time. I groaned and then laughed as I felt the transformation spread through me, my cells and organs changing, growing, adapting. I became a little bit larger, my muscles thicker and stronger. My heart pumped more powerfully and when the feelings finished with my brain, I could think more easily, more clearly, with more detail and complexity. The world seemed sharp, bright, colorful and harmonious. If I had taken confusion nuggets, they were gone from my system. I understood with my entire being the course that was laid out before me, my impending future as easy to bring into consciousness as my recent memories. Easier, even. And in my future memories, I had powers and abilities that I'd never dreamed of. These were things I could not understand, but knew that I eventually would.

"I was amazed and impressed by these changes and sudden mental clarity. A new man, I could feel my destiny pulling me forward, as if a huge attractor of some kind waited for me in the future, just beyond where I could see, drawing my life into a pattern. I knew that this was the experience I hoped for, a change from my stultifying, repetitive life, a transformation of my self and the world. No longer would I have to line up on the jumpway only to repeat my daily behavior so that I could have snapboxes in every room. I'd always had the feeling that something important would happen and save me from my nowhere life and this was, most certainly, it.

"'Yes!' I exclaimed. 'Yes! I accept your quest!'

"'Oh, that's good,' the Great Attractorizer told me. 'I'll see you when you get there.'

"I had questions for him, but there was another bleemer and then I was alone behind the laborium. Somewhat dazed, I returned home. But the next morning, instead of heading onto the jumpway, I packed up a few essential items and walked, like a human being and not, as you say, like a frog. With my new form and my new powers, it was easy to convince several friends to throw in on the venture and come along for the journey. The Great Attractorizer gave me an incomprehensible map and scant clues to find the Valley of Very Fucking Thorny Plants and the resonant chamber, but I knew that I would recognize the place when I saw it.

"Individual vehicles were rare in the era of the jumpway, but one of my friends had an antique floater that he worked on as a hobby. Six of us jammed into the cabin of the tiny flying machine and we set off in search of the Valley. We lifted off and rose high above the lines of, yes, froglike people hopping along on the narrow paths of their lives. For twenty years we traveled the face of the Earth, learning of the many and diverse societies scattered about the planet. I asked many questions and became an expert on local plants, particularly those with thorns and white flowers.

"During our travels, there was plenty of time to fill up as we flew from one place to another. My mind had fixed on some of the things that the Great Attractorizer said to me. One that obsessed me was his question about transforming one thing into another. I did that at the laborium, yes, and there seemed little significance to this. Partly, I did not want ever to do that again, because it reminded me so much of the hated life I'd left behind. However, I was curious that the Great

Attractorizer would consider that a qualification to undertake the quest. So one day, in the boredom of a long flight, I turned a small piece of cheese into an equally small granite statuette of a duck. It was very simple: I created an attractor and drew the cheese into the form of the duck. And I realized that along with whatever other powers the Great Attractorizer had bestowed upon me, these simple transformations were now much more intense to even contemplate, and they felt very, very easy to do. I knew instantly that I could do transformations that would have been impossible only weeks previously.

"I also knew that my abilities were in their infancy and I would develop them in the years to come. In fact, I knew something else. I knew that my powers would be very great at some point many, many years in the future. And that, far in the future, I would have the ability to create an attractor that would draw me to it, that would pull me toward the Valley of Very Fucking Thorny Plants. Eventually, I was able to sense this future attractor and follow it to the cave entrance and down here to the Pool of Shebangs."

"The terrtrych?" I asked. I'd been waiting for Dondelakavin's tale to wind itself back around to the subject at hand. "Was that the future attractor?"

"Yes!" he exclaimed. "How did you guess? I knew a few things about the terrtrych right away. I knew it had to be extremely powerful and that it would help if it could remain in existence a very long time. And also that it would be very, very different from anything else that has ever existed. It needed to stand out in its very difference. It appealed to me that I might create such a magnificent thing, and I had a very compelling idea of the future to move toward.

"Following the pull of the terrtrych, I located the Valley of Very Fucking Thorny Plants and descended into the cave, where I met Perzanto and came to the Pool of Shebangs. When I learned that we might wait yet many years until we could play our song in the resonant chamber, I found a welcoming shebang and set up shop. I knew that the terrtrych would exist one day because if it never did, I wouldn't even be there. I devoted my life to understanding the transformation process and creating meta-attractors, large scale systems of attractors that can alter the shape of space and time. My optimism held for many years, but the years moved on a very, very long time. I worked even harder, with grim determination. It was nearly a thousand years before I mastered the simplest form of meta-attractor and five hundred more before I created the terrtrych.

"The terrtrych was an interesting novelty when it first blurped into existence. Undeniably powerful, undeniably different. I could not have guessed how it would start to throw off transforming objects. In reality it constantly forms attractors, at random or based on some very obtuse pattern. The patterns draw any matter nearby into the shapes of the attractor which, as it comes into physical form, falls away from the terrtrych. So it seems like it is constantly extruding things. This was somewhat of a problem. I had to remember not to bring anything that I valued, or any friends near the terrtrych. All of them would be transformed. With every bit of matter it contacted, the terrtrych seemed to gain energy, to grow in size and intensity. And every bit of matter that was drawn into it and cast out as something else would be drawn in yet again, as the terrtrych grew in size. And every other bit of matter that it encountered was similarly added to it so that it grew and grew even more. It began to take over more and more of the shebang. As it got larger, it also grew in complexity and the forms that it cast off were sometimes alive and fully sentient. A society of sorts evolved and re-evolved, moment by moment, and you are now here within it."

Dondelakavin gestured broadly at the café, which, as we finished our food, was turning into a large, flashy boutique. There was a smattering of applause.

"I could hold the terrtrych in position using sophisticated equipment that I created. But I could not keep it from growing. I did not know what would happen when it swallowed the whole shebang. Would it continue on and devour the Pool itself and the world and universe beyond? Would everything become crazy with transformation? I must admit that the idea had its appeal, but even I had to question the potential cost. I mean, everything near the terrtrych loses its value. By the very fact that something might be something else by the time you are ready to use it, it cannot be sold for any fixed amount. How do you set a price for a loaf of bread that might be underwear or dishwater in twenty minutes? Things in the zone of transformation have value only in what they can be used for now. If you have bread, you must eat it or hope that what it turns into will be equally useful — and, of course, most often it is not. You cannot save money, because it won't be money. You cannot own real estate, because it will certainly be surreal estate. You can't grow tomatoes because they might sprout into waffle irons. It has been a fine world for me to live in, but I have been here for fifteen thousand years. Now the terrtrych is tamed. Don, the boy who could traverse space and time in his dreams, can swallow and even control the attractor of space and time. It is a wonder, a miracle. And I am free."

"I think," said Don Speckler, "that I like it here very much. I want to stay."

"And I want to go," Dondelakavin said.

"What kind of instrument is the lipsquacker?" I asked.

Dondelakavin concentrated his attention and, with a small whoosh, his silverware and napkin turned into a small, complicated wind instrument. It was made of shiny chrome and covered in tiny tubes and valves. Dondelakavin raised the nipple-like mouthpiece to his lips and wailed a jazzy fanfare. It sounded like a cross between a saxophone and a French horn.

"Can you play the blues?" Trent asked.

20. Town

Dondelakavin led us on a short journey to a "place" where brightly-finned toaster ovens played in a shimmering blue lake. A short flight of stone steps led to an arch beyond which was nothing, a fall to the beach. Dondelakavin led us up the steps, pointed to the arch and with a muffled thump reality separated and we stepped through to the Pool of Shebangs. All of us except Don, the angel and the devil. Don stayed behind to be the new Lord of Lakavinland. The angel and devil were his brain trust.

I was a bit turned around. The forest of bright columns surrounded us. They all looked the same and I wasn't sure if I could detect a slight downhill slope, or if it was my imagination. "Which way?" I asked Perzanto.

"We should collect Beezel and Bernard," the big guy said, "and then continue directly to the resonant chamber." He looked around. Our entourage was still emerging from the shebang, a process being observed by a small company of Liana's guards and a motley crew of entities in a dozen different styles of costume. Perzanto pointed in what seemed, to me, an arbitrary direction. "Beezel's shebang is this way, a short walk."

"So, we're close now?" I asked.

"Oh, yes," Perzanto affirmed, "very close."

As we started in the direction that Perzanto indicated, there was a deep rumbling vibration that grew louder and louder. Remember that old movie where they simulated an earthquake with big Cerwin-Vega concert subwoofers? It was like that, except the vibration rapidly escalated to more violent movement of the ground, accompanied by rattling and crashes from all around. It felt like someone was shaking the wide bowl of the Pool, shaking it like it was a pie tin. The columns of light moved along with the stone floor, though more slowly, which was an odd effect. The floor rose and fell, pitched and tilted, and the columns kind of swayed after it. Everything in the Pool that was not bolted to the rock was tossed like salad. Boulders, chairs, bales of unknown cargo, pocket change, fruit, luggage and tons of other crap bounced and rolled, boomed and clattered around us. I was knocked to the floor at the first tremor, falling in a heap along with Perzanto, Oswaldo and Aqualung. In spite of the stench of Aqualung's moldy gray jacket, we clung to each other and were able to stand, more or less, and move on without getting slammed to the ground too often.

"It's the Scrambler!" Liana shouted, on all fours, scrabbling for purchase. "Run! Uh…" As she tried to get to her feet, a very large shipping crate of packaged cheese slammed into her chest armor with surprising force, knocking the wind out of her. She tumbled into the bouncing debris, another piece of flotsam among the jetsam. Several of her guards dived after her and were also deflected and knocked about. I quickly lost sight of them in the chaos.

"This way!" Perzanto gestured frantically and we tried to make our collective, stumbling progress in the direction he indicated. I kept my head down and let Perzanto do the navigating. It must have been only a few minutes, but it seemed like hours of rumbling and abuse before the big guy indicated a particular column of light. "I'm not sure," he began. "I think this one…" He was cut off by something really big that slammed into us from behind and we tumbled over each other into the shebang.

I landed on cool, soft sod, which was certainly preferable to landing on anything harder. Unfortunately, Perzanto, Oswaldo and Aqualung landed on top of me. The guitar case and shotgun banged against me painfully but they also protected me from the sharp corner of the little amp formerly strapped to Oswaldo's back. Assfriend was knocked from the guitar strap where he'd been clinging, and snagged the amp as he fell. He held on and bounced with it. When everything finally came to rest, we untangled ourselves and dodged as other members of our troupe fell to the ground with ballistic force. Birdie appeared, followed by the cats. Tim came to earth in a long, graceful arc and Bob made a perfect four-point landing, digging his claws into the turf. Trenton, Dondelakavin, Esty, Karen and Mark Ratner plopped through in a big, groaning heap. The Tripper fell directly on top of them. Then Captain Head Charge landed on The Tripper. And finally, from a puff of luminous smoke, Jehovah strolled nonchalantly to join us.

"Where's Cleve?" I asked.

"He went after Liana," the old storm god said. "I lost track of them during the earthquake."

"Do you really think it's safe to leave him alone with her?"

Jay stroked His beard, the glow around His head brightening. "Hmmm. Maybe you're right. I'd better go. Remember, if you need Me, you only have to pray." There was another puff of luminous smoke and He disappeared.

As I stood and brushed bits of dirt and grass from my jeans, I could see that we were in the middle of a wide expanse of lawn bounded on three sides by tall boxwood hedges. The sky was blue with a few wisps of high altitude cloud, the air warmed by a bright yellowy sun. Birds were singing, squirrels darted nervously under the boxwoods, and a rattling Model A Ford lurched toward us over the sod.

The car was a real jalopy, of a kind that was already nearly extinct when I was a kid. Our movies and TV shows told us that teenagers had these old relics from the 1920s and '30s, held together with straps and coat hangers. But mostly, by the 1960s, any surviving Model A Fords were in the hands of collectors or had undergone metamorphosis into enamel and chrome hot rods. This one wasn't pretty, but it was running, which was enough of a miracle. It was thoroughly dented and sported a fringe of rusted-out metal filigree around the edges. It had more rust and holes than my old Datsun did just before I junked it in 1973. The back end of the Model A had been converted to a flatbed, thick planks attached to the chassis with big, crudely-wrought bolts. It had another option not included in the standard package: a custom paint job. Actually, it looked more like graffiti, two symbols hand-painted over the oxidation and ancient paint-flecks of the car's hood. The first and larger graffito was a simple figure: two green lines meeting at an acute angle, a narrow A without the crossbar. Just behind that one, verging on the windshield, was an uneven ellipse in brown, a line-drawing of a very short earthworm or a perfect turd, barely visible against the dirt and rust. A man in a wide-brimmed felt hat grinned at us from behind the steering wheel.

We were still straightening up and taking inventory when the old car clattered to a stop. With a creak of the ancient, bent door, the driver climbed out and joined us. His clothing was homespun but with dressy pretensions. He wore a brown suit jacket-type thing with long tails, a flamboyant blue bowtie, and thick, brown, woolen trousers. Slung around his neck were various chains, strings, and lanyards suspending a glittering array of medallions and talismans. He doffed his hat and greeted us with a hearty, "Howdy, new neighbors!"

We glanced at each other, but no one commented. I figured "new neighbors" was a local custom or catch-phrase, just as we might call complete strangers "partner" or "buddy," or address letters for people we don't really know or like to "Dear."

"Oy there," Aqualung tried.

The man took a long stride toward Aqualung, his hand extended for a manly, confident shake. Aqualung raised his hand tentatively; it was immediately crushed and pumped athletically. As the old sot rubbed his bruised hand, eyeing the Ford driver suspiciously, the man said, "Are you the leader of this fine band of settlers? Is this all of your stuff here? It ain't much. Do you serve Mystery, Mastery, Sex or Drugs?"

"I like all those things," Mark Ratner offered. "But I think of myself more as a consumer rather than a server."

The man looked perplexed. "I mean, what do you do for a living? Are you farmers or weavers, root workers or lubers?"

"We're musicians," I said. "And our road crew."

The fellow turned toward me, extending his bone-crushing hand. I ignored it. "Musicians?" he echoed. "Musicians? Well, that's a first."

"Don't you have music?" I asked.

"Sure, but can't everyone do their own singing? I mean, except for in the Time of Prophecy, when the goddess shall sing for us all."

There was a moment of silence as we tried to figure that one out. "This goddess," Perzanto finally asked. "Is her name Beezel?"

The man fiddled nervously with his bling, but replied mildly. "We each call her, in our own hearts, by the name most dear to us."

It was another stumper of a statement. After a moment, Perzanto persisted. "Yes, indeed," he said, "but what does she call herself?"

"Oh, ho," the man chuckled. "Ha ha." He held one of his medallions, a large brass disk engraved with a series of those turd cartoons, and waggled it at Perzanto. "Very good. You are a theologian?"

"No, no," Perzanto explained, shaking his big head. "I'm a mrrlnx player on a quest. We were looking for the shebang of the goddess Beezel. If that is the name of your goddess, then we have come to the right place. If not…"

"And what is your reason for seeking this goddess?" the man inquired.

"We are her friends," said Dondelakavin. "From way back."

The man eyed Dondelakavin for a moment, as if he'd never seen sequins and spandex before. He polished a small replica turd that hung from a leather strap and tapped several times on a wooden square that bore, shellacked to its surface, an image cut from a magazine of a tube of some kind of ointment. Then he grinned. "We are all friends of the goddess, of course!" he exclaimed. "So it is said! My name is Alkashazar, but everyone calls me Buick. I serve Mastery and I drive this here Welcome Wagon." He looked around at us, giving each person or entity a toothy smile. "Come on, then. Load your gear onto Alice here. Don't got room for more than one passenger, but I can at least tote your stuff for you. Come on. Town's only a mile or so yonder. The road's a bit rough and Alice can't go much faster than a trot. You all can walk along behind and we'll be there in no time."

I was hoping that Perzanto would ride shotgun, as he had a slightly better chance of gleaning information from Buick and determining if we were even in the right shebang. Alas, the seats of the ancient car weren't nearly big enough for the hulking god.

Dondelakavin smiled and took a step forward, but Buick avoided eye contact with him and looked at me. I was elected.

Alice the Model A bumped and groaned across the field, jostling my aching bones. With the band and crew strolling behind, we turned onto a deeply-rutted dirt road. The narrow tires of the Ford jolted from one rut to another and I kept checking back to make sure our gear wasn't bouncing off the flatbed. To either side, small farms and woodlots slid jerkily past.

"How come they call you Buick?" I shouted over the clatter and rumble. "I mean, when you drive a Ford?"

"A Ford's a kind of Buick," the man said. "Ain't it? And this here Ford is the only Buick we've got. Only one this side of the Baraquenderos, anyway. By the way, that's a real fine fowling piece you got there."

"Thanks," I said. "It's a Mossberg 500. 12 guage. Pump action."

"Pump action," he repeated. "And what you got in that funny-shaped case that you wouldn't load with your other stuff?"

"It's my instrument," I said. "An electric guitar."

"Electric, you say? Like, it's motorized? Does it play all by itself?"

I looked at him for a moment. He was focused intently on keeping the Ford on the road, which was not an easy feat. His question appeared sincere.

"Uh, no," I said. "I have to play it. It just makes it sound better."

"Well, that must sound something awful special, all that electricity zapping around in there." He suddenly hit the brakes and when the car finished shuddering to a stop, he looked at me. "It's not the Devil's work, now, is it?"

"No, no, of course not," I said hastily. "In fact we, um, left the Devil behind in the last shebang."

He stomped on the clutch, wiggled the gear shift, applied his right foot to the accelerator and we were rolling again. "I sure am glad to hear that you left the Devil behind," Buick said.

I refrained from mentioning the angel, as I thought it might confuse matters. And I wasn't going anywhere near the topic of Jehovah. "I've got something else in the guitar case," I said, working my best gambit to change the subject. I opened the clasps.

"What's that?" Buick asked as I pulled out a handful of buds. "Oh! Well. Everyone likes a bit of the herbs now and then," he told me, fidgeting with a desiccated root that hung from a chain among his other bling, "but best you keep that out of sight, unless you want the brigade to take it from you. You're purely lucky I ain't on such good terms with the b-men."

"Right," I said. "It's kind of like that where we come from, too."

"I sure wouldn't mind a taste of them herbs, though," Buick continued. "I haven't seen none of that in two-three months."

"My pleasure," I said, extracting a king-size rolling paper. I crushed a fragrant bud and twisted it up. Raising the doob to my lips, I patted my pockets, looking for my lighter.

"Allow me." Buick held up a small, brass talisman and, with a snap, the end of the joint glowed red-hot. I toked, nodding my thanks.

"You know," he said a few minutes later, exhaling a deep toke, "for a bit of this kind of herb, I'd be happy to put you all up in my barn 'til you can get your own place built."

"That's very kind of you," I told him. "But we're just here to find Beezel. We'll be moving on immediately, as soon as we figure out which way to go. Hell, this might not even be the right shebang."

"I'm not sure what you mean," Buick said, swerving around a boulder in the middle of the road. "Shebang?"

"This place," I said. "Your world. We came from the Pool of Shebangs, where there are many, many worlds like this."

"I think I know of what you speak." He took another big hit, held it for a little while and then exhaled. "Others, like you, come here from time to time, appearing in the hedges back there. I meet them all, you know, and hear their stories. Most come to stay, to settle, to make a life under the guidance of the goddess. Some, however, talk about 'getting back' or 'going home' as if it were possible to leave the world.

Darned if I know where they get those ideas. We are born or shoved into this place but only death can take us away, I believe." His hand groped through his talismans, finally finding a metal version of one of those acute-angle things. He stroked it with his thumb.

"We were in another shebang," I offered, "and there was a way out, back to the Pool. A set of steps that led up to a doorway and…" I paused here for my own toke. "Surely this place has an exit, too. A magic doorway, a wormhole, a transdimensional portal, a chrono-synclastic infundibulum. Whatever."

"Well, we have stories like that," Buick told me. "But they're only stories. I mean, I believe in the goddess, sure, everyone does, even though we never ever see her. But the story about her palace in faraway Klod where the world splits open and the chosen are taken to a better world – that's a story to keep the children at their chores. And people might have been telling that story for a long, long time, but it don't mean it's true. It don't mean we got to take it all literal." He suddenly looked around, a moment of cannabis-fueled paranoia. "You won't tell anyone I said that, will you?" he asked.

"It's okay," I reassured him. "If anyone asks, I'll swear that you believe in the goddess, Santa Claus and Bugs Bunny, too."

"Bugs…?"

"Never mind," I told him. "You're okay with me. It's none of my business what you believe. I've seen some shit. I'm not one to judge."

He stared at me. I gestured toward the road, hoping he'd take a hint and keep his eyes there. He didn't. We jolted over a series of potholes and rocks. I checked back to see if we'd lost any gear. "You sure are a very strange sort of person," Buick told me.

"Faraway Klod," I said. "Which way is that?"

"It's a story. A legend." He still wasn't looking at the road. He either knew this stretch of road well enough to get away with it or fate was somehow on our side. We kept bumping along and didn't hit anything large enough to stop us.

"Which way does the legend say?" I persisted. "Just point."

"Far to the west," Buick pointed to our left. "The legend says very far to the west."

"You'll have to tell me that legend some time," I said. "But for now, can you give me some highlights? How far to the west does the legend say?"

"There are a few versions of the story," Buick explained. "Some say many days, some say many months, and some…"

"I get the idea," I said. "Klod is far away."

"Even farther since it don't rightly exist." He returned his attention to the road where we rattled toward a collection of single-story wooden buildings that approximated a town.

"As far as my own beliefs go," I told him, "up until a few days ago, your whole world – and thousands of others – didn't rightly exist. Nor did half my friends. And my cat couldn't talk. I've bet my life on legends a couple times now and at this point – legend, reality, stories, myths, life – it's all becoming the same."

"Well, of course your cat couldn't talk." He chuckled and shook his head. "Like I said, you really are a strange sort of person."

With much creaking and thumping, Buick guided the Ford onto a wide avenue of lumpy dirt that served as Main Street and parked in front of a small general store. The store was right out of a depression-era movie version of rural America. Like the several other buildings there in the heart of town, it was built of splintery gray, weathered wood. Stripped logs supported the roof of a rickety front porch. Three large, enormously-horned ox-like creatures bearing saddles were tied to the logs, their coarse-haired hide damp and sweaty in the sunshine. Miscellaneous merchandise was stacked along the front of the porch: shiny metal buckets, various iron hooks and bolts, wooden bird houses that looked as if they'd been there for decades, and brown burlap sacks labeled "winter fuel" and marked with that turd-like symbol. Seated on a long plank bench against the front of the store were two old men and a middle-aged woman.

I gingerly climbed out. The aches and pains were starting to add up: our indecorous arrival added a few new scrapes and bruises to my already quite extensive collection. My ass, much abused recently, had endured another kicking from the worn, pre-ergonomics seat of the Model A.

"Hey new neighbor, you look a little saddle sore," commented an ancient galoot dressed in threadbare, faded denim. "Old Alice can be rough on the posterior."

The other faded coot and the woman laughed uproariously.

"You'll never get me in that thing, Buick," the woman said.

"Aw, you know Gertie won't let me get no other woman, in the motorcar or anywhere else!" Buick replied and they all guffawed like it was the funniest thing anyone ever said. I figured that professional comedians were as rare here as career musicians. If their attempts at homespun singing were anything like their jokes, we'd blow their minds with just our B material.

The rest of our party straggled up, most of them looking a bit weary.

"Had a nice ride?" Birdie asked me.

I rubbed my ass. "Yeah, sure."

"You folks got any money?" Buick wanted to know.

"I've got nothing," I said. Other members of our group shrugged or pulled wads of dollars from their pockets.

Buick glanced at the legal tender and instantly dismissed it. "It's okay. New neighbors never do have any money. We allow for that. But the town elders'll expect you to start pulling your weight on the morrow, if you stay in town. What are your skills?"

"Like I said," I reminded him, "we're musicians. I play guitar and sing. Trenton over there plays keys. Perzanto plays the bass, sort of. Dondelakavin plays the, er, something or other. Birdie sings. The Tripper drums. The rest are our support crew. Management. Roadies. Friends."

"How do you make any money singin'?" the galoot wondered.

"Good question," I said. "It depends on the venue."

"What's a venue?" asked the coot.

"A concert hall," I tried. "A nightclub. A, uh, tavern?"

"We have us a real nice tavern," said the woman. "But we do our own singing there."

"It'll be fine," Buick interjected. "We'll find you some good jobs where you can sing if you feel the urge. Always a call for farmhands around these parts. In the meantime, it's our tradition to feed and house our new neighbors 'til the morrow when you can find work and start building your own houses. Or decide to leave town, if that be your will. You'll have dinner with us tonight, then later we can go down to the tavern and you'll hear how good our singing is."

We split up, a few of us going with Buick, a few going with the galoot, and a few heading off to stay with the coot and the woman who, it turned out, was the coot's daughter. I was in the group who passed the afternoon at Buick's place, a low, rambling conglomeration of shacks that all ran into each other. Aqualung and Karen helped Buick's wife, Gertie, in the kitchen, peeling potato-like vegetables, chopping onions and scrubbing her big, black iron pots. I smoked a joint with Esty and Trent and then took a long nap.

When I woke, there was still some time before dinner and I wandered around a bit. The shebang looked mostly Earth-like, though there were a few trees and plants that I couldn't identify. There was a small blacksmith shop where Buick worked on Alice and repaired assorted tools, a wood shop where a few odd pieces of furniture were in the process of repair, a kitchen garden full of half-grown veggies and herbs, and a medium-sized barn with one of those ox things, six goats, a large flock of assorted birds, and several pieces of hand-operated machinery, purpose unknown.

Dinner began with much waving of talismans – all these people were festooned with sigils and amulets and were quick to wiggle one in your face. The food, though, was supremely satisfying and that wasn't just because of the weed and near-starvation. Gertie could throw down some chow. There were roasted strips of chicken – or something that tasted like chicken – encrusted with chili peppers and poppyseeds. These rested on a bed of multi-colored grain, something like wild rice if rice were red, purple and orange. Piles of round, green pea-like vegetables tasted more like avocado than legumes. There was hot soup that was like a cross between squash and melon, and big bowls full of little crispy bits that went well with everything.

We spent most of the meal complimenting Gertie and in between Buick told a long-winded tale about how, when he was younger, he drove Alice for two whole hours away from town and had a fine adventure. It gave him the distinction of being the only person in town ever to have traveled so far. He saw wonders on his journey, too; in a town near the extreme end of his path where no one had ever even heard of a motorcar, at least not in a way that they believed, they had built a great flying machine powered by the nethermost exhalations of the ox-like beasts. I decided that I didn't want to think about that too much.

Trenton countered this with some tales of the touring life, including a story about how someone spiked the wrong coffee dispenser backstage at a show in New Haven and the entire concert security team tripped their brains out and danced naked on the stage for two days. Buick and Gertie chuckled politely but I don't think they quite appreciated it.

"I still don't quite get how whole stadiums full of people would pay you money so you'd sing for them. I can hardly even imagine what that is, a stadium, but I mean, having someone else do the singing for you, that's like watching someone have sex," Buick speculated.

"What's wrong with that?" Aqualung inquired.

"Sex ain't no spectator sport," Gertie pointed out, waving a spoon for emphasis.

"Try telling that to ten million Internet users," Esty said.

Buick shook his head. "You folks sure do have a funny way of speaking."

"Isn't there anyone who can sing really, really well, that you enjoy listening to?" Esty inquired. "I mean, someone who sings even a little bit better than everyone else?"

Gertie and Buick looked at each other and shrugged. "We all sing pretty good," Gertie explained. "Ain't nobody sitting back and listening to anybody else. When it's singing time, everybody sings. Mystery, Mastery, Sex and Drugs."

I was thinking that those might be the titles of the songs that everyone here sang – and I was right. Later that evening, I worked hard to get comfortable on one of the tavern's rough wooden benches while they sang and sang and sang those same damn songs over and over and over again. It seemed like hours. The Townspeople were, each and every one of them, awful. Truly bad. They shouted, quacked, quavered, droned, and bleated. They bellowed, blasted, belted, and moaned. And no one listened to anyone else, it was true. It was amazing that they started and finished somewhat at the same time. I sipped at a beer and smiled politely. Trent looked entirely flabbergasted. Esty and Birdie kept glancing at each other and giggling. The cats bolted for the door at their first opportunity and were nowhere to be seen.

When the locals finished their last song, they laughed and whooped and clapped each other on the back as if it were a legendary performance.

"How come you weren't singing?" Buick asked me. "I thought you were a singer."

"Just waiting for the din to subside so you could hear it." I nodded to the others and in a few moments we were plugged in and ready to go.

The tavern was a good size for a bar, but what we might call an intimate environment relative to Madison Square Garden. It was fairly full of people, perhaps seventy five or a hundred in all. Clothing was homespun but festive, the men in suspenders and floppy bowties and the women in long dresses, displaying cleavage where available. The room was decorated in the ubiquitous theme of turds, tweezers, tubes and roots.

They stared at us, conversation halted by curiosity. I cleared my throat, momentarily at a loss. I took a step over to Buick, who was seated in what passed for a front row. "What the hell is the name of this place?" I asked.

"We call it the Town," he told me. "It's part of the World."

"Clever," I said.

I stepped back to my place, between Perzanto and Birdie. "Hello Town!" I called to the back of the room. "Are you ready to rock and roll?"

They continued to stare. "Rocky knoll? What's that?" someone asked.

We began their musical lesson with some simpler tunes: Buddy Holly's "Not Fade Away", the Stones' "Jumping Jack Flash", and Blue

Smoke's own "You Need to Be Free." Then, taking it up a notch, we did "Awake (from the Dream of our Distance)". Through all of this, the townspeople sat silently, barely even sipping from their drinks. I played my ass off on the solo and was rewarded with an audience response so subdued that it was unnoticeable. I figured we'd subject them to one more tune and I led the band into "I Could Stay With You." I hope you know this one. It's one of my favorites from *Six Songs*, the first cut on side B. It's a slower song and I really get to sing my heart out and play a very laid-back, free-soaring kind of solo.

"I Could Stay With You" has kind of a long intro, celestial keyboards and a taste of the soaring guitar theme. The townspeople stared, slackjawed. I didn't care by that point – the song always takes me back to when Jane and I first moved to Rosendale in 1978. We'd owned the mountain property for a year or so by then, but it took some time to get our lives untangled from the West Coast and Blue Smoke was at its peak of touring. Our stuff had been moved and even partly unpacked in advance of our arrival, which was good because I was coming off of several months continuous touring, again, and I wasn't looking forward to hauling furniture or sorting boxes. Such were the benefits of stardom.

The first verse came around and I kept it controlled, restrained and sweet.

> "I live my life on the open road
> Earth my bed, stars my roof
> I roll like a stone, wander like the wind
> But I could stay with you"

In those days, I was full of plans. I had more albums I wanted to create than a human band could ever actually record. I had concepts for stage performance, thoughts about big benefit concerts, and a treatment for a Blue Smoke concert movie with a science fiction theme. I saw the way that our music influenced people and I wanted to engage in global cultural engineering through rock and roll. I kept moving and the not inconsiderable amount of work I did turn out never seemed like enough to me. I was impatient for it all to happen.

But then I found myself in Rosendale, surrounded by quiet mountains, ancient oaks and hemlocks, with Jane at my side.

Birdie joined me on the next lines:

"Summer sky arching blue
Contains my world
And includes you"

Man, what a relief it was. For the first time in about eight years – since the band took off and I moved out of my parents' house – I felt like I was home. I enjoyed my time with Jane. We hiked in the woods, rode bicycles into town, and indulged ourselves in local restaurants and nightclubs. All my plans suddenly were overruled by a new set of short term objectives: to see another smile light up Jane's face, to hear her laugh, to feel her next to me. It was like permanent vacation and for a while I could understand the lizard on the sunny rock or the cat curled up by the fire. And there were songs there, too. They were a different kind of song, not motivated by pop charts or money or what anyone else would think. They were pure, they were organic, arising naturally from my connection to this place and to Jane. *Six Songs* would ultimately become our most widely acclaimed album.

"No walls can ever make my home
No place I rest my head
Here I walk alone, freedom at my feet
But I could stay with you"

And Birdie joined me, really wailing with power:

"Winter snow falling white
Enfolds my life
Falls in your night"

I stayed with Jane and spent more time around the mountain. Blue Smoke still toured, sure, but they were shorter jaunts with longer downtime in between. We could do it at that point because we made a lot more money per show and royalties from the albums, in those days anyway, were pretty sweet. There was a feeling that life was crystallizing, transforming from possibilities into its proper form.

One unseasonably warm autumn day, Jane and I packed a picnic lunch and hiked all the way up to the top of our mountain, where a lichen-covered slab of rock capped the top of the ridge. The sun was a blazing jewel against the blue silk sky and below us the oaks and maples were painted with vivid yellow and red. Jane wore a pair of baggy army-green pants, like something designed for a combat harem or a very sexy paratrooper, and a tight yellow tank top. We lay on the sun-warmed rock, a faint breeze tickling the edges of our perception. A pair of red-tail hawks called and circled overhead.

Okay, okay, it was my turn to sing again.

> "When I am old, still loving you
> I may yet feel the road's call
> Have regret for the freedom that I felt
> But I could stay with you
> a-awooo"

"Part of me feels guilty," I said to Jane. "I mean, here I am, up here with you and the hawks, doing nothing when my life's work isn't nearly done."

Jane's voice was soft and musical as she said, "This isn't doing nothing. This is living."

"I know," I said.

"When I was in junior high," she told me, "our next door neighbor, Mr. Waterman, had to go away for a while. We didn't really know why and everyone speculated, but before he left he came over and asked me to take care of his cat, Norman. Mr. Waterman was a strange guy. He was tall, thin and dressed really well. We thought he was a secret agent. Norman was a great big black and white cat who had a bad reputation in the neighborhood. Really, I think it was the

Goldberg's dog that raided everyone's garbage at night, but Norman got the blame.

"Anyway, Waterman gave me the key to his house and told me where the cat food was kept. I was supposed to let Norman in and out periodically and was told to pet him and talk to him and keep him company. I wasn't really too keen on the whole idea. It was a responsibility I'd have to keep track of and I really wanted to spend the summer hanging out with my friends. But my parents encouraged it and Mr. Waterman offered me ten bucks a week to do it."

As I recalled Jane's tale, my fingers were flexing along the frets, playing that soaring solo, squeezing every last bit of each note from the strings. And I sang:

"I live my life on the open road
Earth my bed, stars my roof
I roll like a stone, wander like the wind
But I could stay with you"

"After I'd gone to feed Norman a couple times," Jane continued her story, "I realized that, far from being an onerous duty, having the key to Waterman's place was the key to my summer. Anytime I wanted to get away from the parents and be alone for a while, I could say I was going to spend time with Norman and disappear. Even better, if we didn't mess things up too much, I could bring my friends over, too.

"Waterman's place was pretty cool. It was a three-bedroom ranch house like most of the houses on the street, but he lived there alone. I think he may have inherited it from his parents, because it was full of antique furniture that looked like it had grown old right where it was. There were big shelves full of books in most of the rooms. Some of the books looked really old, but many were current titles. There were a few paintings hung here and there, Hudson River kind of stuff, with big, stormy skies and lush green colors.

"So one of the first nights, I'm sitting on Waterman's living room sofa with Norman kneading my lap. I was listening to his record player and drinking a bottle of Coke I liberated from Waterman's fridge. I'm just sitting there admiring the vines hanging down on the sides of a big bookcase. And I realize that, well, he's got these vines. I looked them up later, they're called Golden Pothos and they were thick cascades of shiny yellow and green leaves. But Waterman hadn't said anything about taking care of the houseplants, just the cat. So I resolved to water the vines, standing on a chair with a cup of water from the kitchen faucet. I mean, I didn't want them to die, I wanted to have friends over to be awed by how cool the place was, and I thought that maybe Waterman would appreciate the extra effort and maybe throw in an extra ten bucks or something.

"Over the first week," Jane continued, "I found a few other loose ends that needed my attention. The milk man kept leaving fresh bottles by the back door, so I brought them inside and put them in the refrigerator. I drank some of it, poured some of it down the drain and put the empties back outside. Waterman's newspaper delivery and mail started piling up pretty quickly, too, so I got in the habit of taking it all inside and stacking it neatly in the foyer. Time stretched on and Mr. Waterman did not return."

Birdie came up beside me and we sang together:

"Summer sky arching blue
Contains my world
And includes you"

The song stretched into the final instrumental part and Dondelakavin took an excessively long, though tasty, solo on the lipsquacker. He played and the townspeople gawked. Jane pulled my thoughts through time.

"The more time I spent in Waterman's place," Jane explained, "the more I began to think of it as my own. I felt liberated and grown-up. The more possessive I felt about the house, the more I did with it. I started to make small, subtle changes in the arrangement of furniture, at first for my own convenience. Then there were some bigger decorating changes as I thought of ways to improve the place. I removed some long-term stains from Waterman's carpet. I found a book on home repair and figured out how to fix a leaky faucet. I replaced the grout in Waterman's shower and I mowed his unruly lawn.

"My friends came by sometimes, but as the summer wore on, they visited less and less. I barely noticed. I didn't want to play, ride bikes, go to the movies, or go to the beach. I just wanted to stay in my place. I was having the greatest summer ever and half of it was doing things that I would never, ever do if my parents asked me to. It was like I was in a trance and I continued to go deeper…"

"So what happened to Waterman?" I asked. "Did he ever come back?"

"Oh, sure he came back," Jane said. "About two months later. I was in his kitchen, arranging flowers in a vase when Mr. Waterman came strolling back in, looking around in amazement.

"'Holy Crap!' was all he said at first. I remember it so well. I was frozen; I didn't know whether to run like hell or laugh my ass off. But it turned out that he was really happy with it all. He'd been expecting the mess that he'd left behind, plus a lot of dead plants in his living room and junk mail on the front steps. While he and Norman had a joyful reunion, Mr. Waterman explained that there had been a huge earthquake in Ethiopia and that he went with a charitable organization that he belonged to, to help out and save lives. I thought that was noble and reflected that most people would want to stay as far away from a thing like that as possible. Waterman paid me an extra twenty bucks for the non-cat-related work that I did. It was more money than I'd ever owned all at one time and I felt rich. I was a different person, almost a grown-up, I thought, and I'd helped out with an earthquake in Ethiopia, sort of, indirectly."

That was the story that Jane told me as we lay basking on the mountaintop. And that's the story I thought of, somehow, as we played to the stone-faced townspeople. I know, I know, it's a little short on plot. But that's the way it happened, so fuck you. Life with Jane wasn't always perfect, don't get me wrong, but in moments like that I knew that I was in the right place, with exactly the right person.

The song eased into its final notes and then there was silence. There's not supposed to be silence when Blue Smoke finishes playing a song. There's supposed to be applause, or at least jeers. I mean some kind of feedback, something to let you know that the audience didn't drop dead during the second chorus. If there were sounds of normal conversation, clinking glasses, and other signs that we were just being ignored, even, I could understand that. The silence suggested that they were paying attention, very much so, but didn't offer a clue what they were thinking. At that moment, I could only imagine that they hated our music, or that it was so alien to them that they entirely failed to get it.

Finally, after what seemed a very long time, Buick cleared his throat. "Well," he said timidly. "That sure was something like I've never heard before."

A few others quietly agreed with Buick.

One man stood, shaking his head. He tossed back a gulp of ale. "What's it all about, new neighbor? I mean, what is all that singing and playing supposed to do?"

"You're supposed to enjoy it," Trenton spoke up. "Let it move you, make you feel something, tap your foot, shake your booty."

"I was struggling real hard not to tap my foot," the man said.

"What's a booty?" someone else asked. "I don't think I got one."

"Whoa," said another one. "I wish I'd known I was supposed to tap my foot. I could have tapped pretty good, I suppose."

The ice was broken and from beneath their chilly exterior the townsfolk offered us a variety of tepid compliments. They explained how they enjoyed it, how they felt like moving but didn't, and so on. One of them even correctly identified the booty as an anatomical object.

And then a galoot asked, "How did you get them guitars and stuff so loud?"

I patted the black box in front of me. "It's called an amp."

"Look at all them wires and such," one of them called out.

"Yeah," said another. "It must be the devil's work."

"Well, that would explain why my booty wanted to shake," an older woman commented. "It was the power of the devil!"

"Nah," Buick told them. "He told me it was an electric guitar. Electric, that's okay. It's like Alice's starting spark, when I crank her up. Or like them old light bulbs we use for the catawaba festival. That shit's trippy on the eyes; this here's kind of funny on the ears, I figure."

"Well, it's not nearly your place to make that figuration," said the woman. "You might be the signbearer, though I never do see you bearing the sign, but you are not the brigade."

"I bear the sign upon the front of my domicile," Buick asserted. "And you should call the brigade, if you believe there's anything actually *electroonic* about these here musical thingabamoms."

We all looked at each other.

"Electroonic?" I asked. "Whatever do you mean?"

"That's electric the way the devil does it," Buick explained. "Instead of honest wires made of metal from the World, electroonic uses chips off the Olde Block, the neighborhood where the devil grew up. Our goddess has declared, from early times on, that electroonics is the work of the devil and she told us much about various nefarious devices – communiphons, telesponders, digipalms and the like – that will rot the mind and corrode the enamel of moral culture."

"It's some kind of telesponder!" The woman pointed at the little amp.

"No, no," said a thin, elderly man in the front row. "The telesponder was more of a thing that was planted right in the head, where it would grow and people could pretend to have long lists of friends and trade pictures of cats, according to Shishkalol's Devilopedia."

"Well, it's some kind of devil thing," the woman said. "Can't you tell?"

"Oh, yes," the old man explained. "It's a blaudiopoop, which is also mentioned by the goddess!"

"A blaudiopoop!" The cry was repeated by just about everyone there.

"It's just a loudspeaker," I tried. "A public address system."

"Call the brigade!" the woman demanded.

"It's been a long time since we had to exit a gig this way," I said to the band. "But I think we should run. Run! Grab the gear! Let's get out of here!"

We had a clear shot to the tavern door, but our gear wasn't properly packed and it slowed us down. The guitar was strapped to me, but I had to make a grab for the case and the shotgun, which I carried one in each hand. The townspeople were right behind us. Outside, on the lumpy dirt of the street, they surrounded us.

We were outnumbered but they didn't seem very scary to me. With all the homespun cloth and superstitious talismans, they reminded me of members of a Vermont commune we once visited back in the mid-70s. I just remembered that they ate a lot of granola and wore big, honking pieces of "orgone jewelry" that was supposed to protect them from the bad vibrations of power lines and fluorescent lights.

The townspeople closed in on us. If they'd been waving pitchforks and torches, I might have been a little more scared, but they were unarmed. I shifted the butt of the Mossberg into my armpit, worked the pump and pointed the muzzle a few degrees over their heads. I was about to fire a warning shot when both Perzanto and Tim snarled and charged toward the townsfolk who were appropriately intimidated, backing away.

"Now, now, friends," Buick said. "Violence never solved anything."

"I once punched out a son of a bitch who said my wife had a large posterior," said a galoot. "That solved that."

"It didn't solve anything for your wife's posterior," another galoot commented, earning a glare from the first galoot.

"I took a club to that moosevark that was raiding our henhouse," a very large and brawny woman remarked. "Solved that problem and made a moosevark casserole."

"Well, they're not moosevarks," Buick pointed out. "And they've only been polite to us and our posteriors."

"They have electroonics!" the old woman who began the fuss crowed. "They might be devils themselves!"

"Electroonics!" some of the townspeople echoed. "Devils!" they cried.

They started toward us again and this time I pointed the shotgun toward the sky and squeezed the trigger. The Mossberg boomed and kicked and the townspeople backed off again. The shot was still echoing when there was a second boom, an answering shot from up the street. We all turned to look.

"Here come the b-men!" the old woman shouted.

"Oh shit, it's the pigs," Captain Head Charge elaborated.

Four men in carefully tailored, dark blue coveralls were striding toward us. They wore serious, somewhat pinched expressions and each one carried a funnel-mouthed blunderbuss. I knew the look. They were cops coming to bust some hippie ass. They were the National Guard marching on Kent State. They were DEA agents looking for the evidence. They were Nazis, checking official papers. They were Inquisitors seeking confessions of witchcraft.

"Oh, fuck," I said.

Nobody had to say anything more. We hugged our gear and ran. We did pretty well, too, with Perzanto blocking for us and the cats hissing and snarling. Most of us broke through the circle of townspeople and gained a few paces, but there was a commotion behind us. We stopped and turned to see that Oswaldo had tripped – or had been tripped. He was lying on the ground and the amp that he carried had bounced a couple yards away. The townspeople converged on him as he struggled to get up.

I set the guitar case on the ground and Perzanto and I hurried back to keep Oswaldo from any further harm. The big god picked up townspeople like they were kittens and tossed them out of the way. I used the stock of my gun to persuade a couple clinging citizens from Oswaldo's side. We got Oswaldo to his feet and realized that we were once again surrounded.

The brigade strolled over and gave us that universal cop, what-do-we-have-here look. They walked in a row, like I imagined British redcoats might have, in another world hundreds of years ago. Two taller b-men were in the middle, two shorter ones on the outsides.

They had the same short dark hair, pencil thin mustaches and billy clubs hanging from ammo belts. The wide muzzles of their guns pointed at us and I could see that they used complicated talismanic mechanisms to ignite the powder, all cocked and ready to spark.

"Put the fowling piece on the ground," one of the shorter ones commanded in a deep voice. I gently placed the Mossberg on the road.

"Now step back from it," the b-man ordered. I took two big steps and they seemed satisfied.

"Are these your electroonic devices?" one of the taller ones asked.

We all looked at each other and shrugged. "They're not electroonic," I explained. It was technically true.

"We'll be the judge of that," one of them said.

"You must be new neighbors," a taller one said. "So let us explain how it works around here. The goddess, she's real busy most of the time and she don't come around here very much these days."

"That's right," continued the other taller one. "So the brigade is here to serve and protect the goddess' interests. And when there's a question of interpretation, it's up to us to do the interpreting, 'cause the goddess don't offer no more words."

"Doesn't answer your phone calls?" Mark Ratner attempted. They glared at him and swiveled their guns in his direction.

"What that means," a shorter b-man said, "is that something is acceptable if we say it is acceptable and something is electroonic if we say so."

"That's our job," the other shorter one emphasized. "Not yours. Not anyone else's. The brigade makes the distinction."

"Can you tell the difference between magic and electroonics?" Esty inquired.

A tall b-man pulled himself up to his full height. "Of course we can tell the difference between magic and electroonics! We are highly trained in the interpretation of doctrine. No one knows such things more than the brigade!"

"Well, okay," Esty said, shaking her head. "Because this is powerful magic from another world. I doubt you've seen anything like it."

I gave Esty credit for a good try, but the b-men scoffed, nearly in unison. "We've seen every kind of magic there is," a short one drawled, jingling a collection of talismans that hung from his belt opposite the nightstick. "And there's nothing here to indicate magic. No symbols. Nothing."

"That's right," Esty continued. "This magic doesn't need symbols. Inside each of the boxes is a magic entity, a little man who sings and makes the sounds louder and louder."

There didn't seem any hope that the b-men would swallow Esty's convoluted attempt at a lie. "We'll see about that," one of the b-men said as they advanced on the nearest amp, the one that Oswaldo had pitched onto the lack of pavement. "I'm sure it's stacked all full of chips off the Olde Block."

With surprising speed, Perzanto got there first and swept the amp off the ground. "Back off!" he snarled at the b-men.

And they shot him.

The big god staggered back a few paces, dropping the amp, which bounced erratically on the uneven ground. Perzanto fell to his knees, pulling open his shirt to reveal a spreading red stain.

The b-men looked at Perzanto with contempt and then went after the amp, which landed rather forcefully in a wagon wheel rut. The front cover of the amp came loose and dangled from a corner. With a dramatic flourish, a tall b-man snatched off the cover and tossed it away, revealing the speakers.

That is, revealing the speakers *and* the magic little man who was riding with them.

Assfriend waved a tiny arm. "Hi!" he called.

21. Light My Fire

While the b-men stared slackjawed at Assfriend, Esty, Trenton, Dondelakavin and I gathered around Perzanto. He had taken blasts from at least three of the muzzle-loaders. The skin of his chest was peppered with metal balls, quadruple-aught shot, much larger than the double-aught I used with the Mossberg. Few of them, it seemed, had penetrated deeply, but he was leaking a steady flow of blood from a dozen or so wounds.

"Ow," Perzanto said. "Fucking ow." I don't think I'd ever heard him curse before.

"Maybe you should lie down," Esty suggested.

"Don't worry," Perzanto winced. "Those little guns can't kill me. It does hurt, though. A lot. I'm going to need tweezers or something to get these things out of me."

The b-men were coming back to their senses. They looked around at us and began to reload their weapons. Compared to pumping a shotgun, it was a complicated procedure, involving various amounts of powder, shot and wadding rammed into the wide muzzles of the guns. Four long strides and the Mossberg was in reach. As the first of the b-men finished his ramming procedure, I pumped a shell into the chamber and took aim. The b-man thoughtfully lowered his blunderbuss. With a little urging, the others dropped their not-quite-loaded weapons, which were collected by Captain Head Charge and Mark Ratner.

"So what do you say?" I asked the b-men, emphasizing my words with movements of the gun. "Electroonics or harmless magic?"

"Magic," said one of them.

"Yes, yes," said another. "Definitely magic."

"There's a… *little… man*," one of them babbled.

"Did the goddess say anything about little men?" I continued my interrogation.

"No, no," the b-men all agreed. "Nothing about little men."

"Hello, Town!" I called in my arena voice. "What do you think? Are we okay?"

"You're good with me," Buick spoke up. "I never doubted you. You seem like good folk. Now you're good with the brigade, too."

"I want to try some of that booty shaking!" a rotund man shouted.

There was a loud chorus of agreement and much waving of talismans. Most of the townspeople seemed to be on our side – or maybe they just weren't on the brigade's side. A few, including an old woman and a thin elderly man, turned and stomped off down the street.

"Stick around," I told the b-men. "We're going to have some fun."

We picked up our gear and went back into the tavern for a second set, this one with plenty of toe-tapping and booty-shaking. We played some of it without bass or mrrlnx – Dondelakavin tooted some low notes on the lipsquacker – but towards the end, Perzanto, freshly bandaged, rejoined us for a song. Even the b-men got up and danced. The townspeople figured out applause all on their own, too, though they seemed to prefer hooting and hollering to clapping. I felt a little bad that we had to lock Assfriend back into the amp for the duration, but he assured me that he was digging the vibration. The decibels made him feel like he was home in Lakavinland.

The next morning we were all given the royal treatment at breakfast. Each Town family approached us with an offer of lodging or work. They were shocked when we politely declined. After this was repeated about half a dozen times, I took Buick and Gertie aside and, as succinctly as I could, told them our story and explained that we had to keep moving on to faraway Klod in search of the goddess, or at least the exit from this shebang. They were amazed by parts of the tale, confounded by others, and skeptical that two of our company, Perzanto and Dondelakavin, had met their goddess, if indeed she was Beezel. But, reluctantly, they accepted our immanent departure. They went into their kitchen and discussed it all privately, in urgent whispers.

When they re-emerged, Gertie looked a bit sour and Buick was solemn. "We believe," Buick said, "that if your quest is truly for the benefit of the whole world, then we are obligated to help you in any way we can. I would like to offer the use of Alice, so that your travels will be smoother and in style."

I wasn't sure about the smoother part, but I figured that a car might be handy so I agreed. An hour later we had the recuperating Perzanto nested in a pile of borrowed blankets on Alice's flatbed. The little bit of space left free from his oversized limbs was stacked with gear, tied down with ropes and orange extension cord. Buick shook hands with everyone and Gertie gave each of us a hug. After embracing me a little too firmly, she took me aside.

"You're going to want some of this," Gertie said, handing me a gigantic wicker picnic basket. She wielded it like it was nothing, but when I grabbed the wooden handle I almost dropped it, it was so heavy. I opened the lid for a peek; it was packed with food.

"I tried to give you what won't turn," she explained. "But there are some sandwiches on top that need to get eaten today."

I thanked her profusely and toted the provisions back to Alice. I went around to the driver's side, pulled open the creaky old door and found Buick sitting behind the wheel.

"You didn't think I was going to let you *drive* Alice, did you?" he asked. "No, no, she's right temperamental and I reckon I'm the only one who can coax her the right way. Hop on in." He gestured toward the passenger side.

I shrugged. I used to say the same stuff about my old Datsun, which usually required a bit of tinkering under the hood and some fancy footwork to get on the road. And I figured that I could literally ride shotgun. Now I knew why Gertie looked so sour. Buick was going to be our guide to faraway Klod, an epic journey for someone who never left home. I climbed in, hoisting the picnic basket onto the seat between us. Before I could slam the heavy door shut, Bob leaped up and settled on my lap. I scratched his wide, fuzzy head and he started to purr.

Farting and rattling, Alice rolled out onto the one and only road. Again, she barely went faster than a walk on the randomly-rutted dirt road and the rest of the band and crew easily kept pace. The morning sun was golden and dozens of small green birds flitted and darted overhead as we rolled and strolled out of Town.

"I thought west was that way," I said to Buick, pointing in the direction I thought he had indicated the previous day.

Buick chuckled. "Well, the road only leads south at this point," he said. "But that's all right, because we're going to need some faster transportation if we want to get to Klod any time soon. We're going to Bemshire first."

"Bemshire?"

"That's where we'd pick up the western road," he explained, "but even better, last time I was out that way, five years ago, they had a gigantic airship. Maybe we can fly to Klod."

We bumped along in silence for a little while and I figured it was high time to roll a joint. I picked out a choice bud, crumbled it into my palm and twisted a fat and fragrant doobie. I held it up to my lips and without a word Buick waved his fire talisman and the joint sparked up. Bob raised his head and blinked. I took a deep toke and passed it over.

"I want to learn how to do that," I said, exhaling a great blue-gray cloud.

"What?" Buick asked, incredulous. "How to light a fire? Surely you've discovered fire in your world."

"We use matches," I explained, passing him the joint. "Or a lighter." I fished in my pocket and pulled out a green Bic, which I flicked into life. Buick eyed it quizzically. "Don't worry," I assured him, "it's mechanical, not electroonic."

"Oh, heh," Buick chuckled. "After seeing how the brigade behaved yesterday evening and talking it over with Gertie last night, I really do suspect that all of that electroonic stuff is a pile of wiffle dung."

I wondered what a wiffle was, but I think I caught his meaning. "Propaganda," I said, "to control people."

He nodded vigorously in agreement. "And it seems to work in their favor that none of us rightly know what electroonic is, anyway. That way they can hassle anyone, pretty much whenever they want. No one can argue with them. Except you, it seems."

"Me and Mossberg," I clarified.

"And your magic from another world."

Bob snorted and I laughed. "That's just Assfriend. He's not magic, I think. Just weird."

"It looked downright magical to me," Buick said. "I never saw anything like it."

"You understand that the whole electroonic thing is, uh, wiffle dung, right?" I waited for him to nod before continuing. "Maybe there's a kernel of truth in, uh, the dung. Not the devil part, though. In our world, though, we have something called *electronics,* not electroonics. Now that's for real. And it uses silicon chips, integrated circuits, solid state technology and a hell of a lot of other stuff that most of us don't really understand. And I guess people really do use it mostly for very trivial things, even stupid things, like texting while they drive, watching television, selling penis pills, putting illiterate captions on cat pictures, and insulting each other's politics. But none of that is evil. It's stupid, yes, but there's no Devil involved. Just stupid fucking humans. And there are a lot of wonderful things people do with electronics, too."

"Such as?"

"They make really kick-ass little guitar amps."

Buick took a long toke, held it for a moment and exhaled. "I get it," he said, wisdom dawning slowly. "The little tiny man doesn't really sing, does he?" He laughed and I snagged the joint back from him while he was still shaking. "You really put a good one over on the brigade. That is purely too good. Purely. I never saw anything at all like that before." He laughed some more. I think the weed was kicking in.

Bob grumbled and tucked his head under a paw.

"Best thing you can do," Buick told me, "when we come to these other towns, you run that same deception. Show them that little old ass friend right up front and make sure the brigade leaves us be. That is, if you intend to make your music."

"We intend to make music," I said. "In fact, I'm thinking it could be fun, opening up new audiences."

Back in the early '70s Blue Smoke took some odd gigs just to keep working. County fairs, local street festivals, an Elks lodge or two, even, Jay help me, a couple bar mitzvahs and a wedding. The audiences weren't always rock'n'roll fans. We could usually get folks comfortable by throwing in a swing number, a show tune, *Hava Nagila*, or even Sinatra and if we were lucky, we might get them to boogie a bit to our own stuff. It was tough to keep a straight face sometimes, but we did it. This was different. The audiences of World, if they were anything like the people of Town, didn't even know how to be an audience. They didn't have the concept. We would have to take them by the hand and lead them every step of the way toward rock fandom. Warping minds is half the fun of playing in a band. Of course we were going to play!

Bob lifted his head, yawned and said, "I smell fish."

Buick hit the brakes and Alice bounced to a stop, prompting a shout from Perzanto.

"Your cat," Buick stammered. "Your… cat. It *can* talk!"

"Didn't I tell you?" I asked.

"What's in the basket?" Bob inquired, his nose twitching.

"Oh, yeah," I told Bob. "Gertie said we needed to eat the sandwiches. Maybe it's tuna."

"He eats sandwiches, too?" Buick wanted to know.

"No, dude," Bob explained. "I only eat the meat. Bread, phhhh."

I set the roach down on the dashboard and opened the picnic basket.

"Is something wrong?" Perzanto's voice boomed out from behind us. "How come we're stopped?"

Buick got Alice back into gear and we lurched forward. I found a fish sandwich for Bob, carefully wrapped in paper. I opened it and set it on the floorboards. Bob hopped down and began to lick and gobble the fishy filling. It tended to slide around a bit as the old car waddled across the uneven dirt and the motion increased Bob's interest.

"You sure are a very strange sort of person," Buick told me.

"You've got some strange yourself," I said, pointing to his collection of clattering symbols.

He looked at his talismans and then looked at me. "You think my magical talismans are strange?"

"I've seen stranger," I said. "But, yeah. They are strange to me."

"I never did think of it like that, how these here talismans might seem unusual to a new neighbor. None of the others ever said anything about them."

Bob looked up from his sandwich. "They were being polite," he said.

"Do you think?" Buick looked perturbed and tucked his talismans into his vest.

"Hey," I told him, nudging Bob with the toe of my boot. "I said they were strange, but they are still very cool. Rockin'. I wish I had some."

Buick brightened up. "I could show you how to use the fire talisman. Then you could light up your herb real easy."

We passed the outer limits of Town and were bumping along between orchards on both sides of the road. They were low, gnarly trees, kind of like the old apple trees we have out past Rosendale, toward Stone Ridge. But these trees didn't bear apples, or at least not any kind I ever saw. The fruit looked more like giant purple and green striped figs. Between rows of trees we had an occasional glimpse of some very Earth-like deer. Overhead, vultures with bare, pale necks and long black wings rode the currents among puffy clouds. They were uglier than our Rosendale turkey vultures, which is saying a lot, but just as graceful, floating with wings outstretched, feathers fingering the breeze. Fat-assed woodchucks sat up and stared from the side of the road as we rumbled by. The ganja was finding its way to my brain and the landscape seemed, for a moment or five, perfectly arranged, every detail in its proper place. I took a deep breathe. In spite of the lurching and bouncing of the car, I felt muscles relax and soften throughout my body.

"Okay," I told Buick. "Teach me your fire talisman. Uh… next time we stop?"

"Oh, no," Buick said. "I can teach you right now."

Keeping one hand on the wheel, he unclipped the talisman from his lanyard and held it out to me. It was a flat piece of brass-colored metal, square, about two inches to a side. There was a small hole through one corner for the lanyard clip and a symbol painted on it in black enamel that looked like a turd with lines radiating from it. A radioactive roadapple. Keith Haring's first dump of the day. The metal was cool and smooth in my hand and a little heavier than I expected.

"The Book of Flashkazar," Buick explained, "says that the use of certain metals is important. Either painless steel or coin will work, but nothing with gold, silver or platinum. When the talisman is forged, the sun must be forty five degrees above the horizon and a white bird must be purchased and eaten."

"I have to eat a bird?"

Buick laughed. "No, no. You're not going to make a talisman; you're only going to use this one. And you can keep it, too. You got more need."

"Thanks," I said.

"But you will have to know about the four energies and their eight signs. There's Mystery, Mastery, Sex and Drugs, those are the four energies. There are eight signs because each energy has two, one calling, one repelling. So this here is the calling sign for Mystery." He held up one of his talismans that had a simple ellipse on it, one turd. "And this here is the repelling sign of Mystery." He flipped the talisman over and showed me.

"It looks the same," I said.

"No, it's not." He told me, waving the thing closer to my face. "It's upside down. See? The calling sign curves up a little and the repelling sign curves down."

I wasn't sure that I did see, but I nodded affirmation. "How come it looks like a turd?" I asked.

Buick grinned and shook his head. "That's because it is a turd! Excrement symbolizes the very cycle of life itself! Everything we eat comes from shit. All our wood and fuel comes from shit. We might use stone and metal to build, but it has to be tempered in fire and fire comes from wood and wood comes from shit. That's the Mystery of life, that we ourselves and everything we do rises up from the lowly dung of the World."

I nodded as if this made sense.

"This one is Mastery," he continued, holding up a symbol with two lines set at an acute angle. "These here are forceps, to show specialized skill. Every part of our life is governed by some kind of Mastery. There are some who are Masters of numbers and finance. Others have Mastery in making cabinets or shingling a roof. Gertie, she's got Mastery of the kitchen. My Mastery is making machines. Your Mastery is with that there electric guitar."

"I do some farming, too," I said.

Buick nodded emphatically. "And if your herbs are any indication, you have some Mastery there, too." He flipped the talisman over and there was another forceps, to my eyes exactly the same as the other one. "This is the repelling one."

I nodded, but my expression must have been a giveaway.

"It's facing the other way," Buick explained. "See?" He turned the talisman over a couple times.

I wasn't sure that I did see, but I nodded with what I hoped would pass for conviction.

"This one is Sex," Buick said, steering very suddenly around a pothole. When he was able to free a hand from the steering wheel, he showed me an elliptical, flat piece of wood with one of those symbols that looked like a tiny tube of ointment. I decided immediately that I really didn't want to know how they chose that particular symbol for Sex, but Buick went for it anyway. "It's a little tube because of, you know, the what-you-call-it *phallic* imagery. And because that's what the sacred love oil comes in. It makes things more slippery and fun. Sex makes the world go 'round. All you need is Sex. Happiness is warm

Sex. Money can't buy you Sex. We wouldn't be here if it weren't for Sex. Everything we do, we do for Sex."

"What about love?" I asked.

"Don't you think that's a part of the whole sexual phenomenon? The sacred dynamic between two people. Not between us two people, but between me and Gertie, for instance, or you and, uh…"

"Jane," I filled in.

He looked around at the people walking to either side of the lurching car. "Have I met Jane?"

"No," I said. "She's dead."

He shook his head. "Well, that is purely unfortunate. Now, this here is the repelling sign for Sex."

Buick flipped the talisman over and this time the difference was obvious. The little tube was rolled up like an empty, old-fashioned toothpaste tube.

He laughed. "That's one I've had rare occasion to use!"

I didn't get it.

"Well, I generally don't have cause to repel Sex! Gertie would stop cooking my dinner forever if I did that but once! Anyhow, here's the next one. This is the talisman for Drugs."

This was a hexagon of some kind of yellow, rubbery stuff with a line drawing of a little root inscribed on it. "The book of Flashkazar," he told me, "says that most things have the property of a drug. Everything we do, think, eat, drink, breathe, chew, or come in contact with nudges our state of mind in one direction or another. The morning air makes you feel different than the evening air. A big old slice of sticky-fly cake will make you feel like taking a nap and a cup of hot joejoe will wake your ass up and send you off to the wifflechute. The smell of cooking pickle fruit might make you think of your mother and the stench of a rotten ducklebear will send you running from the room."

I couldn't argue with any of that, especially since I had no idea what most of those things were.

"Everything changes our minds, from a cool sip of water to a great big catawaba root. That's this right here." He pointed to the little drawing of a root. "Only it's not a great big one, of course."

"What's a catawaba root?" I asked. "I mean, what does it *do*?"

He looked at me in amazement. "You've never gone zooting on a catawaba root? I would have thought that with your fondness for herbs…"

"I don't think we have that, where I come from," I explained.

"Oh, my," Buick said. "Well, we'll have to find you some good root. Maybe in the next town. It's an experience that everyone should have and if you believe the Drug enthusiasts, as often as possible, though I try to keep it down to once or twice a week. Here's the repelling sign." He flipped the thing over and there was the same root, only more crudely drawn, thin and twisty."

"Makes sense," I commented. "Though I'm not sure yet how this all relates to the fire talisman."

"This is the background," Buick told me. "The context in which the talisman can work. You may never use all this information, but knowing it is what gives power to the magic. Knowledge is power."

"I see," I said, though I really had only the smallest of clues. "The fire talisman is a form of Mystery?"

"That's exactly right! Now we need something to burn." He looked around. I held up the roach, which had long since gone out. "That'll do!" he cried. "Now you hold onto that herbal bit with one hand and raise up the talisman with the other. Good. Good. Now give that talisman a couple of shakes, so you can feel its weight and movement in your hand."

I waved the talisman, like I'd seen the townspeople do.

"Now you say the following, to yourself, quietly, in your mind: Mystery, Mystery, Mystery. Fire, fire, fire. Burn, baby, burn. Fire, I'll take you to burn! C'mon baby, light my fire."

I repeated it in my head, and threw in an extra verse of the Doors, for good measure.

"Now look at what you want to catch fire, imagine it burning, see the flames in your mind."

"Got it," I said.

"That's good. Now bring your attention back to the talisman and let your mind run all around the outside of that shape. Like you're feeling the edges of it with imaginary fingers."

I did as he instructed and suddenly felt a very weird rush, like I'd just inhaled a lungful of nitrous oxide and gas was rising into my brain. And with a tiny sizzling noise, the end of the roach caught fire, flamed and sparked for a moment. I raised it to my lips and toked until the tip was glowing orange. I passed it to Buick.

It was a really cool feeling, creating flame from nothing. For a moment I felt magical, powerful in a new and different way. Maybe Ian was god.

22. The Road to Bemshire

I practiced firestarting about a dozen more times as we bounced and rattled toward Bemshire. I only stopped when Buick politely complained that I was leaving charred spots on his rusty and decaying dashboard.

Around us, the orchards came to an end and a dwarf pine forest took over. The trees were scraggly things that looked like mutant pitch pine, charred in places from a recent forest fire. Between the pines, a fragile undergrowth made a tentative attempt to thrive. The road itself grew narrower, branches reaching in to scratch Alice from either side, and eventually resolved itself into two not quite parallel ruts. The ruts ran directly through a series of potholes and rock outcroppings and Alice careened from side to side, accompanied by grunts of pain and disgust from Perzanto. Alice haltingly blazed the way and the rest of our company followed behind. Bob, finished with his snack, jumped back into my lap and quickly fell asleep.

I had a nice buzz going and, finally, some time to reflect on the decidedly unusual events of the past days. I've always been tolerant of weird experiences. Hell, it comes with the rock star gig. You see all kinds of weird shit: drugs, groupies, crazed parties, mental aberration, The Residents, body modification and egos beyond control. For our stage shows we had to *develop* weird experiences for our audiences. It had to be psychedelic, you know? And I always thought that the purpose of psychedelic experience was self knowledge. It was an exploration of an inner landscape. Well, here I was in an outer landscape every bit as trippy as the biggest magic shroom you ever ate.

Make no mistake, World wasn't the kaleidoscopic torrent that Lakavinland was, but it was nonetheless subtly and powerfully strange. Take the sky, for instance. It was blue like Earth's, with white clouds, but when you looked for a while you started to notice that the clouds took shapes that no terrestrial clouds ever took. These weren't cumulus or nimbus or stratus or whatever. They were other shapes and patterns. Bumpy white checkerboards, tiny galaxy-like spirals, and – I swear I'm not making this up – clouds in the exact shape of the Playboy rabbit. But you could overlook that in the broad sweep of the heavens. What you might not overlook, however, were the three moons, each glowing, somehow, a different color, red, green and gold. Rasta moons in the daytime sky.

Had this weird collection of worlds always existed in the cave below my mountain? Or had it somehow come into being, with a complete and very ancient history, on June 23? If it came into being with that history, if someone went back in time now, would it have been that way even if it hadn't been before? These were not questions I could answer, of course, but they were fun and tickled my gray matter. Esty had attempted to explain the shift the world underwent on that day, but I was still unsure what it all meant and how much of my present experience was attributable. I now kind of wished that I had gone to Saugerties that day. But, of course, then I might not have been home for Jane's return and I wouldn't have missed that for all the ganja in a thousand worlds.

The Scrambler. What exactly was it that pushed us into this shebang? I'd tried to be non-judgmental about Liana's nemesis, but I was leaning heavily toward the idea that she was paranoid. Pathologically paranoid. Delusional. She'd been alone too long, too many thousands of years, which was likely why she wasn't the innocent beauty that Perzanto claimed to recall. Or maybe his memories had softened her edges a bit. Either way, she used the Scrambler the way oppressive governments deployed their various semi-imaginary enemies. In the USA, we feared Communists, terrorists, and evil drug users – for the purpose of mobilizing cash toward politicians' favorite projects. Liana had her own crackdown, on anyone she claimed was in league with the Scrambler. But, anyway, something had tossed us here and, while there were very rare earthquakes in the Gunks, they were usually tiny little temblors, the kind that registered only on some sensitive instrument in a laboratory somewhere. And, given the many kinds of entities we'd encountered so far, a malevolent entity remained a possibility, though we had no evidence either way.

Fire magic. Would it work on planet Earth? Or was it bound to the laws of nature in this shebang? Buick barely even accepted the existence of other shebangs and could offer no answer to that question. I resolved to ask Perzanto at the next opportunity. *His* magic worked up there. Well, maybe. Come to think of it, I'd only seen him at work down in the cave. Closer to the surface, somewhat in contact with the upper world, but still in the cave.

Whatever. I was in this world now, didn't see an immediate way out, and was perfectly willing to live by the laws of nature that I found here. I remember a few times, back in my younger years, when the walls started to melt or breathe. Or that DMT trip I took out at Kesey's place, a five minute odyssey through a realm of cartoon jungles and dancing elves. You just accept it and grin or it blows your mind in a nasty way. On a drug trip, if you try to hold on to your narrow reality or your ego, forget it; that's the fastest way to find trouble. You have to relax and breathe and just ride it out. Sometimes the ride is a bumpy one.

On the other hand, I did have some more mundane concerns. The whole journey, as unprecedented and remarkable as it might be, was taking much longer than planned. I prayed for rain in Rosendale, or my plants would wither in the summer sun. I hoped that tour details were working themselves out without us. We were getting rehearsal and warm-up gigs. We were going to be ready when we got back to the surface world. My debts still needed paying and I was still going to need a place to live; with a little luck, the promoters and record label would have it all set up. Maybe, just maybe, we would get out of this crazy place before everything crashed and burned up top.

And Jane. It was all linked. I needed the tour so that I could save the mountain and get Jane back. When I thought about it that way, I found it difficult to remember why I was even in this place. This quest was a distraction, a diversion that got way diverted. I had to find my way back. But, ultimately, it was the old hurry-up-and-wait. Go out on tour long enough and sooner or later it becomes a dominant factor.

Like the time we were supposed to go on stage at the Hollywood Bowl for a sold-out show, but our bus broke down somewhere in the middle of the fucking desert between Las Vegas and L.A. Eighteen thousand people and hundreds of thousands of dollars depended on that bus rolling west, but the engine was a smoking ruin and it would be hours before a replacement could arrive. You watch the clock spinning closer to your deadline and pray that something happens to get you there. Beyond that, you make do, get high, read a book, sleep or do some sightseeing.

And so the miles rolled by. The road began to climb up and around a series of rounded hills.

"This here mountain range," Buick informed me, "these are the mighty Baraquenderos."

As mountains went, they made the Shawangunks look like the Himalayas.

After a while, I became used to the erratic motion of the old car and got as relaxed as I could. Not as relaxed as Bob, who slept pretty much the whole way, but relaxed enough. After a while I used my new-found skill and torched up another number.

"You know," I said to Buick as my synapses shifted gears, "I realize that in our world, we have something very similar to your four energies. Only we've rolled Mystery and Mastery into one: Rock'n'Roll."

"Rock'n'Roll and Sex and Drugs?" he asked.

"Something like that," I said.

"Still sounds like two things," Buick pondered stonily. "Rock and Roll."

"It's more than two things, just as your Mystery and Mastery represent so many ideas. Rock'n'Roll is about leather jackets, tight jeans, driving your car, heavy metal thunder, young love, unrequited love, twisted love, gender-bending, groupies, mosh pits, effects pedals, and really cool hair. It's about blues and the backbeat. It's about freedom and fun and telling authority to fuck off. Tell your parents to fuck themselves. Tell your boss to shove it. Tell the old folks to fucking fade away. It's about cursing and fighting. Get out, get loose, scream and shout, take over, fight the law even if the law wins. Pump it up, start a fire, start a revolution. Shoot the sheriff, rock the Casbah, go one toke over the line. Tear down the wall. Change your life, change the world, spread some love, pass along the good vibrations.

"Rocking and rolling are the motions of the ocean. They are also the signs of spiritual trance states, of mind and body moving to the rhythms of life. Rocking and rolling are the movements of dance and the mother of dance, sex. It's primal. It's what our ancestors did on the plains of Africa, rocking with stones and logs around the flickering fire. It's the central ritual of the human species. Though we try to hide behind the thin veneer of civilization, every one of us longs for the release of a great, rocking orgy. Rock'n'Roll is in our soul, man."

"I never thought of it before," Buick said, "but now that you explain it, I also long to rock'n'roll. Especially if there's an orgy."

"Rock'n'Roll is powerful ju-ju."

"I would like to learn," Buick said, fingering a drawing of a tweezers.

"All right," I told him. "Here's the first lesson." I taught him the lyrics to Ian Dury's "Sex & Drugs & Rock'n'Roll" and we sang it as we trundled down the trail. I encouraged him to listen as he was singing and he even managed to keep it near the right key. Our walking companions picked it up as well and we were all singing as we came to the outskirts of Bemshire.

23. Spondulicks

We rolled down from the not very exalted height of the Baraquenderos onto a wide plain. The first signs of civilization were sprawling wiffle ranches. Weak attempts at fences appeared here and there, never stretching quite far enough to close off one ranch from another or separate ranchland from the road. Great herds of ox-like wiffles grazed on grass-like stuff that covered the ground in abundance. Another few miles and the ranches acquired rickety shacks, like Appalachian shanties from a Snuffy Smith cartoon. Here and there we started to see people – who mostly stood slackjawed, watching us as we waved.

We hit traffic a little while later. Two wagons pulled by long-horned wiffles, loaded high with big shiny brown pods of some kind, hogged the road ahead of us, moving even more slowly than we were. Buick squeezed the bulb of Alice's horn, alerting the wiffle-drivers to our presence with a deep toot. Which, as necessary as it might have seemed, was a bad idea. The wagons stopped.

"Hey," I called, "get out of the way! We've got a flight to catch!"

Buick gave the horn another squeeze.

The wiffle drivers climbed down from their seats, a process that seemed more involved than necessary.

"Oh, no," Buick complained. "They're going to want to trade with us."

"Trade what?" I asked.

"I don't know," he said. "Do you have anything?"

A half hour later, we ended the negotiations with an exchange of about a quarter ounce of buds – and the joint I had to burn to convince them of the quality – for two of the big pods and the opportunity to get ahead of them on the road. I had no idea what the pods were, but was happy to get moving again. I strapped the things on top of our gear and we rolled into town a few minutes later.

It was an odd sort of place. It reminded me of an industrial park near where I grew up in Michigan, except that the only construction materials were sod, splintery untreated planks, and caulking that looked suspiciously like wiffle dung. Next to the low, sprawling buildings were racks of barrels, coils of metal tubing, and spindly machines that might have been built by Rube Goldberg out of giant Tinker Toys. Each building had a smokestack or three and most of them were streaming white or black fumes into the sky.

The road curved around a larger, sod-covered structure and suddenly we were in a traffic jam. Okay, this wasn't New York City or L.A., not by any stretch of the imagination. And the things cluttering up the road weren't exactly cars. Nor were there very many of them. But there wasn't much road either and the crazy contraptions were snarled up in the one and only intersection.

Each of the half dozen vehicles was a unique creation. Two were tall, spidery things that jittered back and forth on long wooden legs. The others had varying numbers of wheels, from three at the low end to something like a dozen at the upper. All of them had open frameworks, mostly of narrow wood slats with metal connecting pieces, gears and rods. Only one seemed to have an engine of any sort. Three had sails. One had pedals.

The problem was that two of them, one with sails and five wheels and one with legs, had become entangled in the center of the intersection. They pivoted erratically around a shared axis, the drivers calling out suggestions and the vehicles making loud clacking sounds as they moved. The other vehicles kept trying to get through but had to repeatedly dodge the careening stuck contraptions. Meanwhile, a small herd of enormous wiffles came ambling toward us from the other side of the intersection. The lead wiffles stopped mere inches from a spidery vehicle and bobbed their huge heads in consternation. I suppose that with our arrival, this was the biggest traffic jam Bemshire – maybe even the World – had ever seen.

Buick tooted his horn and the drivers turned to look at us. He waved cheerfully. Once again, big mistake. Man, I was really going to have to teach these people how to behave in a traffic jam. They all stopped their vehicles, turned off the engine, disengaged whatever needed to be disengaged, furled sails, deployed kickstands, balancing rods, and anchors and climbed down to the dirt of the roadway. They moseyed over and stood in a row, grinning at us. They wore oil-smeared wiffle-hide coveralls, leather Snoopy-vs.-the Red Baron helmets, goggles, and had a strange and diverse collection of tools and gizmos dangling from belts and straps. They resembled greasy steampunk aviators attacked by squadrons of alien socket wrenches.

Buick grinned back at them, stuck his head out the window and shouted a cheery, "Hello, neighbor!"

"Let me handle this," I said. Hell, I learned how to drive near Detroit and on California freeways; I had skills. I urged the cat off my lap, pushed hard against the Model A's creaky door and climbed out. "Hey! You're blocking the road!" I pointed out.

"That's a fact," said one of them. The others nodded and agreed. The drivers continued to smile. Some of our walking contingent came to stand with me.

"Shouldn't someone call a cop?" Mark Ratner smirked.

"Can you let us by?" I asked.

The drivers conferred among themselves, with much head scratching and gesturing between us and their vehicles. Eventually they turned back toward me.

"Well, that there's the problem," said one of them. "You see, the huffler rod on the manipedatruck got a little bit tangled with the Jeffries angle on the rollopuff." Or at least, that's what I thought he said.

Captain Head Charge leaned toward me with a stage whisper. "He talks exactly like this mechanic dude I used to bring my car to. The more confusing he talked, the more I knew I was going to have to pay! I always suspected he was shitting me. Is there such a thing as a polyhedonic framistanter on a Toyota Tercel?"

"No way," I said. "How'd you deal with the mechanic?"

"Check this out," he whispered. He spat on the ground and tucked his thumbs into his belt. "I hate it when that happens," he said loudly to the drivers. "Are those the five inch huffler rods or the eight inch ones?"

"What's an inch?" one of the drivers inquired.

Head Charge waved his fingers ambiguously. "You know, it's about this long, an inch. Standard unit of measure for the new titanium alloy huffler rods, but you're probably still using the old wood ones, right? I'm guessing you've got the fives, 'cause they always hang up on every goddamn Joopries angel…"

"Jeffries angle," one of the drivers said.

"Oh?" Head Charge continued. "You're still using the Jeffries? I see. No wonder you're all tangled up. Now, you boys were going to suggest something about clearing this intersection now?" He folded his arms across his chest and leaned back, waiting for the reply.

"Uh, that's right," said one of them, more timidly. "We were going to suggest that, you know, if you neighbors were in such an all-fired hurry to get through this here, uh, intersection, well, we could call in a fellow to disassemble these here conveyances and put them back together in a less, uh, obstructing sort of way."

"That would certainly be mighty neighborly of the fellow," Head Charge told them, "to help us out of the goodness of his heart. You sure he won't mind pitching in for us like that?"

"Um, well," one of the drivers asserted, "we would have to, you know, compensate him for his efforts. This is, you know, skilled labor here, highly specialized. He's the fellow what built these conveyances and wouldn't you know he's the only fellow in the world who knows exactly how to take them apart."

"A guy I know," Head Charge explained, "once said that specialization was for insects." He crossed to the entangled vehicles in a few big strides, saying, "Let me take a look at those hoppler cranks. I've got a way with machines."

"Huffler rods!" one of the drivers called after him. They all looked at each other and then turned to hurry after the Captain.

Head Charge made a big show of inspecting the machinery. He tapped a strut and listened to the sound it made. He kicked a tire, pulled on some wires, grabbed a long wooden leg and shook both contraptions a little. The drivers stared, either completely mystified or incredulous, or maybe both. Captain Head Charge plucked a tool from the nearest driver's belt. It was a kind of baby claw hammer and he rapped it against a gear with a resounding clang. Then he ducked under some struts and rods and things that I don't have words for and located the place where the two machines ensnared each other. He tapped it with the hammer and made some "hmmm" noises. Then, suddenly, he attacked it with the claw end, wedging the tool between the stuck parts and pulling for all he was worth. The vehicles creaked and rattled. The Jeffries angle, or maybe it was the huffler rod, started to bend.

"Hey!" called someone. "Don't do that!"

"This?" Captain Head Charge asked, really yanking the hammer, causing something in the machinery to yield with a loud *sproing*.

"Hey! Hey! What are you doing?!" We turned and saw the owner of the voice, a small, portly man dressed much like the drivers, only with way more tools and paraphernalia hanging from his wiffle-hide coveralls. His aviator helmet was dangling from one hand and I could see that he had a short fringe of red hair circling a pale and shiny bald pate.

"I'm doing *this*!" Head Charge insisted, leaning hard against the hammer.

I intervened. "Captain! Don't break their contraption."

He looked at me. "No? It's what I used to do with that mechanic. Only he had a Shelby Cobra. He'd start to sweat every time I'd get near it. He'd fix my car twice as fast, if only to get me out the door."

"These people haven't done us any wrong," I said.

Captain Head Charge pulled the hammer out of the works. He ducked under a yardarm and some struts and walked back over. "Sorry," he said. "They were setting us up for some kind of scam. I know when I'm being conned even if I don't know exactly what the con is. I can smell the reek of fresh bullshit."

The little bald guy ran to the vehicles. He inspected the damage, throwing a few dirty looks at Head Charge. He stroked the huffler rods fondly, cooing baby talk to the machinery. Then, it seemed, we were all forgotten, if not forgiven. He whipped a tool from his straps and became entirely engrossed in twiddling bolts and adjusting gears.

"Somehow," I said to Captain Head Charge, "I just don't think they're on your level of sophistication."

"Here they come," he said.

The six drivers lined up facing Head Charge and myself. I looked around at our companions, hoping for some more support. Buick was tinkering, too, his head under the rusted hood. Perzanto, still strapped to the car, took advantage of a moment of stillness to nap, snoring loudly. Dondelakavin had climbed onto the stack of gear lashed to Alice and was sniffing and licking one of the pods we'd traded for in our last traffic jam. Most of the rest were sitting on a narrow verge of grass-like stuff, catching their breath after the long hike. Trenton and Aqualung came to stand with us. Bob jumped down from the car and Tim came over to growl with him, their tails lashing back and forth. Jaguar and shotgun aside, we weren't very imposing, but neither were the drivers, really.

"Now you done it," one of the drivers kindly pointed out.

"That's right," agreed another. "You got Mack out here and he's already at work."

The drivers nodded their heads. "Yes, yes," said one of them, "now you'll have to pay. "Mackshematop doesn't work cheap. Big brubarb, that's what he gets."

"Brubarb?" I asked.

"Brubarb!" one of them affirmed. "You know, smileovians, muloniss, grodogs, pelantychops, wifflebutts!"

"Huh?" I inquired.

"He means money," Buick called from beneath Alice's hood.

"Your money is called wifflebutts?" I asked.

"Yes," a driver admitted. "What do you call money?"

"Dollars," I explained. "Bread. Dough. Do-re-mi. Moolah. C-notes. Spondulicks. Greenbacks."

"A nicker," added Aqualung. "A quid, a bob, a tosheroon."

"Doo-fifty," Esty called musically from the side of the road.

"Bacon, mazuma, jack, scratch," Mark Ratner contributed. "Lucre, lettuce, clams."

"So do you have any, er, spondulicks?" a driver, predictably, asked.

"Are you sure you can accept spondulicks?" I inquired, attempting to make it sound sincere. "It's not brubarb."

"Five brubarb equals half a wifflebutt," one of them explained. "Six brubarb if the butt's still fresh. But even roasted, that's a straight-up five. And that can feed a family of eight for a week."

"We have no wiffles or brubarb," Trenton spoke up. "And not too damn much in the way of spondulicks, unless you can accept plastic. And I don't think it's very fair to ask us to pay to fix your mistakes."

"Plastic?" one of the drivers asked. "You have plastic?"

"Real plastic?" asked another.

Trent palmed his face and sighed.

I reached into my pocket and pulled out a guitar pick. I held it up so the drivers could see. They gathered around.

"It's so smooth and shiny," one of them said.

"Is there much plastic where you come from?" another wanted to know.

"The streets are paved with polyethylene. Now this," I said, holding the pick out to them, "is ten thousand spondulicks. That's a lot of spondulicks. Back home, I can feed my family of twelve for most of a year with that. Here, I imagine you could be up to your eyeballs in wifflebutts and pods for a long, long time."

The nearest one reached out for it.

"I hope you aren't paying those men," said a voice. I withdrew the guitar pick, snatching it away just before the driver grabbed it, and turned to see the short, portly fellow, Mack-something-or-other, right beside me.

"Right," I said, sensing an opportunity. "We should pay you. Here you go." I offered the pick.

"No!" the fellow bellowed. "I don't want your money! I won't take your money! Say, is that plastic?"

I nodded, still holding out the pick.

"No! I won't take your money!" Mack turned toward the drivers. "You fools! Don't you see? This amazing vehicle here – it's Alice! The Buick driven by a man named Ford! It's the inspiration for all of this!" Following his expansive gesture, I saw that the vehicles were now separated and appeared to be in working order, though it was tough to tell.

"My name's Buick," Buick said, "and this here car is a Ford, but that's a kind of Buick, isn't it?"

"Ah, yes, exactly!" Mack exclaimed. "Don't you remember me? When you came through here five years ago, I was amazed and educated! You opened my mind with this ancient artifact. I hope to recapture the lost knowledge and build vehicles that will change our World. Before you came, I was working on a machine that could fly, as we hear about in the ancient legends. But after seeing Alice, I realized how much more personal vehicles would change the world. Why, every man could travel from one end of town to the other, at will or whim! We might even have commerce, you know, with other towns! Think on that!"

"I do recall you," Buick told the man. "You had a remarkable flying machine."

"This is him?" I asked. "This is the person we're looking for?"

"Maybe the World's not as big as they say it is," Buick smiled.

"It stands to reason," Trenton commented. "The person responsible for these inventions would be the brain behind the flying machine, too."

Looking at the rickety contraptions, I wasn't entirely sure that was good news.

"Come along," Mack exhorted us. "Follow me! You are welcome at my place, all of you!" He pierced Buick with a gaze. "You and I will have much to discuss!" Then Mack stepped over to Captain Head Charge, who winced as the inventor clapped him heartily on the back. "Brilliant! Brilliant! I would never have thought to bend the huffler rod into an obtuse angle. You've increased the manifold torque and now the polyhedonic framistanter reverses direction more easily!"

Head Charge shot me a look. "What the fuck?"

The little man climbed up onto the manipedatruck – or maybe it was the rollopuff – pulled some levers, weighed anchor, turned a series of cranks and suddenly was scrabbling down the road on jittery wooden legs. Buick, Bob and I climbed back in the Model A and rolled after him, our entourage following on foot.

24. Wiffle Gas

The flying machine was enormous, at least what we could see of it. Great folds of fabric filled a barn-like structure next to Mack's low, rambling sod home. Packed in with the acres of cloth was some kind of disassembled structure, slats of wood and metal brackets stacked against one wall.

"It will take ten days to gather enough gas," Mack explained to us, after we finally convinced him of our need to fly to faraway Klod. "We can assemble the cabin and engine while we wait for the bag to fill."

Our part of the deal included lessons in internal combustion engines to be delivered by Buick, a half ounce of bud, and a promise of labor, to help prepare the craft. And we also threw in a concert, scheduled for the following night, even though I think Mack didn't really appreciate the concept. The good people of Bemshire seemed even more clueless about music than those of Town. I hoped that our increasing level of musicianship would convince them.

We cleaned out Gertie's enormous picnic basket and made camp on the ranchland beyond Mack's place. One of the drivers, at Mack's insistence, I assume, brought us a sack of something that burned like hardwood but more closely resembled the sigil on Buick's Mystery talisman. So we sat around the turd fire, smoked and sang songs until all the moons dipped below the horizon.

In the morning, Mack showed up with a complicated apparatus of long, fat, rubbery tubes with round metal filters on the ends. About ten minutes later three vehicles appeared, driving a large wiffle herd before them.

"If this is going to happen on schedule," Mack announced, "I'll need everyone to grab the end of a hose and pitch in."

We each took one of the metal filters and waited for further instructions. The drivers hopped down from their contraptions and began to lead individual wiffles toward the hoses. I had a sneaking suspicion I wasn't going to like this.

Oswaldo, who was near me, gaped at his hose end. "It's a bed breezer!" he announced. "A giant bed breezer!"

"A what?" I asked.

"You know," he said. "The simple rubber tube that makes sleeping less stinky. Everybody uses it! Don't you watch TV?"

"You've got to be kidding," I told him. "You're telling me that idiots stick tubes up their…" And at that moment, just as a giant wiffle was parked, ass first, in front of me, I realized what we were expected to do. "Oh, fuck no!" I dropped the hose and backed away from the wiffle's towering butt.

The driver came from around the big-ass bovine and plopped a bucket of goo on the grass in front of me. He apparently caught the expression on my face. "Oh, come on," the man said. "It's easy. Easier if you use the lube." He gestured at the bucket. My expression, doubtless, didn't change. "Cut me a slice," he said. "It's not like anyone's going to stick it up *your* hole. Here, let me show you."

He picked up the hose from where I dropped it, dipped it in the bucket of goo and advanced on the unsuspecting wiffle. I turned and started walking. I've flown a lot of budget airlines in my time; this was a new standard for customer humiliation, well beyond over-booking, bad food, and sloppy schedules.

I refused to participate in the rump-wrangling, but I figured I could help out in other capacities. At the other end of the complex hydra of tubing, Mack, Buick and two other men were slowly and carefully folding out acres of shiny blue and silver-tinted fabric. Mack lined up the great airbag and marked out a series of positions on the field using chunks of "fuel." We slowly rolled the fabric envelope flat on the lawn, up to the first position. Each mark was Mack's projection of how full of wiffle gas the airbag should be by the end of each day. And just as we managed to finish, the gas started flowing into the bag and the fabric began to undulate and rise.

The next big task, as the wiffles contributed their finest efforts, was to haul a great quantity of sand bags over to the airship. For the first couple days, Mack explained, the weight of the fabric would be enough to keep the expanding airbag from lifting off, but after that, it would be subject to any breeze and would start pulling toward the sky. We piled the sand bags in long rows on each side of the airship and began to tie them to loops of thick rope that hung from the fabric.

It kept us busy through the day, until dinner. After we ate, we took time to bathe in the bend of a small creek that meandered through Bemshire. The swimming hole was a big, tame bathtub of lukewarm water and it felt great to finally wash off geological strata of road and cave dirt. Then it was time to start setting up for the show.

Bemshire didn't have a tavern, as such, but they had an outdoor venue that was even better. It was the kind of village green that might have featured a town fair, with pie-eating contests and a chance to dunk the clown, in an old Frank Capra movie. Except that all the buildings were crude sod-and-plank structures and the crowd, such as it was, wore more interesting apparel. Globe-shaped lanterns hung from wires strung over the square, wooden barrels of local wine were racked under a plank lean-to, and a natural amphitheater sloped down to a band shell in one corner. I asked Mack why they had a band shell and no bands, and he said "A what shell?" Apparently the thing was used for some kind of religious pageant, once a year when the moons were in a favorable position.

Mack and the drivers donned fresh wiffle hides, with a few less doodads hanging from them and they left their Snoopy hats at home. Everyone wore hides, often with the hair still attached. There were a few overalls, of the kind we'd seen earlier, but many had more elaborate outfits, three-piece suits, long coats and breeches, and tunics of various sorts. The women mostly wore skirts and dresses, wiffle hide hemlines ranging from floor-dragging all the way up to mid-thigh. They wore short bolero jackets, open in front with nothing underneath, sort of a softcore cowgirl look. People turned out because we were new and there was rumor that something different and unique was going to happen. The crowd must have totaled near three hundred, about two hundred and fifty more than my best estimate of the population of Bemshire.

After most of the audience – and a couple members of the band – had a glass or two of wine, we climbed onto the stage.

"Hello, Bemshire!" I called. Some of them stopped what they were doing and looked up. "Come take a seat!" I encouraged. A few of them did. Most of the rest just stared at us like a herd of wiffles disturbed by a hand grenade. A few even appeared to be chewing their cud, though I imagined it was only schmoozing. "You can stand, too," I continued. "But if you stand, I want to see you shake your booty! I know you don't think you know how, but everyone knows how to rock. I know you don't have the slightest clue what we're about to do here and I'll tell you this: it doesn't matter. Just listen and if you feel in the mood to move with the groove, find the rhythm and move your feet, move your arms, move your head, move your body! Are you ready to rock?"

They stared at me.

"The correct answer," I told them, "is a-awoooooo!"

The band was on it. They caught my cue and launched into "Chicken Fried Blues," one of our early, electric blues numbers. Perzanto, well enough to play as long as he had a chair to sit in between songs, was laying down the rhythm fat and thick and you could tell the Bemshirites were feeling it. We rocked hard and more and more of them found seats and a few booties even began to boogie. By the end of the first set, most of them were dancing – and you could tell that most had never, ever danced before.

At the conclusion of the second set, I introduced the band. After I'd prompted, with only slightly more effort than usual, a round of applause for each musician, I popped the grill off my amp and got a round of applause for the little magic man who made it all possible. Assfriend bowed, the audience hooted and hollered and we never heard a word about electroonics or devils. When we finished, I was exhausted and went back to Mack's place for some sleep, in spite of offers of wine, roots, pods, and a few new-found, wiffle clad (some just barely) groupies.

Over the days that followed, we got into a rhythm of working for Mack until sundown, and playing a couple sets before a packed house in the evening. Each afternoon, the airbag would loom a little larger. The cabin, supporting structure and engine of the airship took shape as well, long slats of wood and metal rods linking together to form a skeletal frame. Every night the crowds would return and we would take them down a slightly different musical path. Days and nights were pretty full, but the work wasn't any harder than planting season in the Gunks. I was getting fresh air and exercise; we were getting rehearsal time, and if it weren't for the hurry-up-and-wait factor, it would have been summer camp in the Poconos.

By the final day, the true size of the airship was revealed. The great gasbag towered above us as high as an office building and as long as a submarine, the blue and silvery fabric sparkling in the sun. Held securely to the ground with a network of fat rope tethers, the actual craft, the part you might ride in, seemed relatively small. It bore resemblance to the ground vehicles that Mack designed, a rickety sculpture created by Rube Goldberg from Tinker Toys, an erector set, and various wiffle parts. The cabin itself was more of a big tent, fabric walls flapping loosely in the breeze over a collection of warped planks lashed to the frame. A smaller gasbag, connected to a system of pipes and valves, contained the driving force of the vehicle. The pipes and valves linked to gears and cams which, in turn, provided power to a series of fins, fans, and giant pinwheel propellers. Mack and his men herded the wiffles back to their pasture and disconnected the hose system from the airbag. We gathered around and strained our necks looking up at the gargantuan balloon.

"So," Mack beamed enthusiastically, "which one of you will be making the voyage?"

"We're all going," I said. "We're all in on this mission."

Mack's grin turned into something more serious. "One of you," he said. "Only one. We've twelve and a half wiffleweights of lift from the bag. The structure itself and the ropes — you would not believe how heavy all that rope gets — account for nearly eight wiffleweights. The main framicam alone weighs over three quarters of a wiff. One wiff of ballast. Two wiffs of water and food. Two deck hands and the pilot, that's another wiffleweight. One of the deck hands is quite large. The wiffle gas hose assembly, in case we need to refuel, that's a quarter of a wiff. There's a quarter wiffleweight left, which is enough for one person and his or her supplies." He looked around at us. "Think about it. Talk among yourselves." He signaled to his men and the final loading of the craft commenced.

We talked among ourselves. It was fucked that we couldn't all go. Every one of us wanted to get out of the shebang and most of us were necessary should we get to the resonant chamber. And there was a concert tour, tax bills, etcetera, etcetera. Was there even any strategic advantage to sending a single person?

"If one of us can make contact with Beezel," Perzanto said, "perhaps we could come back for everyone. Maybe Beezel has faster transportation."

"You and Dondelakavin are the only ones who have actually met Beezel, face-to-face," I said, "so I vote for you."

It was unanimous. Among us, that is, but when we introduced Perzanto to Mack, he just shook his head. "I said a quarter wiff," he told us sternly. "This large gentleman is at least half a wiff. And that's without gear!"

We all looked at Dondelakavin. He held up his hands and shook his head vigorously. "No way," he said. "Not a chance. I'm not getting into that flying flapdoodle. It's an impressive amount of fart gas, that's true. And the smell… I can't deny that I'm in awe, but there's no way in hell that I will dangle from that twisted collection of bent planks and frayed rope. I mean: what the fuck? No."

I didn't argue with him. Hell, I felt the same way. I wasn't going to fly all the way to faraway Klod on that rickety-looking contraption.

"Do we have a volunteer?" I asked, trying to take everyone in with my glance.

There was silence.

"Anyone?" I reiterated. "Who wants a blimp ride to faraway Klod?"

The breeze changed direction and the reeking olfactory aura of the gasbag overwhelmed us for a moment. No one said a word, though there were some choking noises.

"C'mon," I said. "If there's a way to send for help, this is it. You'll be a hero."

"All right," someone said.

"What?" I asked, looking around. "Did someone just volunteer?"

Aqualung raised his hand and shuffled forward a step. "I did. I volunteer. I will be the hero."

25. Dope Run

Aqualung had improved greatly since first appearing in Rosendale. His broken lung seemed mostly healed, though the wiffle gas brought forth a few rounds of nasty coughing, as it did for most of us. Snot no longer ran down his nose and, in case it did, he had a handkerchief. He'd made an attempt to trim his beard – not a very good attempt, but anything was an improvement. Sometime in the last week, Aqualung had replaced his moldy jacket with a long, wiffle-leather overcoat. He was a fairly short fellow, but stood taller now than he had. There was something to be said for spelunking as healthy exercise, I guess, not to mention the lack of hard liquor in the cave. In fact, I noticed that he didn't even drink the weak wine they served in this shebang, though he did sit in on a few doobie sessions. We'd long since started trusting him with gear other than extension cords and he'd proven himself worthy. And Mack liked Aqualung because he was the only one other than Dondelakavin who endured the wiffle gas, coughing fits and all, without complaint.

Above all, I thought, he was an entity and faced less risk of death than a human or god-human. I mean, could you kill a fictional entity from a pop song? Wouldn't he exist until the last album with his name on it disappeared from record collections and yard sales everywhere? Until the last person with that guitar lick stuck in their head lost their head entirely? Or could he be killed by a collection of disco hits? Or some kind of fictional entity bullet? I had no idea. But it sort of made sense that Aqualung should go.

Aqualung had no gear except the clothes on his back. A few items were donated to him by the Bemshirites: blankets, more rope, an aviator's helmet, and a mess kit. It was all stowed in a manner of minutes, lashed securely to the cat's cradle of the cabin with even more rope, and Mack's crew began preparing to release the other ropes that bound the gassy craft to the ground.

I had a sudden thought about all that rope. I picked up the end of a nearby coil and sniffed it. It smelled a bit woody, with a hint of mildew.

Aqualung interrupted my olfactory investigation. "I wanted to thank you," he mumbled shyly. "For all that you've done for me. And…" He shifted nervously.

"Yes?" I prompted.

"I was wondering," he said, "if I could get a little bit of that herbal medicine. You know, for the ride."

I opened the guitar case and retrieved the bag. The gunk shit was greatly diminished, down to the last third of the bag, at least, but I broke off a nice bud for Aqualung. He held it up to his hairy face and inhaled rapturously. I gave him some papers and said, "Don't smoke near the gasbag. Ever see that film of the Hindenberg? Wait until you land, okay?"

He nodded, thanked me again a few times, and hurried aboard the blimp.

Trent, always thinking, conned a couple of Bemshirites into bringing our equipment to the air field. We plugged in and played a stately blues with riffs that soared across the sky as the crew cast off the remaining lines. The blimp, creaking and flapping in the breeze, began a slow, steady ascent. The long craft turned its nose to the west, lined up fins, wings and pinwheels, and sailed up and away. Finally, when it was no more than a tiny dot over the horizon, we unplugged the gear and went to smoke a joint.

"You can come back to Town," Buick suggested, "and stay with us. There will be work and the tavern and whatever all a musical group could want."

I shook my head. No one else spoke.

"Well, I figured you wouldn't, but I did have to make the offer," Buick said. "So I guess me and old Alice will be heading west with you."

"You don't have to do that," I told him. "You have a life to return to."

"A life and a wife," he said, "and I sure do miss them both. But I came along to see that you got as close to Klod as I could help you get. And I am learning the ancient secrets of rock and roll. I'm happy to go. We'll take the road west and maybe, if we're lucky, our flying friends will send a conveyance to take us all the way to Klod in a more expedient manner."

We didn't have any other choice, so when we'd finished the joint, we loaded our gear onto the old car and made our way to the one and only intersection that defined Bemshire. We turned onto the road that went west, which was just as rutted and bumpy as the north/south road that brought us in. Ten minutes later we'd left Bemshire proper and were rattling and stomping through endless orchards and wiffle ranches.

On this leg of the journey, Buick was the only full-time rider. I took my turn walking and spared my ass the bumping and shaking that Alice tended to inflict. Perzanto was fully healed and as wiffle-strong as ever. He walked and even pushed the Model A through some short sections of particularly bad terrain.

The sun was dipping toward the horizon when we came to the next village, called Avantre, if memory serves correctly. It was a bright and funky place, compared to Town and Bemshire, with actual paint over the ubiquitous splintery wood planks. They were just as clueless about rock'n'roll as everyone else in World, so after some negotiations we took over their town hall and blew their minds with a Blue Smoke concert. Afterwards we were treated like the rock stars we were, with plenty of food, drink and social opportunities. Again we had to decline offers to remain as permanent residents. When we were on the road again in the morning, we had three new traveling companions, two young women and a college-age boy. I guess joining our crew was the nearest thing to running away and joining the circus that World had ever seen.

The next night we slept in a field, but the day after that we found another town and another audience. And so it went for the next few weeks. Mostly we were welcome and played for our food and lodging. A couple times we left in a hurry, but more often the audiences were friendly and eager to learn the ways of rock. It was fun, a daily rhythm of traveling and playing, perhaps the most relaxed tour that Blue Smoke ever made. And we were starting to get really good. The audiences here didn't know the difference between an off night and a kick-ass show, but we did. And we kicked major, major ass.

But there was a problem. I ran out of weed.

Well, almost. I had one small bud left when we rolled into a medium-sized town called Gilcrest. We'd happened upon the place in the early afternoon, which meant that we had some hours to relax and get ready. I took the mostly-empty bag and found a quiet alleyway behind the tavern where we would play later that night. A reasonably splinter-free wood box was enlisted as a seat. Now marijuana is generally a social herb. It's more fun to share it, to pass it around, to offer it to your friends. But this was my last little bit, out of that large and excellent bag that began the journey. I wanted some time alone with it. I knew that little bud intimately and I contemplated it in solitude. It was a round nugget, about an inch in diameter, dark green with gold highlights, red hairs, and sparkling crystals of resin. It smelled like a young red wine with hints of honey and cardamom. I could tell by looking which plant it came from, maybe even what part of the plant. I'd watched that plant grow over a season, from a tiny cutting to a big, bud-heavy bush. I knew how much nutrient solution it sucked up over the summer. I could tell you how I picked bugs off it, tied out branches, or pruned sun leaves. The little bit of green in the palm of my hand represented months, years, a lifetime of symbiosis with an amazing plant.

There were more buds in Rosendale, of course, but at the rate we were traveling, it would be a while before I saw my remaining ganja. This little bit was it.

I crushed the bud, wrapped it and licked it. I pulled out the fire talisman and sparked it up. I am my own lighter, I thought as I filled my lungs with sweet smoke. I leaned back against the side of the building. Here the ubiquitous splintery planks were decorated with metal medallions or tokens, nailed into the wood at regular intervals. It made an interesting texture, felt through my shirt. I watched a thread of smoke from the end of the joint rise languidly, twisting and shifting, through a wedge of sunlight. I exhaled and the billowing cloud from my lungs rolled and expanded through the alley. I savored the sweet-spicy taste that lingered on my tongue and then took another toke.

"Oh my," said a voice. "That smells so wonderful."

I looked around and didn't see anyone.

"It's an ancient smell." That time I could tell the voice was female, though deep and husky. "The smell of deeper mysteries and silly secrets."

There was a sound and I looked up to see a stout woman climb down from the roof on a dubious planky ladder. Like the other women in Gilcrest, she wore a big swath of gray cloth, wrapped tightly around her thick body. Shaggy, shoulder-length dark hair framed a heart-shaped face. She hit the ground with a bounce and her large breasts appeared to struggle independently for release from their wrappings.

When everything stopped moving, she asked, "Can I get a puff of that?"

What was I going to do? I passed the joint.

She took a deep toke, held it for a few seconds and then exhaled a fragrant cloud. "Great Goddess!" she exclaimed. "That is fine herbal! Not much like this around here. Plenty mah-wah grown in these parts, but none of it like this. You're obviously not from Gilcrest."

"There's herb grown here?" I asked, snatching the doobie from her hand.

"If you can call it that," she said. "It's grown for rope. Somebody'll bag up the tops and sell them as mah-wah, but it's not the good stuff. You have to travel a bit for that."

I was getting used to World standards of distance and travel. These people were like Manhattanites; most of them never went more than a few miles from where they were born. There were a few traders who traveled "long distance" routes of maybe ten or twenty miles. A hike of more than thirty minutes was considered a major expedition. So when this woman talked about travel, I guessed that a big journey for her might be an hour on foot for me. Not a problem if I could score enough good ganja to last me until I made it home.

"I wondered where all the rope came from," I said. "So where do I have to go for the good shit? I'm almost out of this." I brandished the joint and she snagged it back from me.

"West of here," she told me, toking on the doob, "it's all rope weeds, for as far as a wiffle can run before it stumbles and dies. The good stuff comes from the plains on the other side of the Palacczo range, so I am told. It's a long way and a difficult journey, so we rarely see any of that. A few years ago, a trader came through with some. Oh, my, that was some tasty shit."

"Did you get a phone number from the trader?" I asked.

"A what?"

"A way to find him," I said. "You know, set up a deal?"

"He told me," she said. "He said to travel west to where the mountain road branches off to the south. Then south until the road crosses water three times. And then ask for Wayne."

I laughed. "Typical pot deal. That doesn't sound too difficult, though."

"If the deal is across the Palacczos," she said. "I don't know how far that is. A long, long way. Maybe two hours by wiffle-cart, or so I'm told."

"Where's the wiffle-cart rental?" I asked.

When we finished the joint, I thanked the woman and let her keep the roach. It was the least I could do. I went and found Trenton, who was a bit skeptical when I told him about the quest I was about to undertake.

"We're going to play here tonight," I told him. "We have all day to kill. I'll go score some weed and be back in time for the show."

"If you actually find some good herb," he said, "get me some, too. I'll go in with you on the bag. Which raises the question: What are you going to use for money?"

I reached in my pocket and pulled out a guitar pick. "Maybe they take plastic," I said.

Actually, I did have a small amount of local currency, which looked like little bits of twisted wire. Over the last couple of weeks, I took some odd jobs here and there, during our downtime. Mostly just because I wanted to keep active and help out where I could, I spent some hours picking fruit, helping to build a barn, and washing dishes after a big feed in our honor. I picked up a little bit of extra brubarb that I never really had the opportunity to spend. I had no idea what a quarter pound of bud went for in this shebang, but I hoped I had enough wire, picks, and persuasiveness for at least an ounce. Trenton dug into his pockets and added a few more wires, a tuning fork, and a pink plastic gumball machine ring with a faceted red heart. I didn't ask.

I found Bob snoozing on top of a low stone wall. "Hey, kitty," I said. He looked up and blinked slowly. "I'm taking a hike for a few hours. I'll be back before the show tonight. Stick around here and keep an eye on things. You're in charge." Which is what I always told him when I went out the door, at home.

"You know I am," he said. "So what do I do if you're late or don't come back?"

"I'll come back," I told him. "But if I'm that late, the band can play without me. These rubes have never seen us play, they don't know who or what is supposed to be there."

"Sure, dude," Bob said. "Bring me back some decent food, too. All these people eat are beans and pods. Phthphth."

There were no cart-rental lots and not too damn much traffic at all, so I started out on foot, heading west from Gilcrest. It was one of the bigger towns we'd been in, bounded by a wooden stockade wall. Beyond the stockade, farmland stretched to the horizon. Acres and acres of dusky-green hemp sucked up morning sunlight.

I stepped off the road and into a field. The half-grown hemp was about shoulder high and just starting to flower. The stalks, planted close to each other, were tall and straight, with little branching and long internodes. Enormous sun leaves, nearly twice the size of my hands, waved and fluttered in the breeze. It was all very pretty and it would make some awesome, strong rope – but it wasn't going to produce much in the way of quality ganja, even closer to harvest.

I hiked through farmland for about ninety minutes before I came to the turn for the south road. The roads in this shebang mostly sucked and this was one of the worst. "Road" was being nice. It was a rocky trail, perhaps wide enough for an underfed wiffle and a cart to pass. The path climbed up and away from the hemp fields, winding around boulders and the occasional big tree as it ascended into a low ridge of hills. I hiked that trail for a while, maybe an hour, and it never crossed water once. I was starting to get concerned over the directions. Was there another trail? Had the Gilcrestian woman got the directions wrong? How much farther would I have to go? I was thinking about turning back when I heard cursing and rumbling behind me.

I turned and saw, emerging from around a bend in the trail, the huge, horned head of a wiffle and, above it, the head and shoulders of a gangly man in a floppy hat. The man was rocked and shaken by the lurching movements of the cart on which he rode, eliciting curses and grunts of great variety and enthusiasm. I stuck out my thumb as he approached.

At the cost of a few pieces of brubarb, I had myself a ride, though it was far from first class accommodations. I rode in the back of the cart, on a piece of rough hemp fabric that covered a very lumpy and hard pile of something. The driver assured me that we had yet to reach where the water crossed the road and then went back to grunting and cursing as the cart lurched and jostled. It reminded me of a New York City cab ride, only slower. I managed to find a reasonably seat-like series of lumps and bumps in the payload and I relaxed. The cart rocked back and forth. It creaked and rattled and the driver cursed. The wiffle farted and plopped enormous, soft turds in our path, the aroma blending with the musty odor of the cargo.

And the view was very different. From on top of the cart, I could see out over the boulders and scrubby bushes that bordered the narrow trail. It was fantastic; the steady climb over the last hour put us at some real altitude and I looked down at miles and miles of hemp fields, forests and towns. The sun was warm, the moons colorful and surreal and, oddly, I was having fun.

Every tour we ever did had its side trips and dope runs. There was Trenton weed, of course, which was fine if you were hanging around Trent. Often I could bum a little bud or two to take away if I was in need, but if I wanted to have my own bag of weed, I had to arrange a deal, a dope run. For the most part, these involved following someone's confusing and ambiguous directions, often through strange and foreign cities. Typical would be the time we were playing Madison Square Garden and, on a tip about some Thai sticks, Jason and I took a wild subway ride across Brooklyn to find the acquaintance of a friend who knew somebody who had some. We were lucky that time and scored a quarter pound of golden-hued Thai weed. Extreme would be the flight that Jane and I took to Katmandu to track down the legendary jungli weed, the wild, hyper-resinous cannabis that grows on the slopes of the Himalayas. The wild jungli, far more potent than most commercial strains, was said to be the original sativa, the mother of all the fine meditative, spiritual and psychedelic reefer of the world. We spent a week in Katmandu purchasing samples of ganja and hashish from the shops and streetside sadhus. Some were quite excellent, but there was nothing bonafide as jungli. A wild, blarney-talking Irish guy we met at a rooftop party led us to the Nepali holy men who knew where the jungli grew, many miles from the city and far up the side of a mountain. We followed them to a place where the ganja really did grow wild, on giant, ancient cannabis trees. We camped on that mountain and smoked out for another week. I saved some seeds and smuggled them back into the States in the toe of my sock, which is the origin of my Nepali Gunk strain. So far, this dope run was running a bit too long, but it still wasn't a trip to Katmandu.

The cart rocked forward as it reached the crest of the hill and we started a long, rattling downhill grade. The wiffle, who hardly complained on the way up the trail, really didn't like the downhill side at all and began stamping and bellowing repeatedly. And it dropped more turds than ever. Ahead of us, I could see the trail winding down the slope to a wide plain. On the near side of the plain was a thick stand of forest and just beyond that a creek flowed through, undoubtedly crossing the road. Beyond the creek was farmland, rich green fields, probably hemp, stretching to the horizon.

Rocking, rattling, bellowing and plopping, we eventually rolled down into the trees. The trail widened to the width of a two-lane road and it smoothed out, too. The wiffle seemed much relieved and the driver broke open a flask of sour wine and drained most of it before offering me a sip. For about fifteen minutes we traveled beneath a broad, leafy canopy, cool green light reaching us in shafts of varying degrees of brilliance. Extra-large squirrels leaped and chattered in the trees and flocks of tiny birds scattered, chirping, around us. And then the woods ended abruptly and the wheels of the cart sloshed through a few inches of clear, flowing water. Beyond the forest was grassland, or something sort of like grass that waved and rolled like the ocean in the light breeze. A few minutes later, we crossed another stream and then lurched and bumped into a hemp field. It was a long ride and I was getting a little drowsy in the warm sun. I must have dozed off a bit, in spite of my lumpy, bumpy perch, and as I came back to awareness, I realized that we were stopped. The wiffle was munching the leaves off a small tree and the driver was prodding me gently with his boot.

"Did I miss my stop?" I asked.

"We crossed the third stream," he told me. "Are you sure this is where you want me to leave you?"

I looked around. A small, muddy rivulet crossed the road just behind the cart. Beside the road on both sides was patchy, ill-tended lawn, with a few trees and bushes. Beyond the verge was the deep, rich green of some very spectacular hemp. Other than agriculture, there was no sign of civilization except a side road, an even narrower trail that led off into the cannabis field. It looked promising for one simple reason: this wasn't ropey dope. These plants were thick and branched, big, round bushes a foot or two taller than my head. A skunky sweet aroma settled over the field like a warm, sun-infused blanket. As with the rope hemp I'd seen, the plants were just beginning their flowering cycle – and they were all females. This was a ganja farm. I thanked the driver and started off down the trail.

I'm sure you've noticed by now that I have a deep relationship with this plant. I've smoked weed for almost fifty years, since I was a teenager, and I've smoked it daily when I could. Please don't mistake my frequent use for addiction. Marijuana addiction is a bogeyman of moralistic propaganda. Back in the day, I took more frequent breaks from smoking, sometimes necessitated by travel or work and these days I still take an occasional day or even week off from the weed, just to reset the receptors, as it were. And when I stop, even if I've smoked out daily, all day, for years before the break, there's nothing even vaguely resembling withdrawal symptoms. I may dream more vividly for a couple days, but that's about it and that's far from unpleasant. I was a daily coffee drinker for a long time, too, and that was definitely an addiction. If I stopped, I could plan on three or four days of really painful headaches. I've heard people tell me that they get agitated or grouchy when they don't have their cannabis. Well, fuck that. I get grouchy when I can't play my guitar. It doesn't mean I've got an addiction. I would just rather be playing my guitar.

When I was growing up in the '60s and '70s, the media offered us a decidedly mixed message about cannabis. While beatniks, hippies and rock'n'rollers extolled the virtues of the plant, the government and public moralizers went on and on about how evil and dangerous marijuana was. They lied and even funded an endless series of incredibly biased studies that posed as science, proving that pot damaged your DNA, made men grow tits, and that a single toke led inevitably to death by overdose in a sordid heroin shooting gallery. No one who ever tried cannabis believed any of that shit, but many of us did buy into some of the other bullshit. Let's dispel some of those myths while we're at it.

For a long time, the Reefer Madness department of the U.S. government and their buddies in the media told us that pot turns you into a lazy stoner. Fuck that shit, too. I don't put on a monkey suit and go slave over spreadsheets or whatever in some corporate bunker, but no one has ever mistaken me for a lazy person. Sure, there are times when I'd rather be kicking back, listening to music, smoking a fatty. But I cut and split three cords of wood every winter, I run sacks of compost up the mountain every spring, and when there's a tour to play, I rehearse and perform like no one else. And I was smoking herb when the current crop of government drug warriors was playing with bubblegum cigars. Hypocrites, all of them. Our most recent several presidents and who knows how many senators, congressmen, judges and law enforcement officials have admitted to a toke here and there. You might call Bill Clinton, George Bush or Barack Obama hypocrites, but you're not likely to call any of them – or fellow smokers George Washington and Thomas Jefferson – lazy stoners. In the rock world it was the hard drinkers and narcotic abusers who fucked things up while the potheads did the work and ran the show, or at least they did in my day.

Hell, one of the reasons I like cannabis so much is that it makes me want to do things. It makes me want to play and write songs. It makes me want to kick ass at otherwise mindless chores. It makes me want to eat. It makes me want to exercise, to go for a hike or chop wood or take my mountain bike for a spin down the old rail bed. It makes me want to think. And it makes thinking more fun. My mind suddenly has access to a greater diversity of memories and thoughts than I would otherwise – along with the remarkable ability to draw connections between them, no matter how diverse. Sometimes those connections are just silly – and that's okay – and sometimes they are profound.

And then there's the way cannabis changes time. Or the way I experience time. Sometimes I'll smoke and then start a project, playing or writing or planting, and time will pass with blinding speed. I'll suddenly notice that it is hours later and that I've played, written or planted a prodigious amount. It's a great feeling, like you've got a powerful tailwind flying you home. Sometimes time will get subjected to the cannabis cut-up technique. Short term memory goes out the window and every half a minute or so you forget what you were thinking. When you remember the events later, it all seems to have the usual narrative flow, but while it's happening, you can start speaking a short sentence and get lost and confused before the second word. This happens more with some kinds of pot and usually only when you've gone a toke or three over the line. This sort of thing can be a hazard if you are, as they say, driving or operating heavy machinery, or trying to play a song in the correct order from start to finish, so generally if you plan to do those sorts of things, you smoke the other weed and keep it in moderation. Having no short term memory, however, focuses your attention on the immediate *Now*, exclusively on the present. Every moment becomes a rich feast for the senses, as full and detailed as a whole shebang. Even just a few minutes of this kind of high will leave you with a sense of awe and calm for the rest of the day. It's how I suppose that experienced meditators feel and one of those things that everyone would benefit from every now and then. I've got a Shawangunk Kush strain that will get you there reliably every time. And then, of course, there was the Blue Smoke.

So, back in our world, the deck is heavily stacked against cannabis. It's a low cost, easily produced alternative to a lot of things that the corporate masters make big money from. Heavily invested in trees for paper? Well, you don't want a fast-maturing, renewable source of high-quality paper growing all over the damn place. Invested in petrochemicals for synthetic fibers? All of that groovy brown hemp that could be farmed for pennies just about anywhere might really cut into the profits. Do you sell expensive drugs to help people deal with their moods, sleep at night, or get relief from pain? Hell, I've been to a doctor three times in the last twenty five years, for two broken bones and a cut finger. When Jane was suffering from the side effects of chemotherapy, cannabis was the only thing that helped her eat, sleep, and feel like a human being. My medicine grows in my backyard. Apart from the extra expenses and risks of guerrilla farming, it costs about as much per plant as cherry tomatoes.

But the thing that the forces of status quo really fear, that was the thing that really endeared me to ganja when I was a kid. It was one of the things that I noticed the very first time I toked up. Bobby Margolis, the older kid who gave me my first guitar lessons, gave me a joint and a couple of records to listen to, saying that I would never really understand the guitar until I listened when I was high. One of the 45rpm records was Django Reinhardt, but I can't remember what the other one was. Django's tune "Nuages," after hesitantly puffing up the joint with Bobby, was a revelation. Every note made sense in a new way, revealing complex relationships with all the other notes that were previously hidden. And suddenly, after we listened to both records a couple times, we were ravenously hungry. I was feeling mighty high and a wee bit paranoid about being in public, but Bobby insisted and a little while later we were at a local burger joint, rapturously sucking down chocolate milkshakes and French fries.

After I was somewhat satisfied with the food, I sat back and looked around the place. Everything was brightly painted, orange and red and green. The lights were bright, slightly flickery fluorescents and the room filled with the sizzling sounds of the grill, the chatter of teenage conversation, calls for orders from the counter men, and the gunning of oversized car engines outside. It smelled like grease and beef and ketchup. And I had a moment that was much like listening to Django, a revelation that drew connections between every sound, every sight, every feeling and smell in the place, revealing a whole new level of information. It was like I was graced with the magical ability to see through the façade of society.

The whole burger joint suddenly seemed like a sham, a thin veneer covering desires, cruelties and deceptions. The young couple in the next booth, they obviously wanted to fuck each others' brains out, but made polite chatter about school dances and hamburgers instead. The grinning, polite fellow working the counter really wanted to smack the fat lady he was serving with a spatula, but because of the rules of commerce and his desire to make money, he got her some well-done fries with extra ketchup. Burger joint employees deferred to a man in a business suit, cleaning a table so he could be seated quicker, just because of the fabric covering his body. People greeted each other with handshakes and kisses when they obviously barely tolerated each other. The bright paint and friendly signs of the place were there to obscure the real capitalistic purpose of the place. It was all there to take your money, every bit of it, the cheerful exterior masking a vast conspiracy of bovine genocide. I felt as if, having been revealed, all the social niceties no longer had meaning for me. I could use them or reject them. I could step back from the public show and observe the goofy way humans were ensnared, without giving it a thought, into all these objectively bizarre and ultimately dishonest behaviors. It was both funny and tragic at the same time.

And that's why cannabis remains illegal. Blame that old alcoholic fucker Nixon, who created the DEA and the War on Drugs so that he could bust a few hippies when he wanted. It was obvious that cannabis and psychedelics were blowing minds, opening people to revelations about society and their fellows, removing the blinders from our eyes. The people who were opposing the war and calling for Tricky Dick's impeachment were the people who might, from time to time, take a toke. They were the Enemy and he put the apparatus in place to hunt them down and lock them up. And that became another great deception that the American people and the world – at least those who weren't high – bought wholesale.

And so, because of my world's reefer madness, I'd never really seen a ganja field as big or impressive as the one that I wandered through, even in Nepal. I walked for about half an hour and there was still no end to it. Fortunately, that was when I found Wayne.

26. Blue's Smoke

The trail widened enough for a wiffle-cart to turn around. At one side of the turn-around was a small shack, as splintery and planky as anything else in World. A man in his late twenties, dressed in brown hemp cloth, sat outside on a stool, his head drooping on his chest, a low rumble of snores suggesting a full-on lack of consciousness. I cleared my throat; the snoring continued. I tried it again with the same lack of response.

"Excuse me," I offered. There was a slightly louder snore. "Hey!" Still no response.

I stepped up to him and gave his shoulder a nudge with my elbow. Before I could say anything else, the man leaped into the air, spun around, and landed in some kind of martial arts crouch. If I were intending to fight the guy, it would have been a brilliant move, taking me completely by surprise, except that he ended up facing entirely away from me.

"I'm looking for Wayne," I said.

He spun back, his arms swinging in wide arcs that might have clobbered me, had I been anywhere within reach. I had my hand on the Mossberg, but my intuition said it wasn't necessary. I've dealt with paranoid pot dealers before.

He blinked. "Who's asking?"

"I'm Ian," I said. "Ian Better. I'm a musician. I'm just trying to find…"

"You expect me to tell you that I'm Wayne?" He looked at me accusingly.

"I hope you will," I said. "But only if you are."

"And what if I am? Are you from one of the brigades? I don't see a squad."

"I'm not from the brigade. And, really," I told him, "I don't give a shit if you are Wayne or not. I'm looking for some herb."

"Hmmph," he said. "And what makes you think I've got herb?"

I looked around at the fields of gorgeous green ganja that surrounded us.

"Oh, right," he said, the martial stance relaxing. "Ah, wiffleshit. I know you're not brigade. They never come this far from their little towns. We've been here for twenty years and no sign of the brigade, ever. But Blue still makes us cover the watch shifts. Just in case, he says."

"In my world," I told him, "we use these to guard our crops." I hefted the shotgun.

He squinted at the gun. "Scares off the brigade, does it?"

"In fact, it does," I said, "and it makes the deer run like hell."

The man stuck out his hand and we shook. "I'm Wayne," he admitted.

"Can I get some herb?" I asked. "I was hoping for about a quarter pound. I've got some brubarb…"

"Hold on, hold on," Wayne said. "There's no dry herb out here. These here plants ain't ripe by a couple months. And if you want any quantity, you'll have to talk to Blue himself. Come on. I'll walk you up to the house. We've got some dry goods up there. You'll like Blue's smoke. Everybody does."

He started to walk away, beckoning me to follow, but I just stood and stared. "Did you say Blue Smoke?"

"Come on," he urged me. "Blue really does have the best herb."

I shut up and followed.

Ten minutes down the trail brought us to a sprawling two-story farmhouse set in a grassy clearing. The house was remarkable in how un-splintery and planky it was. It looked quite a bit like an Earth house, with white-painted siding cut from smooth timber and slate shingles on the roof. In fact, it had a floorplan similar to my own house, including a big front porch. To either side of the house were barns and long, low wood-sided buildings. As we approached, I could see that the porch was occupied by two figures. There was a younger woman, perhaps in her twenties, and a very tall man of indeterminate age. The woman had brown skin and dark dreadlocks down to the small of her back. She wore a brightly-printed sarong draped around her hips and that was all. She was sitting at a small table, rolling joints as fat as my thumb. The man, similarly attired, stood leaning against a four-by-four pillar; as we got closer, I guessed his age at maybe forty-five or fifty. His dark brown hair was pulled back in a short ponytail and a long beard hung to the middle of his lean chest. There was something about him, even beyond his height, that was a little larger than life, more vivid than you might expect. I encountered people like him from time to time: Morrison onstage in his prime, Hunter Thompson on a wild run, Ken Kesey mobilizing the prankster troops. Back home it signaled charisma and some extra vitality or something. Here, my first thought was "god."

"Hoy!" Wayne called and they looked up.

The woman stood and waved happily, small breasts bobbing. "Just in time!" she said, holding up a spliff.

"Hold it right there," the man commanded. "Who is this?" His gaze struck me like a laser, across the remaining expanse of front lawn.

"His name is Ian," Wayne reported. "He's looking for herb."

"You're not brigade, are you?" the man asked me.

"Not likely," I said. "I'm a musician. And a farmer, too. I've been admiring your crop."

"Where's your farm?" he asked. "Why do you need my herb?"

"I'm traveling," I told him. "I'm far from home and I ran out."

"My crop is already spoken for," he said. "I have contracts with merchants to the south and the rest goes to the medical men in the Crosober Circle. But you are welcome to come share this spliff with us before you turn around and go away."

Wayne led me up the steps. The woman ran to him and gave him a big hug. His arm around her waist, he turned to me and introduced her as Caroline, his wife. She grinned at me and wriggled in his grasp. Wayne kissed her and then led me over to the man.

"This is Blue," he said. "This is his farm, the biggest herbal plantation between the Sustenx River and the Palacczos mountains."

"Nice to meet you, Ian." The tall man shook my hand. His grip was firm and strong and being close to him reinforced the otherworldly impression. If you looked at him closely, he seemed just a little too vivid, maybe with a hint of sparkles that could have been something I saw or something in my mind.

"Your plants are beautiful," I told him. "I've never seen a farm so big. In my country, weed is illegal, so we have to grow small plots and hide them. An acre would be a huge farm. I suppose there are some big farms in Mexico or Afghanistan, but I've never seen one. You've got what, forty or fifty acres that I saw coming in here?

"Seven hundred and fifty-five rope squares," Blue said. "That's about three hundred and seventy-five of your acres."

"Holy shit," I commented. And you can't spare a few ounces? I kept that last part to myself.

Caroline lit the spliff from a kind of talisman I hadn't seen before, something that looked like a small brass ring.

"What strain are you growing?" I asked, hoping that I could gain some rapport through farm shop-talk.

"We grow over forty strains," he told me. He accepted the spliff from Caroline, took a solid toke and passed it to me. "This one is Hogberry, a cross of Shiskaberry and Hog Balls."

"I never heard of Hog Balls," I croaked, trying to hold in a lungful of expanding smoke. "But it tastes like a fat and fruity indica."

Wayne and Caroline nudged each other, nodding at my astute appraisal.

"Good call," Blue said. "Seventy-five percent indica. The buds look like they're covered with sugar. It's been curing for almost ten months and it's getting a real nice flavor."

"Cannabis Cup winner for sure," I agreed. "There are folks where I come from who don't believe you can grow outdoor this good. They always think my shit's hydroponic."

"Cannabis Cup?" Blue gave me a stare. "Where are you from, stranger?"

"Another world," I said. "I'm not sure I can really explain how I got here."

"Through the Pool of Shebangs?" he asked. "Are you from up above? Earth?"

"That's right," I said. "And you're the first person I've met in this shebang who was even aware of the Earth."

"I thought so. Cannabis Cup – no one here knows what that means. I lived up there for a while," Blue explained, toking on the joint which was making its way back around. "Ever been to Amsterdam?"

I nodded, taking the joint from him and toking carefully.

"I've been there. I've been to the Cannabis Cup. Hell, I won one year."

"I went the first year," I said. "Blue Smoke was playing the Netherlands and Steve Hager from *High Times* gave us an invite."

"Did you just say Blue Smoke?" Blue asked.

"I did. That's my band."

"You know," Blue said. "I think I got you wrong. I thought you were from around here. When someone comes here and says they need a little weed, we're talking wiffle-carts. You're from Earth! A little weed… what? You're talking about head stash! To smoke on your journey, right?"

I nodded. "I was thinking about a quarter pound, if you can spare it."

"That's a fair amount of head stash. Do you have any money?"

"I've got some brubarb. And plastic."

"Ha! You know a pot dealer who takes plastic? Show me your brubarb."

I fished a handful of wire bits from my pocket and held it out for him.

He looked at it and sniffed. "What's that?"

"Money," I said. "Brubarb from jobs in Gilcrest, Avantre, Town and a few other little dots on the World map."

"We use a different kind of brubarb this side of the mountains," Blue informed me, "made from colored pieces of wiffle hoof. I don't know anyone who would take this wire stuff. Do you have anything else?"

"Do you take spondulicks?" I tried.

He chuckled. "Let me see."

I pulled out a guitar pick and held it up. "This is ten thousand spondulicks. Worth a whole lot of wiffle butts."

He laughed, a good long one. When he finally stopped, he said, "No, really. Got anything else besides your spare guitar pick?"

"Shit," I said. "That worked really well in Bemshire. No, I don't have anything else. Just my guitar. I could play a few songs, if you like."

"I can always use more farm hands," Blue said. "You could work it off. Say, a week on the farm for four ounces of primo?"

I thought about it. I thought really hard. Here was a chance to work on the greatest ganja farm I'd ever even heard about. Farming excellent quality herb in that quantity was unheard of anywhere. On Earth, farms a quarter the size of Blue's grew seedy commercial crap, because there simply wasn't enough time or labor to bring in a top quality crop that large. My pothead nature would not be denied. I wanted to learn all his growing secrets. I had an image in my mind of a huge field of gigantic ganja plants covering the Rosendale mountainside.

"Tempting," I said, "but I'm supposed to be back in Gilcrest before evening. We have a gig there and then we travel on in the morning. As much as I really want to – and really want that bag of weed – I don't have the time."

I probably said that last sentence at least a few times back when we were on tour. People never seemed to realize how tight the timing of a tour usually was. We always tried to leave some leeway in the schedule for relaxing, side trips and dope runs, but it was rarely enough. There were a hundred cities that I knew only from airports, hotel rooms or a fast-paced bus ride through town. And a hundred parties that I ducked out of early because we had to roll. Left to my own devices, I'd still be on the beach in Ibiza, or roaming the streets of New Orleans long after the tour was over. But it usually fell to me or Trenton to keep everyone on schedule, including, sometimes, our road manager who tended to fall asleep at inappropriate times. And wasn't I looking out for the band on this journey the same way?

"Hold on," Blue said. "I'll be right back." He disappeared into the house, screen door banging closed behind him.

"It's hard work," Wayne said, "but we have fun, too. And you can get high whenever you want."

"Stay and tell us all about where you come from," Caroline insisted. "We never go anywhere except Calstanus, when we take the herb to market."

The screen door swung open and Blue stepped out, holding a big glass jar. He handed it to me. "Here you go," he said.

The jar was made out of thick brown glass and could have held about a half gallon of water or preserves. I unscrewed the metal lid and removed a rubber seal. There weren't any preserves in there; it was herb, probably three or four ounces of what was easily the finest cannabis I had ever seen or smelled.

I picked out a bud and held it up. This was no fat fruity indica. This was a sativa with light bluish green calyxes, bright red hairs and a generous coating of gold-tinted resin crystals. The buds were long, delicate little torpedoes that smelled like lemon meringue pie with a touch of sweet hash. Moments after the jar was open, the aroma filled the porch, overpowering even the skunky reek of the growing crops all around us. I had a moment of déjà vu.

"That's what you would be working for," Blue told me. "That's what you would be farming."

You know, I'm generally a responsible guy. So, yeah, I let the taxes on the mountain slide for a few years. I was working on that. All right, maybe not *that* responsible, but I am when it comes to playing. I've never missed a scheduled gig, even that time in Sydney when I broke my leg, or most of a European tour when I had the flu. I always made it there. It was part of my identity.

But here was a jar of wonderful weed. I mean, I've seen a lot of weed. I grow ganja better than anything I could ever buy. I appreciate the finest, and I don't usually go slackjawed at the sight of a q.p. I pull much larger quantities out of my own garden. It's just that this stuff looked really familiar. It was the closest thing to Blue Smoke that I've seen since back in the days when Trenton used to get it for us. In fact, this looked better than any bag Trent ever produced. Fresher. Less crushed and broken up, all the buds solid and intact, every little crystal in its rightful place. Not that Trenton's herb was too crushed or anything – it was just that this was perfect. Farm fresh and never in a plastic bag.

And let's not forget that in recent years I became much more of a farmer than a musician. I played a bit here and there, but growing cannabis filled my days. I had a decision to make now. Farmer or rock star?

Blue was determined to sway my decision. "I'll tell you what," he said. "If you stay and work tomorrow – just one day – I'll give you an ounce. Then you can return to your quest or stay longer, if you decide that's what you want."

I thought about it. I'd already told Bob what to do if I didn't make it back in time for the gig. They would do fine without me and, failing all else, they could play some of Trenton's stuff or some of the standards we had rehearsed. I would stay and work most of the day, I figured, then excuse myself toward late afternoon and make my way back to Gilcrest.

"Okay," I said. "I'll stick around for one day."

"Great!" Blue enthused. "Why don't you hang onto the jar, as a measure of good faith? Smoke what you want, too. Everyone smokes as much as they want while they are here, just as long as you can do your job."

I thanked him and inhaled the fragrance of the bud I still held in my hand.

Today, I thought, I'm a farmer.

27. Ganja Time

I was given a room on the second floor of the farmhouse, with two big windows overlooking the backyard acreage. The room was small and reminded me of a spare room that my parents kept for the occasional guest in the Santa Cruz house. There was a mattress on a varnished wood frame, a small dresser, a nightstand, a spindly chair, and a closet about the size of a phone booth. One window was propped open with a thick piece of hemp stalk and a warm breeze and skunky aroma wafted through.

The chair didn't look very comfortable, so I sat on the bed and opened the jar. I pulled out a few buds and laid them gently on a smooth area of brown hemp bedspread. They were beautiful, exquisite bouquets of tiny dried flowers. I turned one over and let the resin sparkle in the afternoon sunlight. I didn't intend to smoke any; I was pretty high from the spliff of fruity indica. But it was hard to resist. What would it be like, after all these years, to smoke the ganja that once defined our band and our lives?

I fished a pack of papers out of my pocket and pulled out a leaf. I could at least roll one up. I picked out a particularly lovely bud and crushed up about half a gram. The spicy-floral smell was intense and my fingers quickly became coated with sticky resin as I rolled. I ran the length of the slim doobie under my nose and inhaled the fragrance. I stuck the end in my mouth and toked gently, without lighting it, and was rewarded with a sweet taste that immediately transported my thoughts to the days of doobies gone by.

When Trenton would get some really special ganja, he would deliberately underplay it. A typical session went something like this:

"Did you get some grass?" I would ask.

"Yeah, I got a little," he'd say.

"Is it good?"

He would shrug, say "It's okay," and pass me a lit joint. One time, he handed me some kind of African weed and I took one toke and forgot where I was before I could even pass the joint. Another time he broke out this dark brown Colombian stuff called Wacky Weed that produced, after just two tokes, the most intense laughing jag I'd ever experienced.

The day he offered me the Blue Smoke I was hip to his ploy. I could tell by the way he worked to keep a poker face that this was something interesting. But that still didn't prepare me.

We sat outside on a concrete wall near the train tracks, a mile or two out of town. The railway was used sporadically by freight trains carrying timber from Olympia, so it was usually a quiet place and we had a nice little pocket of woods where no one could see us. We did some of our serious smoking out there and if a train did rumble through while we were high, it was always a rush. I also liked the place because it reminded me of another secret spot, one that I had near the tracks back in Flint, when I was younger. The trains in Michigan were more frequent than in Santa Cruz, both passenger and freight, and my hideaway was a clump of trees next to a golf course, rather than the California woods. I spent a lot of time there, watching the trains and daydreaming.

So, with a shrug, Trenton passed me a thin doobie. I took a small toke and tasted deliciously smooth and sweet herb, which encouraged me to keep toking. I filled my lungs and held it for a few seconds. I barely finished exhaling when the feeling started creeping up the back of my skull. Just at that moment, a train clattered into earshot and my mind took me twenty five hundred miles away and I was back in Flint, by the tracks. It wasn't like any vision or daydream I ever had; it was a full sensory experience. I found myself seated on a grassy patch between the trees, looking down toward the tracks and an old locomotive was heading my way, lumpy clouds of black smoke pouring from its stack. I could feel cool, damp grass, not concrete, under my butt and a light breeze rearranged my hair. I felt as if I could stand up and just walk into this memory, as if I were right there.

So I tried it. I tried stepping into the scene that I saw. And I came back to reality in Santa Cruz, sitting on a concrete wall, with freight cars full of timber rolling past and Trent laughing hysterically at the expression on my face.

That's what the Blue Smoke did. Memories that you recalled while high became a full sensory experience. It became real almost to the point where you could touch it, but if you tried to do that, you would usually end up back where you started.

I couldn't resist. I pulled out my fire talisman and I lit that little joint. I toked and the smoke flowed into my mouth like some kind of sweet syrup.

We knew the weed was special, but it took us a few sessions to understand how consistent the special effects of Blue Smoke were. A few times we smoked it as we would our usual daytime smoke, expecting to get involved in activities or play some music. In fact, the first time we lit up the stuff with the band was in preparation for rehearsal.

Another couple tokes and there I was, observing that rehearsal. While it started out as a regular memory, from my own point of view, as the high kicked in, I found myself looking at the scene as if from one side of the room. Once again, like my Blue Smoke experiences of the past, it was amazingly real, like I was right there.

I could see myself, absurdly young, rolling a joint on a *Sgt. Pepper* album cover. A scattering of seeds dotted the orangey shag carpet that lined Trenton's basement. My guitar was propped against the wall, next to the funky old armchair I sat in. Trent, in a dapper pinstripe suit, was fiddling around with the electric organ. Cleve and Jason shared the couch, looking a little unsure of what to expect.

After a moment, Trent looked up and said, "So, like I told you at the auditions, we're an electric blues outfit. This band is about musicianship and authenticity. You dig? We're going to play some real-deal blues. Are you in for that?"

"Oh, yeah, man," Cleve said. "I'm in for some blues."

"Yeah," agreed Jason. "Sure."

"I thought we could jam a little today," Trenton said. "Some Robert Johnson, some Howling Wolf?"

Everyone was down with Johnson and the Wolf.

"I hope you guys get high," I said, torching the joint with a big, smelly Zippo.

"That's always the best way for me to play the blues," Cleve grinned.

"Yeah, sure," said Jason.

I took a big toke, held it and passed to Trent. We didn't say much as the joint went around for the first time. It was a solemn ritual, all of us getting high together for the first time. Cleve was the first one to go off, just freezing up like a statue with the joint still in his hand.

"Hey, man," Jason complained. "Puffing or passing."

I saw the moment that the Blue Smoke took my mind. I exhaled a big cloud that rolled through the room and then my eyes got a far away look. Trenton plucked the joint from my fingers. I could smell the smoke that my younger self exhaled.

I remembered, now, what I saw, what I experienced then. And the Blue Smoke took me to that memory, too. I saw us performing, although it wasn't the four of us. Jason was missing, there was someone else on drums who I couldn't see clearly, and there were other musicians sitting in as well. My view was apparently limited to the stage. I could see the band, though not the amps and speakers which must have been somewhere else nearby because the music was really loud, so loud I could feel it in my body. Nor could I see the audience. The lighting was really bright, too, brilliant yellowy-white. The air itself seemed bright, like maybe there was a fog machine or something. I looked good, perhaps a few years older than I was when I had the vision, a healthy, non-arthritic young man who strutted and leaped around the stage.

We played like the spirit was on us. We rocked. It was glorious and inspiring. Really inspiring because we'd never really played together and here was this vision of how good it could be. It was a great song, too, one I'd never heard. I tried hard to track the chord changes. It was electric blues, sure enough, but it was something more. It had an intricacy, a maturity, like it was some kind of psychedelic symphony. I listened with amazement until, quite abruptly, the experience ended midsong and I found myself back in Trenton's basement.

And we were all blinking and looking around.

"Holy shit," I said. "What a trip!"

"Yeah," said Jason. "That was a definite groove."

"I saw the band," Trent said. "I saw and heard us playing the most incredible song."

I picked up my guitar and tried a few bars, from memory. I wasn't sure if I was getting it right, but they were all staring at me.

"That's not what I heard," Jason said. "I heard a kind of uptempo thing, you know, like a radio hit. It was coming out of the coolest hifi I ever saw. The records were real futuristic, man, little silver disks. And it sounded sweet, really sweet."

"Wait," Trent said to me. "Play those chords again."

I did and he joined in with the melody, pretty close to what I heard.

"That is fucking cool," Cleve said, picking up his bass. "That's what I heard, too." He played a few notes of the bass line, much like what I'd heard.

We stopped playing and stared at each other.

"I saw us playing," I told them. I didn't mention that Jason was not there. I didn't know what that meant and I wanted him to feel part of the band. What a show! Great lights, man! We had back-up singers and horns. Psychedelic!"

"We've been privileged," Trenton said, "with a vision, a glimpse into what we can be. I don't know how. I never heard of that kind of thing happening, different people seeing the same vision, I mean, outside of a science fiction story. And it's more than the blues, man. It's…" He struggled for words.

"Transcendent," Cleve filled in. "Spiritual. We were *rockin*! Think we can really play like that?"

"Beyond psychedelic," I said. "A whole new thing. A new level of music."

Now Blue Smoke was not the only band, by far, that evolved through shared mystical experience. Hell, half of the bands, from the Beatles on down, tripped together. I knew a lot of them and I'm quite sure some weird shit went down that no one ever spoke about. Morrison told me a few tales of trips in the desert with the band. The whole San Francisco scene evolved around the Acid Tests and bands including The Jefferson Airplane and The Grateful Dead came out of it all smelling like paisley roses. The Who would do it right on stage, not necessarily trip, but become possessed, at one with their music. We did, later on, capture some of the experience in our live performance.

"Hey, what I heard was pretty cool, too," Jason said.

"Cool, man," I told him. "Play us some."

"Uh, I gotta remember." Jason stepped over to his drum kit, which he had lugged down into Trent's basement in big, black cases. "It was sort of like this."

He started knocking out a very strange rhythm. It reminded me of that Desmond Dekker hit from a few years earlier, *The Israelite*, only a little different. It was a compelling rhythm. He wasn't playing the downbeat, like we always did. And it sounded cool.

"Cleve," Jason said. "Check it out. Play a bass line like this." And he hummed a few bars of syncopated rhythm. Cleve joined in. "There was a melody on top of that," Jason explained, "but I'm not sure I can do all that. But check this out."

They were playing a reggae rhythm. Unmistakable to me now, but back then, beyond that one Desmond Dekker song, I don't think any of us had actually heard any reggae. It would be another year or so before the Jimmy Cliff movie, *The Harder They Come*, came out and a few years yet before Clapton covered "I Shot the Sheriff."

"Well, that is very cool, too," I commented as they came to a conclusion.

Trent looked around at all of us. "We've been given a glimpse. Hell, we've been given *music!*"

"What the hell was in that joint?" Cleve asked.

Trenton laughed. "Nothing but grass."

"That's some heavy grass," Cleve said.

"It's called Blue Smoke," Trent explained. "I have no idea where it comes from."

"Where'd you get it?" Jason wanted to know.

Trenton shrugged. "From a pot dealer. You know. Some guy."

"Oh, yeah," said Cleve. "We got the same dealer. I get my weed from Some Guy, too."

"Can you get some more?" Jason inquired.

"Oh, he's never got the same thing twice. Almost never," Trent said. "But I can ask."

"Just in case," I said, "maybe you should put that bag away. And we only use it for the band, at special times. I mean, it's your weed, you decide, but that's my suggestion. We'll chip in and buy you a lid of regular grass, if that's all you've got to smoke."

"I've got other smoke," Trent said. "And, yeah, I'll put it away."

We never did score any more of the Blue, but we made that bag last about six months. We had other experiences with it that brought us music, usually from other times and places. We never went back to that first vision, though, and most of the rest, when the vision included the band, included all of us. One of those visions, one that only lasted a few minutes, was of the band playing in front of a huge crowd somewhere in Japan, judging by the signs and advertisements plastered all over the arena. It was great encouragement to us, a sign that we could be huge stars. That one actually happened, years later in Tokyo, and we all recognized it, about halfway into the first song. Deja Blue. We talked about it after the show and then never again. I stuffed it away in the mental file for weird shit that happened even long after we smoked from Trent's special bag. Now that file drawer was open again and the Blue Smoke took me to Japan and forty thousand screaming fans.

I watched as my younger self danced at the front of the stage. And, yes! There was Jane, in the wings, shaking her very sexy booty. I soloed and the crowd roared, a mighty blast of sound that echoed across time, repeating itself at other concerts and I found myself in

Athens, watching Blue Smoke rip through a mighty jam, the audience screaming, clapping and stomping. Then I was seeing a concert in Philadelphia, at the JFK Stadium, the din of seventy-five thousand fans rivaling our huge sound system for sheer power. And then the inside of a civic arena someplace, a concert I didn't remember. I was near the front of the stage, just holding my guitar, looking young and healthy in a silvery costume that I also didn't remember. What looked like an extended version of the band, with back up singers, dancers and horns, stood in the distance behind me. Even though no one appeared to be playing, the audience shrieked and howled like it was the Second Coming.

And then I was back in the room on the second floor of the farmhouse, smoldering doobie still in my hand. I took another deep toke.

As cannabinoids found their way to my brain, I wondered about this whole journey. The whole thing, the quest for the resonant chamber was predicated on the idea that time was weird, somehow, that some of these gods lived for tens of thousands of years, that some of the gods and entities were scrambled in time. Was this all just some kind of weird trip that began on June 23? How could it be ancient *and* new at the same time? What exactly was all that?

And the Blue Smoke showed me. I stared out over a sea of people that stretched away to a big outdoor stage about ten acres away. It was an amazingly mixed crowd; young people, old folks, conservative-looking people, wild hairy freaks, and people of every race, creed and drug balance gazed toward whatever was happening up on the wide platform. Flanking the stage were two enormous video screens, the biggest I've ever seen. Other than the expansive crowd and the stage, there weren't many real landmarks: some trees in the distance, a parking lot very far off to one side.

"Where am I?" I mused to myself. "Is this Saugerties?"

"Yes," said a voice. "Good call."

I didn't see anyone, but as I looked around, a foggy figure began to take shape, accompanied by a kind of fizzing sound. The fog resolved itself into a young man with wild, black hair, holding a big, gray cat. If my Blue Smoke visions were like looking through an open window, this guy appeared inside the house. He was with me, seemingly also gazing out at the vast crowd.

"Is this the… uh…" I didn't really have a word for it.

"Hoo-ha," the man said.

"And who are you?"

"I'm called Atem," he said. "I'm the show's producer, you might say."

There was a flurry of activity. A voice that had been speaking over a big P.A. system was now interrupted by a shout. The big video screens filled with a purple glow. If you saw this on TV, you know what it was, but it was all new to me. I could see Joe Maloney, who I sort of vaguely recognized and, with him, Esty. A lifetime in rock, I've seen crazier things, you know. More shocking. And even if this was, as it appeared, a glowing purple sex act, the crowd seemed more awed than anything else. A vast "Oooooooooooooooooh" rolled through the audience.

A voice said, "Push whatever through the center of everything."

"What's going on?" I asked Atem. "What is all this about?"

"Think of it as a ripple in time, as if a stone were tossed into a pool and the wave travels through the aeons, transforming what it passes through, crashing against an island here and there. This is one of the places where the wave breaks." *

There was a deep, booming bass note and a blinding purple flash. The purpleness pervaded everything, pulsing and throbbing like a reggae bassline for a very long moment. And then, wham! It exploded in brilliance. There was a tinkling crash that seemed to come from everywhere at once and, everywhere on the big field, entities began winking into existence. Big ones, little ones, humanoid ones, reptilian ones, mechanical ones, ridiculous ones, gods, goddesses, demons, angels, heraldic beasts, dragons and who the fuck knows what else. A big vortex of some kind appeared in the sky and stuff started coming

---

* For the full story of what happened in Saugerties on June 23, see *The Great Purple Hoo-Ha: A Comedy of Perception*, by Philip H. Farber (Mandrake of Oxford, 2010). – Ian.

out of it. There was a big whoosh and, yes, there it was, the alien spacecraft that buzzed my mountain, looming huge in the sky.

"Goddamn," I exclaimed.

"It's all right," Atem said. "It's a minor change to the neurology. Harmless, really. And you can see her again."

"Thank you," I said, as the Blue Smoke took me off again. Jane. Yes, I *could* see her again. Now. I saw her, beautiful and radiant, as naked as I had just seen Esty on the big video screens. And there I was, too, a younger self, also naked but not nearly as radiant. I remembered this. It was at the hot springs at the School for New Learning in northern California. Somehow we had the springs all to ourselves. We made love in there for hours. There were no purple explosions, but it ranks as one of my best ever memories. I'd never seen it from this angle. I could see in my eyes how much I loved her. It was fascinating and the Blue Smoke took me off to Rosendale, many years later, Jane ill and frail on the sofa in a nest of blankets. And there I was, bringing her tea, and I had that same look in my eyes. And then a much more recent memory, the night of June 23, this time in Rosendale. The young-looking Jane-entity in the arms of the old, arthritic, mountain-man Ian, and there was that look in my eyes again. I watched as I fell asleep and she sat up in the bed, naked except for the sheet across her lap. My point of view was very close and I wanted to reach out and hold her and…

That brought me back to the room in Blue's farmhouse. The sun was getting low on the horizon over the ganja field, spreading golden light across the vivid green. I could hear voices from downstairs and the dinner bell began to ring.

28. The Fields of History

The next day, as promised, I worked in the fields.

Growing up as a pothead in Twentieth Century America, repression sometimes leads to outrageous fantasy. Over the years, with the resources and connections of a rock star, I explored as many of my cannabis fantasies as I could. Other fantasies, too, of course, but we're talking about big-ass fields of ganja here. In the '70s, there were rumors that John Lennon had a forty acre farm in upstate New York and that sounded pretty appealing to me. I could only imagine what that was like. Even just a few acres would be magnificent and way more than I could smoke or sell to my friends. I visited grow ops when I could and I already told you about the trip to Nepal. But I'm not sure there's ever been anything like Blue's farm on planet Earth and my most outrageous fantasies didn't even come close. It was inconceivable. The only thing comparable that came to mind was an image from a favorite comic of mine from '72, Dr. Atomic #2, *The Giant Grass of Bangagong Valley.*

Standing between the rows of plants was like standing in a New York apple orchard. The ganja plants were eight feet tall, nearly ten feet in diameter and just starting into their flowering cycle. They would be as large as trees by the time the buds were ripe. The growth was so vigorous that you could already get a sense of just how monumental the colas would become. And looking down the row, the plants stretched off into the distance, as far as the eye could follow, finally losing distinction in endless, vivid green.

A small army of us moved up and down the rows, trimming away small sucker stems from the lower parts of the plants, tying out branches to give the inner parts of the plants more sun and air, and picking off any obvious parasites. Back home, with my little plants, it was twenty minutes work to trim and pamper. Here, there was no limit;

you could keep going all day. We kept up a good pace, with breaks for smoking and lunch, until late in the afternoon.

Throughout the day, I kept looking for an opportunity to talk to Blue. He came to the fields, but we were all so busy, I didn't have the chance. Finally, as we were finishing dinner, he came over to see me.

"I expect you'll want to get paid and get out of here," Blue said, lowering himself onto the mess hall bench beside me.

"I have to rejoin my friends. But I did want to talk to you first…"

Blue snagged a small roll from the center of the table and stuffed some of it in his mouth. He chewed, swallowed, and then said, "What about? Oh, don't worry about that jar of weed. You keep the whole thing, okay?"

"The weed in the jar," I said. "It's Blue Smoke, isn't it?"

"Oh, yes," he affirmed. "Nice isn't it? That's also what your band is called, you said?"

I nodded.

He laughed. "I saw you play once. On the Museumplein in Amsterdam. Great show! You guys rocked. You're a god!"

"Don't believe everything you read on t-shirts," I said. "Can you tell me? Where does the Blue Smoke come from? Why does it do what it does?"

"It comes from right here." He gestured toward the fields of monstrous cannabis. "Maybe it's just an extra twist on the THC molecule, maybe it's a new cannabinoid chemical altogether. Ganja almost always has time distortion properties. It quiets the cerebellum, the part of the brain that, among other things, helps to create our illusion of linear time. Blue Smoke is just a little bit stronger in that direction."

"But," I stammered. "It was all so real! Like being there. I…"

"Okay," Blue said. "That's the power of your mind. Your brain can build whole worlds of sensory detail. Like dreams, you know, which sometimes seem very real. The Blue Smoke just taps into your memories, brings them out."

"I don't think they were all memories," I told him. "There were things I don't remember. And the very first time the band smoked it, way back when, we had a vision. Well, three of us did. We saw the band playing and we'd never played together before. How could that be a memory?"

"I use the term memory," Blue said, nibbling some of the roll, "because it is the common term. But most people make a lot of assumptions about what memories are and how they work, that aren't exactly accurate."

"What do you mean?"

"We have an illusion that time runs in a line. The future is ahead of us and the past is behind."

"Right," I said. "And there are people in Peru who have the past ahead of them and the future behind."

"Peru?" he asked. "I don't know. But there are enough weird ways to perceive and describe time in the different shebangs to account for not only timelines, but circles, squares, trapezoids and spirals, among much else."

"So what shape does time really have?"

"It doesn't," he grinned. "It doesn't really have a shape except what our minds make of it. So when we recall something, memory is rarely linear. Memory happens more by association than chronology. Our perceptions and experiences are organized by state rather than calendar."

"State?" I asked.

"Sure," he said. "If you are happy, it's easy to recall happy memories. If you are sad, it's easy to recall sad memories. Your state of consciousness blocks out information related to other states and gives you access to the memories that relate to the particular state you are experiencing now. For instance, have you ever walked into a room of your house, the kitchen, say, and then stood there, wondering why you came?"

I laughed. "I put that down to age. Or reefer."

"It happens to everyone," Blue said. "From time to time. And maybe a little more with age and reefer, too. But it's an example of *state dependent memory.* When you are sitting in the living room, watching TV, you are in one state. When you stand up, your blood pressure drops, your perspective on the world changes, and you enter a significantly different state of consciousness. And when you relocate to the kitchen, you forget what it was you thought of in the living room state. But then you go back to the couch and suddenly remember that you were supposed to make popcorn."

"I don't watch TV," I explained. "But I take your point. I still don't understand why, then, I saw things that weren't what I would call memories. The performance we saw never happened."

"Well, maybe not *yet*, if we try to understand this as linear. It's not, though."

"Linear or not," I said, "I looked young there. Now I'm older and I look older. It never happened when I was that age."

"Oh, you're much too stuck in the straight line frame of mind," he told me. "Anyway, the brain sorts time by association, not linearly. Memories line up with similar memories. Every time you get high, your brain associates to every other time you ever got high or will get high. Let me ask you this, what are the limits of your consciousness?"

"There are too many ways to take that," I said. "But how about this? My consciousness is limited to me, this guy, right here." I thumped my chest. "Because once anything is outside of the limits of my body, it's no longer me." I wasn't entirely sure I believed that myself, not being a big believer as I've already mentioned, but I wanted to hear Blue's opinion.

He peered at me. "Are you sure about that? You keep breathing in and out. The air keeps flowing through you, interacting with all your organs and cells along the way." He scarfed another baby roll. "And all this stuff, goes in and interacts. Some of it stays inside, becoming part of your body, and some comes back out. If you could look closely enough at your skin, you'd see gases and particles and all kinds of weird things, continuously going in and out through permeable membranes. Is this stuff part of you when it's inside you and then suddenly becomes not part of you? If you look that closely, it's kind of a fuzzy boundary, indistinct. It's more like you sort of fade off into what's around you. Let me ask you something. Can you imagine a big bag of weed, sitting on the table – even better, on that table over there?"

"Sure," I said. "I can imagine that."

"So is that inside you or outside you, that imaginary bag of weed?"

"I suppose there is some kind of physical process going on in my brain," I speculated, "and the imaginary bag over there – that's imaginary."

"Right," Blue said. "Now how about the table itself."

"That's outside me," I tried.

"Are you sure? Is that the table you're aware of, or only your brain's interpretation of a table? If we assume there actually are external things that we are sensing, then they are both outside us and inside us. Or at least, the boundary between outside and in becomes somewhat less distinct. What we consider to be our internal mind may be largely composed of experiences and ideas from outside; and our behaviors based on that experience influence and become part of the so-called external world. We start to understand, I hope, that we are parts of a system. We can't survive or even exist without the world that we fit into. Consciousness is a continuum and we are the way it delineates itself."

"We?" I asked.

"Entities of all types," he said. "Humans, shebang entities, linguistic entities, gods, imaginary friends. In a lot of ways, we're all the same."

"I've had similar thoughts," I told him, "usually after a nice spliff. My wife used to say that we are the eyes of the universe, the cosmos' way of perceiving itself. But I'm not sure where you're going with this."

"The point is that memories don't necessarily have to be personal. Our personal reality is inextricably wedded to a greater or higher existence through which we have access to a much broader range of information than we usually can perceive. The brain normally blocks a lot of it, filtering out the bandwidths of information that don't directly apply to our survival. But in certain altered states some of it slips by the cerebral sentries. And it is infinite. If you are in the right state, your personal consciousness may recall someone else's memories, may witness future memories, or may connect to almost anything, anywhere in a great and diverse universe. A fellow from your world, Lon Milo DuQuette, once said, 'It's all in your head… you just have no idea how big your head is!'"

"And Blue Smoke…" I began.

"Blue Smoke allows your brain to follow those occult connections in a very specific way. The experiences are personal, but may come from anywhere in time and space. Everything you see and hear while high on Blue Smoke relates to you in some way. And it all seems so real because it is. Just as your brain makes an accurate real-seeming representation of that table, it can make accurate and real representations of anything it receives information about. In practice, it's the same as seeing those events across time and space exactly as if we were right there."

"Are you telling me that I was really looking at my younger self?" I asked. "Damn, it sure did seem that way."

He nodded. "You can learn to control it. With a little training and practice, you can become a time traveler. Or, as I prefer to say, a spectator of time and space. I can show you. Come on." He wiped crumbs from his mouth with a random, used napkin and stood.

We went back to the house and Blue directed me to one end of the living room, next to a big, dark wood bookcase. He ignored excellent-looking armchairs and stretched out on an old oriental rug, propping himself up with a collection of embroidered cushions. He gestured for me to do the same. As I settled in, he produced a medium size joint from somewhere in his clothing.

"Ready?" he asked.

I told him I was and he torched the thing with a big old Zippo. He puffed big clouds of smoke and, when he was sure it was burning properly, passed it to me. I filled my lungs with sweet Blue Smoke.

At that moment, the thought crossed my mind that I really needed to get on the road if I hoped to rejoin my friends. Bob had instructions for one evening and I was well past that now. Would they wait for me? Would they come looking? Another toke, the Blue Smoke did its thing and there I was, gazing at Trenton, Perzanto, Captain Head Charge, Bob and Tim. They were walking through the gate of a planky stockade, into a town that I had never seen. As they passed into the town, I saw Alice rattling along behind them, followed by the rest of the company on foot. They must have done well in Gilcrest because they'd picked up some new fans who were along for the tour.

"They're going on without me," I said. "Why would they do that?"

And there was Blue, right there with me, looking out at my band-mates. "Where are they headed?"

"We were going to faraway Klod, to find Beezel and the exit to the Pool of Shebangs."

We watched as men from the town pulled the stockade gate closed behind our troupe.

"That's quite a journey on foot," Blue said. "Give 'em about four months to make it that way."

"Four months? Fuck."

"There's a saying in this shebang," Blue told me. "'It's a big world'. And they're not kidding. It's even bigger, given the lack of any decent roads, or vehicles to drive on 'em."

"We sent someone ahead in an airship, in case Beezel had faster transportation she could send back for us," I explained.

Men and women came out in the streets to welcome the band to town. Either the band's reputation was spreading, or they were exceptionally warm and friendly people.

"If that works out," Blue told me, "we'll give 'em two months. Either way, there's plenty of time to catch up and rejoin them."

"How could I possibly catch up?" I asked.

"Ever ride a dirt bike?"

"A long time ago," I said.

"Never mind. You'll be fine," he told me. "Now let me show you something."

The scene changed like a cross-dissolve in a very detailed 3D movie. We were looking at a mountainous landscape, a view from high up on a precipitous ridge. In the foreground, a field of snow sloped steeply to where bare boulders sat on the edge of a great fall to nowhere. In the distance, other snow-capped peaks emerged from a field of clouds. A strong wind blew through the valley between the mountains, dispersing the clouds in long streamers. Below, where the snow ended and the clouds cleared away, was the rich green of mountainside jungle, patterned with irregular shapes of cleared land.

"Where are we?" I asked.

"Yunnan Province, China. Or whatever they called it in the year 2,000 B.C."

"Why here?"

"Over there." Blue pointed across the valley.

I followed his gaze and our point of view shifted in another cross-dissolve. We now gazed out over a cannabis field. Compared to Blue's plants, these were midgets. They were just about ripe and the tallest were perhaps five feet tall. But they were dense little Christmas trees of ganja, thick bud cones that must have weighed over a pound per plant when dried. I would have been proud to have any one of them in my own garden.

"Beautiful," I said.

Our point of view kept changing, moving into the field, as if we were taking a stroll through the farm. Plants came right up close to us, and then passed off to one side. The buds, waving a mix of red and white pistils at the sun, were coated in thick, sparkling resin.

"These are some of the original medicinal cannabis plants," Blue said. "On the local linear time scale, these plants have been farmed here for thousands of years, at least, even at this early date in history. Big and stinky, I'm sure, if we could smell them. They are one of the ancestors of Blue Smoke."

I wanted to look closer at the flower tops, but something started to happen, obscuring my view. A small whirlwind set the plants waving and wobbling. The whirlwind filled with luminous mist and then cleared away a moment later, revealing two human figures. The figures looked around at the farm and slowly turned so I could see their faces.

It was Trenton. And me.

I didn't look that much older, just a bit dirtier.

"What the fuck?" I asked. "How did I get to prehistoric China?"

"Couldn't tell you," Blue said. "But I know you're going to find out. In time."

29. Some Real Noise

I couldn't leave Blue's farm. I just couldn't bring myself to turn around and get back on the road. How could I? It was the opportunity of a lifetime, an experience so fantastic, I had to stick with it. I mean, the greatest ganja farm in the universe was spread out all around me. I could work the fields and watch the magnificent plants ripen under the summer sun – and a variety of moons. And the mysteries kept deepening every time I thought I had them plumbed. The Blue Smoke. My appearance in ancient China. Entities, gods and June 23. The nature of Time itself.

Blue suggested that he could train me to be a spectator of time and space. That was intriguing. I wanted to learn. I thought maybe I could see the future, or at least some clues to my mysteries. I thought maybe I could see Jane.

So I stayed and I hoped that my friends, wherever they were, would understand. If they were in my place, I thought, they would do exactly the same. Trent at least. Hell, Cleve went off with Liana. Don ate the Terrtrych. Fuck it. It was only fair that I got to explore my own dreams.

So every day I worked in the fields. It was wonderful, blissful. And it was hard work. For the first week or so, I went to bed with sore muscles, but then I started to feel really good. The physical activity, fresh air and fine ganja made me feel years younger. My arthritis stopped bothering me and my stamina was up. I could prune plants all day – and I did.

In the evenings, I would sit with Wayne and Caroline and some of the other field hands. We would smoke the regular ganja, drink lemonade, and I would play a little bit on a battered old Martin D-18 that Caroline found stashed in a closet. It was in shabby condition, but it sounded okay and reminded me of an acoustic guitar I'd owned many years ago. These people were a little more music savvy than the others we'd met in World, but they'd never heard the blues played with a bottleneck slide.

Two or three nights a week, I would meet Blue in his big living room for a session with the Blue Smoke. He taught me, slowly and with much fumbling about on my part, how to follow mental associations toward specific ends. We followed our thoughts from the personal out to the universal. In the process, we visited important moments in my own life and some great moments in history. We solved a few historical mysteries. I can tell you what happened to Amelia Earhart (it's sad). I know why the dinosaurs died off (in part, because they pooped where they ate – the comet impact was just the clincher). I saw who really built the Sphinx (they didn't look Egyptian, and they talked to each other through devices called communiphons). At very long odds, we confirmed some of the improbable stories of my traveling companions. I glimpsed Dondelakavin's frog pond home. I saw Liana eating the primordial stew at the dawn of time.

It was the kind of mental exercise that I've always enjoyed when I was high and, with the Blue Smoke, it was something else again. After a few weeks, I started to get the hang of it.

Meanwhile, the plants grew thick with fragrant buds and the farm was increasingly spectacular. Every day I wandered through the fields for a while, admiring my favorite plants. And then, one day, Blue decided it was time and brought out a fleet of big, mechanical harvesters from one of the side buildings. Similar fleets, he said, were being deployed from identical buildings scattered throughout the vast farm. The harvesting machines looked as if they had been cobbled together out of odd parts, right here in World. They weren't quite as baroque as Mack's various conveyances, but were still downright weird. Each harvester had a pair of rattling engines that drove a big, slotted drum mounted on an open metal framework. The drum rolled over the ganja trees, separated branches from the stalks and gently deposited colas into a giant, cloth-lined box.

When a harvester filled its payload, we'd haul the full box off the machine and onto a hand truck, switch it for an empty, and roll the harvested tops back to the trimming shack. In the trimming shack, the buds were poured into the hopper of a big, hand-cranked trimming machine. Each bud rolled on top of a set of rotating blades that cut away sun leaves and bud trim, producing a clean, tight nugget of flowers. We checked it all by hand, trimming off leaf that got past the machine. With a crew of about fifty people working our part of the farm, it all took about ten days before many tons of buds were hung to dry. The smell of terpenes, like a freshly cut lawn, mingled with the intense fragrance of cannabis resin, pervading the countryside for miles around.

And then the harvest was in and it was time to go. Blue continually assured me that I still had time to catch up with my friends. I suspected he had some temporal magic to whisk me across World to faraway Klod or wherever the band was.

"I guess it's a kind of time machine," Blue said, pulling a hemp-cloth tarp off a motorcycle with big, knobby tires. "You'll be moving faster than anything else in this shebang. Figure your friends are making a top speed of about four miles an hour, when that old Model A hits a smooth, downhill straightaway. The bike will do ninety on a smooth road; figure a safe speed of about forty or fifty on most of the roads here. If they've gone about fifteen hundred miles over the last two months, you can cover that ground easily in under a week. We'll load this thing up as much as we can with food and extra fuel. You may need to find more fuel along the way, but that's possible, too. Not much petroleum in World, but she runs on pretty much anything. Hemp biomass ethanol in it right now."

Even better, Blue refilled the empty weed bag in my guitar case with as much as we could stuff in there and still close the thing. It was one of his top sativas, a spicy-tasting strain of Worldly origin. And I still had the jar of Blue Smoke, mostly full.

And then Blue said, "Oh, yeah. Remember to get the seeds."

"Seeds?" I asked. "What seeds?"

He laughed. "When you get to China in 2,000 B.C., collect some seeds from those plants and bring me some."

"I don't know if I'll be able to," I said.

"You will," he told me. "I've seen it."

Wayne, Caroline and a few of the farm hands came out to see me off. I was variously shaken, hugged, kissed, clapped on the back, and wished all kinds of good fortune on my journey. Three different kinds of amulets were pressed into my hands. Someone drew a sigil in chalk on the back of my jacket and a big spliff was stuffed in my face.

And then I was roaring off down a dirt road, the bike bouncing and leaping across the ruts. The suspension was way better than Alice's, but it was still a wild ride. To spare my old bones, I had to take breaks and ride more slowly from time to time before gunning the bike back up to top speed. The wind whistled around my borrowed helmet as I flew past hemp fields, orchards, woods and wiffle ranches. I avoided the towns as much as possible; I only stopped to ask directions and to learn when my friends came through. At night I slept beside the road wrapped in a blanket, the Mossberg at my side.

On the fifth day of my ride, I discovered that I was getting close and I pressed on a bit more into the evening. Just after dark, I rolled into a town called Snutwore, a fairly populous place by World standards, with tall, planky buildings adorned with bright paint. The streets were largely empty, but light and noise spilled from a big, peaked-roof structure at the end of the main street. It was familiar noise. Or sort of. It was one of Trenton's songs, "Underwater Arabesque." Trent was singing and covering a lot of ground on the keyboard, accompanied by mrrlnx, lipsquacker and dumbek. I pulled up and parked, leaning the over-packed bike against the side of the building. I unstrapped the case and took out the Gibson, carefully stuffing the sacks of ganja back inside. As the song ended, I stretched my legs and limbered up my fingers, which were a little stiff from the ride.

The next song began, Blue Smoke's "You Need to Be Free," and I knew it was my cue. Carrying the guitar, I crept inside. The stage was brightly lit by gas lamps in glass globes. The rest of the place was dim, ineffective guttering candles on each table. It was a capacity crowd, occupying all the chairs and most of the standing room as well. Heads rocked, toes tapped, a few booties shook. Keeping to the darker shadows along the wall, I made my way up to the side of the stage. I spotted Oswaldo, sitting in the wings on the object that I wanted: my little amp. He looked up at me with dawning surprise. I motioned for him to keep quiet. I pointed at my guitar and then at his seat. It took him just a moment to comprehend and he stood and swept the amp off the floor.

As the song came around to the usual place for a guitar solo, I was plugged in, switched on and out on stage. Trenton grinned in amazement. Esty, who was dancing on the front of the stage, made room for me. The Tripper gave an extra flourish on his drum. And I was jamming.

Damn, it felt good to make some real noise again.

30. Declan Bean

I spent a couple months playing bottleneck slide on Blue's old Martin and very little of it was from the concert set list. But it turned out that I was only moderately rusty at full-on electric Blue Smoke and my licks now took a wilder, rootsier form. I kept it loud and rocking. At the end of the song, the crowd who, I was certain, had no idea who I was, gave me a huge round of stomping and clapping. They pointed at me and shouted. And the band gave me an ovation as well. I bowed formally. I looked at Trenton for the next song cue; he smiled and tipped his hat, deferring to me. I pointed at The Tripper and grinned, which was the signal for "Awake."

I got into the groove pretty quickly and we rocked out the rest of the set. In fact, I felt refreshed. I was back from one of the best vacations of my life. I was relaxed, my cannabis ya-yas were appeased for the moment, and I was ready to play. After the show, I was hugged, kissed, shaken, clapped on the back, offered drinks, roots, pods, and groupies. Bob appeared from the shadows and swirled around my legs. I picked him up and held his fuzzy, buzzing body in my arms. When we managed to get away from the crowd, I told my friends an abbreviated version of my ganja farm adventure, leaving out the stuff about Blue Smoke and weird time-related experiences. They were amazed enough and slightly disbelieving at my tales of ganja farming on a mass scale, so I opened my guitar case and showed them. And then we smoked a whole lot of it.

Later, after most everyone had wandered off to bed, I broke out the jar of Blue Smoke.

"I got some other weed that's not bad," I said to Trenton.

"Yeah? Is it as good as what we smoked?"

"It's okay," I said and handed him the open jar.

He recognized it at once, of course. His eyes widened and his jaw dropped open.

"This is it," he said. "This is it!"

I nodded. "The farm I told you about," I said. "That's where it comes from."

"Holy shit."

"You remember how Blue Smoke would take us places, almost as if we were there, watching and listening?"

He nodded. "Sure. You'd never know where you were going to end up."

"Blue showed me how to know. How to control it and go wherever I want."

"I was never sure," Trent said, "If we really saw things that happened or if it was only imagination."

"We tested it," I told him. "We used it to view things we knew nothing about, but could go and test. Simple things, like what was under Blue's old porch. Or what kind of animal was tearing up plants in the back forty and where it lived. But then there were a few other experiences that, well, they couldn't have happened."

"Such as?"

I told him who I saw walking in the field in ancient Yunnan.

"I'd love to see a pot patch like that," he said. "Or Blue's farm. But 2,000 B.C.? I don't think so. You were hallucinating."

I shrugged. "It didn't seem like a hallucination. I'll show you. I can take you there."

"I'd love to, but it'll have to be another day," he said. "I smoked a whole spliff of your other weed by myself and we've got ground to cover tomorrow."

"That's the other thing I wanted to tell you." I told him about Blue's estimates of travel time to faraway Klod.

"Two more months?" He sighed. "Fuck."

"That's what I said."

"So much for the concert tour," he said.

I had a vision of my little Rosendale farm, dead from neglect, and the Ulster County sheriff coming to foreclose on my mountain. And Jane, very angry, which was never a good thing.

"Good God!" I swore. "I wish there was a faster way to get to Klod!"

At those words there was an impressive but not very destructive explosion, a deep and rumbling boom, a burst of very smoky flame, and Jehovah Himself stood before us, brushing bits of soot from His robe.

"Ian!" Jay exclaimed. "Trent!" He favored us with a broad, omnipotent smile. "Need a miracle?"

Of course, we did need a miracle and after we got Him Most High, Jehovah agreed that in the morning he would teleport our entire touring company to faraway Klod.

"You mean, we could have just teleported there right from the start?" I asked.

Jay nodded. "I told you, you only have to pray! I always grant prayers. I mean, except for the stupid ones. And the ones that are too much work and not enough fun. But anything for you, man." God was a fanboy.

"I thought you were busy," Trenton tried.

"Well, yes," Jay said. "I'm always busy. Running the show, you know! Well, not so much these days. I mean, apart from a few cataclysms and P.R. appearances, this job was mostly about the first six days. But there's still plenty to do…"

We made camp under a pavilion in the local park. The night was warm enough and someone also built a crackling fire in a barbecue pit, so it was soporifically toasty. Apart from sporadic snaps and pops from the flames, this part of World was a very quiet place. A thin chorus of frogs or insects chirped from the tall grass around the edges of the park. Occasionally a night bird would call. And humans snored, farted and rustled around in their bedrolls. I don't remember falling asleep; the next thing I knew it was late morning and I was waking to the sounds of a tour in full mobilization.

Just outside the sleeping pavilion, Buick was giving Alice a check-up, pulling dipsticks and topping off fluids. "I thought I'd get an early start," he said. "I've got a lot of driving to get through."

"You're going to keep driving?" I asked. "But…" I gestured toward our friends, who were packing and toting.

"I'm going home," he told me. "I did my part and I'm honored that I could. You don't need me anymore and I have a life to get back to, too."

"Wait," I said. I ran and got the dirt bike and wheeled it over to Alice. "I'm not planning on coming back this way, so why don't you take charge of the bike? If you can get back to Blue's farm one day, that would be good, but if not, maybe you can put it to use."

He agreed and we loaded the bike onto Alice's bed. Then we exchanged three different kinds of handshakes and a fist bump. Buick waved an assortment of talismans at me and gave me another one to keep, for good luck. I gave him a bag of weed for the ride and a group of us waved as he rumbled off, back to Town.

I slugged down a large mug of the local version of coffee, ate something that resembled a big, spicy pancake, and then carried my gear over to where Jehovah Airlines issued baggage claims. One of our new-found groupies tagged checked items and stacked them in a neat pile, while another recorded the claim number on a clipboard. Jay nodded and smiled at each of us, saying "Have a divine journey!"

When everyone was there and all the gear collected and inventoried, Jay lifted His hand in a gesture of benediction and said, "Ready?"

His hand came down, there was a burst of light and frankincense that obscured my vision for a moment, and then, as the smoke cleared away, I could see that we were somewhere else.

"This is as close as I could get and still ensure a safe landing," Jehovah told us, pointing up beyond our heads. We turned to look.

It was a steep-sided mountain, very tall and somewhat out of place on a vast plain of waving grasslike stuff. On the upper reaches of the peak, a great structure had been created from the native rock. It was somewhere between a Tibetan Buddhist temple and a fairytale castle. The whole thing had a mashed-up Disney-like quality; "It's a Small World" perched on top of the Matterhorn ride. Like some mystical mountain in a kung fu movie, a stone staircase climbed relentlessly up to the castle. The mountain and castle were not the only things looming above us, however. A great blobby shape floated awkwardly across the moons. Mack's airship, looking much worse for the wear, climbed slowly toward the castle. We had arrived at the same time.

"Please enjoy your stay in Klod," Jehovah told us, "or wherever your final destination may be."

We all thanked God for His help, gathered up our gear and started for the base of the great staircase.

Jay hurried after us. "Hell," he said. "I'm coming along, too. You might need Me again."

"What about Cleve?" I asked. "Is he okay?"

"Never better," Jehovah explained. "I don't know how he managed it, but that big, old warrior bitch is as googly-eyed for him as he is for her. Two's company, trinity's a crowd. He'll pray if he needs Me."

We started to climb. As tall as the staircase seemed from below, it seemed infinitely taller and longer once we were plodding up the treads. The cats loved it. They bounded up ahead and disappeared in the distance. The rest of us kept stomping along. It was not only a lot of work, but repetitious and mind-numbing, too. Only one thing for that; when we took a rest break, I rolled half a dozen fat spliffs of Blue's sativa. We smoked them as we walked, passing them up and down the line until we were all giggling and singing.

As we got higher on the mountain, a breeze started to blow. I didn't think this was anything unusual; most mountains I was familiar with were wild and windy places. However, as we got a little further up it very suddenly got a lot stronger. A *lot* stronger. This was gale-force, hurricane-strength wind that roared around the mountain like a barrier, preventing the merely curious from climbing any higher. And a few of our party, some of the fans and groupies who joined us in the last few towns, did in fact turn back at that point. But the rest of us had no choice and we pushed on into the wind, hanging onto the stone wall that lined the staircase.

After what seemed like a very long time, but was in reality only about half an hour, we climbed above the windy barrier. The hurricane blast diminished to a natural breeze and we stopped on a landing to catch our breath. I started to roll a joint, blocking the breeze with the guitar case. I had just crushed a bud when it suddenly got dark, as if a big cloud passed before the sun. And that's when we heard the shouts.

I stuffed the unrolled weed and paper back into the case and turned to look. The airship was very near and we were in its shadow. It hadn't fared well passing through the wind barrier. A rent in the lopsided gasbag gushed wiffle gas into the atmosphere. Broken fins and wooden struts hung loosely. The shreds of a hempcloth tarp flapped in the breeze.

And then, right before our eyes, a fresh gust of wind, a stray eddy from the barrier, caught the blimp and pushed it against the side of the mountain. It hit with a crash, smashing fins and pinwheels, crushing pipes and valves, tearing the smaller propellant gasbag, and knocking loose planks and struts. Perhaps a bit of metal crashed against the rocks and struck a spark, I don't know, but a great *whump* of blue and yellow flame blossomed from the break in the bag. The crew leapt from what was left of the cabin. The nose of the ship was right against the mountain, so the men who jumped from the front part of the structure did pretty well grabbing onto rocks or trees. But one crewmember was forced to jump from the tail of the ship and had a much farther fall onto very hard rocks.

By the time all the crewmembers found the ground, the gasbag was half consumed by flames, the burning fabric peeling back in big sections. I set the guitar and shotgun on the landing and started to climb over the stone wall, to see if I could help retrieve the airship crew. Perzanto was ahead of me, already scrambling over rocks toward where Mack was lying against an outcropping, conscious but apparently in a lot of pain. I started down toward the next crewmember, who was pulling himself up a steep and very uneven incline. I wedged myself securely against a boulder and lowered my left leg down to where he could grab onto my ankle. Using the boulder for leverage, I pulled him up to where it was flat enough to stand. He assured me he was able to get to the landing himself, so I looked for the next nearest crewmember.

Captain Head Charge, Mark Ratner, Dondelakavin and Jehovah followed me over the stone wall and were now assisting two crewmembers. The only man unaccounted for was the one who had fallen much farther below. What else could I do? I returned to the stairs and started back down. Perzanto joined me, as did the airship crewmember I pulled to safety. We went back into the wind, stumbling down the steps, near-blinded by flying grit and debris. Finally the wind died down again and we could see where the crewmember lay, another fifty yards below us. Like the other members of Mack's crew, he wore a long wiffle-leather overcoat on top of coveralls adorned with strapped-on gear, and a steampunk aviator helmet. He wasn't moving, although from this distance it was hard to tell if he was resting or deceased. And then I had a thought about the one airship rider I hadn't seen higher up on the mountain.

The crewmember clambering down the stairs at my side must have seen my face. "He was a hero," the man said. "It was a difficult journey. We were blown off course. He fought and worked with us to complete the mission. And, at the end, when the rudder fin cable broke in the wind, he went to the tail of the ship and pulled the rudder by hand. He saved us all!"

"He did?" I asked. "Aqualung? A hero?"

The man nodded emphatically.

"That is Aqualung?" Perzanto asked and, when I said it was, he leaped down the stairs, five at a time and climbed down the rocks to Aqualung's side. I'd suspected the big guy was a Tull fan and I guess I was right.

"We don't call him Aqualung," the crewman told me. "He wanted to be known by his birth name, you know, since his lung healed up."

I'd never even considered that he had a birth name, but I suppose that for anyone not born into the Cousteau family, Aqualung could only be a nickname.

"What's his birth name?" I asked.

"Bean," the man said. "Declan Bean."

By the time we had climbed down to his level, Perzanto was stepping back over the stone wall onto the staircase, Declan Bean over his shoulder in a fireman's carry. The big guy looked grim and I didn't have to ask about Aqualung's condition. But I wondered, not for the first time, was it possible for an entity from a popular song to die?

We staggered back into the wind one more time, another century of plodding up stairs in a forty mile an hour blast, gripping the stone wall for life. Man, I was getting tired of this shit. Just a little shroomy jaunt over the mountain to play a song. Only a day's hike down to the resonant chamber. A quick trip to faraway Klod. Fuck that. I was supposed to be onstage, rocking the house. Not having the crap kicked out of me by weird and unnatural wind. Better yet, I should have stayed on the farm. What did they have to do there, now that the harvest was in? Sit out on the porch and smoke and play music. That was the life for an arthritic, sixty four year old musician. Not climbing some endless fucking stairway to God knows what? And I can't even ask God what He knows, because He's on the other side of the fucking wind.

And, of course, we eventually came out the other side, though our timing couldn't have been worse. As we emerged from the wind barrier, the airship completed its disintegration and rained down on us as fragments of charred wood and metal and a swirling cloud of black ash. We all hit the ground and covered up as best we could until it passed. Finally, it was over and I lay down on the landing to catch my breath. Bob came and sniffed at my head. Perzanto put Aqualung on the flat stone about ten feet away and everyone gathered around.

Trent looked at Jehovah. "Can you resurrect him?"

Jay laughed. "Resurrect him? Aqualung?" He laughed some more. "Nah. I stopped doing the resurrection thing a long time ago. People always seemed to take it the wrong way, you know? Besides, he's not mine." He looked at Birdie.

"Why are You looking at me like that?" she asked.

He shrugged, a bit too dramatically.

Tim, crouched at Birdie's feet, raised his head and let out a series of hair-raising yowls.

"What's he saying?" I asked Bob.

Bob licked at an errant bit of fur, blinked a couple of times, and sauntered over to Tim and Birdie. With some effort, I sat up.

"He says that he's one of yours," Bob told Birdie. "And it's time to step up and meet your responsibility as Guide and Protector Between the Worlds."

"He said that?" Birdie asked. "Meet my responsibility?"

"No," said Bob. "He said" and here Bob repeated Tim's feline dialect. "But it means the same thing."

Birdie snorted. "So what am I supposed to do?"

Tim growled a bit, followed by a small yowl.

Bob translated. "He died because he changed. Aqualung – he's in a song and cannot die. But he became someone else; he strayed too far from his legend. Declan Bean, no one knows well enough. He can die."

"And this concerns me how?" Birdie asked.

Tim yowled and then growled.

"Take him to your shebang," Bob translated. "That is where the dead go. And they stay there or they come back to life. You must take him and determine the fate of Declan Bean – and of Aqualung."

"Right," said Birdie. "Take him. I don't know how. I don't know where."

A long and very eerie jaguar howl.

"Place your palm on the chest of the deceased. Your skin must contact his skin. Then you will feel the jaguar power within you and you will know what to do. Do it now!"

"Touch his skin?" Birdie asked. "Eew. He's dead."

Tim growled and showed his teeth. Bob didn't have to translate. Birdie leaned over Aqualung and unfastened the top of his coveralls. Screwing up her courage and her face, she placed her palm on his hairy, scrawny chest.

Her expression changed. From confused and disgusted, she shifted to serene and powerful. She looked regal, spiritual, and her eyes made it clear that she was a force of nature. She looked much like she did when she was singing, but the only sound to come from her lips was the word "Yes." And with a snap, she and Declan Bean were gone from World.

31. Funky Town

After a while we regrouped and resumed our ascent. We climbed the staircase until the sun was low in the sky and the moons were doing weird things. My muscles ached and my knees popped with every step, but we didn't want to camp on the staircase and we pushed on. The castle loomed larger and larger the higher we got, until we were right underneath it, walls of great stone blocks leaning ominously over our heads. Up ahead, the staircase ended at a landing with a huge and ornate wooden door. It was, of course, locked.

After I caught my breath, I knocked on the door with the stock of the shotgun. It boomed and echoed, but no one answered.

"Maybe no one's home," Captain Head Charge suggested.

Perzanto came and pounded. The sound was deafening, but still no one answered.

"Can anyone pick a lock?" I asked, pointing at the enormous cast iron lockset.

"I can," Jehovah said. "Watch this!"

He stepped up to the door and pointed His finger. His fiery nimbus flared and a fat arc of lightning leapt from His fingertip to the door. With a sharp *crack*, the lock and about a third of the door splintered into fragments and fell, smoking, to the ground.

"Nice special effects," I said. Jay bowed modestly.

"Yeah," Captain Head Charge commented. "Very fucking precise."

Perzanto grabbed a black iron handle in the center of what remained of the door. The muscles of his mighty arm bunched into boulders and the wood disintegrated in a cloud of dust and debris as he pulled. A dank breeze from inside cleared the dust as the bits and pieces of door settled in a heap. We clambered around the mess into the opening. Inside it was dark and smelled faintly of mushrooms. Just beyond the door, a big torch waited in a sconce. I gave it a flick from my fire talisman; it fizzled and then crumbled entirely. In a moment, flashlights and more esoteric sources of illumination were exhumed from packs and deployed. Perzanto sent a small ball of pale white brilliance through the doorway and into what we could now see was a wide, upward-sloping hallway.

"Do you think Beezel is here?" Dondelakavin asked.

Perzanto shrugged.

"I don't think anyone's come this way for a very long time," I said. "But maybe the exit is in here somewhere."

"Damn," Esty harmonized. "I was hoping for a hot bath and a soft bed."

"I'm hoping for dinner," Head Charge said. "Do we have any food?"

"Let's find someplace better to sit down," I told them. "Then we can eat and rest and figure out where we're going to camp."

So we hiked up the long hallway. It was an easier ascent by far than the mountain staircase, but we were fully exhausted. There was little talk, just the sound of tired feet shuffling on stone. I imagined that everyone else, like me, was fantasizing about a hot meal and a soft bed. Without Tim to pal around with, Bob stayed closer to my side. The bounce was gone from his step; he trudged listlessly like the rest of us.

Finally, at the end of an hour's uphill march, we came to a vast hall. The stone ceiling towered thirty feet above us and great, square flagstones covered a floor the size of a six thousand-seat concert venue, including the stage. Two enormous fireplaces filled the walls at both ends and three other wide, stone corridors opened into the hall, two on each of the longer walls. Between the exits, big, curved stairways rose up into dark openings in the stone.

And there was no sign of life. The fireplaces were empty and cold, patches of brownish dust nearby indicating where wood may have been stacked, long ago. Dust dunes and drifts covered about a third of the floor. There was no surviving furniture, only a few corroded nails and other little bits of metal. There was no one home, nor had there been for eons.

There was too much territory to explore and absolutely no energy to do it. Without a word, most of us unloaded our gear and sat on the bare stone floor. We broke out whatever food didn't need cooking and gulped it down, barely tasting anything. A few of us were asleep, wrapped in bedrolls or right there on the bare floor, before the meal was finished. It wasn't long before I slipped into an altered state, too, a gently purring cat at my side.

When I woke, narrow beams of sunlight pierced the room from tiny windows high on one wall. The windows also accounted for the chilly draft that trickled through the place, I reflected as I climbed out of my bedroll. Breakfast, again, was whatever we had that didn't need cooking, washed down with a hot cup of ersatz coffee from one of Perzanto's pea-devices.

We decided that the best way to search the huge building efficiently would be to split up. Captain Head Charge and Mark Ratner, veterans of any number of guerilla adventures, both insisted on a buddy system. We left our gear stacked beside one of the stairways and assigned a pair of very tired groupies to stay there and keep watch. I buddied up with Esty and we started up one of the stairways. Bob ran ahead.

"I saw your hoo-ha," I said as we climbed. "Wait! That doesn't sound right."

Esty laughed musically. "Millions of people saw my hoo-ha. It was glowing purple on international television! Welcome to the not-very-exclusive club."

Now you know that Jane is the only one for me, living, dead, or imaginary. But Esty is a sex goddess and she earns the title. I challenge any heterosexual male to discuss her glowing purple hoo-ha, to her very beautiful face, and not suffer from confusion and instant awkwardness. I did what I could to keep my cool and, with only a minimum of stuttering, I explained about my vision. "Who the hell is Atem?" I asked.

"An entity," she said. "A proto-entity. He's the one responsible, more or less, for the way we perceive all entities."

"Is he the Master Inscriber? Or the Scrambler, for that matter?"

She shook her head, waves of glossy black hair flowing around her. "I never thought of that, but no, I don't think so. Doesn't match Atem's description, or his M.O."

We climbed through the ceiling and came out on one side of a wide hallway. It was as dark as every other part of the castle – darker, even, since there were no windows. Our flashlights made very little of it visible. We aimed the beams along the walls and moved along slowly. After a few minutes, my beam shot through a doorway, into the darkness of a room.

In the ray of pale, LED light there were two eyes shining luminous green.

"This place is weird," Bob said, strolling toward me.

"You scared me," I told him.

"What?" he asked. "My eyes?"

"Yeah."

He seemed pleased. As he swished his tail and swirled around me, Esty came up behind us.

"Go see what's in the back of the room," Bob said, aiming ears and nose toward the darkness.

"What's in the back of the room?" Esty asked.

"Go see," Bob urged.

Following the wavering beams of our lights, we entered the room. I swung my beam in an arc, and we could see stone walls rising up to a vaulted ceiling. The room was long and reaching the back of the room involved a bit of a hike. As we approached the far wall, a giant shape loomed from the darkness. I explored with the light and it was revealed as a giant penguin. Or what appeared to be a sculpture of a big, all-white penguin, with no markings or features.

Esty giggled musically. "I know what that is."

I stated what I thought was the obvious. "It's a giant penguin."

"It's a hoo-ha," Esty giggled.

"Say what?"

"Actually," she explained, "it's only the clitoris. Not the whole hoo-ha."

"The clitoris is a, um, little tiny thing," I said. "A button. The little man in the boat. It's not the penguin on the telly."

"The penguin's beak," Esty laughed, "the very tip of the beak, that's the only part that sees the light of day. The rest of it, the, um, wings and stuff, run down along the sides of the vaginal walls. You have to stroke them from the inside."

"You learn something new every day,"

"A penguin?" Bob commented. "Phhtt. I think it's a Romulan warship."

"What do you know about Romulans?" I asked.

"I napped through every single one of your Star Trek tapes. VHS. Phhtt. When are you going to upgrade to HD, anyway?" He arched his back, stretched, and then strolled off into the darkness.

"So why are we looking at this hoo-ha?" I asked Esty. "Why would anyone create such a thing?"

"Beats me," she said. "Maybe this was a medical school, female anatomy department."

"Ah, we're getting sidetracked anyway. We need to find the exit."

"Right," Esty said. "Which way?"

"This way!" called Bob from the darkness.

I turned the flashlight until his eyes glowed back at us. He stood in an open doorway, across the room. We made our way around a bit of debris in the center of the room and joined him. We aimed our lights through the door.

"Well, it's not only the female anatomy department," Esty said.

In the pale beams of our lights were more hoo-has. Male ones, this time, and roughly life-size. Or life-size for Ron Jeremy, anyway. And there were a lot of them. The floor and much of the walls were covered in rows of evenly-spaced, erect penises. I stepped in and prodded one with the toe of my boot. It was stone, the outer layer of it crumbling with extreme age. We stood and stared for a long moment.

"Strange," I said. "A number of questions come to mind, mostly beginning with *who*, *why*, and *what the fuck*. But we may never know, and this isn't the exit."

We continued on, following a zig-zag path through the stone cocks toward a door on the far side. I thought that door might lead back to a corridor, but I was wrong. It led into an alcove that was bare except for a double set of glass doors, grimy with age, set against one wall. The doors featured a series of bolts, operated by turning small metal handles, and a big lever protruding from the wall beside them.

"Is it the exit?" I asked. No one had an answer for me.

I started working at the bolts, ten of them, running down the center crack between the doors. They were frozen with age but each started to work loose after a few minutes of twisting and several whacks from the butt of the Mossberg. Finally, they were released and Esty leaned on the big lever. With a loud creak and hiss of hydraulics, the doors slowly swung open. It was an airlock, with an identical, but much cleaner, set of doors on the opposite side. Bob ran inside, sniffing around the periphery.

The inner doors, bolts and all, were in much better condition than the outer and in a few moments they swung open. Again there was a hiss of hydraulics, but also something else, equalizing air pressure. If you could call it air. It smelled awful.

But it looked really nice. I mean, compared to the parts of the castle we'd already seen, it was fabulous, but a planky-wood hovel in the slums of Bemshire would be luxurious compared to the dusty emptiness we'd found. At first glance, I thought we were looking into a hotel suite. There were sofas and armchairs in chrome and pale, polished wood. And that's what it was – in the past tense. As the slight air current from the opening door washed against the nearest sofa, it crumbled almost soundlessly to the floor. A haze of dust rose from the wreck of the couch, carrying an even more intensely awful aroma to our senses. I remembered a time in high school when some nerd kids spilled a chemical called butyric acid in the hallway as a prank – it smelled like hot vomit mixed with month-old kitchen garbage. The butyric acid was almost as bad as what assaulted our nostrils in that decaying room. I choked and pulled my shirt up over my face, hoping that the stench of unwashed pits would overwhelm anything else. Bob growled and tried to back up into the airlock. He bumped into Esty's leg, but she didn't notice. Her face was rigid, screwed into an expression of mixed horror and fascination.

"Come on," she said, striding into the room, her gown swirling around her legs.

I shrugged, pressed shirt fabric tighter against my nose, and followed. Bob did too, although under protest. He walked like he was trying hard to make as little contact with the ground as possible, while holding his breath. In our wake, the furniture and everything else crumbled into foul dust, a denser stench pursuing us through the room. Through the heinous haze, we came to another doorway, standing open. We paused to look, before our presence destroyed any interesting evidence.

There was a body in there, sitting in a leather office chair. It was mummified, withered beyond any recognition of sex or identity.

"Beezel?" I gasped.

"I sure hope not," Esty choked, her voice reduced to a single, almost ordinary tone.

We crept in, trying in vain to disturb as little as possible. By the time we reached the mummy, though, the room was awash in stink fog and the desiccated body was in pieces, beyond any identification. This time, however, a few objects survived. A console on one wall, opposite from where the dead person had sat, remained fairly solid, though it was covered in dust and random chunks of other things. Esty strode over and brushed away the layer of crap to reveal a stainless steel surface.

At the top right of the surface, a green light burned steadily. In the center of the steel plate was a small screen. There was a moving image on the screen.

"Woohoo!" Esty exclaimed and then coughed and choked on a lungful of funk.

I leaned in to see what it was.

It was pornography.

Or that's what it looked like, anyway. There were two naked people, seemingly floating in a dark void, doing what naked people tend to do when they rub up against each other. One was a woman, as voluptuous as a centerfold model, with a great wave of brunette hair streaked with blond. Her partner was a slim, athletic man who was hung like a moose. A very large, mutant moose. The way they fit together, over and over, was almost improbable. I mean, he was really big and she was normal sized. I know the vagina can stretch to accommodate a baby's head, but that's usually kind of traumatic without anesthetic. The images on the little screen were fascinating in a freak-of-nature kind of way, but at that point my shirt utterly failed to filter nastiness and I started coughing and choking. I ran for the airlock, Esty and Bob right behind. When we were all inside, I worked the bolts as best I could with tearing eyes and a wracking cough. A few long, stinky minutes later we fell out on the stone floor of the alcove, gasping fresh air and moaning.

"What the fuck," I said when I was able. "I mean, just what the fuck was that?"

Bob frantically licked at his fur. "Nasty!" he hissed.

"Um, I'm not sure." Esty's multi-tone voice was beginning to return. "Everything decomposed right where it was, undisturbed for centuries."

"I really don't want to go back in there," I said. "Let's finish searching out here, then go back and find the others. If no one's found the exit or Beezel, we'll go back into Stinkland. With gas masks or something."

You know where this is going, right? None of our friends found a damn thing. Dust, debris, and the odd – and I do mean *odd* – sculpture was all there was in the whole gigantic building. So we had to go back into Funky Town.

The whole crew marched past the giant hoo-ha and through the room of cocks. When we reached the alcove and the outer door of the airlock, Esty and I reiterated the warning.

"It really stinks," I said. "We didn't last five minutes."

"It *really* stinks," Esty emphasized. "I mean, *really, really* stinks."

"You're saying you didn't like the smell?" Mark Ratner smirked.

"Perzanto," I asked, "can you make gas masks? Respirators?"

"I can make anything," he told me, "if I understand how it works."

"Okay," I tried. "Something that covers the nose and mouth and allows you to breathe through a filter."

"What kind of filter?" the big god asked.

I was stumped.

"Charcoal," Captain Head Charge offered. "Charcoal that's crushed up really fine. Best charcoal for gas masks comes from burnt coconut husks. We used to make masks in case the cops tried to tear gas us."

"Damn," Ratner said. "I wish you were around back in '67."

"Charcoal," Perzanto explained, "is difficult. It's more like something I would use to make something else. It takes more material. How much food do we have?"

"As much manna as you'd like," Jehovah grinned graciously.

"Finally," I said, "a good use for that shit."

So Jay zapped goop into existence and Perzanto converted it to coconut charcoal. It took twice as much manna to make a quantity of coal, but twenty minutes later there was a sizable pile of black granules and we turned our attention to the masks themselves. What we eventually came up with was a mask that covered the nose and mouth, fitted with a foot-long tube stuffed with charcoal and covered in fabric at the nether end. A bag of mixed nuts from a town along the road served as raw material for Perzanto's efforts and a little while later we were handing out the finished products. As he transformed each nut into a mask, I was able to follow it a little bit. It felt sort of like using the fire talisman, but more complex. The masks smelled like the Almond Joy factory burned down, but that was preferable to what awaited beyond the doors.

The airlock could comfortably fit five people, three if one of them was Perzanto. I went through in the first group, along with the big god and Esty. We went straight through the ruined hotel suite and into the porn room. On the little screen, the improbable couple was still going at it.

"Check that out," I said to Perzanto. "Ever seen anything like it?" It sounded funny. My muffled voice seemed to emanate from the end of the filter a fraction of a second after I spoke.

"It is only sex," he said.

"I know," I explained, "but he's… I mean… just look."

"Oh." Perzanto smiled a little. "I thought perhaps it was impolite to mention. And really, he's not that tiny. I suspect that many of you mortals are much smaller. It's not the meat, it's the motion. Be thankful for what you've got."

"Uh, right," I said.

Esty stared at him, eyes wide.

Perzanto examined the screen and the stainless steel console. "The signal is coming from in there."

We followed a cable that ran along the base of the wall toward the darkness. With every movement we made, the contents of the room that had succumbed to dry rot swirled into the air, a foul, nearly impenetrable fog. Out of the haze, our flashlight beams picked out a wall with a long, shuttered window. A small green light winked from a steel control box alongside the window. Under the light were three large buttons, one blue, one yellow, and one red. On impulse, I poked the blue button. Nothing happened, so I poked the yellow one. A weak whine came from inside the wall and the metal shutter on the window began to haltingly roll up. There was a faint glow from inside.

"Are they in there?" I asked. I wasn't sure I wanted to disturb them.

"No," said Esty as the shutter revealed more of the window. "I think there's only one, er, person."

Esty produced a handkerchief from somewhere inside her robe and wiped clean a small area of the window. Through the streaky glass we could see a kind of ergonomic medical table. Lying in a human-shaped recess in the center of the table was a mummified woman. Her bare, dry skin lay against pale bone; she wasn't much more than a leathery skeleton. The woman was wired into some kind of machine, a dozen leads jacked into her head and body. At first glance, you'd think she'd been dead for centuries.

But she wasn't dead. She was moving. Her pelvis rocked with a movement that would have been erotic, had she not been so dead and creepy-looking. Her skeletal jaw opened and closed and, very faintly through the glass, we could hear sighs and moans of ecstasy.

There were footsteps behind me and I turned to find Oswaldo, Ratner, The Tripper, Jehovah and Captain Head Charge.

"That's fucked up," Head Charge declared through his filter tube.

"I agree," I said. "But the question is, 'what do we do?' Do you think she can tell us where the exit is?"

"It is worth a try," Oswaldo pointed out, "if she can even speak at all."

Perzanto and Head Charge nodded agreement, Esty shrugged, and Mark Ratner just grinned. I reached over and poked the red button on the console. We heard a mechanical grinding inside the wall that went on for a rather long time. Lights came on, on both sides of the window. The mummy woman stopped rocking and looked up, her expression one of surprise and maybe a little annoyance – it was hard to tell from her skeletal features.

There was a deep *clunk* and the entire windowed wall began to rise into the ceiling. Funky Town haze rolled into the cleaner air that was inside. The woman began coughing and choking.

"Quick!" Esty said. "Do we have a spare mask?"

Perzanto produced a mask and he ducked under the rising wall and carefully fit it onto the woman's face. Her coughs subsided, but she didn't look happy.

"Who are you?" she demanded, her voice muffled and weak. "Where is Ernst?"

"I do not know Ernst," Perzanto explained.

"There was someone out here," Esty said. "But he was dead for a very long time."

"I was only supposed to be in here for a few hours," the mummy woman said. "Something must have happened to Ernst."

"We won't bother you any more," I told her. "You can go back to what you were doing. But we're looking for the exit."

"Or for Beezel," Perzanto said.

"The exit is close by," she wheezed. "And I…" She coughed again. "I am Beezel."

32. Cyberbator

We made a kind of sling or stretcher out of jackets and gear and very carefully carried Beezel out of Stinkland. She weighed almost nothing and seemed as if she might crumble to dust like the furniture in her rooms. When we were back in the more breathable part of the castle, we set the stretcher on the stone floor. Someone covered her naked, withered body with a blanket.

"I'm so hungry," Beezel moaned. "I forgot… I forgot about eating for so very long. Oh, God, I would love some food."

Zap. Jehovah offered a handful of bug poop. She must have been incredibly hungry because she slurped it up and looked at Him for more. Several more globs of gooey manna followed the first, plus a long drink of water. Life came back into her as we watched, her skin transforming from dried leather to pinkish, living flesh. Now she looked like a very, very old woman who lived and breathed, though she might be on her deathbed.

"How long?" she asked in a dry, raspy voice. "How long was I in there?"

"A very long time," I said. "I don't know."

"How long from when you arrived at the Pool did you go into that room?" Perzanto asked.

"Perzanto!" she exclaimed. "I remember you. How could I forget? Oh, it was many years before I went in there the last time. A hundred and fifty, I think. Was I in there for months? A year? Good gods, it seemed like forever."

Perzanto was silent for a long moment. "You were in there," he said, "close to fifteen thousand years."

"So it *was* forever!" she exclaimed weakly. "A long, timeless, wonderful…" She sighed and closed her eyes.

"Do you remember me, too?" Dondelakavin asked.

She spent a few moments trying to focus her eyes on him, then gave up. "Yeah, I remember," she said. "You're the cute one of the group."

We figured that rest, food and medication would be necessary before we could, in good conscience, demand information from Beezel. We found her something better to eat and moved her onto thicker bedding. I rolled a joint and got her to take a few tokes before she fell into a deep sleep.

She slept until the next day when she ate a whole lot more and then spent a rather long, noisy time off in a dark corner remembering how her body was supposed to work. I mused over the idea that gods still had to crap from time to time. I considered that the food itself had to go somewhere. And if Beezel were like the other gods on this particular quest, she may have begun her career as a normal human and might still have human digestive organs in there with whatever it was that gods were full of. The organs kept her healthy, godhood kept her alive.

And she looked much healthier now. She was still pretty skinny, but noticeably fleshed out. Her skin mostly lost the leathery look and she moved around like a stiff middle-aged person. All in all, a big improvement from barely-mobile mummy.

I asked if she was ready to come with us, back to the Pool of Shebangs and the resonant chamber, to sing a song.

"Oh, God," she said. "Is that why you pulled me from the cyberbator? I put that silly quest behind me a long time ago. You really think there's something to it?"

"Fucked if I know," I said. "Maybe you should talk to Perzanto."

I called the big guy over and he gave it his best effort. While he was making an eloquent appeal about the state of the world, the time spent on the quest as an investment that demanded a return, and the probability that this was the best, last chance to make it happen, Beezel listened skeptically and scarfed down another meal.

"But you say Gardangulon and Mortimer never arrived," Beezel pointed out. "How is this going to work?"

Esty wandered up and offered her take on how Blue Smoke was the greatest band ever and Ian was a god.

"Sounds kind of iffy," Beezel insisted. "But that's some voice you have, sister. Who the hell are you?"

"I'm just a fan," Esty said.

Beezel stared at her, squinting a bit. "I don't think so," she said. "He told you to come here, didn't he?"

"Who? Who told me?"

"The Big Head," Beezel said. "You know, the one who sent us all on this untamed snarlobite chase."

"The Master Inscriber?" Esty asked. She glanced furtively at me. "No, it was someone else."

"Hmm, I see," Beezel said. Her unrelenting stare at Esty's perfect face became even more unrelenting. "There's someone else in there with you, isn't there, dear?"

Esty nodded. "Yes. Syzygia."

"Sizzy what?"

Esty sighed musically and lowered herself to the floor. She arranged her gown around her and explained. "Syzygia was a famous woman in ancient times who became a goddess. In the long-forgotten civilization of Teehsloob…"

"I have not forgotten," Perzanto interrupted.

"No," said Esty. "I imagine you haven't. But most everyone else has, it all happened so long ago. Teehsloob was an advanced civilization, though little of it remains today. Syzygia was a stateswoman, an inventor, a social engineer, a sex goddess and a spokesperson for an array of quality products. After her death, at the end of a long and amazing career, the legends about her grew and spread. They became stories, books, movies, and sensifeeliums. She achieved the status of saint, then of goddess as her legacy became increasingly important. Statues were constructed and temples in which she was worshipped. But like Ozymandias, even her greatness, in time, was forgotten."

"But what does that have to do with *you*?" Dondelakavin wanted to know.

"The stuff that happened in June was not the only project we were involved with, the GPHH, Incorporated, I mean. Testing out some of the principles that were more widely manifest on June 23, William Wilderman, the founder, called forth a being that matched his perfect partner. It turned out to be Syzygia, to simplify a bit. But she couldn't stay, not in corporeal form like that. So she wrote down a set of instructions. After she was gone, Wilderman gave me her book and I did what she said. And Syzygia, across time and space and whatever else there is to cross, became part of me. She merged with me and transformed me. That's how I appear and sound the way I do."

"So you really are human," Trenton said. "Sort of."

"Everything about me is human," Esty told us. "My body that I was born with, Syzygia, even the legends that made her a goddess, are all human and human-created phenomena. This is something that everyone is capable of, I believe. One day, I'll write a book and explain it for others. Although it's not the only way a person can make this kind of transformation." She looked at Perzanto and Dondelakavin, who were listening with great interest.

"You don't need to explain it," Beezel said. "You only need to do it."

"You want me to…?"

"Yes, dear." Beezel nodded her head, a little less feebly than just a few minutes before. "I don't want to leave here. Screw that old quest. It ruined my life. I want to go back in there." She nodded toward the cyberbator. "If I have to hang around someplace for eons, I want it to be pleasure, you know? But you can take me aboard, like you did the other one, and I can be there when you play the song. Kind of. Enough so it might work and I can stay home. Are there any more of those cookies?"

"Okay," said Esty. "I thought that might be it. Why I'm here, you know. So, okay. You'll have to tell your story, Beezel. In enough detail so it becomes a legend, omitting the merely-human and sticking to the gloriously-human."

"I can do that," she said. "But can I have some more food first? And some of the old guy's herb?"

"Who you calling old?" I asked, even though at this point she looked decades younger than I did. But I rolled one for her and a few more for the rest of us.

A meal and a spliff later, Beezel looked like she was in her mid-thirties and in pretty good health. The rest of us weren't getting any younger, but we were a little more mellow and receptive. Beezel propped herself up against a stack of loaded backpacks and bedrolls. Esty sat cross-legged on a folded blanket, an old-looking book open on her lap, a pen in her hand. Her aura of sexy wisdom leaned harder on the wisdom than it usually did.

Beezel cleared her throat, took a sip of "coffee" and began. "Everyone listened to my songs," she said. "They uprouted them by the millions, onto their communiphons, digipalms, and eye blowers. Gliding through telespace, I would zing my product code on the status updates of everyone I saw. I would hear my own voice coming from poopsites wherever I went. I was good, you know. Venster Behad, the famous telesponder critic, said that I could sing into the heart of every listener. I thought that was good, too, because that's what I tried to do."

Esty gave Beezel her full attention, as did we all, and made notes in her book. The rhythmic scratching of her pen became background accompaniment to the tale.

"I had a great life," Beezel continued. "Really, really great. I can't tell you how much I enjoyed it. I had luxury mobilators waiting to take me anywhere I wanted to go, whenever I wanted. I traveled by flying montyback and ate in the finest places. Did you know that the correct way to serve broiled smackacia root involves rubbing the underside twice with fresh fingersauce from the Belarian handtoad? I didn't even know that Belarian handtoads made fingersauce until the waiter at Spanorcas explained it all to me. And you have to rub it twice, not once, or it doesn't work and it ends up tasting like chicken. One time I went to Spanorcas with six boyfriends and the rest of my entourage and we ate so much popped ticklefish that they ran out! Can you imagine, Spanorcas running out of ticklefish? Wow! *That* was legendary.

"I had more boyfriends than I could handle and my publisher set up a special department to keep them organized. My boyfriend department had twenty-five employees and over five thousand boyfriends! Do you believe that? It was insane. If it weren't for my dedicated employees, I would have had no time to make music. They would connect my boyfriends one or two at a time and they would message all the rest with updates on a regular basis. Sometimes when I couldn't message, they would message for me, as if it were me messaging. I think they liked to do that, because my boyfriends were very hot and had incredible fingers and excellent devices.

"My life, all our lives, happened through our electroonic devices. That's how we met each other, how we socialized, how we did business, how we had sex, how we made art. All of it mediated through the signals that went from communiphon to telesponder to digipalm to feeloray. Like everyone else, I carried my communiphon with me everywhere, so that I could c-message, c-massage, uproute, downdump, dimensionally express myself and get discounts at my favorite retail outlets. I loved my communiphon and my telesponder, too. I used them to make my music, you know, and to downdump it to my publishers. I had my own poopsite and handsheet pages that got a million hits a day. My publishers made sure that I had every possible technological advantage and they bought me new telesponders and communiphons every month, to make sure I was up to date.

"I spent my days exploring the world that I could access with my electroonics. Sometimes it was a real wonder that I ever made any music at all! What with poop gliding and mexting all my friends, all the time. I was connected! Seriously! My connections were legend! No one had more handsheet friends than me! And part of making music was all about using the interface, you know, making the communiphon do what you want it to. That's part mental focus and part knowing the commands. Everyone can do it, of course, but some of us are better than others. I was very, very good. I was a big star, the voice of my generation, the queen of poop. My songs were so powerful, they actually changed the circuits in the communiphons and telesponders! It blew people away.

"My first collection of songs was all about modern love. You know, finding romance in the telespace, unrequited uprouting, and finally, dimensional expression, though I had to watch my language on that one. You couldn't just talk about dimensional expression back then. No, you had to say things like 'affection downdump' or 'fucking,' you know, metaphors, euphemisms. The title was 'The Up and Downdump.' Everyone loved the collection and millions and millions were uprouted. The next collection was called 'Bananaphon' and that was another hit. The title song went mega contagious and everyone played it everywhere. That was the collection that had the song about dancing ferrets – but I guess you don't know that one. It had an image that I programmed of cartoon ferrets dancing, lots of them, and I would sing 'Ferret, ferret, ferret' while they danced. It was big. Really mega contagious. I made five more collections. The last one was called 'Resonance,' which was kind of a coincidence, you know?

"It was all so wonderful and so fascinating that years flew by while I was engrossed in phonic interactions in telespace. It was so much fun! There were poopsites where you could aim flyamatics at streets and houses and actually see where other people actually, you know, were, in physical space, in the world. It was so awesome, really. You could even put it on the eye blower or the feeloray, if you had the right cable. And there were always conversations on my handsheet pages and friends who wanted to mext. People used to take pictures of thylacines and put funny captions on them, like 'Ai ken haves cheezwonger?' or 'I nots hapi, my teef too bhig to clov mouse.' You get it? A thylacine? With big teeth? That was epic.

"And then one day there was this actual person, standing there in my room. Not on handsheet, but really there, in the flesh, you know? It was like a blink mob, with only one person. And what a presence! He was tall, young, and wore some kind of weird silver suit. Nice hair, too, kind of long and wild. It was rare that anyone would take the trouble to actually speak to me, I mean, right to my face, so I was impressed. Maybe a little too impressed.

"'Are you Beezel?' he asked.

"How could he not know it was me? My image was everywhere in 'space. I thought, did he live in the wilderness or, like, in a small town or something really primitive? I stared at him in disbelief.

"'Right, then,' he said. 'How would you like to be a really big star?'

"'Hmmph,' I told him. 'I'm the biggest star there is.'

"'Oh, I'm sure you're big enough, in this provincial backwater. But I'm talking about the world. No, I'm talking about worlds, thousands of them. You will join with the, um, greatest stars of the rest of the world and go to a, um, special broadcast studio called a resonant chamber, where you will play a song together that will be heard by everyone, everywhere! We're talking about a whole new level of big. An order of magnitude greater than whatever fame you already have. Better than Empty Vee. Or the internment. No, several orders of magnitude. Distribution beyond anything you've ever imagined! It's the chance to make a real difference to untold billions of people. You'll save the Earth and all the other worlds, too, and people will remember you forever! It will be the stuff of legend and myth. Even better, to prepare for this journey, er, I mean, this tour, you will be given powers and abilities beyond those of mortal, er, women. Are you with me?'

"I c-zapped my publishers and they were skeptical at first, but I had the silvery stranger, the Big Head, explain over the communiphon. He spoke as if he knew the secret language of music publishers and explained the ancient, secret practices of leveraging the product and maximizing Arrowai, whatever that is. Soon the publishers were enthusiastic, and they insisted that I let the stranger change me, right away. I was amazed and impressed by the stranger. No one persuades my publishers to do anything they haven't first decided for themselves. No one except the Big Head, anyway.

"So the stranger changed me. He pointed his finger at me, waved his hands, and shuffled through a bunch of junk he had in his pocket. Then he mumbled something that I didn't quite catch and *blam*, I was a goddess. What an upgrade to my image! I was taller. My breasts were larger. My hair was longer. I was stronger, smarter, and when I went to sing – Wow! My voice was more powerful, had a bigger range, and listeners would feel it through their whole body. I was sexier than ever, both in the way I looked, sounded and moved and also in my appetites, which were greater than ever. I suppose I always had a lot of desire, but now I had a hundred times more."

"The Big Head gave me a crappy map and I was ready to go.

"Better pay for Romans on your self-own,' he told me. Or something like that; I had no idea what he meant.

I wanted to take a hundred of my best boyfriends, but most of them wouldn't leave. Only fifteen came along. I took my communiphon, plus a couple of spares, a telesponder, a digipalm, and a pocket-sized blaudiopoop, really the bare minimum that I would need. We loaded all our things into six big mobilators and we rolled out of town, toward the Valley of Roses, which was very far away. It was so far away, I figured, it might take us all day to get there.

"We traveled a full day and I began to understand the scale of the map. The world was so much bigger than I ever considered! Worse yet, three hours away from my city, telespace disappeared. At first I thought that there was something wrong with my telesponder, but the boyfriends had the same trouble on theirs. I was convinced, then, that something horrible happened to the big c-routers deep under the streets. I felt so powerless. I couldn't even make a handsheet update about it. I almost turned back, but I thought about what chaos the city would be without 'space. Better to stay out until they got it fixed, I thought. Five boyfriends left me, then. It was three days before I figured out that we were very, very far away from any place that I knew and that was certainly why I couldn't reach telespace. I began to despair. Again, I almost turned back, but we were lost and the map was incomprehensible.

"We wandered for a full year, mobilating over smooth roads and rough terrain. Each day we would breakfast and explore the local area for whatever food we could find while the mobilators charged in the sun. Then, by noon, we would be rolling again. In some places, where there were people, I would sing and they would feed and fuck us in return. It was strange without mexting, but I survived.

"My devices would still work without telespace, of course, but they made no connections, there was no one else there and it was lonely business. Without the big city computers, my devices would not even link with my boyfriends' devices. I spent a lot of time re-reading my c-mail and listening to my old messages. I listened to the songs I had stored on the digipalm. I made new songs, even if no one heard them. And, grudgingly, I talked with strangers face to face. Eww. It wasn't too bad with the Big Head, because he was only one man and fairly clean, I think. But in some of the places we passed through, there were crowds of people who smelled horrible. They had things wrong with their faces and their teeth. They limped and coughed. It was nasty and I avoided it when I could. It was a little better when I was up on a stage and I couldn't really see them all because of the lights. I could hear the applause, which was good, and I could imagine they were all listening to me on their communiphons.

"And so it went until one day I recognized a landmark that was described on the map, a rocky island in the mouth of a river. I hadn't looked at the map in months, but I pulled it out from under the mobilator's seat and we soon realized that we were close to the Valley of Roses. The problem was, as we followed the wide river north to where a smaller tributary forked west, the terrain became too rough even for our mighty mobilators and we were forced to leave behind most of our luggage and walk. We hiked for two days until we came to the cave.

"I was amazed. I was jubilant. Finally! It was happening as the Big Head said it would, a little slower and with much more effort, but it was happening and I was going to be big. Interstellar. And then I could go home and enjoy my fame and fortune. I could already imagine the sensation that I would cause in telespace. The c-traffic would fill all the pipegirth, up and down the pooposphere. You know what I mean?"

Before anyone could reply, Beezel continued on. "Of course, I ended up in the Pool of Shebangs. There was nothing happening in the resonant chamber. I met the big guy here and the freak." She nodded toward Perzanto and Dondelakavin. "Which didn't do much to instill confidence in the quest, you know? And worse, I was having real problems without my connection. My devices were a plague to me rather than a comfort, a constant reminder of what they could be doing, what they should be doing. I played the games that were loaded on them too many times. I listened to the thousand or so songs on my digipalm over and over and over on my journey. I felt limited, stifled.

"I wandered for a while, first in one shebang, then in another. I never found a world where there was good telespace access. I mean, there must be one, right? But I couldn't find it and no one could point me there. My boyfriends left me, one by one, as they found better lives in the shebangs. At some point I think something in my brain snapped. I couldn't have telespace, so I became vehemently opposed to it. I decided to find a shebang where the level of technology was so low that the idea of telespace itself had no meaning. That's how I came here.

"After my first few months in World, I realized something. I hated it. I hated the dirty lifestyle. I mean, there's dirt everywhere. And you have to touch things. And people. Who you don't know. They worshipped me as a goddess and I couldn't stand it. So I decided to go as far away from the people as I could. I hired the best magicians in the shebang and had them create this castle at the exit point.

"I tried to keep busy, to make my life worth living. I made songs and eventually I experimented with visual art and sculpture. I suppose I was a bit starved for attention, you know, and I think the Big Head must have increased my sexual appetite along with my size. My art was a bit, um, masturbatory. But I was alone and my body had needs…

"I wasn't entirely alone, always, though. At first curious people would climb the mountain, to find out what was in the castle. Some would be men following some romantic vision of a goddess, looking for me. Sometimes, if they were fairly clean when they got here, I would fuck them and then send them back down with a warning to keep the fuck away. Every once in a long, long time, someone would make the climb looking for the exit point. Like you, these were usually visitors from another shebang, lost or trapped. That's how I met Ernst.

"Ernst was an electroonic genius from a shebang where they built gigantic robots. He hated the robots and left to find a better life, but accidentally fell into World and could not get out. He sought the exit and came here, much as you did. We fucked a few times, but it was messy, smelly and not satisfying. When I told him about the electroonics of my world, he was amazed. I had one device, my telesponder, that I kept as a reminder of what I must reject. I showed it to him and he worked to figure it out. Suddenly, with the hope that maybe he could get me connected again, I wanted my electroonics again. I wanted it so badly!

"But Ernst had both good and bad news for me. He could understand the circuits, but without the big c-routers of the city and all the people, there would be no shared telespace. He could, he told me, make a personal telespace, a realm inside a machine that could simulate almost anything. I could create my own world in there, with programmed c-people and all the connections I could imagine. I agreed and he started to work.

"Before Ernst could create a tele-world for me, he had to start with individual characters and actions. I showed him the sex-connect app on the telesponder and he went to work. With programming that he once used for running big robots, he was able to create artificial people who could connect to the sex app. They would be able to respond to me almost as well as a living person. It was better than nothing, so I agreed and we tested out a prototype.

"It turned out that I liked it, in a way, better than a living person. The personal telespace was much cleaner and nicer than being around live people. It was very responsive and with subsequent tests, we were able to make it even more intense than a person could be. Eventually, we created the chamber with the direct neural interface." Beezel tapped her right temple, where a series of jacks were implanted.

"Ernst took a turn first. After twenty minutes, I pushed the red button and he came out covered in sweat and out of breath. Sticky fluids dripped from his penis. I made him wash off the table before I went in there. When everything was clean and dry, I lay down. Ernst jacked me in. With each connection he made, the telespace took form. At first I seemed like I was floating in a gray void and then scenery began to appear, a clean, comfortable room with soft lighting. Although I looked like I was standing on the carpeted floor, I still had a sense of floating. And then the c-person began to appear, first as a floating assortment of lines and vectors and then acquiring texture and dimension. He was beautiful, an athletic man with nice muscles and a large pabloonga. And he was somehow human enough to arouse my lust but also artificial enough not to be totally icky. It was just like using the sex-connect app with a real person, only more so.

"He touched me and stroked me and I touched and stroked him. He entered me and we found a rhythm. It went on for a long time and I wondered where Ernst was. I didn't wonder too hard, because the c-person was taking me to pleasures I rarely experienced. After a while I noticed that he was accommodating me in other ways, that as I grew used to the size or shape of his pabloonga, or any other part of him, it would get slightly larger, or longer, or warmer, enough to push me a little bit further into ecstasy. The ecstasy filled my mind and it went on forever. Sometimes I would notice that I was hungry or tired, but those were abstract concepts and the eternal fucking would take me again. And then, suddenly the thing stopped and disappeared and here I am. But I wonder, what became of Ernst? Did he leave me there?"

"There was a corpse," Esty said. "But it's dust now. I don't know if that was him."

"Who else could it be?" Beezel asked. "There was no one else here."

"He must have died, somehow, while you were in there," I suggested. "Maybe a heart attack after all that virtual sex."

"Now I'm sad," Beezel said. "I'll miss him. But it was all so long ago. I don't know." She sighed. "Esty, do you have what you need?"

Esty flipped back through the pages she had just filled. She looked different somehow, her hair bigger and wavier or something. She nodded. "Yes," she said. "I've got it."

"All right, then," said Beezel. "Let me get another bite to eat, then you can put me back into the cyberbator."

Esty began to sing. Her multi-toned voice had at least one new tone and it soared and dipped with melody. I didn't know the words –

they were in a language I didn't recognize – but the song made my heart swell with happiness.

33. The B.C. Deal

Beezel pointed out the exit; it was through a door we hadn't noticed before in the haze and funk of Stinkland. We brought her back to the cyberbator, strapped her in and, carefully following her instructions, plugged the wires back into her body. Once she was happily doing her thing – and, really, it was much less difficult to look at now that she had flesh – we gathered up our stuff and finally departed from World.

I stumbled as I stepped through; the shift from dim lighting and a flat floor to the brilliance and incline of the Pool was slightly disconcerting. I grabbed onto Perzanto, a step ahead of me and solid as a mountain, and caught myself. Bob landed smoothly and strolled off with a smug look.

"First step's a doozy," said Mark Ratner, lurching through behind me.

Following Perzanto, we started upslope toward the cavern wall, which was hidden in the distance and glare. The others joined our procession as they came through and, after a short hike, we passed the last row of columns and came to the wall. Between the columns and the cave was a relatively flat area where shebang entities, as we'd seen before, made camp.

"I suggest we stay here for the night," Perzanto told us, as we gathered around him. "We can search for Bernard's shebang in the morning."

"How the fuck do you know it's night?" I asked. "Wasn't it late morning in World?"

Perzanto looked around. "How come *you* can't tell? It's night here."

"Why search for Bernard's shebang?" Jehovah inquired.

"Because Bernard is the final god," Perzanto said. "At least the final one that we can find."

"No, no," Jay said. "I mean, why go through the bother of searching, when you can simply pray to Me for the answer?"

"You know where Bernard's shebang is?" I asked.

"Duh," God said. "Of course I do! I'm God. I know all kinds of things. I keep telling you I can help, but do you listen? To think that I went through all the effort and suffering of Creation so that I could have ungrateful creations. Huh! But I suppose it's My fault anyway. Why did I go and give them free will?" He looked right at me. "You don't pray for years. What's a Creator to think?"

"You sound like my mother," Esty said.

"Wait a minute," I said. "We *want* You to help us! If You can lead us to Bernard, so much the better. We'll be done all that much sooner! I mean, we've been in this fucking cave for months. Let's fucking do it."

"All right," God said.

"Go on," I said. "Let's go get Bernard and finish this thing."

"Okay, yeah," Jehovah said.

"Well?"

"It's late," He said. "I'll do it in the morning." With a puff of frankincense, and maybe a little kaneh-bosm, He was gone.

My biological clock was telling me that it was not late at all, but what could we do? We set down our gear and made camp. Camping skills were now as natural to our road crew as I hoped stage skills would be when we returned to the upper world. Bedrolls were deployed, a small cooking fire was lit, and dinner preparations ensued. Trenton and I wandered along the edge of the Pool, looking for a good place to sit and smoke a joint. After a short stroll, we came to an area where campers were not so numerous and there was a shallow alcove in the cave wall. We sat facing the omnipresent glow of the columns as I rolled a joint of Blue Smoke.

"I got pretty good at this, practicing with Blue," I told Trent. "So just stay with me and I'll take you along for the ride. I really want to you to see Yunnan, 2,000 B.C."

"Was it even called Yunnan in 2,000 B.C.?" he asked.

"Couldn't tell you. And not a history book in sight. Maybe we can ask someone."

I torched the joint. The technique Blue taught me was a little bit like using the fire talisman. I would visualize what I wanted to happen while simultaneously holding a sigil or diagram in my mind. Both parts were tricky. How do you visualize a place you've never visited? Often, the best you can do is to visualize times that were sort of like the one you want – and you let your mind play through a range of times, getting closer and closer to the feeling that you want. Creating the sigil is another little job. It has to represent the coordinates in space and time that you want to snoop and it needs to be simple enough to hold in your mind.

But Yunnan was easy. I'd already been there and I knew what it looked like and what the sigil would be. I toked deeply and passed to Trent.

"Ian," he said, somberly puffing on the joint. "I think this may be the right time to tell you. I've waited so many years to explain this to you."

"What?" I asked, getting another puff for myself. "What are you talking about?"

"I know what we were doing in Yunnan. Remember back in 1976 when I had that bag of Chinese weed?"

"Hold that thought," I said.

The Blue Smoke was starting to creep up my brain stem and I had to be ready to focus my attention. I started to formulate the sigil. But something else happened then, something totally unexpected.

The Pool of Shebangs, as if someone turned a knob on a light board, got brighter. Not only brighter, but it appeared less like a collection of columns and more like a pool, like a deep basin full of light. The light was a bit lumpy, as if denser in some places and thinner in others. And it kept getting brighter. It was really fucking bright, right?

"Holy crap," Trenton said.

The sigil I started in my mind continued to form, by momentum or by its own volition, I don't know which. And the memory of Yunnan popped into my mind.

And we popped into Yunnan, 2,000 B.C.

For real.

Or at least it seemed very damn real. As real as anything else down in the damn cave. Are shebangs more or less real than the upper world? Was this a shebang of ancient China? Or ancient China visited through a shebang? Or did the Blue Smoke and the Pool take us to the actual, historical place? Fucked if I know.

We stood in a field of prime, ripe cannabis, fat little pine trees of sparkling indica bud.

"What the fuck?" I inquired of no one in particular.

"I was trying to tell you," Trenton said. "My weed connection all those years. It was us. You and me. Or more often only me. I never told you because they… we… told me not to, that I had to wait to tell you. Until now, I suppose. Because, well, damn."

We walked between rows of the fragrant little shrubs. The smell was intoxicating. Green-clad mountains rose on all sides, brilliant in the sunlight. A striped bird with a long beak landed on a nearby cola. It raised a feathery crest, tilted its head, looked me in the eye and said, "Oop oop oop." Then it flew off, fluttering its wings like a big, goofy butterfly.

We were actually in China, in a very ancient time. No question about it. We wandered through the plants in silent amazement for a while.

"So, do we just take some?" I asked. "It'll take weeks to dry properly. That's dense bud. We don't have any place to dry it, no racks, no dehumidifiers."

"I don't think that's it," he said. "And I don't want to steal it. We could get shot. Uh, with an arrow or something."

"We're not going to rip off farmers," I told him. "But the farmers are who we need to find. And work a deal."

"A deal? What language do you think they speak? English wasn't invented in 2,000 B.C."

I laughed. "You haven't made a pot deal with anyone except yourself, your whole life. Back in the day I was really good at it."

"Okay," Trenton said. "What will we trade?"

I started pulling stuff out of my pockets: A collection of various talismans, both lucky and practical; a few stray bits of brubarb; two guitar picks; one Assfriend; and the Bic lighter. And, of course, what was in the guitar case, but that might be like selling ice to Inuits.

"Assfriend! Goddamn it. How did you get in there?"

"Sorry." He stretched and yawned on the palm of my hand. "I was tired. It's a great place to sleep. Like swinging in a hammock, when you walk. Hey, this is a nice place. Gonna take some of this weed?"

"No," Trenton said. "We're going to make a deal."

"With those guys?" Assfriend pointed down the row of plants.

A group of three women and two men walked purposefully toward us. They weren't Chinese, I'll tell you that. They were tall and dark-skinned, with big, bushy eyebrows and long faces. From their heads sprouted great, drooping deadlocks, hanging down to the backs of their knees. And they wore black vests embroidered with pot leaves over brown hempcloth trousers and shirts.

"Yeah," I said to Assfriend. "Probably."

I set the little guy on the ground, stepped forward and held out my hands, palms up, in what I hoped was the universal We Come in Peace sign. They made an even more peaceful sign. The woman walking in front held up a huge, smoldering chillum. We all broke into big grins.

When the bowl made its rounds and was done, I loaded another from Blue's excellent sativa. The chillum circled again and the grins got wider and wider. These people grew the mother of all indicas, but I don't think they'd ever tasted sativa. They were impressed and a bit glassy-eyed.

One of the men reached into his vest and pulled out a parcel wrapped in big, flat leaves. He sat cross-legged on the earth between the plants, opened the wrappings and laid them carefully on the ground. On top of the leaves was a great, big dried bud. He gestured toward it and we joined him on the ground. He said something in a language that I've never heard before and he gestured again. The meaning was clear; I picked up the bud and took a look. A dense indica bud like those on the plants around us, this one was especially fine. It was cured to perfection, a golden brown with just a tinge of green, dark red hairs still intact, and covered in glistening crystals of resin. It smelled of faraway pine forests, with a hint of sandalwood. Suddenly it came back to me: the bag of Chinese weed in 1976! Yes! I nodded and smiled and passed the bud to Trent.

While Trent sniffed the indica bud, I opened the guitar case and pulled out a hempcloth sack of World bud. The sativa buds weren't as huge and chunky as the ancient Yunnan stuff, but they were exceptionally nice. The only thing better was the Blue Smoke, and we weren't sharing that. I laid out six torpedo-shaped sativa buds, totaling about the same weight as the indica, as close as I could estimate. I gestured at the ganja and the B.C. farmers gathered around to inspect. They sniffed it, they pinched the buds between their fingers, and they held it in the sunlight and squinted at it. They smiled, they exclaimed to each other in their language and they kept admiring the buds. Then, abruptly, they placed the buds back on the leaves and crossed their arms over their chests, staring past us with stony expressions.

"Is that it?" I said. "Do they want more? I tried to make it even. All right."

"Kind of greedy, isn't it?" Trenton commented. "Don't give them too much more, okay?"

I laid a couple more buds on the pile. They leaned forward, pupils dilating, eyes bulging. They looked at each other and made a gesture that even I could interpret. They shrugged and held a brisk discussion. One of them leaned forward, gestured to my buds, gestured to their buds and then made a short speech that was complete gibberish to my ears. I mean, as a language it sounded more like baby talk than poetry. Then they sat back, stony-faced again.

I tried again. I picked up their chunky bud and mimed putting it in my guitar case and walking away. They stared at me, seemingly without comprehension; but just then things changed. The Blue Smoke was starting to wear off, I suppose. With a weird feeling up and down the center of my body, we transitioned and were suddenly seated in the rocky alcove, facing the brilliant light of the Pool.

I was still holding the indica bud.

34. Deliveries

"Holy shit!" I exclaimed. "That was real! We were really there! Look at this!" I waved the bud around wildly.

"That didn't happen before?" Trenton asked.

"No way," I told him. "When I did this with Blue, we only watched. We were spectators. It must be the Pool. The Pool changed somehow with the Smoke… and… and…"

"Hey," said Assfriend, who was clinging to the guitar case. "You stole their weed!"

"It was a fair exchange," Trenton pointed out. "We left an equal amount. Hell, we left more."

"Yeah," I said. "And, anyway, we didn't mean to take it, we just popped back here."

"Give me a break," Assfriend complained. "I'm fucking with you. Like you were doing with them."

"I wasn't fucking with them," I said.

"I wasn't either," Trent added.

"Acting like you couldn't understand them." Assfriend shook his tiny head. "You guys are such assholes."

"We weren't acting," Trent said.

"What do you mean?" Assfriend asked.

"We couldn't understand them," I said. "I mean what kind of language was that? Ba ba doo doo wah wah?"

"Really?" Assfriend asked. "Wow. I misread that whole thing. I thought you were working a scam. Hey, they wanted you to take the bud, don't worry about it. They just didn't want to make the deal."

"I'm still confused," I said.

"The bud was the deal," Trent clarified.

"The bud was a sample," Assfriend said. "The field was the deal."

"You could understand them?" I asked.

"Yeah."

"How?" I inquired. "You never visited China before, B.C. or A.D."

"I listen," the little guy said. "And I hear. I don't know. It happens, you know?"

"So what did they say?" Trent asked.

"They thought you were trying to buy their crop with weed. They wanted to have your sativa, you know, to smoke, but they needed food and other trade goods for the big deal. They thought you were crazy, trying to buy ganja with ganja. Why would you do that? But they were perfectly willing to trade head stash."

"I wish you'd told us that," I said, "but the deal went off exactly like we wanted and like they wanted. Mission accomplished."

Even if we weren't time tripping anymore, I was still quite high. I gazed into the brilliance of the Pool, which was congealing back into columnar form. Little flecks of color seemed to swirl and dance in the brightness.

"Light that up," Trent said.

He gestured toward the Blue Smoke joint where it lay on the stone floor of the alcove. I picked it up. It was mostly intact; we'd only had a couple tokes each before the trip to Yunnan.

I held up the fire talisman. "Where are we going?"

"We have deliveries to make."

I looked at the indica bud. "Oh, yeah," I said. "Give me a moment to figure out the sigil for 1976."

The target was Trent's apartment in Santa Cruz in March of that year. We were taking a short break between a world tour and a recording session. I was off in northern California with Jane. Trent would drive up a few days later to bring us the ganja. I knew what his apartment looked like. I knew what Santa Cruz looked like at that time of year.

I lit the doobie and took a deep one as the sigil formed in my mind. I held the image as we passed the joint back and forth and with an audible – or at least it sounded audible – *pop*, we were in Santa Cruz, in the living room of the younger Trenton.

"Cool," I said.

Trent had a great pad. He'd spent some of his rock star fortune on top quality furniture. Not weird or abstract, groovy-looking stuff in any way, just incredibly comfortable and durable. There was a lot of nicely polished wood, on walls, floors and chairs, some rectangular areas of dark stone on table tops and entryways. A rack of keyboards and stereo gear filled most of one wall. And the young Trenton – complete with dark suit, narrow tie, and fedora hat – sat in a very comfortable chair, grinning at us with no apparent surprise.

"What's the date and time?" the older Trent asked.

"March 5, 1976, at 1:05p.m.," the younger Trent said. "You're right on time."

"Cool," I told him. "I guess this is for you." I passed him the bud. "It's Chinese, sort of."

He took the bud and looked at it with an expression of wonder. "Uh, I've got your stuff, too."

He handed me a brown paper shopping bag, folded over at the top. I opened it and found a large box full of Bambu wraps in red and white packages. There were also two rolls of premium toilet paper. If you knew what passed for T.P. at the Pool of Shebangs, you'd be as grateful as I was. And there was a box of shotgun shells.

"Thanks!" I said. "We were running low!"

"Want to put one of those to use?" the young Trent asked. "The rolling papers, I mean. Not the other stuff."

I looked at the older Trent, who grinned and nodded.

"What the hell," I said, tossing a pack of wraps to the young guy.

He began crushing a piece of bud between his fingers, crumbling it onto a copy of *Led Zeppelin IV*. Seeds rolled down the cardboard image of *The Hermit* into a big ashtray.

"Whoa!" he said. "Look at the size of those seeds!"

"We've got another delivery to make," I said to the older Trent. "You're going to love this." I scooped up some of the seeds from the ashtray. "Got anything to put them in?" I asked the young Trent.

He found a black plastic film canister, opened it to check that it was empty and passed it to me. I poured a dozen or so oversized indica seeds into the container, pressed the lid on firmly and slipped it into my pocket.

Trenton – the young one – quickly twisted up a fatty and gave it spark. These trips through time and space got me quite stoned, it's true. As we finished the joint, though, and the soft indica high was coming on even stronger, the Blue Smoke started to lose its grip and we slipped back to the Pool of Shebangs.

We recharged our time travel abilities with a few more tokes and followed another route familiar to me, back to Blue's farm to deliver the seeds. While Trent took the tour and gawked at huge quantities of drying bud, Blue and I sat on the front porch and smoked.

"You made your choice already, I think," Blue told me.

"What choice?" I asked.

As he spoke, he poured the Yunnan seeds out of the film canister and then refilled the container from a bag of seeds that he took from his pocket. He stuck a piece of adhesive tape on the lid and wrote "Blue Smoke" on it with a marker. He handed me the refilled canister. I stuck it in my pocket. "You chose to go on tour, you chose to go back to the band. If you hadn't, did you know that you would have ended up where I am? You chose rock star instead of farmer. I salute you!"

Maybe it was the truly massive amount of cannabis I'd consumed that day, but I wasn't quite following the point of the conversation. Before I could ask what the fuck Blue was on about, Trent returned, laden with a collection of bags and loose buds. He thanked Blue and, with an odd expression, shook his hand, and then we were back at the Pool.

"So what do you think of Blue?" I asked Trent, as we regained our bearings.

"I think he's *you*, man," Trenton said. "Did you look at his eyes! They're your eyes! Ian, I've known you too long to mistake it. He's you, but not quite. He's you if we never formed the band. Or you if you never moved from Flint. I don't know, you from the alternative lifetime in which you became a farmer."

"Yeah," I told him. "That's what he said, that I chose rock star instead of farmer. You know, when I was a kid and I just started smoking grass, before we formed the band, I would have been very happy to have the biggest pot farm in the World. That was my epic life goal. I spent a lot of time imagining how cool life would be among the giant ganja trees."

"Well, there you have it," Trenton said.

"Is that possible?"

"You've met your dead wife, had lunch with Aqualung and smoked a joint with God Himself. Why not?"

I couldn't argue with that. "Fucked if I know."

"Can I try one?" Trenton asked. "Can you show me the basics?"

I looked at the partially-smoked doob. "Sure, why not?" I explained, as best I could, what Blue told me about time spectatorship and we practiced making a sigil, without the smoke, of course. Trent's smart; he had it pretty much the first time.

"Pick someplace that you are very familiar with," I told him. "It's easiest if you know it really well and spend a lot of time there."

"My studio," he said. "Hey, I've got something there I want to show you, too."

"Cool," I said, lighting up the joint. I guided him through the process. With a *pop* we were in his studio.

"Damn!" he exclaimed. "I did it! That was easy! It makes sense, too, the way the sigil forms. Did you ever dream that we'd be doing things like this?"

"Not exactly like this," I said. "But I've always felt that there was more to life than we usually perceive."

Trenton's studio was amazing, the dream studio of any musician with a technology fetish. It was a big room with windows that looked out into a hallway where other windows looked out toward the Oregon coast. Out there, the sky was blue and gulls tilted over the top of the wind. Inside, keyboards and computers rolled around on wheeled racks. More racks against the inner wall held a vast variety of instruments from around the world: shakers, bangers, tooters, whirlers, buzzers, things with little keyboards, things with odd numbers of strings, and stuff too weird to identify without asking.

"Oh, wow," Trent sighed. "It's good to be home. Come on, over here." He gestured toward a thing that looked as if parts from three or four laptop computers had merged with a bank of theatrical strobe lights.

"Cool!" I said. "What is it?"

"It's a psychocollaborative stimulator. A friend of mine builds them. Funny thing is, I doubt he ever imagined what they would do on June 23."

"I have only a sliver of a clue what you're talking about," I told him.

"The strobe lights flash at frequencies that activate centers in the brain associated with visualization and imagination," Trent explained. "A seed image forms in your mind and then you see it as being real, only not quite. It was supposed to be special effects for a concert tour, like a super-psychedelic light show, you know? But now it does something else. On June 23, some of the seed images started to come out of the stimulator and stick around for a while. I mean, these entities that are all around us now, they come from somewhere, or from nowhere, but this thing makes them appear on command. Well, not exactly 'command,' but they appear. Watch."

He flipped a series of switches and tapped something on a keyboard. The psychocollaborative stimulator started to hum and make computer noises. Suddenly the strobe lights switched on and started flashing. It would have a made a great lighting effect; at first the flashes seemed like rainbows that shattered like glass.

"So if I keep staring, Bugs Bunny is going to pop out of the center of this?"

"Bugs Bunny?" Trenton repeated. "If you'd like."

The lights were beautiful and I thought that Bugs Bunny was great, but for all-out Looney Tunes laughs, you couldn't beat the Roadrunner and Wile E. Coyote. And swelling out from the center of my vision, Wile E. Coyote appeared in three dimensions, floating toward me rapidly. Instinctively, I dodged and momentum carried him past and he collided with the rack of instruments against the inner wall. He slid down to the floor in a heap. A beat and then the whole collection of instruments fell on him in a great, clattering, banging pile. A thin coyote arm reached up through a collection of little drums, waving a flag that said, "Ouch!"

Trent switched off the device. We were still laughing when the Blue Smoke wafted us back to the Pool of Shebangs.

"Pretty cool," I commented, catching my breath. "We could use it in the show, but there might be some collateral damage."

"That's still got a couple tokes in it." Trent nodded toward the roach of Blue Smoke.

"Where should we go?"

"Your call," Trent said.

I applied fire to the roach and we finished it. I visualized my mountain garden in Rosendale. I was concerned about the plants – they were either dead or ready for harvest by now – and wanted to pick up a few things, like clean clothes and guitar strings. I started to create a sigil – and my mind wandered. You know, it was a short mental leap from Rosendale to Jane. The sigil squiggled in my brain and, with a *pop.* we were in Rosendale.

We stood outside the house. Green leaves half-turned to yellow and red flickered in the afternoon sun. A loony woodpecker laughed from the treetops. It was early fall, which was right, but my Toyota 4X4 was parked in front of the porch – and I junked that old pickup in 2000. Now it looked only slightly rusty and it hadn't yet acquired the big scrape that adorned the passenger side in its later years. Hanging from the porch and flapping in the breeze were Tibetan prayer flags that Jane purchased at the monastery near Woodstock. Which meant that Jane was inside and that this was maybe 1995 or '96. Jane would be ill. She would be dying.

"I think I fucked up," I told Trenton. "I was aiming for my garden, now, er, I mean in our own time, but this is the past. Mid-nineties. Jane…"

"Jane's here? Can we…" He saw my face. "Oh. Okay."

"I… I have to see her," I said. "I can't be this close and not see her."

"I get it. Do what you have to. I'll keep watch. Birdcall if someone's coming."

"Forget birdcalls," I said. "Too many real birds. Just yell and we'll run until we're back at the Pool."

He nodded and I walked briskly toward the back of the house. If I could get onto the back porch, I could look through the window and see Jane, if she were in the sitting room we'd made for her, which was likely.

The back porch was enclosed, with a short flight of steps leading up to it from the lawn. At the top of the steps was a door with heavy, old-fashioned glass shutters, opened with a metal crank. The door was always unlocked; I can't remember ever having a key for it. The stairs creaked gently as I climbed and I did what I could to silence them. I could see a light coming from the inner window and as I slowly opened the door, I heard voices.

Both voices were disturbingly familiar. One was Jane's, weak and whispery, yet still beautifully lilting. The other, a raspy growl, was mine, of course. I crept onto the porch, closing the door behind me as quietly as I could. The big freezer chest was humming to itself under the window. I was about to climb on it so I could look through, when I had a thought. I reached into my pocket and found the film container with the seeds from Blue. I opened the chest and stuffed the canister down beneath the tubs of ice cream and boxes of freezer-burned meat. Then I climbed on top, where I could see above the window sill. My younger self bent over the couch where Jane was nesting in a pile of pillows and blankets. My beard was a little less shot with gray, but my face was lined with worry.

"Do you want your other blanket?" my younger self asked.

"No," Jane whispered. "I'm good. Can you turn down the lights on your way out?"

"I'll be in the kitchen. Use the buzzer if you need me."

My younger self walked out. Jane settled deeper into her blankets.

"Why don't you come inside?" she whispered a little louder.

"Are you talking to me?" my younger self reappeared in the doorway.

"No, sweetie, just talking to myself. I'm sorry."

With a nod, younger Ian went back toward the kitchen.

"Quietly, dear," Jane whispered.

I pulled the back door open and slipped inside.

Jane saw me and gasped. "It *is* you. I could feel it. Hey, you look good, rock star."

"I look fifteen years older," I said, as quietly as I could. "But you look great. I can't believe…" I guess I started to choke up.

She snorted. "I do not look great. I'm dying, Ian. Already I feel like I'm halfway into another world. Like now, I see you here, but also a kind of glow around you. It's very strange. Like there's a video image superimposed on you, an image of a rock god. I know you're not the real Ian. He's in the kitchen. You're Ian the god that everyone talked about back then."

"Don't believe everything you read on t-shirts," I whispered. "I'm not a god. I'm from the future."

"The future? You know, don't you?" she asked. "How long do I have?"

"Not long now," I said. "A few months more, I think. But, Jane… It's not the end…"

"Yeah, yeah," she scoffed. "Everyone says that, all my newage friends. I thought maybe you were here to tell me truth, not platitudes."

"It's not a platitude," I said. "In fifteen years. On June 23. You come back. You're resurrected. So are a lot of other people and, um, other things."

She smiled. "That's a nice story," she told me dreamily. "I know it's a story, but it makes me feel better anyway."

She kept smiling as her eyes closed. She looked like she was slipping into sleep.

"Ian," she whispered. "Ian from the future."

"Yes?"

"I love you."

"I…" It went unsaid because, with a *pop*, I was back at the Pool of Shebangs with Trenton Augustus.

35. Shining Girl

"Are you okay?" Trent asked.

I was a little disoriented and the scab over my heartbreak had picked loose a bit. I was also very, very stoned. I think it helped. Cannabis always helps me focus my attention on the present. And when I'm in the moment with enough woohoo, it's pretty damn tough to obsess over the past or get anxious about the future. And besides, I knew Jane would come back. Maybe I would even see her again, soon.

"Yeah," I told Trent. "I think I am. How about you?"

"That was fantastic!" he exclaimed. "I mean… it's real! I kept it secret for so long! All the times I wanted to tell you. All those years meeting my older self, I wondered when I would finally get to be that guy, when I could travel through space and time and search for the legendary weed. And it really, finally, happened! This is now!" He ran out of the alcove, making woohoo and yippee noises, like I'd never, ever seen him do before.

He was at least as stoned as I was. It made me giggle.

Our travels were over for the day, for the simple reason that if either of us smoked another puff, we'd arrive at our destination too giggly and incoherent to accomplish much, so we returned to camp and went to sleep.

I woke feeling refreshed and actually optimistic about the whole resonant chamber thing. I mean, we were pretty close, right? We only had to get Bernard and then we were off to finally play that song. And I guess that I was never too far from believing that something weird and magical would happen when we played our resonant chamber gig, but now I was fully committed. Why the hell not? I could light giant spliffs with a single thought, move through time with a toke, and I saw other people do even stranger things. I saw Esty and Joe do what they did on June 23 that changed the world. That was pretty hot, but as far as a stage show, taking into account the actual dynamics of a performance, Blue Smoke blows them away. It's what we do.

We bartered a bundle of wood from an old man who wandered the periphery of the Pool with a mountainous pile of kindling strapped to his back. He seemed to consider the joint and the good luck talisman as the better end of the deal. We cooked our breakfast over the fire and broke camp.

When we were all packed and ready to roll, Perzanto clapped a big hand on God's back and said, "All right, Jay. Lead us to Bernard's shebang."

"Aw, why do you want to go there?" Jehovah asked.

"You know why we want to go there," Perzanto attempted. "You said you would take us."

"You don't think I can, do you?" God asked.

Perzanto sighed and turned to me. "I'm sure the shebang is on this side of the Pool, so if we start, I don't know, maybe asking around a little…"

"Wait! Wait!" Jay called. We turned to look at him. "I can take you there."

"Okay," I said.

"I can," he reiterated. "But… what's in it for me?"

"You're God," I told him. "What could we possibly give you that you can't get yourself?"

He raised his eyes to the distant stone ceiling and tapped his foot.

"Some weed?" I offered.

More foot tapping.

"Some food that doesn't taste like bug shit?" asked Captain Head Charge.

"Hmmph," God said.

"A virgin sacrifice?" Mark Ratner tried. "Or maybe a nice goat?"

"No, damn it!" Jay cursed. "Prayer, you mortal morons! I'm God, damn it. I want some fucking prayer every now and then!"

"*Fucking* prayer?" Esty asked.

"Feh. You know what I mean. Blasphemer."

"I did not blaspheme."

"Hmmph."

"Our Father," Oswaldo began, "who art in, um, heaven?"

"Hallowed be Thy name," a few others joined in.

"Thy kingdom come," we all said, "Thy will be done, on Earth as it is in heaven. Um…" There was a pause as we tried to remember the rest.

"Give us this our daily bread," Esty prompted us.

"Bread," Captain Head Charge emphasized. "Not bug shit." Ratner and a few others giggled.

"And forgive us… um…" We were getting stumped. Prayers weren't really our thing; we were much better with classic rock lyrics.

"And lead us forth to the shebang of Bernard," I added.

"Amen!" everyone else said.

"Hmmph," Jay said, his nimbus smoldering. "I suppose that will do. We can work on it later. None of you went to Sunday school, I take it. Oh well. Such is life. Come on."

The caravan began to wend its way back to the Pool, following Jehovah down into the pillars of light. Jay took us on a winding path through the columns, first one way, then looping back in the other direction. His expression was always one of supreme confidence. He knew where He was going, His body language kept telling us. But I will confess that after forty five minutes of wandering, I was starting to lose faith in the Lord.

Finally, though, He stopped and pointed at a column of light, no different from all the columns around it. "All right," Jay said in His most omnipotent tone, "in you go!" He gestured magnificently, nimbus flaring.

"This is it?" Perzanto asked.

"Yes." Jay was not pleased to be questioned.

"Are You sure?"

Jay's nimbus flared wildly. "Oh, thou unbeliever!" He pointed His crackling finger.

I wasn't sure that Jehovah could hurt Perzanto, but I intervened. "Come on, Perzanto, in you go."

Grumbling, the big guy stepped into the column of light.

"Thank You, Lord," I said to Jay. "Catch me later and we can get Most High."

I stepped into the shebang.

And I stepped out into the center of a busy urban square surrounded by tall, glass and steel skyscrapers. It was a beautiful, modern city and the square was obviously established to provide some clear space for the arrival point – and also for the exit, an archway facing us on the other side. As I watched, a group of three men in dark suits stepped into the arch and disappeared. My side of the square was marked with a big purple circle, and I stood exactly in its center.

"Move along," a trim woman in a uniform told me. "People behind you may be coming through. I wouldn't want someone to materialize where you are. It can be very messy."

I quickly stepped from the purple circle and, indeed, Esty appeared right behind me, followed almost immediately by The Tripper, Dondelakavin, Ratner, Head Charge, and Bob. None of them materialized in the same place, so it wasn't *that* messy, but as each had aimed for the center of the column of light and had a little momentum coming through, they all collided with each other and fell in a heap. Bob was the only one able to dodge the multi-entity pile-up. The uniformed woman had her hands full for a moment, untangling limbs and keeping the traffic flowing smoothing. Messier collisions were averted as the rest of the company popped through one by one.

At the end of the procession, Jehovah appeared in a cloud of pungent smoke. As he strolled past, he leaned toward me and whispered, "I'm pretty sure this is the right place!"

I went to the uniformed woman and asked directions. "We're looking for Bernard," I said. "A god? Can you point the way?"

"A god?" the woman asked. "Surely you are confused. Bernard was not a god."

"I don't understand," I said. "We were told he was…"

"He? I think you have the wrong Bernard."

Perzanto came up next to me and intervened. "We are looking for your goddess," he said. "I hope Ian did not insult you."

"Goddess?" I asked. "*Bernard* is a *goddess?* You told us he was a god."

"I use 'god' as a generic, non-sexist term," Perzanto explained. "But to these people she is their goddess."

"I'm just stumped on the 'she' part," I said. "I assumed Bernard was a man. It's a man's name."

"Not where she came from," Perzanto told me. "Bernard is all woman, the human parts, anyway."

"I can't wait to meet her," I said.

The uniformed woman stared at us through this exchange with a look of wide-eyed horror. Surely my gender-blunder wasn't that shocking.

"I… I don't know how to tell you this," the woman said. "Bernard, the goddess, is… is…" She started to sob.

"Female," I said. "Yes, I got that part. I'm sorry I called her male. I've been set straight…"

"No!" the woman howled. "Bernard is *dead!*" She burst into full-on blubbering.

"Oh, shit," I said.

"I am so sorry if you came here for her blessing," the woman moaned. "But she passed away a little over two years ago. It was a tragedy. To lose a goddess… it is unheard of… goddesses do not die… but she… she…" And the sobs took over again.

"Some goddesses die," Esty commented. "It's in their nature. It's not as common as dying male gods like Dionysus or Jesus, but they do croak from time to time. For example, the Sumerian goddess Ishtar could be considered a dying-and-rising goddess."

"Dying," I asked, "and rising?"

"Sure," Esty explained. "That's part of the whole myth, that she comes back up and redeems the world. Her male counterparts do it, too. Even Jesus ends his act with a resurrection."

"It's not like that," the uniformed woman interjected. "Bernard was working on a chemical experiment of some kind. We don't know exactly what, really, but it went wrong. There was an explosion, a really big one, and there was nothing left of her laboratory except her corpse. It remains there now, untouched by decay or worms, though the remains of the lab have been cleared away and a shrine constructed around her."

"May we see her?" Perzanto asked. "Please?"

The shrine was public, the woman said, and she gave us directions.

The city was like a cleaner version of London, with a bit more sparkling glass and polished metal. Earth cities could learn a lot from Bernard's shebang. We saw quite a bit of efficient looking public transportation – electric trams that hummed through the streets, streamlined buses, and a subway of glittering chrome and indirect lighting – and very few personal vehicles other than low-slung recumbent bicycles. The sky, glimpsed between towers, was a darker, more velvety blue than Earth's and the air had a sweet, scrubbed smell, like the fragrance that follows a spring rain. Following directions, we walked down a wide avenue with a center meridian of flowering trees to a terminal where we climbed on board a shiny, silver tram and rode for about ten minutes. When the tram stopped, we climbed out and followed a winding footpath through a series of alleyways and into a small park. The shrine was in the center of the park, under a pillared pavilion of white stone.

There were flowers everywhere. Live flowers of every conceivable color filled beds in the park, wherever there weren't walking paths. And great piles of cut flowers filled the pavilion, everywhere except a narrow passageway and a circular area in the center, where there was a small raised platform. It looked like the floor of a building, with shiny but utilitarian tiles, the rest of the structure long since cut away. On the tiles lay the inert form of a very beautiful woman. She was tall, with statuesque curves and a great wave of dark brown hair nesting her head. Her features were exotic, vaguely Asian, with skin tone of light brown earth. She was dressed in a long, flower-print sarong and bouquets of fresh flowers were arranged alongside her arms and legs. She was very definitely dead, but she looked freshly so, not, as the woman told us, two years gone.

Perzanto leaned over her. "This is Bernard," he said sadly.

"And the quest is at an end," Dondelakavin added.

"What do you mean?" The Tripper asked. "It's not at an end! We can still do this!"

"How do you figure?" I asked. I didn't care which one of them answered. All I wanted to know was, should I stay or should I go?

"We're already substituting new gods, our gods, for the originals," Perzanto said. "A guitar god for an ancient god, that's a good swap. Esty for Beezel, that might work. But we have no substitute for Bernard, no god to fill her shoes. And we still have no idea about Mortimer. That's always been the greatest risk, I've thought, but now it means we're missing two out of six, instead of one out of six. Our chances just dropped enormously, I'm afraid."

"I beg to differ," The Tripper told us. "First of all, we do have Mortimer."

"What?" several of us exclaimed at once. "Mortimer? Where? When?"

"I've decided," The Tripper said solemnly. "I'm Mortimer."

"You can't just decide that," I said. "Can you?"

"Well, why not? I'm a fictional character and I've never had much backstory. My story is much like all of yours. A shaman-figure sent me on a quest. He even gave me a map." He pulled out a battered U.S. road atlas and waved it around. "Most of you wouldn't even be here if it weren't for me. I'm deeply invested in this quest. So why can't I be Mortimer? Hell, now that I've decided I'm Mortimer, I remember *being* Mortimer."

It made an odd sort of sense to me. I'd noticed that each of the other gods, so far, was connected, in my mind at any rate, to one of the tunes on the *Six Songs* album. We met Perzanto as we were singing "All the Way Down." We sang "I am You" for Dondelakavin. "I Could Stay with You" was the song I associated most with World and our quest for Beezel. The Tripper definitely had his song, "Awake." That left a song for Bernard and one for Gardangulon. Now knowing that

Bernard was a beautiful woman, I was guessing that "Shining Girl" was her theme. And if I were to replace Gardangulon in the resonant chamber, the remaining song, "The Deep Stone" was singularly appropriate.

Everyone was silently thoughtful. And in the middle of all that thought, Jehovah said, "Why don't you resurrect the girl?"

We all turned to stare at Him. He cocked His head and smiled smugly.

"I thought you didn't do resurrections now," I said.

"I don't," He explained. "And anyway, she's not one of mine."

"Well, who the hell can resurrect her?" Dondelakavin asked. "Not me."

Jay hummed quietly to Himself and scanned the ceiling of the pavilion.

"Birdie," I said. "The, um, Guide and Protector Between the Worlds. The last time an entity died, it was her responsibility. I don't know if she does resurrection, but I'm guessing dead gods in shebangs are her jurisdiction."

There was a lot of nodding and murmuring. "Fine," Esty said. "But does anyone know where to find her? What shebang is *she* in?"

We all looked at Jay. He worked at looking nonchalant, but the smoldering nimbus gave Him away.

"Our father who art…" someone began.

"Wait!" I said. "There's a better way." I looked at Trenton and he nodded.

"Better?" Jehovah scoffed. "How can you say that? After all I do for the whole freakin' world…"

"Sorry, Jay," I told Him. "File it under 'God helps those who help themselves'."

"Hmmph. Help yourself, then."

"We'll need to take the body," I told everyone, "and get it back out to the Pool."

Perzanto leaned over the corpse and slid a giant hand under her low back. Suddenly uniformed men and women appeared on all sides of us. They wore neatly-creased brown shirts and black pants tucked into big boots with an inordinate amount of lacing.

"Do not touch the goddess!" a large man with a helmet ordered.

Perzanto gave the man a quick appraisal and lifted Bernard over his shoulder. The helmet guy was big, but not in Perzanto's league. Unfortunately, all the other uniformed people had weapons and, in a moment, they were all aimed at us.

"Jay!" I called. "Blast them! Quick! Give them the Finger!"

"Hmmph," Jehovah said. "I thought you were helping yourself." He left the pavilion and sat on a park bench, watching petulantly.

What could I do? I thought about swinging the Mossberg around into my arms, but figured that might draw fire and get me killed. I whipped out my talisman and conjured a flame. No one was impressed. In fact, I'm not sure anyone even noticed.

Perzanto slowly lowered Bernard back onto the platform, carefully rearranging the flowers around her. "Sorry!" he said loudly. "Very sorry!"

"It's a cultural misunderstanding," Esty explained. "In our world, we always, uh, hold the dead as a way of, er, commemorating them. That isn't what you do here?"

I don't think her line of bullshit had any effect, but her harmonic tones and divine appearance may have softened them up, just the slightest.

"We still have to arrest you," the man with the helmet said. "Tell your story to the magistrate, perhaps he'll believe you."

"No, no," I exclaimed. "We're a band! We don't want to hurt anyone. Bernard was a member of our band! She was like family to us!"

"A band?" helmet-man asked suspiciously. "Where are your instruments?"

Two minutes later, we were plugged in and ready to play. I tapped my foot in the opening rhythm to "Shining Girl." The Tripper heard and picked it up immediately. The drum intro came around a second time and Trenton added some keys.

I sang the first verse, low and growly. "Shining girl says she loves me

"When she appears out of the night

"She wraps herself around me twice

"And she turns up all the light!"

On "light" we all hit it, the whole band rocking hard and Esty offering a spine-tingling "Ahhhhhh-ahh-ahh". Apparently the cops never listened to FM radio; they were startled, gripping their rifles tighter. As we continued, though, feet showed the first, faint signs of tapping and booties looked as if they sincerely wanted to shake.

I had a thought, then. Yeah, yeah, it was about Jane and the old days. It must have been around '75 or '76, because Jane was on the tour bus with the band. We came into some mid-size city somewhere. I think it was Syracuse, New York, but when Jane and I talked about it years later, she was convinced it was somewhere out west, Colorado, maybe. Anyway, we turned out for an afternoon sound check at the venue, an old converted opera house of the kind you find all across America. Jane and I stuck around after all the microphones were tested because we were intrigued by the old building and its fantastic décor – and because we were hoping for some alone time, which we definitely weren't getting at the hotel. Oh, believe me, there are plenty of opportunities for alone time in and around an old theater.

The next verse came around, and I really belted it out:

"She says, I'm gonna change you

"Rock'n'roll you 'til you glow

"Gonna blow your mind with information

"And explain what you don't know"

You've heard the song, I'm sure, so you know it rocks hard right on through the first few verses, with plenty room for pyrotechnics. Everybody gets a lick in and I get three. Trent is really the star of the song, though. He runs with this Bach-meets-Sun Ra thing that most of our early audiences didn't really understand. Hell, I'm not sure I do, but it sounds fucking cool, the intricacies of a fugue decomposing into space and returning to order, over and over, to a rock beat.

So, we were in that Syracuse opera house, poking around the stage. The way we set up our gear created a lot of hidden spaces. They were useful if one or more of us wanted to disappear for a song, or wanted to do something for a moment that we didn't want the audience to see. Don't get too carried away by that, mostly it was blowing noses, gesturing wildly for roadies, or catching a quick toke.

Back then, the usual concert setup included great stacks of speakers actually onstage with us while we played. We all wore ear plugs when we played; there was no other way to do it night after night and survive. We saw other bands burn out from sheer volume, no shit. Center stage, about halfway from the theater's back wall to the first row of seats, we set up our biggest, most impressive-looking stacks. Behind them, protected on either side by arrangements of blue anvil cases, was a space about the size of my Rosendale living room. It wasn't quite as comfy, but there was a beat-up old sofa, a couple of chairs, a throw rug on the floor and a small table featuring a large coffee urn. There was also an auxiliary sound board and a place to plug in; occasionally we would hide someone back there to play without being seen. Jane and I had a bottle of wine, a joint of blond Colombian and for the moment, we were alone.

"A secret language passes

"In between and through us all

"She says she'll tune your brain waves

"So your mind receives the call"

The cops were getting into it now. One of them was even dancing a little bit. Only one still held a gun, and she was waving it back and forth to the rhythm. I wondered if they had gun safety classes in this shebang. But it was encouraging.

Have you ever been the only one in an empty theater? It's a little creepy, especially if the building has some acoustic properties. A sound anywhere in the main auditorium sounds like it's right next to you. And old buildings make a lot of weird sounds as the heat comes up or switches off, as ventilation systems go to work and electrical relays clunk and click. Clocks tick, things rustle and scrape. Even though I was pretty sure no one was present, it made our little sanctuary behind the speakers seem just a little riskier, which made it more fun.

Jane was wearing an ankle-length dress of some thin, shiny stuff. It flowed around her body with every movement. And if I couldn't tell by looking, when she pressed against me for a kiss, I could tell she wasn't wearing anything underneath. I've mentioned before how beautiful and sexy Jane was, but I'm not sure I've given her justice. Remembering how she looked that day deserves at least a few moments – and it's important, as you'll understand. Her hair was long and straight, not shiny black, but glossy in a way that gave it a soft aura, like I was viewing her through a vaselined camera lens. She didn't have on makeup, and didn't need it. She had a natural rosy glow in her cheeks and full lips. Her eyes were dark and, to me, sometimes seemed unusually large, like the eyes of some rare nocturnal animal. She was lean where it counted, belly and legs toned by countless hours bicycling and swimming. Her slim body made her breasts seem more pronounced in contrast, beautifully round and swaying gently under the thin fabric as she walked. She was breathtaking.

The song suddenly slowed and Esty harmonized with me on the dreamy interlude of the next verse.

"In the dust of an ancient desert
"On top of a wind-wild peak
"Riding the waves of the ocean
"Let the whole world hear her speak."

And then we were rocking again and it was time for my longest solo of the song. By now, all the cops had lowered their guns and watched with amazement as I cranked up the intensity. I was focused on playing and was dimly aware that Captain Head Charge and Mark Ratner had moved behind the cops. They moved slowly, looking nonchalant. I didn't know what they were up to, but the cops were now fully involved in the song and I worked to keep them that way.

As I said, the old opera house made a lot of odd noises, but we managed to tune them out as we got comfortable on the couch. The kissing was getting pretty intense and I was feeling for a way to get my hand under her dress, which wasn't possible without getting all the way down to her ankles. But she caught my intent, stood up suddenly and, in one sweeping movement, pulled her dress over her head, tossed it at me, and stood there in the dim lighting, entirely naked. She was breathing hard – we'd been making out – the blush in her cheeks spread down her neck to her chest, and her nipples were in the full "on" position, begging for a kiss. I started toward her and she ran, giggling, out onto the stage. I ran after her.

I guess we did a little too well tuning out the background sounds. We also failed to hear the fifteen teenage boys who were on the stage. Fifteen adolescent boys and a fat lady. The lady's back was to us and she was telling the boys, "… not to touch any of the instruments while we do our…"

"Holy shit!" said one of the kids, catching a glimpse of Jane. She slid to a halt, pivoted gracefully and snagged her dress from my hands as momentum carried me past. I'm not sure how she did it, but she slid it back over her head and down to her ankles before a second glimpse was possible. But the kids were aroused and any discipline the fat lady might have imposed evaporated. And then they saw me.

"Oh my god!" one of the kids yelled, in near hysterics. "It's IAN!" In a moment, they were all screaming and I was backing away.

My solo ended, Dondelakavin wailed on lipsquacker for a bit, and then the next verse came around.

"Shining girl will you love me
"When you appear out of the night
"You plug me in to your device
"As you turn up all the light
"A-awoooo!"

Jane was slick. And she was smart. Even though she was most famous for her theatrical work behind the scenes, she had stage presence. "Stop right there!" she boomed out. Momentarily confused, the boys – and the fat lady – stopped and looked at her again. "This is a test zone! We are conducting a test, please clear the area!" She then pretended to notice the fat lady for the first time. "Oh, I'm sorry," Jane said. "Were you scheduled to be in here?"

The lady was flustered, even though I don't think she'd turned around fast enough to see Jane's bare booty. "Um, yes," the woman stammered. "The children will be presenting an award to their church group on Monday and they told us we could rehearse for an hour if we didn't touch anything."

"Oh, yes," Jane responded smoothly. "I remember that being on the schedule. I'm sorry our test has run a little long. I need to ask you to please clear the area. This experimental speaker is very dangerous. When we turn this baby on, it can blow the clothes right off your body!"

The boys were suddenly silent.

"Is that what happened to you?" one of them asked.

"That's right," she said, "it blew my dress away! We're going to do it again…"

"Come on, boys," the fat lady whined. "We'd better be going…"

"No!" the boys yelled. "We want to see her dress get blown off!"

"Now, children!"

By this time, I was back behind the speakers, plugging in a guitar and plugging up my ears. I was pretty sure I knew what she had in mind.

Jane climbed on a riser directly in front of the big speaker stack and struck a pose. I couldn't see from where I stood, but she showed me later – her breasts, nipples still pointing toward the sky, pressed against the thin fabric of the dress, her hip cocked to one side, arms stretched out dramatically. The boys let out a collective moan and the fat lady made sputtering sounds.

"Are you ready, Mr. Better?" Jane called.

"Ready!"

"Initiate test!

I made a note, a long, deep, rumble of a note and, holding the string with my left hand, I used my right to nudge a slider on the sound board. I nudged it and kept nudging it, the note rumbling from freight train to full-on atom bomb volume.

The final verse came around and I sang it low and growly, like the first.

"Shining girl says she loves me

"When she appears out of the night

"She wraps herself around me twice

"And she turns out all the light"

The sound coming from the Syracuse speaker stack carried some force – it sounded like the end of the world, a vibrating wail that shook the floor, rattled the rafters, and shook dust loose from the lighting fixtures, high above. In spite of the promise of full frontal nudity, the teen boys ran for cover, fleeing down the aisles of the opera house, the fat lady waddling after them. After a minute or so, I stopped playing, the room reverberating for a long moment. I looked up to see Jane coming around the speaker stack, howling with laughter. We laughed until it hurt and I'm not going to describe what we did then on the empty stage. Fuck you, I told you more than enough already.

"Shining Girl" finishes on a haunting note and, as there usually is, there was a moment of silence before anyone applauded or reacted. Before there was time for any kind of ovation, Captain Head Charge interrupted the auditory pause with a yell. "Grab Bernard and run!"

Perzanto scooped up the body. Head Charge called again, "Run! Run!"

We grabbed our shit and hauled ass. The cops tried to run after us. And fell on their cop faces. It was an old gag on Earth even when I was a kid, but here it still ensnared legs: Ratner and Head Charge tied the cops' shoelaces together as they listened to the band. Seriously, I think those guys watched way too many cartoons when they were kids. There were plenty of laces to tie, too, and the cops were still struggling to untangle when we sprinted off, out of the park and through the alleyways to the tram.

We waited impatiently for a few moments as a tram car slowed to a stop. We scrambled to sit as the car lurched away, and I saw one of the cops run out of the alley.

Perzanto set Bernard on a seat. She looked very dead. Perzanto and Oswaldo moved in as close as they could and held her somewhat vertical with the pressure of their bodies. Her head rolled around with the motion of the car, but I took it as a good sign that she was not the only person on the tram who appeared to be taking a nap. At least the napping passengers had their eyes closed and wouldn't see her. The less somnolent ones, however, kept a wary eye on us, though I think it had more to do with the appearance of some of our company. Let's face it, Bernard, even dead, blended in better than Dondelakavin.

Trenton leaned close to me and said, "Hey, Ian, got one of those Bambus handy?"

"I've got one rolled already," I said, producing a spliff.

"No," he told me, "I only need the paper. This is for something else."

I pulled a pack of rolling papers from my pocket – not an easy feat while sitting on a crowded tram with a guitar, a shotgun, and the dufflebag full of camping supplies I grabbed during our escape – and I slipped a couple wraps to Trent. I didn't give it too much thought just then. Trent's ideas can usually be trusted to be good ones.

The tram squealed as it pulled to a stop. We hustled out onto the avenue with the flowering trees and half-walked, half-jogged to the park.

They were waiting for us, a dozen cops. Very serious cops with riot gear, helmets, face shields, bulletproof vests that would definitely stop buckshot, and weapons. We stopped and looked at them. They stood, blocking the entrance to the park, and looked at us.

Trent leaned close to me and said, "Take everyone off that way." He nodded toward the far end of the park. "Make sure they see Perzanto and the dead, um, Bernard. Draw them off, I've got a plan."

"What?"

"You'll see soon enough, if it works." Trent slipped off, down the street the other way.

I shared the fragment of a plan with the others and we strolled merrily up the street. The cops stood and watched until we were nearly at the corner.

"Come on," I said in arena voice, "let's climb the fence."

It wasn't much of a fence, just a couple of metal railings that surrounded the park. I put my foot on the lower railing and the cops were in motion, running toward us with weapons at the ready. I lost track of Trenton, but I hoped this was accomplishing whatever it was supposed to accomplish. The cops closed in on us in a moment, stomping through the flowers, before any of us could make it over the railing. I don't know what their weapons did, but I didn't want to find out. We stopped and put our hands in the air. All except for Perzanto, who put one hand in the air and kept a tight grip on the limp Bernard with the other. And Bob, who didn't have hands and ignored the whole thing anyway.

If it was supposed to be a diversion, I decided to make it a good one. I climbed up onto the lower railing, standing on it as if it were a soapbox. "Ladies and gentlemen!" I called in a booming voice. The weapons swiveled toward me. I held my hands up, part surrender, part benediction. "We bring you greetings from planet Earth! We come in peace! Tonight, we want to bring to you the hardest working deity in any world, the Big Guy in our world, the God who can create the world, part the seas, spread plagues, and sacrifice His only Son. Ladies and gentlemen, put your hands together and worship the Great God Jehovah!"

"Hmmph," Jay said.

I jumped down from the railing and dropped to my knees in front of Jay, but I projected my voice even louder to the cops. "Oh, Lord, forgive us for our transgressions. We are faulty mortals, sinners who failed to interpret Your word. Oh, Lord, please accept our repentance."

"Go on," Jehovah said.

"We pray unto You, Oh Lord, to deliver us from our enemies! Jesus, Jay, smite these guys!"

Jay looked at me. Then He looked at the cops. Then, slowly, He raised His finger. His nimbus flared and lightning crackled around His finger.

"You sure about this?" he asked me.

There was a brilliant flash of rainbow light. Or rather, a whole series of very rapid bursts of dazzling rainbow light and they weren't coming from Jay's mighty digit. We all turned to look. I knew instantly what it was, I'd seen it just the day before. It was the psychocollaborative stimulator from Trenton's studio. Remembering that incident, my mind created an image of Wile E. Coyote, who came flying out of the lights, bareback on a flaming ACME rocket.

"No," I said to Jay. "No smiting. I was just buying time and this is even better. But I meant the apology."

"Hmmph." He lowered His finger. "I never get to do any smiting."

Along with Wile E. came a dozen other assorted entities: three scantily-clad women, two naked men, a seven-foot-tall insect with iridescent wings, a furred animal somewhat like an extra fat beaver, a poorly animated cartoon version of the extra fat beaver, a short fat man in an expensive suit and top hat, a middle-aged woman in a housecoat, a medium-sized horse wearing a straw hat, and a blue two-door sedan with a wide mouth for a grill and eyes for headlights.

"Is this what you people think about?" I asked. "Holy crap!"

The rocket-powered coyote, out of control as his engine sputtered and coughed, buzzed low over the cops, causing them to duck and to swing their weapons after him. The weapons made hissing noises and a line of holes appeared along the side of Wile E.'s rocket. Thick black smoke issued from the holes and the rocket swung in a crazy spiral, scattering the cops as they ran for cover. The other entities, less ballistic than the coyote, wandered, flew, and crawled out into the park.

At that moment, there was a loud hum, followed by a *sizzle* and the psychocollaborative stimulator died. Green and pink after-images filled my vision for a few moments.

But the seeds of chaos were sown and the entities, apparently, were there to stay. The anthropomorphic car, like a playful cat, stalked and chased a police woman. The beaver things, animal and animated, began to copulate in the middle of the park, creating an unexpected obstacle in a very inconvenient place. Not only that, but the fucking things drew the attention of spectators, both humanoid and otherwise. The big insect walked around on its bottom-most two legs, trying to initiate a chess game, or a literary discussion.

Wile E. Coyote came in for another pass, hanging upside down from the rocket. He collided with a cop, who grabbed him and pulled him from the missile. They both fell in a heap and the rocket spiraled away, colliding with a statue of a tall man with antlers that stood near the park's entrance. Any cops still standing at that point were knocked down by the blast.

I didn't have to say a word; we all knew this was our chance and we bolted for the exit, Perzanto and Bernard in the lead.

36. Resonance

I emerged at the Pool just behind Perzanto and kept moving because everyone else was coming through behind us, as fast as they could hustle.

"Where to?" Perzanto asked as I caught up with him.

"Near the wall," I said. "Let's get away from this shebang, in case the cops come after us."

We climbed up out of the Pool, dodging columns on the shortest course possible to the outer wall of the cavern. We were out of breath and sweating by the time we made it to where the floor became more distinctly horizontal. Perzanto placed Bernard on the stone floor. I sat down next to her and started to roll some Blue Smoke into a joint.

"I'm coming, too." Trent joined me on the floor.

"Sure," I said. "I could use some help. Nice work with the psychocollaborative stimulator. You were able to use the Blue Smoke and the Pool yourself, I take it?"

"Took a couple tries," he explained, "but, yeah."

I licked the joint, blew on it for a moment to dry it evenly and then used the fire talisman. "Grab her feet," I told Trent. "I'll get the upper end."

We toked a couple times, then I slid my hands under Bernard's armpits and we lifted. The Pool shimmered and flowed into itself, growing brighter, and I visualized Birdie. I saw her as I remembered her and my mind flipped through a few variations, settling on the last moment I saw her, when she was acting as the Guide and Protector. Then, all of a sudden, the background of my image shifted, Birdie's hair and clothes changed and the sigil formed in my mind. *Pop*, we were somewhere else.

"I'll be damned!" said Birdie.

"You already look damned," I said, gesturing at her outfit. "Is that Tim?"

"Oh, hell no!" Birdie said, fingering the dress that hung over one shoulder and draped down the opposite leg to her ankle. "This is faux jaguar. Are you kidding? The jaguars are my family. I wouldn't use a real one for clothing! Say why don't you put that dead girl on the table?"

We placed Bernard carefully on a long table of polished dark stone. The room looked like a gothic cathedral from a vampire tale, if it were furnished by a Mayan priest. Statues of jaguars competed with gargoyles. At one end of the vault-like room, a diagram was carved into the floor, like the mystical circles wizards use in old movies. At the other end, modern furniture created a kind of living room pit surrounded by bookshelves, racks of CDs and a big, shiny-chrome stereo system.

"This place is hooked up," Trenton said. "How are the acoustics?"

"Pretty good!" Birdie sang a few notes. They sounded rich and full, with no echo.

Tim appeared in an arched doorway across the room. He spotted us and bounded over, swirling around us for a few moments and purring loudly. I patted him carefully on the head.

"That's Bernard," I said, pointing at the body on the table.

"Really?" Birdie laughed. "*That's* Bernard? Ha! She doesn't look so good."

"Yeah," I said. "We figured you might know what to do."

"Can you help her?" Trent asked.

"Probably not," Birdie said.

"But you took Aqualung," Trent argued. "We thought you were going to help him."

"Aqualung's back where he's supposed to be," Birdie said, "on planet Earth, in the classic rock section. Old Declan Bean, though, he's going to be living down here for a while. Well, not quite *living*, really. This shebang is set up in levels. Down at the bottom, there's a place for the forgotten people, the ones with no one up above left to remember them. Bean's headed that way, but not until everyone who actually knew him forgets or passes away. I'm guessing twenty years, which is no time at all for this place, and then he'll join the forgotten. Which is where she'll go, unless we know her tale."

"Her tale?" I asked.

"I'm sure she's got one," Birdie said. "She's a god. Er, goddess. Whatever. One of those people, who leave legends in their wake. Which would be very useful for us, if we actually knew someone who knew her legend."

"Perzanto?" Trent asked. "Dondelakavin?"

"I've got a better idea," I told them. "Maybe it'll…"

I was interrupted by a loud pop and the appearance of two people: myself and Bernard. I looked exactly the same as I did, er, then. I mean, I was pretty much a duplicate of myself. Bernard was a bit different, though; she was alive and well. Not only that, as beautiful as she was as a corpse, as a living, breathing goddess, Bernard was stupendous, radiating vibrancy and cool intelligence. She seemed to have a shimmering aura of golden light that pulsated with her breath and the movements of her body.

"This," my other self announced, "is Bernard from the future, after she's been revived. She's here to tell her tale and revive herself."

"This was your idea?" Trent asked. I nodded.

Bernard smiled and shook hands all around. Birdie led us across the room and had us sit on the circumference of the circle chiseled into the floor. She took Bernard by the shoulders and led her into the center of the circle to sit on a small cushioned seat. Then, with surprising ease, Birdie retrieved the inert body from the table and carried it into the circle, where she placed it on the floor in front of the living Bernard. Trent and I took a couple more tokes from the Blue Smoke, to make sure we stayed in that time and place, as Bernard began her tale.

"My first memories," she said softly, "were of the ocean. I lived on an island and the sound of the Pacific was an endless rhythm that set the pace of our lives. Colors were bright and vivid in the tropical sun; flowers, leaves, clothing, the blue ocean, the blue and white sky."

Part of her goddess powers must have been the aura of fascination that she projected. She was beautiful to look at and the sarong clung to her magnificent body, but it was something more, something in her tone or her manner that compelled attention, that suggested she was about to reveal some unsuspected mystery.

"I remember walking along the beach with my father, finding shells and artifacts cast onto the sand by the breakers. I was too small to swim in the heavy surf and the waters seemed to hide some secret of creation. The water was where things came from: the fish we ate for dinner, the shells that I used to make necklaces and bracelets, coconuts tangled in seaweed, crawly things with clacking claws, turtles and dolphins occasionally sent too far landward by a storm or big wave.

"Life was simple in our village. Food was plentiful and easy to obtain. We had no electricity and very little trade with the outside world. Sometimes a boat would come, with strange-tasting preserved foods from far away, odd items of clothing, and other bits and pieces of a society we never really understood. Chocolate and shoes were the most popular things we traded for, but we didn't have much to trade with. Sometimes we had a log of exotic wood from the jungle in the interior of the island. Sometimes cloth woven and printed by our women. We offered them more useful things, like fresh awa root and contraceptive herbs, but they didn't value these.

"In one of these boats was a crate of books, college textbooks left by some long-gone sailor. In making room for the coa wood we gave them in exchange for rugged blue pants and leather work boots, they cleaned out one of the holds and left the garbage on the beach. But to us it was treasure, or strange curiosity, and my mother kept the books, lending them to the few literate members of our canoe for a while until everyone lost interest. Everyone except me. I believed that no one would have spent the time and energy to create these amazing things, full of illustrations and equations unless they held important secrets about the nature of existence. Up until then, my experience of books was limited to the Bibles and elementary primers that the missionaries brought to the island, before we ignored them long enough and they went away. These books were different in that they attempted to describe the world as it was, in detail, rather than the fairy stories from the missionaries' books.

"So, over several years, I mastered a semester's worth of college curriculum. I learned mathematics and the method of science. I became a scientist myself, studying what I could of the biology of the island. I became fascinated with the broader cosmic sweep of physics, though, and I observed what I could of the movements of the stars and planets and deduced what numbers I could about orbits, mass, and gravity. I observed the ever-present ocean and learned about the behavior of water. With tools I made myself, I observed that, if you looked really close, the water was always in motion, jiggling around. I believed that this was physical evidence of a vibration, the motion of things in the water too small to be seen with the tools I had.

"And so I continued my studies as best I could under my own tutelage, until one day a boat came to port and my father struck up a conversation with the captain, a tall Dutchman with a big belly. My father somehow got on the subject of me and the crazy things I did when I should have been pounding taro or having babies.

"'Too bad you cannot send her to school,' the captain said.

"My father asked him to explain, having no experience of schools other than the one that the missionaries tried to set up. That night, my father told me about his conversation, assuming I would also laugh off the idea of traveling to the mainland to attend school. But I knew of schools from my books and of the scientists who worked in universities, researching the mysteries of life. I wanted to meet them, to be among them, working as an equal. The scientists were like our kahunas, learned men who had great skill to heal or change the land. But the kahunas mostly passed along their knowledge and if there was any growth or anything new learned, it was very slowly and over a very long time. The researchers on the mainland, I believed, were learning new ways every day.

"I slipped off that night and ran down the beach to the dock. I found the captain of the boat and told him I wanted to come aboard, to travel to the mainland and go to school, as he had described to my father.

"He looked me up and down and said, 'I don't see how the crew would mind having you around. Do you have any skills?'

"I could pound taro, I said. I could identify the planets and the stars. I could clean. I could predict the tides and navigate by looking at the sky.

"'Cooking and cleaning,' the Dutchman said. 'Aye. We have experienced sailors who can tell the tides and use the sextant. We do not need these things from a little girl who has never been to sea. But you'll make yourself useful, I imagine.'

"So I cooked and I cleaned and after some days, the men began coming to me at night, trying to get me into their beds. It was quite amusing how they would lie to me, or sweet talk, or stammer embarrassedly. One even tried to use force. The sailors who were cute enough, I slept with happily, for I had my urges also and we learned to enjoy sex on our island, not fear it like the mainlanders did. I had contraceptive herbs and I insisted that the sailors cleaned up before joining me. As a result, the sailors I favored with my affection became my allies and my defenders and when one tried to use force, they locked him in a storage closet until the next port of call.

"I also showed them how their sextant measurements were inaccurate, which explained why they always hit shore a few miles wide of their destination. They thought the error was in the instruments or in the stars, but I showed them it was in their calculations. They started coming in closer to target and shaving days off their travel time. That got them more deals and they began to prosper.

"Finally, though, the ship arrived at the harbor of Akarana, in New Zealand. There were many island faces there, but also many more Europeans. It was a greater city than any I'd ever seen, with horse-drawn carriages and trolleys that moved by more interesting and mysterious powers. Here I parted company with the ship. The Dutchman, who knew how much I increased his profits, paid me for my labors at the same rate as his sailors. And the sailors, the ones who liked me, anyway, contributed to my wealth with gifts and money. I needed it. When I went to book passage to Europe and the great centers of learning, I spent nearly all the money on a tiny stateroom and meals aboard a huge, black steamship bound for Hamburg. I was assured that Hamburg was in the heart of Europe and had many great centers of learning.

"On board the ship, I made friends with a German professor, a real professor from a university! I was so excited. He spoke enough English to puzzle out my pidgin and he began to teach me German, both spoken and written. I proved to be an excellent student of languages and, to his great surprise, by the time we arrived in Europe, I spoke fairly fluent German and could read scholarly articles. In a month at sea, I became conversant in the professor's own field of anthropology, which I found fascinating. The professor was so impressed that, when we arrived in Germany, he gave me a recommendation to a university.

"In Germany, I worked as a barmaid to get started, while I attended classes. Soon, though, my academic progress was so rapid that I was granted scholarships for all my classes and I could devote myself full time to science. Eventually, I was drawn to physics and to the papers of a young German named Einstein. He was brilliant and when I met him the next year, we had a brief but intense love affair. He opened my eyes to the nature of things and once my eyes were fully open, I realized that his were closed in some ways. When the conclusions of his work became too different from what he expected, he backed off, calling it 'spooky.' But I liked spooky and I was compelled to know more. We had an argument about it and he stormed out, angry.

"In two years, I had a degree. In four years I was called 'doctor.' I decided it was time to return home, to pursue knowledge on my own and to use the knowledge I had to transform our island society. Some months later, I arrived on the island and began to introduce my reforms. The first few were met with enthusiasm. I taught them how to make filters out of plant fibers and used them to purify our awa drinks. Next, I used some of what I learned from Einstein and created a photovoltaic power supply. We spread it out on the side of the mountain and we could power lights and some of the laboratory equipment I brought back with me. They all liked the lights and the demonstration of glowing gases in tubes that I presented for them. I taught metallurgy to one of them and had him make bicycles, mostly from scrap metal and ocean salvage left behind by the trader ships. The bikes were an advanced design of my own creation, recumbent cycles with highly efficient gears. Men and women zoomed up and down the island trails. They loved those. And the advances in food storage and indoor plumbing that I introduced.

"What they didn't like was when I began to study more seriously the 'spooky' stuff that Einstein introduced me to. With his ideas of special relativity, Einstein was close to a concept that became influential to my own work. In relativity, the frame of reference of the observer is as important to the experiment as anything else. I found that it wasn't only the frame of reference, but the consciousness of the observer itself. Measurement of any kind cannot happen without consciousness. Most physics assumed that an object had to exist before it can be measured. I discovered that it can be measured first and then exist later.

"Early on in these experiments, I built sophisticated measuring devices that could delineate and bring into existence all kinds of things. I focused on what I thought were the most important: fresh water, food, and soft toilet paper, a luxury I had grown used to at the university. While the internal mechanisms of my devices were very complex, the external controls were very simple. All you had to do was set the dials for a quantity and the machine would measure out your food, water or TP. When the devices were working properly, I set them up in the center of the village and taught a few of the women how to run them. Everyone came and loaded up on free supplies.

"I thought this would usher in an era of prosperity for my people. They would be freed from the daily, mundane tasks of survival and, like me, could advance their knowledge, study, and create more innovations. They were freed from their constant need to worry about survival. The water man no longer had to carry water, the fishermen no longer toiled in their boats, and the man who collected house waste never had to smell another drop. The women no longer pounded taro root for flour. But things went wrong. There was no harvest festival.

There were no reveling fisherman, buying awa and poi after the evening's catch was in. There were no dances to influence the weather and no one gathered to watch them.

"These were my friends and family, mind you, the people I grew up with and planned to grow old with. Logically, I thought that if they were to be dissatisfied with the new way, it would be in the loss of culture, the loss of the connection to the Earth they found in fishing, farming or digging for fresh water. Proud men and women who once provided for their families now grew fat and flabby. But they didn't complain about any of that. They complained about what they did not have and imagined that they wanted. A day did not go by when someone would ask me why there wasn't wine or whiskey with the water. I considered building a wine measuring device, but they asked so annoyingly and persistently that I decided I would wait until one asked politely. It never happened. They wanted bigger or faster bicycles. They wanted more indoor plumbing and machines to wash their dishes and clothing. I made some of these, only because they were challenges, but I had more important interests.

"I could not avoid the thought that my machines really worked through the consciousness of the person operating them, not through any kind of direct action of the device. So, after much research, I found a way to dispense with the machines entirely. I could create or transform almost anything, with only a thought. I decided not to demonstrate this to the other islanders, but one of them accidentally saw me create a ripe pineapple when I was hungry.

"And it grew worse. They believed that I would be the source of all these things that they thought they wanted. Their requests grew more and more outrageous. They wanted magic machines that would entertain them, cook individual slices of bread, freeze water into tiny cubes, heat food without fire, cool their huts on hot days and have sex with them when their spouses would not. One wanted bicycles that could fly. Another wanted a machine that would dispense ice cold beverages made from mollusk juices. A woman who was a friend of my mother's insisted that I create for her a device that would hypnotize her children, so that she could leave them in front of it and forget about them for a while.[*]

"I didn't get any peace. I was starting to go crazy from lack of sleep, so I did what I could. I created a fortress, a small castle in which I could hide. I invented devices to watch the building constantly from the outside and defend the building from any intruders with electric shocks and frightening noises. I thought that my defenses were flawless, but one day they ganged up on me. It must have been nearly everyone on the island. I watched them gathering there, nervously monitoring my defenses. Some of the rabble-rousers, I noticed, were those I had hired to help build the castle, performing the menial tasks that my machines could not. They must have figured out some of the secrets of my defenses because they overwhelmed them.

"As they were coming over the walls and breaking down the doors, I knew I needed to figure out something fast. I doubted there was a way to escape, as the islanders were on all sides, so I needed a diversion, an intervention of some sort. I looked around at the materials that were presently at hand in my workshop. At the time, I was working on musical instruments that would make sounds that would influence the human brain. I knew that some of those sounds could make someone very ill, very euphoric, or put them into a trance, but I didn't have a way to play them loud enough to reach all the people inside and on all sides of the castle.

"When I was studying in Germany, I ran into an American who told me a wild tale about a man named Tesla, who nearly destroyed a city block in New York with a mechanical device. Tesla attached a small device powered by an electric motor to a steel support in his laboratory. The device transmitted vibrations into the steel, creating mechanical resonance that built exponentially until Tesla had to destroy the device with a sledgehammer to keep it from shaking his building, and several surrounding it, into dust. The American didn't know how it worked, but I figured it out from his description. Resonance. I figured that if I could create something like that, and use

---

[*] Congratulations! You made it to page 420! Please celebrate appropriately. – Ian

it to transmit not a building-killing vibration, but a frequency that would put people into a trance, I had a chance to escape.

"It took me about twenty minutes, manufacturing parts with my measuring machines, and I knew the islanders were getting close. I could hear them in the hallways, looking for me. I bolted the completed device to a stone column and switched it on. It hummed. It whirred. And the humming and whirring got louder and louder, coming from all around. Hastily, I plugged up my ears so it wouldn't affect me as much and I went out into the hallway. I knew that I had to get outside before the vibration got so intense that it would trance me as well as the others, even with my ears plugged. I ran down the hallways toward the main exit.

"In the hallway was a man with a flaming torch – I'm not sure why, there were electric lights – but he looked deeply relaxed, sitting on the floor smiling and mumbling about fish sandwiches. Even though I was abandoning the castle, I put out the torch; I didn't want anyone to get hurt. A little further on, a group of men and women joined in a group hug had fallen over onto the carpet where they were languidly squeezing each others' genitals. In the kitchen, two men raided the refrigerator, smearing mango preserves on their faces and giggling.

"I was starting to feel the effects, too, a softness in my mind and general amusement at the things I found. The sound of my footsteps on stone was enchanting. The way the lights in the hallway were arranged seemed ludicrous. Recognizing the influence of the vibration, I forced myself to pick up the pace. But when I reached the main exit, a man was entering, blocking the way out.

"He was young and tall, wore a silvery suit and was definitely not from the island. It's a small island and I mostly recognized everyone by face, if not by name. Judging by his brown hair, pale complexion and round eyes, he was a mainlander. And he was slightly befuddled by the vibration, though from what he said, at first I thought he was fully insane.

"He told me that I was chosen for a quest, to change the world. That I would seek out a cave on the North American continent and descend to find a special chamber where vibrations would travel through the Earth. I thought about my device which was, even then, vibrating through the castle and the grounds. He told me I would meet others and we would perform our vibration as a song and make the world a better place. I reflected on how my attempts at making things better on the island didn't work out very well.

"I asked him for proof and he turned me into a goddess. Grinning from ear to ear, the man waved his hand in front of me, giggled, and I changed. I recognized the process as similar to my own transformative experiments. I grew a little taller and my body became stronger. I felt great energy inside me, creative energy, sexual energy, intellectual energy, emotional energy. I was filled with insights and I knew that I could do amazing things with my ability to transform and create matter.

"It was more than enough proof and I decided that this might be my chance to redeem myself. To get it right, with the help and guidance of this man and the others that I would meet. And, since I was about to permanently flee the island altogether, it gave me a direction, something to move towards, while avoiding the chaos behind me. I accepted the map that the man offered and fled down to the beach.

"I stole a canoe and paddled across the ocean to a nearby island where they would not yet know of the chaos I caused at home. From there, I booked passage on a steamship bound for North America. I paid for everything with gold that I measured out of nothing. My journey was largely uneventful. We landed in California and, following an afternoon carriage ride to Sacramento, I took the Overland Route and eventually arrived in New York.

"The map that the silvery young man gave me was very odd. It was cluttered with lines and dots that represented features that did not exist, or at least I could not figure them out. Nor could I discern what a Crumby's was; some kind of shrine to extra-large beverages, I surmised. However, the basic topography was intact, mountains and rivers and oceans, the shape of the coastline, and I was able to cross-reference the mysterious map with a current New York road map. I found my way to Rosendale and the cave, where I met Perzanto and Dondelakavin.

"Following their example, I realized that there might be a long wait until the remaining band members showed up. I found a shebang that I liked, one that was sparsely populated, with a pleasant climate and intelligent residents. I filled up my days with the task of building a beautiful society, a modern and efficient culture with an educated population. Throughout, I worked to improve myself as well, to make myself the kind of wise and visionary leader that these people deserved.

"First I had to surmount the belief that my attempts to better the populace would lead to disaster, as it did at home. These were different circumstances, I was starting pretty much from scratch, I was older and wiser, and who knew what was possible inside the Pool of Shebangs? Logically, I knew it to be true, but I found it hard to convince my emotions and change my behavior. After some experimentation, though, I discovered that I could use a process much like measuring to delineate my own beliefs and how my brain and body processed such things. It worked! I firmly believed that I could create a better shebang for these people to live in.

"Of course, finding that I could change myself so easily opened the door to a lot of other changes. I made myself smarter, stronger, happier, sexier, and wiser. As I integrated each change into my life, I realized that, as deep I thought they went, these changes still barely scratched the surface of the possible. I knew that there was a deeper, transcendent change that would unite my consciousness with the deepest and most unknown levels of reality. As a scientist, I needed to know, to experience for myself in a way I could never do intellectually, the secrets of being. I planned the change, knowing that the result would be beyond anything I could predict. I planned for two years and then I did it.

"And that's the last thing I remember."

On the floor, the inert body of the (slightly) younger Bernard grumbled, then sat up suddenly and sneezed. At that cue, my older self and the other Bernard looked at each other, smiled and vanished.

"Well, damn," Birdie commented. "Welcome back!"

"That was weird," the newly-awakened Bernard said. "I could have sworn I heard my own voice! Uh… where am I?"

37. The Resonant Chamber

There was a *pop* and Trent, Bernard and I were back at the Pool. The light was congealing back into individual columns and people were coming toward us from the glare. Our friends were marching before the weapons of police from Bernard's shebang. Two of the cops circled out from behind the others and advanced on us. And stopped.

"Lower your weapons!" Bernard commanded, her voice carrying confidence and power. She looked amazing, really. I mean, she'd looked good even as a corpse, but now she glowed with energy, as her future self had. And the cops were flabbergasted. They stopped, guns wavering, and sputtered for a moment.

"B… b… ber…" one of them stammered.

"You're… a… a…" tried another one.

"I am Bernard and I'm alive!" Bernard exclaimed.

The cops dropped their weapons and fell to their knees.

"Not bad," Trent whispered to me. We high-fived.

Reunited with our friends, we had a meal and told them what happened in Birdie's shebang.

"So this is finally it," Perzanto said, when we finished. "We've done everything we can to be ready and now we must go to the chamber and find out if this can work."

There were smiles all around. I was feeling good now, fairly excited as I often did before an important concert. We gathered up our gear, said goodbye to Bernard's police contingent, and started to hike down toward the center of the Pool in a wavering line. We walked between the columns of light, through the eternal glare. Inhabitants and visitors to the Pool stopped what they were doing to stare at us as our caravan passed by. I was thinking that it was going well, that we finally had an unobstructed path to our destination when there was, inevitably, a commotion.

It was a familiar kind of commotion, though. Sprinting between the columns as fast as they could, shouting loudly, was Liana. And right behind her was Cleve.

"Run!" Liana yelled. "Run!"

We didn't run. We just stared.

Wild-eyed and panting, Cleve ran up to us and grabbed me by the shoulders. "It's the Scrambler!" he exclaimed. "It's the Scrambler!"

Jehovah stepped up next to us. "It's okay," Jay said to Cleve. "You just stick with us. Follow Me. I can handle the Scrambler, whoever or whatever he might be."

Cleve looked into the face of God. "Yeah?"

"Yes, My son," Jay said.

Cleve relaxed. The manic expression faded. He took a deep breath. "I'm sorry I doubted You." He turned to Liana, who was hopping about trying to pull him off for another full retreat. "It's okay," he told her. "Jay will protect us."

Liana gave Jehovah a skeptical look. "Yes?"

"Yes," God said. "And don't fuck around."

"We're on our way to the resonant chamber," I told Cleve. "Right now. Come with us."

"But," Cleve said, "the Scrambler was right behind us…" We all looked around. There was no sign of the Scrambler, or anyone else for that matter. We were momentarily alone in that part of the Pool. "Oh, hell yeah," Cleve said after a moment. "What song are we going to play?"

"I was thinking 'The Deep Stone'," I said, looking around at everyone.

After our first experience with the Blue Smoke, we tried to reproduce the song that we witnessed in the vision. For years we played around with what we could recall of the melody and beat. Our efforts rarely came close to the awesomeness that we remembered and we would drop it for a while. Finally, when we were working on *Six*

Songs, I came up with a version that we liked enough to record. In short, I forgot about trying to reproduce the song that we'd heard and simply played around with working the beat and melody into a song that we could play. The result was "The Deep Stone." It wasn't much of a radio hit, but we often saved it for the climax of a concert and it always knocked 'em dead.

"Works for me," Cleve said. "I can play that."

There was general agreement all around.

So we hiked for a while, down the gentle slope of the Pool floor, and then, finally, after all our wandering through caverns and shebangs, one delay after another, one prolonged tangent after the next, we came to the center of the Pool and the entrance to the resonant chamber.

The solid limestone hub of the Pool was pierced with openings at regular intervals, archways twice as tall as the tallest of us and twice as wide as Perzanto. We entered the nearest and began down the long, sloping tunnel. The light from the Pool faded quickly as we descended and we broke out our flashlights and luminous orbs. Eventually we came to the long stairway and stomped downward into darkness. We traveled in silence. There was no conversation and no song, only the sound of boots on stone.

After quite a while, we could see yellowy light at the end of the tunnel. As we got closer it rivaled our flashlights and we turned them off. Finally we came to the landing at the bottom, walked through a stone archway and into the glowing yellow light of the resonant chamber.

We agreed that we would set up in the very center of the flat stone floor, beneath the great dome of the ceiling, leaving all the camping gear and extra stuff on the landing, outside the chamber proper. I set down the Mossberg and guitar case and brought the guitar and one of the little amps with me. I plugged in and hit a chord. The acoustics were stunning, every note magnified and intensified by the parabolic stone. Trenton set up his keyboard on my right and Esty took position on my left. Our two bassists, Cleve and Perzanto, were, more or less, behind Esty and Bernard and Dondelakin stood behind me. Dondelakavin held his lipsquacker at the ready. Bernard held a small measuring device in her hand. Behind them, the Tripper held the dumbek under one arm. Our crew and friends arranged themselves around the periphery to watch and listen.

"One," I said. "Two. One, two three…"

"Hey!" Liana yelled suddenly. "It's the Scrambler!"

No one played. There was, in actuality, a man standing in one of the archways, staring back at us. He was in dimmer light and we were in the brightness of the chamber, so it was impossible to make out his face. It didn't matter; he turned and started inspecting our gear that was stacked there.

"Who are you?" I called.

He didn't answer. Instead he picked something up and turned suddenly, advancing toward me through the archway. And, with an echoing, resonant *boom*, he fired the Mossberg at my head.

That's when I died.

38. Nothingness with Twinkles

I didn't know that I died, not right away anyway. In fact, as I woke up, I felt pretty good. A little confused, but okay. I stretched my legs and arms. They seemed to be working and, indeed, felt remarkably free from arthritic aches and pains.

"Coming around?" someone asked.

I opened my eyes. Everything seemed just a little too bright and colorful, glowing almost, like I'd smoked a couple tokes of sativa. My eyes focused slowly and I saw a familiar face leaning over me.

"I knew that shotgun was going to be trouble," Birdie said. "Right from the first. I thought, 'That gun's going to be the death of him!' Hmmph. But maybe it's for the best."

"Where the fuck am I?" I asked. "How did I get here?"

"Shotgun blast to the head," Birdie told me. "You died. Now you're my responsibility."

I checked the much-neglected file drawer in the back of my brain that held my deeper philosophy and thoughts on death, resurrection, ghosts and things that go bump in the night or day. The drawer slid to the end of its runners and a gagging cloud of dust filled my mind. I tried to find anything at all in the confusion.

"Shotgun? Blast? To the head? Died?"

"That's what I said."

"The Scrambler!" I exclaimed. "The fucking Scramber!"

Birdie chuckled, which I thought was odd. "Yeah, right," she said. "The Scrambler."

"I'm dead? Really?"

"You're dead, but don't take it too hard, Ian. You look pretty good for a dead guy." She held a mirror over me and I was startled by the image I saw. I recognized that face, the young guitarist that Annie

Leibowitz once immortalized on the cover of *Rockin' Bones.*

It took me a few moments to process this. I sat up, discovering that I was lying on Birdie's long table. I swung my legs over the edge and saw that I was dressed in a shiny silver garment. "What happened to the song? The song in the resonant chamber?"

"The gig was canceled on account of your demise," she said. "The others all gave up and went home. They didn't even try. They walked away. Left most of their gear, there, too, rather than carry it all the way back up to the surface. But, you know, there's someplace you're supposed to be. A time and a place. Can't you feel it? They're calling you back. That's why you're *here.*"

I thought about that. I was dead; where the hell was I supposed to be other than Birdie's version of the afterlife? Jehovah's version? That didn't seem likely. Can you imagine me growling out the blues to harp accompaniment? The stringy kind of harp, I mean. Not fucking likely. And, I decided, I'm not the praying sort. Was I supposed to be with Jane, who was also dead? More likely, but there *was* something else, a pull, a feeling drawing me somewhere else. And yes, Jane *was* there. I explored that feeling with my mind and the world got all twinkly and started to fade.

"See you later," Birdie said.

Nothingness with twinkles, someone once said. But what twinkles! I could see in their facets the essence, the structure of the universe, the keys to time and space. There was a rushing sound, like an ever-increasing wind washing light rain across a beach, forever and ever. As the rushing grew louder, I had an epiphany. An uber-epiphany, a comprehension of the basic transformative nature of reality. Everything was always in flux, some fluxing faster than us, some slower. When we stopped changing from one thing to the next, there would be nothing. I'd always considered myself, through the power of music, to be an agent of change. Now I knew that my very presence was an act of transformation, the universe willing itself to change and grow. Not just me, of course, but all of us, every extension of the infinite into matter. Jane and I had often spoken of ourselves as the eyes of the universe. It was true, and we were its arms, legs, brains and hearts, too. I understood the role I had to play.

The rushing sound got even louder and I heard it for what it was: applause! The twinkles coalesced into Planet Earth, New York State, the stage at the Mid-Hudson Civic Center in Poughkeepsie, where Blue Smoke was playing the first gig of its tour as a memorial concert for the recently departed guitar god, Ian Better. Everyone who had been in the resonant chamber was on stage, plus Jason on drum kit, Don Speckler in a sharkskin suit that seemed to change colors under the stage light, and some kid named Jack White filling in for me on a battered old guitar.

Trenton, I later learned, had just made a speech in my honor, detailing the highlights of my career, talking about me personally. The audience was chanting my name when I appeared center stage, young, dressed in silver, and very much alive. The crowd went wild.

I suppose they accepted me as me because everyone had grown a bit used to the miraculous since June 23. And because, hell, I was a fucking rock god now, for real, summoned back to existence by my own legend. I felt like a god. I knew I was in command of elements of the world that were hidden to me before. Time, space, and rock'n'roll were mine. Ganja was my sacrament, the shotgun my will and my self-transformation, the guitar my spirit and my power.

A blizzard of joints, thrown by the crowd, pattered onto the stage around me. Trent hit a note and the band followed into the opening of "You Need to Be Free." They hit it hard and, damn, I wanted to join in, but I didn't have a guitar. Fuck, where had I last seen that thing? I hoped it wasn't lost. It was a classic guitar. Gibson only made the SG Les Paul for two years before it became the SG Custom. The SG Les Paul had three warm-sounding pickups, instead of two, and a heavy brass whammy bar. Some guys remove the whammy or replace it with a lighter one, but I've tried those guitars and they just don't sound the same. Mine was all-original, in perfect condition apart from a few little chips in the white laquer finish. And it had history. That was the guitar I played on most of our tours. It was the instrument I used to record most of *Six Songs*.

An instant of twinkling and my mind found the guitar, at a distance in time and space though near by association, in the resonant chamber. I transitioned there.

And arrived just as Blue Smoke, aided and abetted by a variety of gods and entities, was about to play "The Deep Stone" and rock the chamber. My old self, looking a bit battered from his travels, had the guitar in his hand.

"Hey! It's the Scrambler!" someone shouted. I looked around, but didn't see who they were shouting about. Oh yeah. Me. I realized that I was as close to being the Scrambler as anyone; all the rest was Liana's paranoia, probably too ill-defined to ever manifest clearly.

"Who are you?" the old Ian asked in arena voice.

"Ultimately," I said under my breath, "you'll appreciate this." I picked up the Mossberg, pumped a shell into the chamber and I blasted the old fart in the head. I've never, ever killed anyone before, but I had no problem with this. It was my decision and I knew it wasn't permanent, so I let me have it. Hell, it was my own head to blast! I ran into the chamber and grabbed the guitar. I tried to transition back to Poughkeepsie, back to the concert already in progress, but somehow it wasn't working. There weren't any twinkles, and Perzanto was moving toward me.

I grinned at him. I waved sheepishly.

"You?" he asked.

And I felt it, a pull somewhere in time and space and since I thought I needed to leave the scene of the crime quickly, I went with it. Twinkles and a moment of eternity. The information of the twinkles filled my mind and I knew, then, what I had to do.

Crumby's. I had to go to Crumby's but I found myself on the front porch of my Rosendale home. It was night, and the porch light was on, surrounded by a cloud of moths in spite of the yellow color. My Dodge 4X4 was parked out front. There was a light on inside, but when I went in, there was no one home.

"Jane?" I called. There was no answer. "Bob?" Silence.

A digital clock on the living room table told the date and time: the concert in Poughkeepsie was happening right now. But I felt no urgency. I knew that time wasn't what I once thought it was. Linearity was a lie; I could arrive whenever I wanted. I could stay for an hour or a decade and still get there when I needed to.

There was a pleasant smell and my nose led me to a back room where fresh buds were drying. Who harvested my crop? Who watered it? It looked to be the whole crop, and it looked good. The plants yielded big, fat, smelly buds. And there was plenty of Blue Smoke. At one end of the drying rack, nearest the dehumidifier, I found some samples that were already well-dried. I tucked a couple small buds into a pocket of my silvery suit.

I found the keys to the pickup on the hook by the front door and I went back outside. I drove a couple miles down White Bush Lane and made a right onto Route 32. Ten minutes later, I pulled into the Crumby's lot and parked under the big blue and white sign on the front of the building. Fortunately, there were only a few people inside, but they stared at me as I found the rack of road atlases, near the magazine stand. I brought four of them up to the register and realized that I had no money, not even any brubarb, in the pockets of the silver suit. I stuck my hand in one of them anyway and to my surprise there were a couple of twenties. I smiled, knowing I would put them there later. It was enough for the atlases, a turkey sub and a large cup of coffee, which I toted back to the house on the passenger seat of the truck.

I brought my haul into the kitchen and sat at the table to finish my sandwich. Some of this god stuff was about intuition, I realized. I could feel the directions that I was able to move in time and space. It seemed that I couldn't get back to the concert unless the concert actually existed, which meant that the living, older version of myself had to get to the resonant chamber, along with the rest of the band, and I had to kill him. So I'd killed him, but the underworld adventure apparently needed to be ensured in other ways. We needed ancient gods on a quest and it was up to me to recruit them. For which purpose, I needed maps to Rosendale.

I spread the road atlases out on the table, found some marking pens and highlighted the Valley of Roses on the maps. I tried to think of some way to make the atlases seem more magical, but ultimately figured that they would seem weird enough on the other side of time and space. I was pretty sure that Crumby's didn't have a franchise in most of the places I'd be going.

I took the altered maps with me and went into the living room where I rolled a joint of Blue Smoke. With my god powers, I knew, I didn't need it or the Pool of Shebangs to trip through the cosmos, but it's a damn fine smoke, you know. And fuck you, no one said a god can't have fun doing his business.

After a couple tokes, I set the joint down in Jane's big ceramic, art project ashtray and I let the molecules bind to my brain. The twinkly stuff started up again, but this time, perhaps helped along by the smoke, it all happened in slow motion and I noticed more of what happened and how. Blue told me that time was organized more by association than chronology and I believed him, up to a point. Now I could see, feel and hear the lines of association, the paths, roads and boulevards of time. I followed one of them and, with a very unusual sound and a bit of a rough landing, I found myself under streetlights, behind some factory or warehouse buildings that looked like they were designed by Doctor Seuss. The walls tilted and leaned and wavered. Also tilting and wavering was a man dressed in green and purple.

Dondelakavin, sort of. Dondelakavin before he achieved god status. Dondelakavin kind of wasted.

He giggled. "Good noise," he said.

"Oh, it's you," I said. "I'm here already? Okay. Good." I figured why not get down to business? I pointed at him dramatically and suddenly realized I hadn't quite thought it through. I'd never changed a person before, but I supposed it was much like making fire with a talisman or creating a time/space sigil.

"What are you doing?" Dondelakavin asked.

"I suppose I should tell you about the quest before I do the transformation thing," I said.

I explained about the quest and the resonant chamber and all that.

"Roses," I was forced to explain, "are very fucking thorny flowers."

He told me he played the lipsquacker and some stuff about his job. I thought he'd agree to the quest right away – I mean, I knew he was going to go, right? – but he started to protest. He wasn't godly enough, he worked in a sex toy factory or something, he was just an ordinary weirdo in green and purple, and so on.

"It doesn't matter," I told him. "Just hold still." I aimed my finger at him, Jehovah-style, and recalled him as he would be, when I met him thousands of years later. A sigil formed, there was a burst of energy, and he transformed into the strange creature who would, someday, create the terrtrych and rule as the surreal god of a shebang.

As a god, he became eager for the quest. "Yes!" he exclaimed. "Yes! I'll go!"

"Good," I said, handing him a road atlas. "I'll see you when you get there."

And I twinkled on out of there. The next temporal line of association took me to a young woman who was poking around at electronic devices in a richly furnished room. She looked familiar and I thought she was Beezel, but I hadn't seen her for very long while she had flesh on her bones.

"Are you Beezel?" I asked.

She gave me a look that unmistakably said, "who the fuck else would I be?"

"Right, then," I told her. "How'd you like to be a really big star?"

"I'm the biggest star there is," she informed me.

"Oh, I'm sure you're big enough, in this provincial backwater," I told her, remembering the kind of spiel that record companies used to spin, back in the day. "But I'm talking about the world. No, I'm talking about worlds, thousands of them. You will join with the greatest stars of the rest of the world and go to a special broadcast studio called a resonant chamber, where you will play a song together that will be heard by everyone, everywhere! We're talking about a whole new level of big. An order of magnitude greater than whatever fame you already have. Better than MTV. Or YouTube. No, several orders of magnitude. Distribution beyond anything you've ever imagined! It's the chance to make a real difference to untold billions of people. You'll save the Earth and all the other worlds, too, and people will remember you forever! It will be the stuff of legend and myth. Even better, to prepare for this tour, you will be given powers and abilities beyond those of mortal, er, women. Are you with me?"

She had to call her agent. I took the phone from her and gave whoever was listening an earful about return-on-investment and ancillary rights. It was sheer bullshit, but they swallowed it whole and became rather enthusiastic about the whole thing so, with everyone's agreement, I turned her into a goddess.

I gave her a road atlas, which she looked at in puzzlement. "You're going to travel a long way," I told her. "Better pay for roaming on your cell phone."

And I twinkled away down another line of association. I found myself in a very luxurious room with walls made from massive stone blocks. It was a very nice place. I knew that because I felt kind of warm and fuzzy and happy. It was kind of like smoking a fatty after drinking a few beers. Really, I didn't mind at all. I think it made it easier.

I saw this skinny Polynesian girl in a blue flowered sarong. She looked at me with alarm at first, in fact she seemed to be in a state of general alarm, despite the warm fuzziness of the place. But I explained the situation. I was undoubtedly very witty and clever about the whole thing, though I don't really remember too many specifics. Like the others, she asked for proof, so I zapped her into a goddess and she was pretty happy about it, and not quite so skinny anymore. I tried to ask her where I could find more of whatever was causing the buzz, but she grabbed the map and ran off.

So I twinkled on, following the next line of association to someplace I really didn't expect. I was in what appeared to be a pagan temple of some kind, a sacred space lit by candles and hazy with sweet and swirling incense smoke. Two black-robed worshippers knelt before an altar. Seated in a throne upon the altar was a radiant goddess in a flowing white gown. The worshippers placed offerings before the throne — goblets of wine, small dishes of food, a long green stalk of marijuana flowers, glittering jewels, occult talismans, and an odd book with a shiny silver cover. The goddess smiled benevolently, lovingly, as she watched them. She radiated love and oozed with erotic beauty. Her hair cascaded in shiny waves, framing her perfect face, tumbling and crashing over her shoulders. The gown draped her body the way a river flows around hills and through valleys.

I knew her. "Esty?"

"Who are you?" she asked in her incredible multi-tone voice. I felt a little dizzy. The two worshippers turned toward me and I could make out, dimly under the hoods, the faces of two men, perhaps in their forties or fifties. They said nothing.

I didn't really know what I was supposed to do, though it did occur to me that we needed Esty on the quest just as much as we needed the others. It wouldn't happen without her ability to incorporate Beezel's story. She needed recruiting, too. I only had one map left, for Perzanto, but I knew she could get a ride with Trent, when necessary.

"I'm Ian," I said. "Ian Better."

"Holy crap!" she said. "You're a god!"

"Don't believe…" I caught myself. "Yeah, I guess I am."

"Nice," she intoned. "Me too."

"Do you know Trenton Augustus?" I asked.

"Not personally," she said. "But, yeah. Of course I know who he is."

"Would you like to meet him?"

"Sure! It's an odd thing to ask, though."

"I'll arrange it," I said. "Consider it perks for being a goddess. About a week after your, uh, hoo-ha thing. Just tell him you want to come along to the Blue Smoke rehearsal. Tell him 'backstage rules'."

"Backstage rules," she repeated. "A Blue Smoke rehearsal? You're getting back together? I am so there. That's historic!"

"Okay, glad you're on board." I told her. "I'll be old and I won't remember you. Alzheimer's, or too much weed. Something like that. Don't let it worry you. See you then!"

And I twinkled down the next most compelling line of association and found myself in what looked like a fantastic, futuristic city. Except that I knew it wasn't the future; from my old perspective it was the very distant past. From my present perspective it was simply the next association. It was Perzanto's city, a large, complex and daunting place. Much of it would have been incomprehensible to my ordinary human mind, but my god mind processed it all pretty well. There were people everywhere, even if it was tough to identify all the forms they took. They floated in bubbles; rolled on wheels; soared in angular flying machines; walked on mechanical legs of varying numbers, styles and lengths; peddled, wiggled, waggled, spiraled and levitated in various ways. Some wore identifiable clothing – shirts, pants, hats – and others seemed ensconced in their wearable devices, most of which I could see no use for. Things popped into and out of existence all around me, at the command of a human, either right there or somewhere else entirely. And everywhere there were nut vendors.

I was there for about a week, looking for Perzanto and upgrading my wardrobe in the city's incredible shops. It was a huge city, at least as big as New York, and my search was doomed. But I had a plan and you know what it was. I announced that I, the Master Inscriber, would hold a competition to decide who would be the champion of his species and save the Earth from some vague but certain end.

A lot of young men wanted to prove their prowess in the competition and we held it in a big, central arena. The media coverage was amazing. Cameras flew everywhere, following me, darting among the competitors. The participants went crazy. I didn't even have to tell them how to do it, they just went at it, practice sessions turning into earnest struggles. The guys who were there to transform things transformed every damn thing that wasn't nailed down. They toted in big sacks of nuts and then, when those were used up, they started on their clothing, on the grass of the field, passing insects, and even their own finger and toenails. Transformed stuff flew everywhere, gadgets and gizmos that I didn't bother to try understanding, along with purely aesthetic displays of flags, animals, skyrockets and so on. Musicians made the damnedest racket, everyone playing to overwhelm the other. Tough guys tried to out-tough each other. A few might have K.O.ed Muhammad Ali or wing chunged Bruce Lee. But most of them were just sincerely goofy. I worked hard not to laugh, seriously. The whole competition idea must have triggered some fundamental urge to act like buffoons, a cultural tendency that transformed sophisticated, high-tech people into the Three Stooges.

After a little while, I spotted Perzanto, sitting across from me, observing the action. Finally, after half a day of slapstick, it came down to three contestants, a real big dumb ox of a guy who crushed all his opponents, a diminutive musician who was actually pretty good on a tiny stringed instrument, and a nerdy fellow with rumpled clothing who would have passed for a computer programmer in our world. I started to point as if I were going to select one of them, but ended with my finger aimed across the arena at Perzanto. The contestants sputtered and complained.

"You!" I called in arena voice. "Come closer!"

Perzanto obeyed, making his way down into the arena.

"Think you can take this dumb ox in a fair or unfair fight?" I asked Perzanto.

"'He may be larger and stronger than me,' he said, 'but I watched him wrestle and I believe I am faster and smarter. I think I could kick his ass.'

I dismissed the ox, who grumbled something under his breath and wandered off.

"Can you play the sqwth better than this guy?" I gestured at the musician.

"I don't play the sqwth," Perzanto said. "I play the mrrlnx. But I think I play pretty well."

"I believe you," I said. And I sent the musician home. "Can you turn a twig into a sqwth?"

"I've never tried, but I know I can turn a nut into a mrrlnx."

"Good enough," I told him. "Congratulations, kid. You got the job."

I dismissed the nerd and stepped closer to Perzanto. "It doesn't really matter any way," I told him. "I spotted you as soon as I came in. I knew you'd be the winner, because I can see through time. But most importantly, you were the only one with enough sense to sit your ass down and wait. If it came to a wrestling match with any of these…' I gestured toward Moe, Larry and Curly, licking their wounds on the sidelines. "You would certainly win. You are rested and fresh; they're all battered and worn. And you display a quality that is more important than mere physical prowess, musical or inscribing skill."

He waited patiently to learn what that was, but I turned and walked back up onto the dais. I turned back to Perzanto. "Get your ass up here, kid," I said. When he climbed up to join me, I projected my voice. "You have been selected to make the journey to the Valley of Roses where you will find the five other candidates and descend to the resonant chamber to play a song. You are a fine, strong young man. You have knowledge and skill. But that will not be enough. Only a god may play the song in a way that will return harmony to the Earth. There was a ceremony when you were born and there was one when you became a man. This gathering, this ritual is the ceremony of your becoming a god." Pretty good for some bullshit I made up on the spot, right?

I knew how Perzanto would look as a god and I made him look that way, humongous limbs and all. There was a big old party after that and I'm sure Perzanto got laid a few times. I had other places to be, so I honored a couple of the losers with the job of sending the big guy on his way in the morning, with a road atlas and a shove in the right direction.

I went twinkly and found a nice, strong line of association to follow. I assumed it was my line back to the concert in Poughkeepsie. Instead I found myself at the Pool of Shebangs, standing near an archway in the central hub. I tried again, searching in my mind for an association to the Mid-Hudson Civic Center. Concerts I'd played there, concerts I'd seen. I would get nice and twinkly, grab onto a line and find myself back at the Pool. Frustrating. That kind of thing, I thought, shouldn't really happen to a god. I stopped for a moment to puzzle it out, searching the pockets of my clothing for a bit of bud. I had changed my silver suit for other finery in Perzanto's city, and I could find nothing to smoke in my new threads. I heard footsteps and voices approaching and looked up. To my surprise, all of my new gods, the humans I transformed and sent on a quest to Rosendale, New York, were near me now, closing in on the hub. There was Perzanto, accompanied by Liana. Beezel had a few very tired-looking men with her. Bernard was alone, dressed in a safari outfit and laden with camping gear. Dondelakavin had a flock of ducks with him.

What the fuck? Why were they all here now? Where was Blue Smoke? *When* did this happen? I couldn't fathom it. I needed advice and ganja and I found a strong line of association to it. I twinkled to Blue's farm.

Sitting on his porch, we smoked a bowl of World bud and I explained what happened to me.

"Ian is a god." He laughed. "I knew it all along. I knew you had it in you."

"So what do you think happened?" I asked him as my brain registered the arrival of awesome cannabinoid molecules. "How did they all show up at the same time? I realize that linearity is irrelevant, especially in the Pool…"

"Yes," he said. "It definitely isn't chronological."

"Associational?" I asked.

"That's my guess," he said, taking a nice big puff. "You sold them on a line of association, to a scenario that they believe in. Reality got a little more surreal on June 23. And you're a god. The universe has to be at least a little malleable to a god, plastic, molded by your thoughts. You've imagined two different storylines. Now you have a choice. Does it happen as they believe? Or does it happen as you experienced it already?"

"Let me get a few more tokes," I said. "I'm going to need it."

Properly stoned, I thanked Blue and twinkled back to the Pool. Perzanto was closest to me and I put on the big voice and played the Master Inscriber for him again. I summoned him down into the chamber and he followed eagerly, Liana on his heels. We walked quickly, to get further ahead of the others.

We descended the long stairway and came down to the landing outside the chamber. I gestured for them to enter.

"No!" Liana yelled. "Don't do it, Perzanto! It's a trap! He's some kind of evil magician who will destroy you!"

"Silence!" I ordered.

She attacked me, but I twinkled out of her reach, reappearing on the other side of the doorway. "You will remain here!" I told Liana. I beckoned Perzanto through into the yellow glow. As I entered, I transformed some of the air into a long crystal staff. It was a little newagey, sure, but impressive anyway. I strode into the center of the resonant chamber and aimed the staff at the stone floor. I knew what needed to happen.

"Perzanto," I said in my normal voice. "She's a crazy bitch. Let Cleve deal with her, he's got God on his side."

He looked at me in confusion. We could hear the others coming down the stairway, so I knew I had to act fast. I pointed the staff at the stone floor and let the thought of what must happen come into my mind. It formed a sigil and the world cracked and shifted. I twinkled then, along a very strong line of association and materialized on stage, right where I'd been standing, a fraction of second after I disappeared, center stage at the Mid-Hudon Civic Center.

It was an impressive costume change in the blink of an eye and, of course, I now had the guitar. The audience went wild. So I plugged in and played.

39. The Deep Stone

We rocked through "You Need to Be Free," one of the best performances of that song, ever. Blue Smoke was smoking. We were well rehearsed. We'd taken a long warm-up tour, albeit through another realm. We had amazing musicians sitting in, an enthusiastic audience, and a reunion across the limits of space and time, life and death, to celebrate. We jammed on "Awake" next, the Tripper getting a special solo on dumbek and everyone taking extra-long solos that blew many minds in that boxy civic auditorium. While I was playing my solo, I wondered about the Tripper. It was odd, I thought; I was the one who sent each of the gods on the quest. But I hadn't sent the Tripper. If anything, he was the one who sent me. Who sent him? Who was the shaman he talked about? Maybe I had yet to do it, sometime when the right line of association led me to it. Perhaps my thought processes were still trying for too much linearity. For now it remains a mystery. Fucked if I know.

After "Awake" faded away, I motioned for quiet. "Here's one that I'd like to do as a favor for a friend who should be here now."

I started playing solo on the guitar, a familiar melody, making up the lyrics as I went along, giving it some feeling:

"Declan Bean my friend
"Your life was never easy
"You flew so high
"And you became yourself"

The band caught where I was going and joined in.

"A-awooo!

"He died alone
"The rocks they showed no mercy
"He saved his friends, that is all we know"

The audience was getting into it, clapping their hands to the rhythm. They knew the song, but not these lyrics and they strained to hear.

"He was a song
"Trapped inside an old man
"He changed his life, a beacon to us all

"Declan Bean my friend
"Your life was never easy
"You flew so high
"And you became yourself"

With a flash of sizzling, blue-white light and a sound like Velcro being pulled apart, Declan Bean appeared on stage, looking a bit confused. I repeated the first verse and, this time, some of the audience sang along.

Bean looked touched, appreciative of his rock'n'roll resurrection, but a bit awkward. Oswaldo and Karen ran onto the stage, shook Bean's hand, and ushered him into the wings. The crowd applauded enthusiastically, though I'm not sure they realized who he was. Or rather, who he no longer was.

We played a few more songs, keeping the energy level way up, rocking hard and extending the jams. Jack White turned out to be pretty good and we jammed together on "Shining Girl." Jason took a modest solo on "Picasso's Blues," with enthusiasm, though not really matching the power of the rest of the band. He certainly hadn't practiced as much as the rest of us. The audience didn't notice, and we blew them away with "Dangerously High," anyway. We ended with

"All the Way Down." The crowd roared. We all lined up at the front of the stage and took a bow before running offstage.

Where Jane was waiting for me. Damn she looked good in a floor-length, very slinky evening dress. We were in each other's arms instantly and it felt really fine to feel her heart racing as much as mine.

"I harvested your plants," she murmured into my ear.

"I went by the house," I said. "I saw. Thank you."

"I brought some with me."

"Blue Smoke?" I asked.

"Mm hmm, what else would I bring to a Blue Smoke concert?"

"I love you," I said. "And not only because you brought me weed."

"Oh?" she asked. "There's something else?"

"Yes," I said and kissed her for a very long time. Now that I was no longer entirely human, let me just say that kissing is a very good thing for gods. My feeling of love for Jane rose like a quick tide, filling me and spilling over into ecstasy. And I could feel, from her, the same.

The noise level around us rose as well; the audience was demanding an encore with more than usual persistence. Applause, stomping and shouting increased in volume until we figured we had to play something or they would tear the place apart.

They were chanting, "Blue Smoke, Blue Smoke. Blue Smoke! Blue Smoke! Blue Smoke! BLUE SMOKE!"

We started back for the stage, but I stopped and motioned for the others to gather around.

"Let's give them the encore they deserve," I said. "Fuck it, let's play one for the whole world."

Perzanto knew what I meant. "In the resonant chamber?"

"BLUE SMOKE! BLUE SMOKE! BLUE SMOKE! BLUE SMOKE…"

I nodded. "I can take you there now," I explained. "But I'll need a little assistance. Jane, got any of that rolled?"

It turned out that she did. In a moment, half a dozen joints were passed around. Jason, who confessed to being in rehab, declined. My mountain crop of smoke tasted sweet and spicy and went right to the receptor sites. As soon as I felt the buzz coming up and could gauge it on the faces of my friends, the twinkling began.

"BLUE SMOKE! BLUE SMOKE! BLUE SMOKE! BLUE…"

I found the strongest line of association, made sure everyone was with me, and we materialized in the resonant chamber. Standing with me, amazed, were Jane Better, Trenton Augustus, Don Speckler, Cleveland White, Esty Westheimer, Mortimer aka the Tripper, Dondelakavin, Perzanto, and Bernard. We had a small audience along with us, too: Oswaldo, Declan Bean, Mark Ratner, Karen, Captain Head Charge, and Jehovah. There was a flash of light and Birdie appeared, Tim at her side. And from one of the archways my good friend Bob strolled nonchalantly into the chamber.

"How did you get here?" I asked.

Bob sniffed. "I told you. This is my mountain. My cave."

I scratched his head and he swirled around my legs.

Someone had cleaned up my blood, apparently, but the Mossberg was lying there and some of our traveling gear was still stacked in the landing, including the baby amps. So we set up and plugged in.

I felt that I needed to say a few words, so I motioned the others into silence. I let the silence stand for a long moment, soaking in the brilliant yellow light.

"The prophecy that sent us all on our unprecedented quest," I told them, "could never happen as it was told. It wasn't meant to, I think. Rather, it was to initiate events through time and space that would bring us all here now. At this moment, our minds are connected, by association, to where we just were in the Civic Center, to our homes, our families, our friends, to everyone we ever met, in all parts of time and space. Allow the resonant chamber to carry our intent down those lines of association to the whole world. Allow this cave to vibrate and transmit the power of our music through the Earth. My friends, let's rock this stone!"

We took a few more tokes of the good stuff as Trent began the long and winding intro to "The Deep Stone." I joined in, repeating chords merging with his fugue-like keyboard run. Then, after a few bars, the Tripper started up his rhythm and Cleve kicked in on bass. As each musician added a layer, the sense of intensity and vibration in the chamber increased. Bernard began to measure out an improvised melody around Trent's efforts and Perzanto hit a mighty note on the mrrlnx as we began to rock. I sang the first verse.

"In the center of the Earth"
"Before the dawn of time
"We were all together
"And everything was fine"

We could now feel the vibration in the floor and it was making a sound, a deep harmonic that blended and empowered our efforts. I looked over at Trenton and he was looking back with an odd smile, nodding his head. And I remembered that moment, seen from another perspective. This was the concert that three of us saw and heard, the first time we toked the Blue Smoke together.

My vision began to get twinkly, the twinkles dancing to the vibration, though I had no sense of going anywhere. It was more like the lines of association were opening up, dozens of them, hundreds of them, thousands of them, flipping through my mind with snatches of images, sounds, feelings, flavors and smells.

Esty cut loose with a long, multi-toned wail and I started on the next verse.

"We're born between the deep stone
"And the fire of the sun
"Each of us a part of the whole
"No need to ever feel alone"

I was in a hammock, under enormous redwood trees, holding Jane in my arms. She said, "Can you feel the trees, how they know the whole world through the breeze, the rain, the birds that nest in them, the soil and rocks that support them? The wisdom…" And then Jane and I were hiking a trail in Nepal, a Himalayan valley spread before us on a vast scale. A mountain wind threatened to lift us up and toss us into the sky and we clung to each other, feeling a play of forces far beyond our humanity. The great snow-capped crags above us and the verdant valley below seemed to embody the thoughts of the Earth, the wisdom of a celestial body, the mother and father of us all.

I saw my parents, leaning over me as I lay in bed. I saw Jane, lying next to me on a California beach. She turned to me and whispered, "The sun…" I was looking at the sunrise, smoldering red as it spread over the Rosendale mountaintop. A hawk called and a vulture circled against the sky. Green serrated leaves reached up to the golden midday light. Westerly clouds flamed crimson as the sun dipped into the tree-lined horizon. A flashpot at the front of the stage exploded into glory as we jammed before a crowd of 100,000. I laughed and my laughter echoed through a hundred thousand years of time, with millions of people laughing back, feeling joy with me.

The focus flipped to three thousand of those laughing people, dancing at the Mid-Hudson Civic Center, rocking to the beat even though we were twenty miles away and deep underground. So far my associations concerned only Jane and me but now every member of our troupe was with me on stage, feeling mighty connection to each other and to every member of the audience. We rocked as one and I howled the next verse.

"We all come from the deep stone
"As below, so above
"We are all and nothing
"Divided for the sake of love"

The chamber was resonating intensely now and whatever associations flashed into experience, the vibration continued. It was as if we became the carrier wave for the vibration, the means to take it wherever our minds led. Somehow simultaneously in the resonant chamber, in the civic center, and before crowds all over the world and through time, we rocked on.

"Every single moment
"Is really only now
"We are the eyes of the universe"

We played harder and harder, the intensity steadily building and the resonant chamber responding. As I tore through the most powerful solo I ever played, Blue appeared to me, his face floating in my vision as other associations rose, fell, and flitted away.

"Rock the stone," Blue said and was gone.

I could feel the stone all around me, vibrating to our rhythms and, through the stone of the chamber, I could feel the stone of the Earth, the stone of the mountain, the pressure and heat far below the stone, the soil above the stone, the trees and plants and animals in the soil, the sky above and lines of association leading away to the sun, the moon, the planets, the stars. I could feel even more associations radiating out from every person there, and every person not there, genetic connections, families, ancestors, descendents. I saw my own children yet to come and their children's children. I heard the voices of a million humans, names forgotten, who shared genes with me. I felt the joy of millions more who shared my ideas, music, and actions. All these connections made their impression on me.

And I knew that we could make our impression through them. I sang.

"Come on, let's rock this stone!"

Esty joined me, singing like the chorus of the gods.

"Come on, let's rock this stone!

"Come on, let's rock it nooooow!"

There was a thought behind the music, a trigger for a chain of associations that opened us up to more information and experience than it was possible to even think about following, even for the mind of a god. It was partly expressed by the lyrics, more by the music, and even more by the thing we felt in our hearts as we played. It was a blast of exuberance from the center of every one of us, from the center of the planet, the center of the universe and it tied every association that we had, every ranging thought across every damn thing everywhere into a single impossible sigil.

"a-awooooo!"

The Primal Moan erupted from me and shook the cosmos, which melted in a blast of lightning and reformed in the sound of the thunder. Or that's how it felt, anyway. I sang.

"The earth is our ancestors
"And we are their desire
"The bridge from stone to stars
"We are the eyes of the universe"

The thundering shock wave of the sigil carried our minds with it to ten thousand places and times. We heard the first music of our ancestors, chanting and stomping around a fire. We felt the joy, the release they felt and we touched the minds of great composers, both famous and unknown, lost in the ecstasy of their sounds. We saw huge crowds at Glastonbury, the Isle of Wight, Woodstock, Central Park, Watkins Glen, and a thousand other venues. We touched the core of the music, the essence of rock'n'roll that remained through all the changes in sound and style and culture. And we guided the sigil to crank out, through time and space, a surge of rock'n'roll power, manifesting through every single performance and recording ever, through everyone who hummed a tune or played air guitar. We turned the dial of every amp in every studio, on every stage, in every garage, up a few notches. We fired up the passion of every rock'n'roller everywhere. Kids just learning to play electric guitar could now shred like a pro. Garage bands found ecstasy in their sounds. Girl groups got grittier. Boy bands found soul. Classic rockers on their geriatric rounds of county fairs found new life in their riffs. Elvis impersonators grew extra testicles. And the musicians who were already rocking hard blew minds and melted faces. The whole world rocked a little harder, listeners felt it build in their hearts, audiences danced with wild abandon and everyone who heard it, everywhere and everywhen, felt a little more free.

"Let's rock it now"

We jammed like no band has ever jammed. Our connection to each other and to our audience, everywhere, was perfect. Every note elaborated the next, every sound triggered a response from every heart. I sang.

"In the center of the Earth
"Before the dawn of time
"We were all together
"And everything was fine"

And then, it was silent and I was somewhere else. I heard a voice, Jane's, say, "We're home, Ian," and it came into focus, our living room on the mountain. My vision was bright and crystal-sharp, I heard birds in the distance like jazz, and I could feel the warmth of Jane's body next to mine on the old sofa. All was very calm. Taxes were paid, debts settled, the harvest in, and a new song was in my mind. It was a moment I'd live in forever.

On the other side of forever, the band rocked into the final verse.

"We're born within the deep stone
"And the fire of the sun
"Each of us is part of a whole
"No need to ever feel alone
"A-awooo!
"Come on, let's rock this stone!"

40. Epilogue

Apparently, we were seen in visions, drug trips and on stages by people around the world. I don't know how many; a million or more? It was great promo for the tour and we sold out at every stop. Did we change the world and put everything back in harmony? Or was it just a crazy trip? Fucked if I know. But it sure changed every one of us. Most of us are no longer entirely human and the rest are so changed that their old selves wouldn't recognize them.

Trenton and Bernard are married with a growing collection of children. Jane and I have two kids of our own. Bob has at least twelve. Perzanto is the star of a reality TV show in which viewers try to set impossible tasks and he uses brains, magic and brawn to accomplish them. He's getting movie offers, too. The Tripper writes books, makes the lecture circuit and leads groups of hippy seekers to shamanic hotspots in South America. Cleve and Liana live mostly in her shebang, but sometimes come up to visit. Esty is back with her boyfriend, Joe, the TV show host and, I understand, is working on a book herself. Don Speckler lives in Lakavinland and Birdie remains in the land of the dead. Dondelakavin owns the most popular nightclub in L.A., where he is considered a cultural icon. Oswaldo and Karen teamed up to run one of the biggest rock management companies in the world, starting with a major success for the reunited Blue Smoke. Everyone comes out when it's time to play. Even Jason, sometimes. Mark Ratner and Captain Head Charge disappeared from sight soon after we returned to the surface and strange events have been happening around the world. The fart-smelling gas released at last year's Republican convention seemed more poetic than the usual terrorist act and I thought of those guys. Declan Bean is a search and rescue pilot in the Rocky Mountains. Jehovah is back in his heavens, though he sometimes visits on holidays, when he's not too busy.

So that's what happened after my wife came back from the dead. Yeah, yeah, I know. When I was just a human, I wouldn't have believed it, but you know I never was much of a believer. If you don't believe it, fuck you. Just wait until this kind of shit happens to your life.

Acknowledgements

Thank you to John Lee Cooper and Chris McNeil for guitar advice. I hope that the musical side of this novel doesn't sound too much like it was written by a non-musician, even though it was. Thank you also to the books of Ed Rosenthal, Jorge Cervantes, Robert Connell Clarke and Mark Merlin, and Julie Holland for cannabis information.

And additional thanks must be offered to DJ Reese, to the residents of Rosendale, New York, and to everyone who read my previous novel, *The Great Purple Hoo-Ha*.

About the Author

Philip H. Farber is the author of *The Great Purple Hoo-Ha*, *Brain Magick*, and *FutureRitual*, among other books. People seem to like his non-fiction books a lot, but you're special because you've just finished reading one of Phil's lengthy novels.

Hoo-Ha Books

Hoo-Ha Books is a new, independent company dedicated to publishing high quality fantasy and science fiction that might not otherwise see the light of day. *Legendary Blue Smoke* is our first novel. Visit us on the web at **hoohabooks.com**.